Sweden ...

Recalling that time, and the events that flow through these pages, you get a sense that the official explanation — *The Version* — was not true. That suspicion is well founded, but perhaps not in the way you might expect. The truth is still only an occasional guest.

It's the afternoon, the eighteenth of June 2014.

The location: the town of Bruket. He has returned there, one last time.

Sweden. What happened was a serious crime, with a long history, and it began, as it so often does, with two people forced to share a secret.

He was there when it happened, in the winter of 1980, when soot and ash were all that was left behind, and he was there when the water took them, four years later. You did get a sense of it, even back then, but it wasn't until much later that the full extent of what had gone on became clear.

Sweden. What follows will force the guilty into submission.

Forgive them.

JUNE 2014

Something's wrong, I can tell. Something is definitely not as it should be.

I ...

I'm not sure how to carry on.

My name is Leo Junker. I'm thirty-four years old, and I'm sitting on my balcony. Sometimes it's as though time's gone backwards and in my memories I feel older than I do now.

I'm running through the outskirts of Salem. The world has enormous teeth, a forked tongue, and if you're not careful, it can bite you. I'm ten, maybe eleven. I'm on my way home from Rönninge, and I've just got off a bus on my own for the first time, worried that I might have got the stops mixed up and that I won't recognise the surroundings.

It's late autumn and the leaves on the trees are drying out, and I'm relieved when I see the familiar blocks of the Triad. I don't go straight home, although I should. My newly earned freedom — that's what it feels like — has made me cocky, and I keep going. I've got my rucksack on, with my new Walkman in; I put the headphones on, listen to the beat. When I get up to the water tower, it looms over me like a temple.

I spot a few kids. They're several years above me in school. They're sitting in a huddle, sharing a cigarette. It looks like they're laughing, but I can't hear them. I prowl along the edge of the gravel

MASTER, LIAR, TRAITOR, FRIEND

CHRISTOFFER CARLSSON was born in 1986. The author of several previous novels, he has a PhD in criminology, and is a university lecturer in the subject. *Master, Liar, Traitor, Friend* is the third volume in the Leo Junker series.

MASTER, LIAR, TRAITOR, FRIEND

Christoffer Carlsson

Translated by Michael Gallagher

SCRIBE
Melbourne • London

Scribe Publications
18–20 Edward St, Brunswick, Victoria 3056, Australia
2 John St, Clerkenwell, London, WC1N 2ES, United Kingdom

Originally published in Swedish as *Mästare, väktare, lögnare, vän* by
Piratförlagets 2015

First published in English by Scribe 2017
by agreement with Pontas Literary & Film Agency

Printed and bound in the UK by CPI Group (UK) Ltd, Croydon CR0 4YY

Scribe Publications is committed to the sustainable use of natural resources
and the use of paper products made responsibly from those resources.

9781911344117 (UK edition)
9781925321821 (Australian edition)
9781925548020 (e-book)

CiP records for this title are available from the British Library and the
National Library of Australia.

scribepublications.com.au
scribepublications.co.uk

path, notice one of the guys putting his arm around one of the girls and another putting his hand on her thigh.

I want to go up to them, but I turn around. I head home.

That's my childhood.

That, and the smell of my mum and dad when they get home from work. It's the sun sparkling on roof after roof, and the smell of cooking fat and exhaust fumes, blue lights that start flickering in the silence just as suddenly as fear; it's the older graffiti writers, it's *tags* and *pieces* and *punitions*, and us all watching, memorising the movements, the bright colours. It's waiting for the train into town that doesn't always turn up or has already rumbled past, and it's cigarettes, and, later, joints, and money changing hands and the blue-grey smoke cascading through my fingers and realising that I've blown the month's allowance again, and later that day me and Grim, my best mate, nicking clothes from a shop on Birger Jarlsgatan, laughing at that, and it's Nas and *Illmatic* and *the city never sleeps* … and me and Grim sitting right at the top of the water tower, and me being struck by the notion that maybe the world, beyond all this, has made room for me, too.

During the first summer days of 2014, I spend a lot of time thinking about what once was, all that water under the bridge. And in the course of sleepless nights, a remarkable insight emerges. Something momentous is about to happen.

And then, just after lunch on the nineteenth of June, by way of confirmation, comes the phone call.

When she was little, Tove Waltersson asked her mum where all the buildings and trees and people came from, and why Bruket was so big, and why there were great expanses of open fields and thick woods. The bushes' long branches seemed to wrap themselves round each other and anything that happened to be in their way: logs, stones, dead cars, and abandoned buildings.

Mum replied that God had not been too pleased when he looked down to admire his works. It was too small, crowded, and stuffy. To remedy this, he pushed his great hands down over them, got hold of the ground on the outskirts of Bruket, and pulled, the way you stretch a T-shirt that's getting a bit small.

That was a long time ago — well, almost thirty years have passed — but the feeling hasn't changed. It's easy to forget it when you haven't lived here for a while. People who come to visit complain of sweats and dizziness, being more sensitive than usual to the sun. On the nineteenth of June, shadows are few and far between, and the tarmac is so warm that steam rises from its surface.

Alvavägen is cordoned off with blue-and-white tape, hung loosely between the lampposts. Tove stops the car, puts her hair up, and takes her sunglasses off.

Two patrol cars are parked along the line of the tape.

Brandén and Åhlund are talking to each other, both perched on their cars' bonnets, each holding a can of Fanta.

4

'Number ten,' Brandén says.

'Who's that?' Tove asks.

'An older gentleman.' Åhlund takes a swig. 'Charles Levin.'

'*The* Charles Levin?'

Åhlund looks over at Brandén, who raises his eyebrows.

'Who?' he asks.

'Police Superintendent Charles Levin.'

'Klas and Östen were first on the scene, so they're in there. Ask them. A technician left Halmstad half an hour ago, so he should be here in about fifteen.'

Alvavägen 10 is a light-grey wooden house, old and uncared for. From a distance, it almost looks more like a hut. A letterbox with no name on it hangs off the fence, and the front door is wide open. The lights are off, and if there's anything to be grateful for here, it might well be that. There's something unsettling about the lights being on in a dead man's house.

In a room to the right, Östen Vallman is standing there, phone in hand, apparently looking for something. A sofa guards a glass coffee table, and on the wall next to a large, empty bookcase is a Carl Larsson painting. The other walls are lined with piles of packing boxes, each marked CROCKERY, GLASS, or BOOKS.

She takes her shoes off and walks into the small hallway. She finds the sound of the wooden floor as it creaks under her feet quite pleasing.

'There,' Vallman says, 'on the left, in the kitchen. He's in there.'

There's a table and two chairs by the window. He's lying on his side, wearing blue jeans and a pale-yellow polo shirt. From the wound, which is level with his right temple, a significant amount of blood has spilled out, and there are no tracks or other marks anywhere near him. He was probably sitting on the chair when it happened, and then slumped, falling to the floor. The other chair is pulled out a bit from the table, as though whoever was sitting there just got up and left.

On the wallpaper, at head-height, tiny scattered droplets form a blurred cloud of dried blood.

The victim is a tall, spindly man. Must be sixty plus, but it looks like he's put some effort into keeping trim, and the first weeks of summer have left him with a bit of a tan. His features are distinctive yet elegant, with a hawk-like nose and high, well-defined cheekbones.

It is him. Fuck.

'When did the call go out?'

'An hour ago, two minutes past eleven,' Vallman says, with his eyes on the phone's screen. 'An old friend of the victim's, Lars-Erik Sunesson, made the call. They spoke on the phone yesterday and arranged to meet for a coffee, at eleven this morning. When he got here and rang the bell, and no one answered, he got worried and tried to see into the kitchen. He saw some blood on the floor, so that's when he called us.'

'Where is he — Sunesson?'

'Klas drove him home. He was going to take his statement there. He was pretty shaken.' Vallman lowers his voice, despite there not being anyone else around. 'I think he might've needed a snifter, if you know what I mean.'

Farmer's son Östen Vallman had the face of a dog and the hands of a labourer. As a teenager, he had been Bruket's best shot-putter, and once won the regional championships in his age group, something that merited a mention in the paper. He's good-looking, in the way that boys in their mid-teens sometimes can be, precisely because their expressions are so blank.

'Do you think he might have done it himself?' he says, looking at the deceased.

'Shot himself?'

6

'I'm just thinking,' he goes on, 'the damage it's done and the way he's lying.'

'Can you see a weapon?'

Vallman looks around, hopefully, holding his phone, which looks like a miniature in his huge hands. When he fails to find anything, he turns to Tove.

'Might it … ?'

'And the two cups on the table, does that indicate that he was drinking coffee alone? An imaginary friend?'

Vallman looks at her and cocks his head to one side.

'You know, it wouldn't hurt you to be a bit nicer. No wonder no one likes you.'

'They'll transfer me soon enough. Don't worry about that.'

Vallman shrugs.

'Yeah but still.'

Four thousand people live here, at most. Lots of the homes are in the area behind the square, close to the main road, from where smaller, narrower roads spread out. She lives on one of those now, on an estate where the houses are old, and small. The kind of home you only live in if you can't afford anywhere better, or if you don't want to feel guilty about not giving a shit where you live. Either way, it's impossible to make it feel cosy.

Tove moved away when she turned twenty-one, and got a place on the Police Training course in Stockholm, three years behind Markus, and while he graduated with great grades and references, Tove barely scraped through. She never did get the posting she'd been hoping for in Gothenburg or Malmö, just places like Trollhättan, Nässjö, and Varberg.

Six months ago, she ended up back here again. Her brother used to say that people like them were doomed to a life here, and that all you could do was live it with as much dignity as possible.

Sometimes Tove thinks he was right and that his fate served to prove just that: leaving Bruket had meant that Markus had to die.

Over the last ten years, it's got worse. Every time she's approached the outskirts of Bruket, she's had to turn around. She gets nauseous, her hands start shaking, she gets the sweats, and her teeth chatter until she blacks out and has to stop on the roadside and *breathe, breathe, breathe* for several minutes before she can drive again.

And then she drives back.

She was on sick leave for nine months after Markus' death, full-time at first, then 50 per cent; three months ago, she was deemed well enough to go back full-time. When she went back on duty, it was at the local station in Bruket, since that was the only place that had room for her. Besides, as they pointed out, she lives here now.

As if that was going to make things better.

Her new colleagues, acquaintances from her past, or old friends of her mum and dad gave their sympathies, told her how they remembered the two of them as children. How they'd stood and peered in through the main entrance, wide-eyed and inquisitive. Did she remember that?

Yes, she said. She remembered it.

They asked how it felt to be home again, how her mum was. Sometimes they'd see her mum, up by the graveyard.

It's okay, Tove lied. She's okay.

They don't need a detective here, nor do they want one, so she's neither needed nor welcome. Even her boss, Ola Davidsson, considers her to be surplus to requirements, and above all most of them are probably hoping that she'll collapse and go back on sick leave.

A car stops outside the house. Tove and Vallman head out to meet the technician, who introduces herself as Fanny Söderlund, notices the stripes on Vallman's shoulders, and asks for his boss. When he points at Tove, the technician looks surprised.

'I was expecting a man,' she says.

'So was I.'

Söderlund has dry hands, fine lines on her face, and silver hair in a bun. She grabs her black bag, which more than anything resembles a toolbox, before moving along the path that leads up to the steps and beginning the forensic investigation.

It's a while before she enters the house, and once she gets to the kitchen and looks at the deceased, she frowns slightly.

'I would have appreciated a heads-up that it was him,' she says.

'Did you know each other?'

Söderlund shakes her head.

'We just knew of each other. But he was still a colleague.'

'We could call someone else out.'

'The day before Midsummer? Good luck.' Söderlund looks at Vallman, who's on the phone to someone. 'Get him out of here. He's skipping around like a chihuahua.'

'So,' Tove says, 'up until a month ago Levin was a superintendent at the National Police Authority?'

'Yes.'

'So what's he doing here? Does he live here? Is this his house?'

'No idea.' Söderlund stares at Vallman. 'Get rid of him now. His plodding is driving me mad.'

Tove leads Vallman into the hall and out onto the steps, leaving Söderlund alone in there.

The warmth of the sun is getting stronger, and it's only going to get worse. The air is still, yet somehow almost pulsating. Heavy beads of sweat trickle from her scalp, down behind her ears, and along the front of her neck. Tove's headache is getting worse. She goes back inside, pulls out a pair of latex gloves from Söderlund's bag, and asks if it's okay for her to have a look around the house.

'Not really.' Söderlund sighs. 'Just … tread carefully, okay?'

The living room has a back door, which was intended to lead

out onto a patio or a terrace that someone forgot about or couldn't be bothered to build. Now it opens straight onto the lawn.

Several of the drawers are empty and the wardrobes are only half-full of clothes. In the bathroom cabinet, there's a wash bag containing a toothbrush and some toothpaste; in the shower, a single bottle of shower gel. That's it. The rest of it is in boxes. There are some in every room, these packing boxes. He's hardly bothered to furnish the place.

He was busy doing something else.

You can almost feel that in the air, in the silence.

In one corner of the bedroom, there's a laptop charger, and one for a mobile phone, on a little desk. Next to the desk is a packing box, gaping open and full of books and paper in an unsorted pile. It looks like how the inside of Tove's head feels.

Tove gets down on her knees, and examines the floor under the table and the bed. Nothing. There's a little office chair in front of the desk. Tove sits down on it and peers out of the window. It looks out across the little garden at the back.

She pulls the packing box towards her. A hole-punch, stapler, bits of paper, and countless books. She puts them to one side. At the bottom of the large box, there's a pile of ring binders, four altogether, a couple of the old metal variety, the remainder modern plastic ones. She lifts one out. It's full of photocopied documents, parts of preliminary investigations and forensic reports from cases she doesn't recognise. Someone — perhaps Levin himself — has made notes and comments in the margins. She flips through the other three binders: similar content, but relating to other cases.

The books: *Blackwater* by Kerstin Ekman, *The Spy Who Came in from the Cold* by John le Carré, and *Wise Blood* by Flannery O'Connor. Underneath that, *The Judge and His Hangman* by Friedrich Dürrenmatt. Tove flips through the pages. Nothing, apart from old turned-down corners and the odd page that's coming loose.

Something is poking out from the unsorted pile of paper, a Polaroid photo of a man, a woman, and a girl, maybe five or six years old. The man is wearing a short-sleeved white shirt and jeans, the woman a blouse and a beige skirt, and the girl is in a blue dress. They look happy.

On the back: *Me, Marika, and Eva, spring '78.*

The picture makes something tremble inside Tove, and at first she doesn't know why.

She turns around, and looks at the walls. Behind the three of them in the picture, she can see the same pale-green patterned wallpaper.

Then it hits her.

The picture was taken in this room.

Tove is driving along roads that are so familiar yet alien, unpredictable. That's how it goes: places that you leave and then return to, they are as they always have been, feel just like they used to feel, and yet not quite.

A wide pick-up truck, laden with beer, pulls out in front of her. The man at the wheel is wearing a cap, and he's alone in the cab.

The house in which Lars-Erik Sunesson has spent most of his life is discoloured by moss and surrounded by mature deciduous trees that look as though they might soon envelop it. A lawnmower stands abandoned on the lawn, which is enclosed by a sparse, spindly fence. The gate is open.

Sunesson and Police Constable Klas Mäkinen are sitting at the kitchen table. Mäkinen holds both hands round a coffee cup, while Sunesson empties his glass and reaches for a bottle. The bags around his eyes are puffier than usual.

'Ma'am,' Sunesson says. 'Midsummer is off to a bloody awful start.'

Mäkinen's gaze is fixed on Tove — an imploring stare. There's a pad lying on the table in front of him, but he doesn't seem to have committed much to paper.

Tove pulls up a chair, sits down at the head of the table, and turns towards Mäkinen.

'You're more useful at Alvavägen than here.'

Mäkinen, a charmless man who really ought to have become a caretaker rather than a cop, gets to his feet.

'Good luck,' he says.

'What a fucking day,' Sunesson says as he fills his glass, his eyes a bit moist.

The worktop is straining under piles of unwashed plates and glasses. A coffee machine is spluttering away in the background. Then, before long, the sound of Mäkinen starting his car and driving off.

Sunesson sighs and holds the bottle aloft, a Polish 'Famous Grouse' lookalike.

'You want one?'

'No. But thanks.'

Hanging on the wall behind him is a framed needlepoint canvas: *Beautiful things, howe'er begotten, in this place all soon forgotten.*

Sunesson, like his father before him, worked at the glass factory that gave Bruket its name. When the plant closed down, he started driving heavy goods vehicles for a haulage firm, where he stayed, as far as anyone knows, until he retired. Tove's colleagues are pretty certain that, besides delivering the haulage firm's freight, he was also smuggling alcohol in his load. They were never able to prove it, though, and now it's too late. She never sees him at the alcohol store, down by the market place, and she's been there a lot since she came back.

'How are you feeling, Lars-Erik?'

'What a fucking day.' He sips the whisky. 'Blood,' he continues, shaking his head. 'Blood, blood, blood. Jesus.'

'When did you last speak to Charles?'

'Last night — I called him, and we arranged to meet for coffee today, at eleven.'

'What time did you call?'

'As I told your colleague — what's his name ... Gösta's son ... Klas — it was about half-nine.'

'How did the conversation go?'

Sunesson looks confused.

'Well?'

'What I mean is,' Tove says, 'what did you talk about?'

'Nothing in particular. I met him down by the market square when I was out getting some shopping the day before yesterday, and asked him what on Earth he was doing here, and he said he lives here now. I said I'd like to hear more about that, so we exchanged numbers and said that we'd be in touch. I rang him yesterday and suggested meeting for a coffee. We arranged a time and then we hung up.' Sunesson takes another swig. 'I hardly knew the bloke, hadn't seen him for over thirty years.'

'He's lived here before, then?'

'In the Seventies. It must have been seventy-one he moved in, because I remember I'd just bought a new car, a P1800. There I was, bragging, you know how it is, proud as a peacock of that car, and I was down at the square just showing it off. I suppose that's when he spotted it.'

'Who?' said Tove. 'Who saw what?'

'Oscarsson's boy, Malte. The one who stole it.'

'Did he steal your car?'

'That same evening,' Sunesson says glumly and takes yet another gulp of whisky. 'Bloody miscreant, that lad. But then I had to go down to the police station, and it was closed, so I went to the one in the city, and there he was. I hadn't seen Charles before, you know, back then ... How old are you, by the way?'

'I was born in eighty-one.'

'So you might remember what it was like. There were a lot

more people living here then. I think it was nearly eight thousand. Now it's a different story — the hotel's closed down and the alcohol store is going after Christmas. Did you know that?'

'No.'

'The thing is, you didn't necessarily notice a new face back then. Anyway, he took my statement. He was nice, too, even if he was from Stockholm. And,' Sunesson adds, raising his finger, 'he tracked down the car in no time. Two days later, it was back in my garage, even though the investigation was left to the clowns down here. That's when I realised he was a good bloke.'

His lowers his gaze to the tabletop, nodding slowly at his own words.

'When did he move?'

Sunesson looks up, his eyes cloudy.

'Eh?'

'He came here in the Seventies. He must have moved away again.'

'Oh yeah. He left in 1980.'

'When did he move back again?'

'I don't know, but quite recently, I think.'

He drains his glass, holds the whisky in his mouth before leaning back, crunching his neck, and gurgling loudly and then swallowing. He licks his lips.

'Where did he live then, the first time?'

'Same place.'

'Do you mean in the same house? What made him buy that particular house?'

'Damned if I know. He was a quiet fella, Charles.'

'Can you imagine anyone wanting to hurt him?'

Sunesson reaches for the bottle again.

'What, here?'

'Yes.'

'No way.' He pours a few fingers' worth into the glass and then clunks it onto the table, as if to emphasise his point. 'No way.'

'You seem very sure of that.'

'Just my *supposition,* officer. But that's the sort of thing the authorities ought to be able to establish without any help from me.'

'Indeed we can. Thank you.' She taps the pen on the pad. 'Can you think of anyone who might be able to tell us a bit more about him?'

Sunesson can't. Or else he can, but he's sick of talking to her.

She shows him the photo from 1978.

'Do you recognise these people?'

'Well, that's Charles for a start, I can see that much.' He raises his eyebrows. 'And then that's got to be his little family.' Sunesson waves his hand dismissively. 'But you'll have to talk to someone else about that. I don't remember all that.'

'This is a small place. Everyone knows everyone. You must remember something?'

'It was a very long time ago. I think it was a car crash. Awful.'

'A car crash,' Tove repeats, studying him carefully.

'Or something. I can't remember.'

He's not lying, you can tell, but he's drunk and slurring so much that it does nothing for his credibility. Bollocks — she should've shown him the photo before doing anything else.

Tove repeats the question, but Sunesson simply raises his glass, takes a swig, and shakes his head. His eyes now stare blankly.

'Oh, did you see my favourite chair?'

'No.'

'It's out there. It belonged to my gran — in fact, you know, I think she even made it herself. A good woman. Charles should've had someone like that, and then this would never have happened. I'm always sitting on it on days like this, having my coffee. Speaking of which, I'm going to have some now.' He laughs. 'I never got any at Charles'.'

Tove stands up and leaves without saying anything to Sunesson, who doesn't seem the least bit surprised, and it's only once she's back in the car that she notices it: the old metal rocking chair, alone on the lawn, rusting away.

When she gets back to the cordon, he's there — Superintendent Ola Davidsson. Standing legs apart, hands on his sides, beer gut first. It grows bigger every year, Davidsson's belly, and whenever anyone points that out, he just pats it and smiles, says that it's all paid for.

'We'll have to take this ourselves to begin with,' he says. 'I've been on the phone to Stockholm for nearly an hour, just trying to sort out the bureaucracy. We haven't got the resources to run this investigation, and even if we did, we wouldn't be allowed to, given the victim's identity. The National Crime Squad are coming down — they've already put a team together up in Stockholm. They'll get copies of everything we do.'

'When will they be here?'

'Sunday night at the earliest, probably Monday. When they're not locking horns with the media, they're busy trying to help their local colleagues with the double-murder in Krokom. And it's Midsummer.'

'But there's five of us, at the most. We can't run a murder investigation.'

'That's not how it works,' Davidsson says, propping his hand against his side again, and nodding towards the house that's waiting there in the sunshine. 'You know that as well as I do. The region will send reinforcements, of course, but not a huge number. What a fucking Midsummer this is going to be.'

Inside the house on Alvavägen, Söderlund is moving from one room to the next, armed with her camera. Either she's done with the body or else she needed a break. Davidsson and Söderlund say hello to each other, and then he asks when Levin died.

'I'm not a pathologist, but I'd guess somewhere between ten and eleven last night.' Söderlund fiddles with one of the dials on the camera. 'Shot in the temple, probably from a revolver held by someone else. I haven't found the weapon yet.'

Davidsson notes the coffee cups on the table.

'So he'd arranged to meet the suspect?'

'Maybe,' Söderlund replies.

She takes a photo of the room's light switch. Davidsson has a stretch and looks grumpy. Tove strains not to smile.

'If you don't mind awfully,' Söderlund continues, 'perhaps you could go somewhere else.'

There's a buzzing in the room, and Davidsson pulls his phone out.

'Stockholm again,' he asserts, without answering the call, and points the phone at Tove. 'You're staying here.'

Tove and Söderlund watch him as he trudges out of the house.

'Is that a good human being, that one?' Söderlund asks, which makes Tove laugh.

It's the first day of my summer leave, and I'm spending it on the balcony, feeling cheated.

Someone, I don't know who, has told my boss, Anja Morovi, that I'm still not clean, that I'm still on the tablets. Whoever it was did so with the help of a tube of Halcion that came from my pocket.

It wasn't like I'd got them straight from the chemist's either, which is why she called me in to see her yesterday.

'Leo,' she said. 'You'll understand that we can't turn a blind eye to this. We have to take action.'

Morovi comes from the Domestic Violence Team, and she's only been here since March. Her degree certificate — a Masters in Criminology — hangs in pride of place on the wall of her office, and if that wasn't bad enough she's reputed to be one of Stockholm's best marksmen. She was offered the post leading the Violent Crime Unit — the Snakepit, as it's known in the force — and for some reason she said yes.

'It was Olausson,' I blurted out. 'Wasn't it?'

Olausson is a prosecutor, a slippery character who's never liked me.

'Leo,' she said again, more wearily. 'Try and keep your focus on the right things here.' She leaned in towards me. 'I can make use of you here, but only if you're *clean*. Functioning. You understand?'

'Yes.'

That was true. I did. I do.

'I'd like to suggest that you take a longer break. According to the rota, you're not off until …' She stared down at the sheet of paper in front of her. 'The thirtieth of June. I think you should adjust it,' she went on, passing over a new, blank holiday form, 'so that you're off from tomorrow, the nineteenth. Use some of the days you carried over, too, and we'll see you back here on Monday the eighteenth of August. Between now and then, you go for treatment and therapy, starting straightaway. I'll get a counsellor to give you a call and arrange the first session. Next time we meet, I want you to be clean.'

I looked at my hands. It must have been Olausson. How many others know? Gabriel Birck, of course, my colleague and the closest thing I have to a friend in the force. He knows, but he'd never drop me in it. Or would he?

'Do you understand, Leo?'

'I understand that you're suggesting that,' I said. 'But is it just a suggestion?'

'No.'

'I thought it might not be.'

Later that day, the phone rang, a number I didn't recognise. The counsellor. I didn't bother answering, just sat there on the balcony, smoking cigarettes and staring out across Stockholm.

Yesterday became today, the nineteenth. The first day of my summer holiday.

The phone ringing that afternoon, that ringtone chiming four times in the sunshine from the balcony table in my flat on Chapmansgatan — I've been waiting for it, for something to happen.

I answer, and then hear Morovi's cold voice.

'How are you feeling?' she asks.

'Wonderful.'

'Sarcasm doesn't suit you.'

I contemplate what I ought to say, how much lying I will have to do.

'I'm okay. I'll be alright.'

She takes a deep breath.

'I thought you should hear it straight from me.'

'Hear what? What's going on?'

'Levin.'

'What about him?'

Silence. On the radio over in the tiny kitchen, someone's singing *is there somebody who still believes in love?*

'Hello?' I say. 'Hello, what is it?'

As she's telling me, Kit appears beside me, quiet at first and then, when he realises that something's wrong, meowing gently. I prop the phone between my shoulder and my ear, pick him up, and head inside, closing the balcony door behind me.

Levin is dead. They're treating it as suspicious.

I'm not sure if I'm expected to say something, so I say nothing. The music on the radio makes way for a newsflash: a bomber has walked into the Moderates' party HQ in Gamla Stan, and is threatening to blow the place up.

'Is there anything you want me to do, Leo?'

'What might that be?'

No reply. I can hear her breathing; I wonder whether my own breaths sound as shallow as they feel.

'This wasn't really the summer I was hoping you'd have.'

'I know.'

'Are you spending the weekend with Sam?'

'She's off to London tomorrow, with her mum. It's been planned for ages.'

More silence. The radio informs us that the bomber in Gamla Stan is heavily armed. And then new information: a TT News

Agency bulletin reports that the Social Democrats' HQ is also under threat.

'Sounds like you've got plenty to be getting on with,' I say.

'Let me know if there's anything I can do,' she says as she ends the call.

My mentor is dead. Maybe I ought to be thinking that my *friend* is dead, but for some reason I just can't. There's something about friendship that just doesn't apply to my relationship with Levin.

I never knew him, despite working closely with him for a long time, first at the Violent Crime Unit when he was superintendent there and then later at Internal Affairs. I like to think that he took me under his wing. It felt good, for once, working with someone who noticed your potential and helped you nurture it.

I trusted him.

I really did.

Levin could get you to talk, to reveal things you wouldn't normally say to anyone, without giving away a single detail about his own life. But it *felt* like he did, that he shared things, at the time. You could easily come away with the impression that he wasn't hiding anything. It was only later, when the spell wore off, that you realised that Levin had never said a word about himself.

And then it all went to shit in Visby harbour, just over a year ago.

The Gotland affair. A mistake. *My* mistake.

The dead still follow me, in my thoughts by day, and in my dreams at night.

The police had to cover their own backs after the incident. I was thrown to the wolves — politicians and the media got the scapegoat they wanted. I needed the pills to survive, Serax, and I stayed on them to keep myself afloat. I went on to Halcion later.

I was starting to suspect that Levin had betrayed me, that I'd been put on Gotland for precisely that reason: should anything go wrong, the spotlight would be pointed at me.

Our contact became sporadic, and our conversations characterised by awkward silences. Sometimes I wanted to scream at him, and I got the feeling that sometimes he wished he could tell the truth.

I grieved for him back then, for the mentor I had lost. The rift between us was incredibly wide, at the end.

Now he's dead. Maybe the truth will remain shrouded in secrecy. Perhaps the toughest cases always remain unsolved.

The air is muggy, like the grief, and I sit here on the balcony, waiting for the rain that never comes.

My girl, my girl, don't you lie to me someone sings out of the radio over in the office kitchen, *tell me where did you sleep last night?* It's the afternoon now, and Tove should be going home.

Instead, she's sitting on a chair in the meeting room, waiting for the little station to muster some kind of first briefing. The windows have been wide open since early morning, to keep the room cool. It hasn't worked — her hair is sticking to her neck, and her armpits are moist, her hands slippery.

She did try and find the table fan, but no one knows where it is. It's probably in Davidsson's room.

In the time that she's been there, she's learnt which objects are coveted by colleagues, and which are not: no one wants television sets anymore, but they're not allowed to get rid of them either. Whoever ends up with one or more in their immediate vicinity considers this to be a punishment. If you want one of the big mugs, which you do, you need to be there early, because there are only a few, and whoever gets one keeps hold of it for the rest of the day.

And so it goes on. It's pointless, all of it, yet somehow these are the things that end up meaning something.

The office is situated on the first and second floors of a building on Paulsgatan, just on the far side of the square. It's a brick-built boxy hulk from the turn of the last century; one of the first to be built after the glass factory opened its doors and began its gradual expansion. On the inside, it's all much newer than that, but uglier. Davidsson likes to explain how he was one of ten employees here when he first started. That number has already been halved, and after the restructuring they're likely to be fewer still.

On the table in front of her are the beginnings of a little biography of Charles Levin, which she's compiling using details from readily available databases and those she's received via email from the NCS. Which doesn't amount to much.

Christ. She could really do with a fan.

Charles Jan Levin is born on the twenty-fifth of January 1947 and registered in the parish of Maria Magdalena, on Södermalm in Stockholm. He grows up in a family comprising his parents, and a brother, Mark Levin, four years his senior. Mark will later die of pancreatic cancer, in August 2008. Charles' dad is a carpenter; his mother divides her time between domestic duties and a job as a cleaner, at a hotel close to their home on Wollmar Yxkullsgatan. Charles is mischievous, finds it difficult to sit still, yet still gets top marks at school — the kind that would surely have fuelled the dreams his working-class parents had for their son's future; he starts his police training in 1966.

In autumn 1969, he arrives at Stockholm City Police, District One, and becomes a detective soon afterwards. Besides working, Levin takes evening classes in politics, law, and psychology at the university. He goes on to graduate in political science, and is — at least by police standards — an educated and well-read man. He is, nonetheless, considered a good cop, a really good one, and he is showered with praise.

By autumn 1971, Charles Levin is twenty-four years old and he moves job, from the Stockholm Police to the Halland regional force over on the West Coast, at which point he becomes a detective at the station in the city centre.

At the same time, his entry on the electoral roll changes, and he's registered as living on Alvavägen in Bruket with an Eva Alderin, born in 1949.

They marry on the twelfth of December 1971. Eva Alderin becomes Eva Levin. A winter wedding.

The following year, their daughter, Marika, is born.

Tove looks at the old photograph, reads the text again. 1978.

She turns it over, studying first the girl's face, and then the mother's. Eva Levin, who would die in the winter of 1980. Her resting place since then is the local graveyard.

'In fifteen minutes,' Åhlund says, standing in the doorway of the meeting room, cheese roll in hand.

'We've just finished the door-to-door. I'm waiting for Brandén, who's busy developing a photograph.'

'A photograph?'

'That's what he said.' He takes a bite of the roll. 'Davidsson's on his way.'

Tove returns to the paperwork.

In 1981, there's another entry on the roll, and Charles Jan Levin is once again listed as resident in Stockholm, in a little two-bed apartment in Gärdet, along with his daughter Marika.

Images flash past: Charles Levin's dead body, the two cups on his kitchen table. The computer and phone chargers in the bedroom, the packing box, the wallpaper in the study. Sunesson raising his glass to Tove, the lonely rocking chair on the lawn.

It's one of the strangest things about this job, something you never get used to: how you get thrown into people's lives without the slightest warning, and how you're forced to root around in them to understand what they've been through.

'We spoke to a witness,' Brandén says, his eyes flashing back and forth between the pad in front of him and Davidsson's stony face.

Davidsson drums his fingers on the file.

'And?'

'Well ...' Brandén is like the messenger boy who's somehow stumbled into the boardroom. 'We spoke to quite a few, didn't we? I think we crossed off about thirty people around the crime scene.'

'Yes.' Davidsson lifts his hand to his face and sneezes. It echoes round the room. 'Fuck me.'

'I think there are about twenty-five houses in the area — most of them are on Alvavägen, but several are scattered around the woods, along the lanes and the meadows around there. We checked those, too. In two of the houses on Alvavägen, there was no one home, and we haven't got hold of them yet.' Brandén turns a page in his notebook. 'Pretty much none of those we spoke to had heard the gunshot.'

'What do you mean *pretty much* ...' Tove says.

'You mentioned a witness,' Davidsson interrupts. 'Was there something in particular about him? Or her?' he adds, glancing at Tove.

'Him,' Brandén says, while finding the right page in his notebook. 'And yes, in answer to both of your questions, he's probably the only one who heard it. An Alfred Berg. Ester Annerberg gave us his name. Ester lives at Alvavägen 16, a few doors down from our crime scene. She's eighty-two, widowed ten years ago, and is eighty-six-year-old Alfred Berg's lover.' Brandén clears his throat. 'Her words. Right, anyway. Yesterday, Alfred apparently cycled over — yes, he can still ride a bike — in the afternoon, and sat with Ester until about half-past nine in the evening. He then cycled home. That takes him back down Alvavägen, the way he came, and on his way he saw a dark car, which, he says, "slowed right down as if to stop". He can't remember the colour of the car, though it may have been dark grey, dark blue, or black. It stops outside the victim's address. He's sure of that, because he turned around to have another look at the car, since he didn't recognise it.'

'So that might have been the suspect arriving,' Tove says. 'At half-nine.'

'I believe so.' Brandén changes page in his notebook. 'Alfred had his old SLR camera with him, because Ester had asked him to take some photographs of her plants. She's very fond of those plants by all accounts, and she wanted them captured now, when they're at their most impressive. When he'd finished, he put the camera down on her kitchen table. Then, when he's very nearly home, having cycled a little over twenty minutes, he realises that the camera's still back at Ester's. By now, it's probably about ten-to ten. He doesn't bother ringing Ester, for the simple reason that she's almost completely deaf — something which, by the way, I can corroborate — but simply cycles straight back. The dark car is still there when he arrives back at Ester's house. He gets there at about ten-past ten and goes into the kitchen — he's got his own key, since her hearing is so bad — to collect the camera. Ester is in the toilet at this point. Just as she flushes, Alfred also hears what he describes as a bang.'

'A bang,' Davidsson repeats to himself.

'Yes,' says Brandén. 'A bang, that was the word he used. He didn't give it a second thought, which might be perfectly natural. Instead, he goes and says goodbye to Ester again, and they chat for a couple of minutes.'

'How do you chat with someone who's basically deaf?' asks Davidsson.

'Well,' Brandén begins. 'Gestures. By shouting and bellowing. That's according to Alfred.'

'Go on,' urges Tove.

'Then he heads out again. It's now somewhere between ten- and twenty-past. Just as he emerges from Alvavägen 16, with the camera around his neck, a man approaches the car parked outside

Alvavägen 10. When the man gets into the car, Alfred gets out his camera and snaps this photo. As you will notice, it's not much of a picture, but it's all we've got.'

Brandén gets out the photograph, holding it carefully between his fingertips, and places it on the table.

It's grainy and out of focus. Perhaps Alfred Berg was breathing out while the shutter was open. The man sitting in the car is blurred, in motion — looks like he might be bending to put something on the floor by the passenger seat. It's impossible to discern any features. If it weren't for the pair of shoulders underneath it, it would be difficult even to say whether or not it was a face you were looking at. He's sitting in a newish dark Volvo. The car looks expensive, and the grille makes it look a bit like a predator.

The registration plates are just about legible.

'Why did he take the photo?' Tove asks.

'He just said that he "had a funny feeling",' says Brandén. 'He's got a little darkroom in his cellar. We made several attempts before we managed to develop the registration plates. I think, after having stared at it for a while,' he continues, more carefully, 'that it's either FOR 528 or FOR 523. And FOR 523 is a thirty-year-old Opel Kadett, so I don't think it's that one.'

'Nice work.' Davidsson inspects the photo carefully. 'FOR 528 then?'

'Well … yes, that's the problem, you see.' Brandén clears his throat again. 'That car doesn't exist.'

'Eh?' says Davidsson. 'What do you mean, doesn't exist?'

'Well …' Brandén glances at the photo. 'It doesn't exist. As in, it's not on the vehicle register.'

Davidsson drops the photo, and it lands in front of Tove. The cabin light is harsh and white, so the face looks more like a silhouette than a person.

Davidsson gets up from his chair, rounds the table with his hands in his pockets, and closes the window. Brandén studies his notebook.

'False plates?' says Tove.

'I assume so.'

The door opens — Söderlund. She has a file under one arm and doesn't bother to shut the door behind her.

'I've got an hour until I need to go to Halmstad.'

She sits at the head of the table, where Davidsson was sitting. This seems to annoy him, but she either doesn't care or doesn't notice.

'Right,' Davidsson says as he flops down next to Brandén, onto a chair that creaks conspicuously under the strain.

'In terms of evidence, this seems like a pretty tame crime scene to me,' Söderlund says, opening her folder, then unfolding a hand-drawn floor plan of the house. 'There's the hall, with the toilet and bathroom straight ahead, kitchen on the left, living room on the right, and then beyond that is a combined study-bedroom, which I will refer to from now on as the study. On this side of it is a smaller room, which is empty. This investigation has turned up very few fibres, hairs, or anything else we might have hoped for. Most of the potentially interesting stuff has already been bagged up and sent off to the National Forensics Centre or Halmstad — when it gets there, it'll end up in a queue. That's where it's likely to stay, for a few days at least, until such time as someone from the National Crime Unit makes a call and asks for it all to be prioritised.'

Davidsson sniggers. Söderlund turns the floor plan around, presumably just for the sake of doing something.

'There's hardly any forensic evidence. As an example: I've inspected that second coffee cup very carefully, and the only person who's touched it is Levin. Surprisingly enough, the kitchen is of very little interest in terms of evidence. There wasn't even a bin liner in the dustbin. I've checked the bin itself, of course, but again, nothing but Levin's fingerprints. This makes the study all the more interesting. Because,' she says, pulling a photograph from the file, 'there are a number of items missing from that room. A computer, a mobile phone, and what I believe to be a scanner or perhaps a printer.'

The picture she hands over shows the area around the desk in one corner of the room.

'How do we know ...' says Brandén.

'The dust,' says Tove. 'Or rather the absence of dust.'

'Exactly. You see, the lighter areas of the desktop — that's dust.'

'Did you say scanner?' says Davidsson. 'Who the hell has a scanner nowadays?'

'As I said, it could've been a printer,' Söderlund replies coolly. 'Or both, one of those combined things. But, yes, judging by where it was on the desk and the size of it — a scanner.'

'You don't go killing people to get hold of a computer and a scanner,' says Brandén.

'I'd say that depends on the content,' says Tove.

'Or else you see your chance to make some cash selling it to a fence, while you're at it,' Davidsson suggests. 'Stranger things have happened.'

'These parts of the puzzle might actually make more sense in the light of what the other evidence might reveal, when we get word from Halmstad and the National Forensics Centre,' Söderlund continues. 'But then there is one more thing, a little detail that takes us outside.'

The detail in question is small rubber tracks on the floor, like those left by a sack truck, in the bedroom as well as the living room.

'Sack truck?' says Davidsson.

'Yes.'

'What the hell is a sack truck?'

'One of those little L-shaped trolleys, with two wheels, the sort of thing you'd use for moving big boxes around.'

'I'm not convinced that those tracks come from one of those,' says Söderlund. 'I took some scrapings and sent them to NFC, so we'll see what they have to say. We often find them in houses or apartments where people have just moved in. So it's not worth getting worked up about. We haven't yet found the trolley itself though, which might point to this being something else entirely.'

'He might have borrowed one?' Brandén suggests.

'Yes.' Söderlund doesn't look like she believes that. 'Perhaps. Or the suspect might have taken it with him. If indeed it is tracks from one of those trolleys, we'll see. They lead to the back door in the living room, which was locked — and shows no signs of having been forced, I might add. After that, I inspected the area around the door quite thoroughly, inside and out.'

'And?' says Davidsson.

'It could be that someone has left — with a trolley, for example — and gone out that door. The grass outside seems a bit flattened, like what two wheels might do to it. If it was a trolley, it must have been heavily laden to leave tracks like that. But,' she goes on, 'this is all speculation. I found similar tracks on the step by the front door. Let's say that it was a sack truck, and yes, maybe the suspect did leave via that route, with packing boxes, computer, printer or scanner. But it might just as well be that someone — Levin himself, for example — used both the front and back doors to *enter* the house, to move a load of heavy boxes in.'

'He moved in about a month back,' Tove says. 'Those tracks round the back must be more recent than that though?'

'That's right,' says Söderlund. 'But you've seen what the place is like. He'd hardly unpacked anything, and, in as much as he did so at all, it looks like he did it in stages. What I want you to be aware of is that there are tracks in and around the house that are somewhat ambiguous.'

Davidsson rolls his eyes and jots something down in his notepad.

'Good,' he says. 'Good. Thanks.'

Brandén seems to be stifling a yawn. Tove feels like throwing something at him.

'Anyway,' Söderlund continues, returning to her file, 'I've examined the rest of the lawn, and part of the woodland behind the house, too. There's almost a little path down there. There weren't any similar tracks or prints. But,' she adds, 'the path meets others a little way in and it looks like some kind of walking route. I've taken several casts of shoe-prints, and even the odd boot-print, but they won't be of any use to us until we've got something to compare them to.'

Söderlund turns her piece of paper over. Davidsson coughs.

'A bit further away, there's a little clearing where dog-walkers tend to park. I've taken photos, and tried to get casts of some tyre tracks, but the ground's no good for that — far too dry — so the photos are the best we've got, if, once again, we ever get anything to match them with. Those tracks come from at least two types of tyre, although they're all from ordinary cars.'

'Could one of them be this one?' Brandén says, flipping the photo of the Volvo over to Söderlund.

She looks at it briefly.

'Impossible to say.'

'But I mean, it's not as though we think this Volvo was parked in the woods, as well as round at the front of the house?' Tove protests.

'I'm not one for guessing,' Söderlund replies. 'But, if I was going to interpret the crime scene, my considered opinion would be that the tracks outside — on the path in the woods for example, or in the clearing — are unlikely to be connected to this incident. I did make casts anyway — to rule them out of our investigation, if nothing else.'

'Good,' Davidsson says, coughing again. 'I've caught another bloody Midsummer cold. My assessment of the whole situation would be to say that the car is our best lead. We'll have to distribute the picture to our colleagues around the country, and ask people around here whether they saw it. That's if it's even worth making the effort before the National Crime Squad arrive.'

'What kind of bloody attitude is that?' Söderlund stares at him. 'This is a fucking colleague we're talking about.'

'Yes, okay.' He avoids her stare. 'That's true.'

Silence. Söderlund is still staring at him. Everyone knows that this case already belongs to NCS. All of them want to be absolved of their responsibilities. They all want to go home.

'Tove,' Davidsson says, when no one can bear the silence anymore. 'You went through his belongings, didn't you?'

'Yes.'

'Can you fill us in, please?'

'It's not immediately obvious what he was up to.' Reaching into her bag, she pulls out copies of the papers from the packing box. 'He might have been the type who spend their retirement trying to clear up unsolved crimes.'

She gives a brief summary of the events detailed in the documents in the box: four serious violent crimes, all of which took place in or around Stockholm. A fatal stabbing in Farsta, 1997; a rape in Enskede four years later; a murder on John Ericssonsgatan; and notes relating to an attempted murder in central Stockholm in 2005.

Davidsson shuffles the documents.

'Where's the rest of this one?' He's flipping through one of the piles of papers. 'The others are heaving with material, even psychiatric analyses and witness interviews, yet for this attempted murder from 2005 I can't find anything other than this memo. Not even the first incident report.'

'That was it,' says Tove. 'That's what's so weird about it. We don't even know who the victim was.'

Davidsson raises his eyebrows, before pulling out the memo.

'A Rodrigo Serraz writes the memo at three minutes past four in the afternoon, on the tenth of May 2005. A woman of around thirty attacks a man twice her age on Vasagatan. The victim manages, according to his own account, to catch a glimpse in his peripheral vision of a person coming at him with something in their hand. He parries the object but is stabbed in the side. He then struggles to defend himself until passers-by intervene and call the police, who arrive on the scene within two minutes. An ambulance takes the man to Sabbatsberg Hospital and a police car takes the woman to Kornberg's remand prison.' He looks up. 'That's it.'

'Could it be,' Brandén says, 'that the perpetrator of one of these crimes found out that Levin was working on the case, suspects that something's up, and fears that the truth will out?'

'And then shoots him, you mean?' Davidsson says. 'I see where you're coming from.'

'But if that's the case, why take the mobile phone, computer, and scanner?' says Söderlund.

'He said it, didn't he,' Brandén nods towards Davidsson. 'To make a bit of cash while he was at it.'

'We'll see.' Davidsson suddenly looks pleased with himself, having received some support for his theory. 'Go on, please.'

'There were a number of books in the box, too,' says Tove. 'Crime and espionage novels. And this.'

She shows them the Polaroid: the man, the woman, the child, and, on the reverse: *Me, Marika, and Eva, spring '78.*

'He's so young in that.' Söderlund's voice is thin, so very thin. 'Just thirty, thirty-one, or something.'

'It's taken in the same room as the case was in,' Tove says slowly. 'In the house at the crime scene, I mean.'

'The same house?' says Davidsson.

'The same room,' Tove stresses.

'Well whaddya know? This is starting to get weird. His family — what were their names?' He turns the photograph over. 'Marika and Eva. Are they from here? I don't recognise them. No, hang on.' Davidsson squints, holding the photograph so close that the tip of his nose nudges against it. 'Fuck me, isn't ... Hold on.'

'Eva A.,' he says. 'A-something. She's got a funny surname. Where the hell have I seen her?'

'She's dead,' says Tove. 'And her maiden name was Eva Alderin.' Davidsson looks disappointed.

'You might have mentioned that?'

'It's in Levin's biography, which, I assume, you have read.'

'Of course,' Davidsson mumbles, still holding the photo. 'Eva Alderin. That's right.' He nods twice, to himself, informed by his own memory. 'So tragic. It was a car crash, if I remember rightly.'

'That's what Sunesson thought, too.'

'A night one December,' Davidsson continues. 'I was a new constable then. She'd been to pick up her daughter from a friend's house and lost control of the car, skidded off the icy road. The girl survived the crash.' He drops the photo. 'The mother did not.'

'Jesus,' Brandén says. 'What a tragedy. Not surprising that he moved after that.'

'Are we sure that her death isn't connected to Levin's?' asks Tove.

'No, we certainly aren't.' Davidsson scratches his cheek. 'We can look at the material detailing the accident, but as far as I recall there was nothing unusual. Sometimes an accident is just an accident. I'm going to talk to my friend Dan, too — he knows everything about everyone round here.' Another cough. 'And we'll concentrate on the car, and the man inside it. Someone else must have seen or heard something. Make sure NCS get all of this,' he goes on, addressing nobody in particular. Eventually, when nobody responds, Tove makes a note on her pad.

'There was one more thing,' says Brandén.

'Okay?'

'One witness we spoke to had noticed something that might be of interest.'

'Okay?'

'A young man, Fredrik Oskarsson, lives on the other side of the wood, at a guess about half a mile away, as the crow flies, from the crime scene. Around half-nine on the evening of the eighteenth, he's out in the garden, putting his parasol down. That's when he sees a man walking along the edge of the woods.'

'And this man,' says Davidsson, 'he doesn't happen to be waving a firearm or anything like that?'

'No. Just walking.' Brandén looks up. 'That was it.'

'So that was that,' says Davidsson.

'Yes. I made a note of it.'

'Oh good.'

Davidsson blinks; he's tired.

Moments later, Söderlund leaves the room, on her way to catch a train. She seems relieved at being able to leave Bruket, and hopeful about not having to come back. Tove looks down at her notepad. Without thinking, the pen in her hand has traversed the page: *Beautiful things, howe'er begotten, in this place all soon forgotten.*

'You still here?' Brandén has got changed and is standing in the doorway with a rucksack on one shoulder. He takes two steps into the room and glances at the papers fanned out in front of Tove, then at the open window. 'It's like a sauna in here. Same every summer.'

She wonders how old Brandén is, whether he has kids. Perhaps.

'I was thinking,' he says, before changing his mind. 'I looked at the duty rosters we got hold of. He, Levin, was with Internal Affairs last year.'

'And?'

'When ... when Markus ...'

It's harder than it sounds, pretending not to know what someone's talking about, especially when what they're saying puts a knot in your stomach.

'What do you mean?'

'I wondered, if, er, well, if you knew him.' Brandén's eyes glide off towards the window, something invisible just behind her. 'Or knew of him.'

'I never met him.'

Brandén seems to be trying to work out what that means.

'Okay,' he says. 'Listen, I ... I really am sorry about what happened to Markus. I didn't know him, he was much older than me, but I knew who he was. He was a good man.'

Tove stares at the desk in front of her.

'Mm hmm.'

From the corner of her eye, she sees Brandén's still standing there, waiting for the conversation to continue, before eventually turning to leave.

'See you tomorrow,' he says.

'Mm hmm.'

In truth, to begin with she kept as far away as possible from anything that had to do with Markus' death. She knew that the events in Visby harbour had been widely reported, but she had only read the headlines. He'd been with the SWAT team a year when he was shot dead.

She remembers how he changed. The men of the SWAT team soon grew into their roles. In the National Police Authority's strict hierarchy, Markus' group was the most renowned, the most in-demand. He was different, somehow. Or maybe *she* was different, and that had changed her view of *him*. Maybe it wasn't her brother that had changed, but she herself who — by virtue of her membership of the force, and her lower standing in that same hierarchy — had begun to see her brother, his opinions and values, and even the wider world from a new perspective.

Charles Levin was in charge of Internal Affairs at the time of Markus' death, although she didn't know that then.

It wasn't until later that she could face reading about it. Levin featured in the case notes: his exact witness statements, with a well-balanced signature; his carefully chosen words spoken during a supplementary interview, conducted in the aftermath of the incident.

Charles Levin was ever-present; always behind the curtain, just out of the limelight.

It's almost dark by the time Tove arrives home, gets undressed, takes a long shower, and thinks about the dead policeman at Alvavägen 10. When she comes out to the kitchen, her phone is on the table with a missed call showing on the display.

'A year ago,' Mum says when Tove calls her back.

'What's a year ago?'

'The interring.'

Mum sniffles.

'I know,' says Tove.

Getting him down here took time, and Mum insisted that he should be laid to rest here. He'd been dead three weeks by the time the funeral took place.

She asks whether Tove remembers that last summer with Markus, when they had their leave at the same time and spent two weeks at home in Bruket. Tove doesn't say anything.

'Is it a good line?' Mum asks. 'I think it's a bit crackly. Hello? Can you hear me?'

In the darkness, the phone in her hand, Tove crumples slowly into a heap on the floor.

'Yes,' she whispers. 'I'm here.'

I push the buzzer on the intercom, and the ringtone beeps out from the speaker. The doors are not open. It's seven thirty in the evening, and the staff might already be dreaming about tomorrow.

'St Göran's secure unit,' says a gruff voice.

'This is Leo Junker.'

'Leo. Well I never. The night before Midsummer.' The sound of slurping from a coffee cup, of a magazine being put to one side. 'Come in, come in.'

There's a clicking sound, and the doors open in front of me.

I wish that I'd been able to leave town without doing this first, but I feel like I've no choice.

St Göran's secure unit is home to men and women who are guilty of crimes that they themselves do not comprehend. That, at least, is the verdict of the courts. The premises are cool, quiet, and white, each corridor isolated by heavy doors with code locks.

'Leo Junker,' Plit says as he approaches me, coffee cup in hand. 'It's been a while.'

He chuckles. Plit is a former prison guard and a great bear of a man with a shaven head, freckled skin, and a red goatee.

'I'm going away first thing tomorrow,' I say, 'and I'd like to see him before I go. Is he awake?'

'John Grimberg is almost always awake.'

We head towards the first of the heavy doors.

'How's he doing?'

'He's got used to his new medication now, so he might be slightly less unpleasant to be around, but he's not someone I'd want to go for a drink with. Not unarmed, anyway.'

That makes me laugh. We stop at the door, and I stand with my arms outstretched while Plit pats me down.

'Maybe you ought to know,' he says, 'that he's asked for a move.'

'Where to?'

'Somewhere with less security, but that's not going to be approved. He might soon be able to get parole though, despite the best efforts of Westin, who is middle management here.'

'Isn't it called day-release?'

'Same thing, isn't it? I heard about the murdered cop, by the way,' he continues, kneeling in front of me, rubbing his coarse hands down my thighs. 'Is it right that it was Charles Levin?'

'Where did you hear that?'

'One of your colleagues was down here this afternoon. I think it had just flashed up on the intranet.'

He gets to his feet and inspects my shoulders, back, and waist. At chest height, in line with my breast pocket, he stops. 'If I ask to see that tube, you're not going to be able to take it in with you. Isn't it time you knocked it on the head?'

'Yes.'

Plit opens his mouth, as if about to say something else, but then seems to change his mind. He turns and enters the code on the keypad instead, and holds up his card against the door's little black reader. The door clicks.

'Charles Levin. Fucking hell.'

'Did you know him?'

'Not exactly. He interviewed me a couple of times, back in my hooligan days. He was a sly bastard, could wheedle the truth out of you. I remember thinking that I never knew what was going on in his head, or what he was going to ask next.'

'Levin used to be around here, right? He'd come here now and again?'

Plit opens the door to the visitors' room.

'There are some questions I can't answer, however much I'd like to. Grab a seat — I'll get John.'

John Grimberg was my best friend, once. Maybe he still is, I don't know.

We grew up together in Salem and we shared a special bond, until it snapped, when I was sixteen. Our paths diverged, and I thought we'd never see each other again. And, if it hadn't been for Grim himself taking the initiative to step back into my life, a little less than a year ago, we probably never would have.

While I had joined the police, Grim had cultivated a criminal career and an addiction that left him in the gutter. The thing that had brought him back up was his gift: his talent for making other people go up in smoke.

He made a living from providing people in the underworld with new identities, and was living under an assumed name himself — he had made *John Grimberg* disappear.

When we did come across one another again, towards the end of last summer, he tried to kill me. He failed.

Now he's a resident of St Göran's, but if he were to disappear again, I know — and he knows that I know — that he would be gone for good.

Grim is brought in through the open door. He's awake and alert. So alert, in fact, that I almost suspect he's taken something. He might have done. Time and again, Grim succeeds in getting hold of lighters, cigarettes, and mobile phones. The box containing contraband possessions confiscated by staff is almost full. If you can get a lighter in, you can get other things in, like drugs. And weapons.

He smiles when he sees me. Grim's teeth are getting a bit yellow.

'Well, happy Midsummer, I suppose,' he says, after getting Plit to help him sit down and we've been left alone in the cool room.

'Yes, happy Midsummer. How are things?'

'I need a new phone charger.' He stares out the window, and I feel a sudden pang inside me. In profile, he looks like he did when he was seventeen. 'It broke, the one I had. They took it off me.'

He's been in here for over six months now, and during that time I've been visiting him regularly. I don't really know why I do it — perhaps he is still my best friend. Over time, we've learnt how to deal with each other. I've learnt to ignore a lot of what he says.

'It might take a while,' I say. 'I'm going away.'

'On dut—' Grim coughs, a deep wheezing noise. 'Fucking cough. On duty?'

'Not exactly. I'm off to Bruket for a few days.'

'Bruket? Where's that?'

'I don't really know.'

'What are you going to do there?'

'Levin is dead.'

Saying it feels strange.

'Charles Levin?'

'He moved down there in May, when he retired. And today, they found his body. They think it happened yesterday.'

'How?'

'I don't know, but they're treating it as suspicious.'

Grim's mouth tightens to a little 'o'. I can see the teeth in his bottom jaw.

'So you — the master detective — are planning to head down and find out what happened?'

I don't know what I want, just that I can't stay here. Perhaps I

43

need to see him one last time. It might actually be that simple.

'Do you remember last winter,' I say, 'when we talked about Levin? You said that he'd been here.'

'You thought I was lying.'

'But a couple of days later, I spoke to Levin about it.'

'What did he say?'

'That he'd been here.'

'And what was his explanation?'

I laugh.

'It's not that straightforward. First you can tell me, again, what happened.'

Grim leans back on his chair, looks like he's thinking.

'This was December. I saw him in the corridor when they were leading me down for lunch. He was with one of the other inmates. He was quite discreet, being careful not to be seen, but he must have noticed that I'd seen him, because after lunch he came to talk to me.'

'And?'

'I was supposed to keep quiet about having seen him. To make sure I wasn't going to squeal, he gave me a mobile phone. That's it.'

'Who was he with?'

'A woman.' Grim cocks his head to one side, and smiles. 'Your turn.'

Levin had started on his memoirs, despite the fact that he really should have waited until after retirement. He was getting a head start, he said, perhaps because he needed access to information that he could only access whilst on duty. He kept the work a secret; I think I was the only one who knew about it. In the memoirs, he dealt with a number of cases that had never been solved. Since his memory was getting cloudy and he needed to check a few details, he visited one of the people concerned, and she happened to be a resident of St Göran's.

I don't know in any detail what the investigation was about, other than it being classed as murder and that the statute of limitations for that offence was abolished fairly recently. If word got out that Levin was going through old case notes with older and significantly wiser eyes than back then, it might have given false hope to the victim's family, and that was something he wanted to avoid. He wanted to keep it under wraps, out of consideration for them.

'That's what he said,' I conclude.

'And you believed him?'

'I didn't believe anything. I had nothing to do with it.'

'That's never stopped you before.'

'This woman he was visiting, do you know who she was?'

'Why do you ask?'

'I'd like to speak to her.'

Grim laughs and tries to wave his hand dismissively.

'Give me a charger.'

'If I sort that out,' I say, feeling my pulse speeding up around my temples, 'you'll tell me then?'

'I should think so.'

'Grim, for fuck's sake!'

He raises an eyebrow. Plit's face appears, tense and uncertain, in the glass pane in the door.

'You shouted,' Grim says. 'What's wrong with you?'

I don't actually know, myself.

'I just wish that, just this once, we could talk, like normal people.'

'Normal people don't go around destroying each other's lives.'

Those words hurt me. I don't want to admit it to anyone, *can't* admit it, but there's no mistaking that feeling: when I think about Grim spending his days and nights in here, my chest burns with guilt and shame. It's thanks to me that he's here.

'Is it true you've asked to be moved?'

'Why?'

'Why have you done that? You know that's not how it works.'

'I have the right to ask whatever I like — we'll see what they have to say about it. How long have you been thinking about having kids?'

'Eh?'

'You and Sam. That's why you got a cat, isn't it?'

'No, it is not.'

Grim smiles.

'Lying again are we?'

'No.'

I look down, despite doing my best to avoid doing so.

'So you are lying,' he says.

'I don't want you to get …' I say but don't finish the sentence, because I can't say what I'm thinking.

'I doubt I'm going to be lying on a beach somewhere with a cocktail and a copy of *The Corrections*. I wouldn't worry.'

That's not the point. Wherever he ends up might be so far away that I won't be able to visit, and I don't know if I'll cope without seeing him.

I tell him that I'll try and arrange a charger. Then I leave the room, and Grim is left sitting alone, waiting for Plit to come and lead him to his room. His cell.

On the way out, I have to sign a register declaring that I have visited him. In reception, two staff members are going through the day's drugs round. One of them reads out the patients' names while the other one ticks them off a list, and it's annoying me. They shouldn't be doing it here, in front of visitors, because you can't help registering the names when you hear them, even when you're trying not to.

'Hello?' I say, but neither of them reacts.

By the time they do come over, I've got quite impatient, which must be obvious because they're scoffing and rolling their eyes at me, and not even trying to hide the fact.

Then I leave St Göran's, with my thoughts drifting off onto Levin, his death, and tomorrow's journey.

FEBRUARY 1984

Sometimes Charles is a stranger and Stockholm is a city he has never known. It's just unfamiliar faces, another street corner seen for the first time, new smells and new feelings.

That's his imagination, a mere momentary distortion, because he knows it so well. He knows the streets as though he himself had created them, at some point long, long ago. He crosses Sveavägen near its junction with Adolf Fredriks Kyrkogata. Hunched against the wind and the snow, he turns up the collar on his coat, nearly slips over in the slush.

The café door doesn't jingle as he opens it, despite being fitted with a little bell. He's not hungry, but still orders a roll to go with his coffee. The woman at the till is friendly — she has nice teeth and chubby fingers, asks him if he would like a paper.

He wouldn't. Someone's singing *we all need someone to talk to* and the chimes sound foreboding and lonely. They sound like his mood.

Paul is sitting at one of the window tables that has a view of the street outside, with a half-full glass of water and an unread newspaper in front of him. Charles hangs his coat on the back of his chair, sits down, and drinks a mouthful of coffee.

'Any news?'

Paul shakes his head and puts the paper away.

'Not since this morning.'

'We should have got an apartment for this. There are people

48

here. I'm sure people will have seen.'

'I know.'

Paul looks at him, his blue eyes as light as polar ice. A patrol car glides past the window and along the street. It's one of the new type, with blue-and-yellow decals, and the blue lights are attached to the roof bar. Charles doesn't recognise the officers' faces, and over the rooftops, above it all, the sky is heavy like wet snow.

Paul eats some of the roll. Charles lights a cigarette and takes a puff, closing his eyes. Straightaway the world seems far away, muted. He's been working under Paul for three years now. Charles is thirty-seven, although most people say he looks younger. Eva always said so, even if he had aged unnaturally fast recently.

He opens his eyes again and drinks some coffee, which is strong and black.

'How many of them are there up there?'

'Three, I think. You would be able to see them if they weren't being so careful to keep away from the windows.'

'Do they suspect something?'

He shakes his head.

'It's just their ordinary, everyday paranoia at work.'

On the radio, the music makes way for the news: the navy are ending their operations concerning the suspected submarine that was thought to have been present in Swedish waters off Karlskrona. Thunborg makes a statement, but everyone's waiting for Palme — the only one who remains silent.

Then come the reports in the wake of Sarajevo. The jubilation in Sweden as Svan and Wassberg returned with their medals. In Sarajevo, all that remains is the deserted Olympic village, foreign correspondents, and a tense political climate. *Vacuum* is the word on everyone's minds, but no one actually says it. And now: the weather.

'Strange times, Charlie,' Paul says, taking another bite of the roll.

'To say the least.'

'The bell on the door,' he says then.

'What about it?'

'It didn't jingle when you came in.'

'I noticed that, too, thought it was odd.'

Paul smiles.

Across the road, the door opens, and a man in a leather jacket comes out. He has dark hair and is wearing thick gloves; he moves with the jerky gait of an addict.

'Showtime,' says Paul.

Charles gets to his feet and pulls on his coat. It's still damp. He leaves the café without a word, or a thought.

Sometimes it's like he's not even there.

Inside his coat pocket, Charles' hand cradles the camera, scarcely bigger than a cigarette packet, as he follows the man through Stockholm.

While they're waiting for a train at Tekniska Högskolan, the man disappears into a shop. Charles stays out on the platform and lights a cigarette.

A little way away stands a woman carefully reading a public-information pamphlet, *In the Event of War*, with a suitably furrowed brow. Charles recognises the publication from his childhood: he was fourteen when it arrived, and he and his brother both read it over and over again, until they knew it off by heart. He still remembers them — the instructions and the recommendations, and Tage Erlander's illegible signature, accompanied by his name in elegant slanted handwriting at the end of the foreword. The exhortations and the insecurity, *the paranoia*, a result of the world's fear that the war might yet be more hot than cold, that it would come sooner rather than later. *Sweden wishes to defend itself, can defend itself, and will defend itself. Any messages claiming that the resistance is over are false.*

The world was a threatening place. You could be shaken awake on any given night, forced to begin the evacuation and the flight from impending doomsday.

The man re-emerges. Minutes later, they board one of the Roslagsbanan's narrow-gauge trains.

Shadowing someone is pretty taxing for the senses. At first, it's quite a pleasant sensation — paying such intense attention to a single individual makes the world's contours sharper, and one's thoughts clearer, cleaner. Everything except the object of the surveillance sinks away and becomes mere background noise. But it's also tiring, constantly being on guard, and being careful not to fall too far behind or get too close. At the wrong place, at the wrong time, losing focus, even for a second, can mean complete failure.

He observes the man, sitting there at the far end of the carriage. The world outside flashes past.

The streets in Täby haven't been ploughed, and the ground is slippery. Tyres have left tracks in the snow.

Håkansson. He's going to Håkansson's house.

The man turns into a driveway that leads up to a bungalow built of dark brown bricks and that has its own garage. Charles can hear voices: one man and one woman; they're in the garage, but the main door is closed. *There*, the door on the side of the garage. It's slightly open. Charles pulls out the camera and moves towards the garage wall, then hugs it as he makes his way along its length. When he gets within earshot, she's in the middle of a sentence:

'… not going to be able to talk to him for weeks.'

'Where's the key?'

'Can't you arrange for me to speak to him? I just want to hear his voice — he's my husband after all.'

'No.' He sounds harsher now — more demanding: 'Give me the key.'

Silence.

Her: Anette Håkansson. The man she is talking about is her spouse, Sven-Olof Håkansson. Owner of electronics firm Sunitron, and currently on remand.

A cupboard opens, a jar or a bottle is lifted down, a lid squeaks as it is screwed off — and then, the quiet jingle of a key.

Charles moves to the end of the building, waits for him. *There*, he's walking back out onto the road. He keeps his hands in his pockets, and has a determined look about him.

Charles gets him in the viewfinder, holds his breath, and catches him in mid-stride.

The shutter clicks, a light, discreet sound.

The woman leaves the garage, closing the door behind her. Her shaky legs take her back into the house, and only then does Charles dare to go back onto the road himself.

Bagarmossen district.

Up there, on the surface. He can breathe again — that's how it feels, after a long time underground. The man slips a bit, a stone's throw ahead of him. He's heading for the apartment blocks a little further down. They're the same colour as a chain-smoker's fingers.

Someone who's shadowed a person long enough will know it when it happens. Sight is a slow sense; it just confirms what the rest of your body is already telling you. Charles turns in at the first corner of the building and looks for him, but, sure enough — he's lost him.

Bollocks.

There are several entrances, all visible from here, the windows in rows above them. The odd dead shrub here and there; a light green bicycle that has been propped up against the wall of the building but has toppled over. A woman with a walking frame, out for a walk. Charles can hear her grunting, but that's it.

He walks between the blocks, keeping his footsteps calm and gentle.

What he really wants is to scream at the top of his voice. There's too much at stake.

Steps at the gable end of one of the buildings lead down to an open steel door. Beyond it, a basement storage room. The door glides to, slowly at first, before abruptly slamming shut.

He stands at the corner of another of the blocks, as if he were waiting for someone, and from there he has a clear view of the cellar door. The cold of the ground beneath has seeped up through the soles of his boots. His fingers are tight and stiff.

Now.

The door opens, and the man emerges. Charles pulls out his camera and studies him through the viewfinder. Then, click: captured on his way up the steps. Click: a profile shot; he's at the top of the steps and heading towards the metro. A third, final picture — the outline of the man's scrawny back through his leather jacket.

Nearby, the sound of sirens — an ambulance. Charles puts the camera back in his pocket.

He's doing this 'naked' — which is how secretive intelligence agencies such as The Bureau refer to working without support or protection. He's not even armed. If something happens, he's got no back-up, no guarantees to call on.

The cellar comprises a single long passage with numbered storage cages on either side. First is number 515, with the sequence continuing upwards. These storage spaces are separated from each other by chicken wire and thick wooden beams. Everything is bathed in a warm yellowish glow emanating from the roof light, and he can feel the warmth on the top of his head as he walks underneath it. A spider the size of a large coin darts across the floor in surprise. He stamps on it.

It smells of old furniture and mould down here. Some of the cages are full to bursting, others hardly used. The great thing about them is the ease with which their contents can be identified: an old ping-pong table here, a bookcase there, a set of winter clothes, a bike.

Surely they should be visible. If they're down here somewhere, they should be obvious.

There. Way down on the left, in a cage marked 536. Right at the back, an old sofa is just visible, as is an old refrigerator with its door ajar. They're almost completely obscured by whatever is in front of them: something large, which has been covered with a thick dark-green tarpaulin. That could be them. The height — about chin-height on Charles — is right. Whatever it is, it's just inside the door, where you would expect to find something that had only just been left there.

It has a serious-looking padlock. Charles has a search around. He pulls out the camera and squints into the tiny viewfinder, adjusts the aperture to the low light level, and holds his breath. Two rapid clicks.

The chicken wire has a slightly larger gauge mesh closest to the floor. He squats down and pushes a hand through one of the holes, manages to grasp a corner of the tarp, and lifts it slightly to get a glimpse of what lies underneath.

They look like drying cabinets, heavy-duty steel boxes with vents in their doors.

At the bottom, little markings are just visible, figures scrawled in felt-tip on a bit of masking tape:

VAX 11/782.

Charles counts: two, three, four of them.

He pulls the camera from his pocket with his free hand.

The computers don't look much, but they're worth their weight in gold, in blood.

As he leaves Bagarmossen, snow is falling.

It's the end of February 1984.

JANUARY–FEBRUARY 1971

Charles and Eva's having met was not simply down to chance, although for a long time he thought so. Hindsight has made him wiser. It was a test, sent by an unknown higher force, something that forced him to display his true colours.

He was an ambitious young man, who after his training had been assigned to District One before being recruited to the Surveillance Unit. It was there he learned the ropes under the guidance of the legendary Sivertsson, a man so cunning he was widely known as 'The Fox'. Charles lived in a one-bedroom flat on Kungsholmen, and he studied when he wasn't working.

The world was changing. Nineteen seventy was one of the last true 'record years'. Growth remained strong, making Palme's social reforms possible, but the idealised notion of the 'People's Home' had begun to reveal its true nature: an illusion, a mirage, an apparition that found its way inside peoples' heads. Nineteen sixty-eight was still an open wound, and Charles' early days as a policeman had been unsettling, full of revolt and unrest. Now, a few short years later, the city's ugly concrete-and-glass estates were soaked in drugs and dirty money. The only ones who didn't realise that something was happening were those still spellbound by Erlander's utopia.

In late-January 1971, he was summoned to Sivertsson's room. As he stood in the doorway, Sivertsson looked up from the file that was almost as renowned as its owner: thick, leather-bound, and with an indexing system that people of average intelligence would never be able to decipher. The binder itself was said to be the only one of its kind in the building, and when it wasn't on Sivertsson's desk it was safely contained in his safe. Rumour had it that he collated the surveillance reports from the private detective he had employed to keep an eye on his wife and her alleged affairs. Other, more persistent, rumours claimed that the file contained intelligence collected in collaboration with the Security Police, SEPO — data so sensitive that only Sivertsson himself was allowed to handle it.

'Isn't it about time we sent you off on a conference trip?' he asked.

Sivertsson's voice was a lot like his personality — thin and sharp, and, since this was the way he would always give his orders, Charles simply asked where he was to go and when.

It took place from the twenty-eighth of February to the first of March, at a conference centre that had been hurriedly assembled in the no-man's-land between Halmstad and the little settlement of Bruket, some eighty kilometres inland. The National Chief of Police himself, Carl Persson, was to attend the opening day.

The evening brought a choice between travelling into Halmstad for continued discussions or going to Bruket. The thought of Halmstad's nightclubs held little appeal for him, so he went with Bruket. Abrahamsson and Knutsson, the colleagues Charles travelled down with, were both twice his age.

They took Abrahamsson's car, and with each mile travelled the streetlights became fewer and further apart. By the time they arrived, it was already dark, so they had no idea of the look or feel of the place. That might also have contributed to what happened next, because the first four hours he spent there felt like being in a black bubble, another, separate, version of reality.

He wouldn't even have been surprised if things had tasted

different there: apples like pears, wine like blood. Something about the place made that seem perfectly plausible; it made everything seem slightly distorted. Or perhaps it wasn't the place, but her.

And yes, that's where she was, almost as though she'd been waiting for him.

The bar they went to was the only one in Bruket, down by the illuminated square. It was an old brick building, with a pavement terrace and a neon sign above the door.

'I take it you've got some ID with you, Levin?' Knutsson said as they got out of the car.

Knutsson was that type of Gothenburg man who, when he opens his mouth, always sounds as though he hasn't quite made up his mind as to whether or not he is being serious. The corners of his mouth twitched, but it could just as easily have been an attempt to conceal his irritation as the beginnings of a smile.

Abrahamsson slapped Knutsson on the shoulder.

'Stop winding him up. For that, you're driving us home.'

'I'm not winding him up,' Knutsson replied, somewhat confused.

It was immediately obvious that the people spending that evening at Brukets Bar were the people who always did: lonely men with pinkish, swollen faces and a beer in front of them.

Behind the bar stood a man with a silver-flecked moustache and soft features, with notes in his hands and the till drawer open.

Charles and Abrahamsson ordered a beer each from the barman and sat down at one of the tables. Knutsson sipped on a soft drink, expressionless. They didn't say much.

Four women came in, one after the other. She was last, and the other three were laughing at something she'd just said. They called the man behind the bar 'Magnus' when they ordered, and one of them asked if he'd fixed the sink in the toilet.

'Do you think I've got time to be doing things like that?' he sniggered.

From their seats, the three policemen watched the women making their way through the bar. They must have noticed, but didn't seem bothered. Maybe they were used to it. The women sat down at a table behind the officers, and one of them said that they should've gone straight to Monica's, and that they never should have come here. She slurred her words.

Charles soon felt woozy in the warm, heavy lighting, and he listened to their strange accents, their guttural Rs and their extended vowel sounds, and with a melody that would be very difficult to imitate.

'That would do you, wouldn't it Levin?' said Abrahamsson.

'Which one?'

'He doesn't get it,' Knutsson said. 'Leave him alone. You're getting tipsy.'

'So innocent,' Abrahamsson said and cocked his head to the side, looking at Charles like you might look at a kitten. He shook his head. 'So unspoilt.'

Behind the barman was a large wall clock. According to that, it was half-past six. Charles doubted its accuracy.

He went to the toilet, which, in a previous life, had served as a cloakroom. It was small and cramped, and smelt like an old man's clothes. When Charles turned on the tap, it delivered nothing more than a foreboding creak, and he quickly turned it off again.

She was outside the toilet, with her arms folded across her chest. Shoulder-length blonde wavy hair, petite, half-a-head shorter than him, with narrow shoulders and fragile wrists. Her nails were unpainted and her eyes were inquisitive and alert. She was wearing a black dress that reached her thighs, and black stockings. A matching black lace rose was fastened in her hair.

He held the door open for her. She smiled. Her teeth were small and uneven, almost like a child's.

Charles stood at the bar, which at that point was missing its barman. The man was outside with a cigarette in one hand, a beer in the other, and all the time in the world.

'You didn't wash your hands.'

She was standing next to him, holding money. He could smell her hair, or her perfume. Maybe both.

'The tap didn't work.'

She laughed.

'I know. I didn't either.' The notes rustled in her hands. 'Where is he?'

'Outside. Smoking.'

'Of course.' She glanced over her shoulder, through the door to where the barman was by now halfway through both the bottle and the cigarette. 'I'm Eva.'

'Charles.'

'You're not local.'

'How do you know?'

'Can tell by the way you talk.'

'Where do you think I'm from then?'

'Stockholm, I would guess,' she said. 'But that seems painfully predictable that someone like me would guess that. So I'll say Uppsala.'

'Stockholm,' said Charles — and something in her deep-blue eyes made him smile — 'I'm afraid.'

Her friends giggled. Charles blushed.

'Stockholm,' Eva said, seemingly testing the implications in her mouth. 'What do you know! How have you ended up out here?'

'We're at a conference, half an hour away, towards Halmstad.'

'So those are your colleagues?'

A man is defined by the company he keeps; his companions were a sneaky pisshead and a man who, above all else, was grey.

Was this how it was going to be? Would he end up like them?

'Yes,' said Charles, reluctantly.

He stared at Eva's mouth — it was only for a second, but he couldn't help it.

'What do you do?'

'I'm a policeman. What about you?'

'I work at the supermarket on the other side of the square — the red neon sign, if you noticed that when you arrived. That's where I work.'

The barman returned. The beer bottle in his hand was empty. Without looking at them, he went back behind the bar and put the music on, an antidote to silence rather than something you'd listen to. As he stood back up, he exhaled, as if it had been something of an effort, and the smell of beer and smoke hit Charles in the face.

'Now then,' he said.

'Another one,' Eva said, holding up her notes.

'Same here,' said Charles.

She told him that she was about to turn twenty-two. Charles said he was twenty-four. She'd never been to Stockholm, was born and raised here. He looked at her ring finger: nothing, just smooth skin and tiny downy hairs. They were heading to an old classmate's, Monica's, for dinner, but they'd wanted to wet their whistles first. *Wet their whistles*, that was the phrase she used, and Charles thought that was odd.

'Do you like being a policeman?'

'You get to come to places like Bruket, I'll give it that,' he said, which made her laugh and touch his arm.

Then one of her friends called over to her, asking if it wasn't time for them to go.

'How long are you around for?' said Eva.

'We leave the day after tomorrow.'

She looked at the barman, who was leaning against the wall, reading a newspaper. Charles was starting to feel intoxicated and had to squint to make sure: it was three days old.

'Magnus, can I have a pen and paper?' She wrote down a telephone number. 'Call me if you'd like to meet up.'

Charles carefully folded the little scrap of paper and put it in his trouser pocket.

It wasn't until they'd gone and he sat back down with Abrahamsson and Knutsson that he noticed the music and the lonely voice, deep yet twisted and sharp, and he remembers the lyrics to this day: *I wasn't sad, I was just dissatisfied*.

He should have thrown her number away, thrown it away and forgotten about ever having met her.

FEBRUARY 1984

It smells bad in here, but perhaps it would've been naïve to expect anything else of a junkie's home. Through the living-room window, the Sofia church tower and the dead treetops can be seen, the sky hanging low. A radio is playing 'Love of the Common People'. Despite the austere furnishing, which consists of a simple table and chairs, a sofa and armchairs, the flat seems messy and grimy.

Jan Savolainen is shaky and fragile, smoking his cigarette. Sitting there opposite Charles, he looks even thinner than he did yesterday on their journey through Stockholm.

Charles picks up the cigarette packet from the table between them.

'Okay if I take one?'

'I suppose so.' Savolainen taps his cigarette with his index finger, causing the ash to tumble into the ashtray. His gaze shifts from Charles to the door, and then back to Charles again. 'What do important types like you want with me?'

Charles pulls a cigarette from the packet, and rolls it between his fingers. The tobacco crackles audibly in the silent room.

'Sven-Olof Håkansson,' he says. 'How do you know each other?'

'What did you say his name was?'

'Sven-Olof Håkansson.'

'How we know each other?'

'Yes.'

'I've never heard that name before.'

'How about *Anette* Håkansson?'

'Who the hell is that then?'

'His wife.'

'Right. No, dunno.'

Charles lights the cigarette. Savolainen's nails are long and black.

'That's unfortunate.'

'What?'

Charles leans back in his chair and blows out smoke, watches it float out into the still air. When his eyes meet Savolainen's, the junkie has had time to get a bit nervous. Charles pulls a photo from the inside pocket of his jacket, and slides it over to him.

'Can you identify the man in the picture?'

Savolainen picks it up, squints at it. It's a good image, and despite the man keeping his eyes on the ground, the profile is still clear and in focus.

'That's me.'

'Do you know where the picture was taken?'

'No.'

'You don't recognise it? Don't you know where you've been?'

Savolainen clams up, so Charles keeps going, in the same monotone voice; he might as well have been reading from a page: 'This is you leaving Håkansson's place in Täby. Yesterday, after you'd been in his garage. I'm saying that's unfortunate, because it must mean it was breaking and entering.' Charles picks up the photo. 'Shame.'

'You threatening me?'

'What I want to know is how you know Håkansson. That's all.'

Savolainen gets up from his chair with such force that it topples over and hits the ground with a clatter, wood on wood. He puts his palms on the table and leans over Charles.

'Get out of here before you need carrying out.'

Savolainen's saliva flecks his face. Charles folds the photograph and puts it in his pocket.

'Would you please sit down?'

Without waiting for the answer, Charles pulls out the next photograph and holds it up in front of him: Savolainen leaving the basement in Bagarmossen in a hurry.

'Sit down. Now. We need to get to the bottom of this.'

Now he does as he was told. Charles leaves the picture on the table and gets out the little bag of speed from his trouser pocket, then places it next to the photo.

'How do you know Sven-Olof Håkansson?'

Savolainen holds the bag between his thumb and forefinger, his lips tight as he admires it.

'I don't know him. I just got asked to do a job for him, that's all.'

'And what was that?'

'It was for his company, Sunitron. I don't know why. I was just told that I had to check that a delivery had been made.'

'And where was it supposed to be? The delivery?'

Savolainen nods at the picture.

'There.'

'And was it?'

'Eh?'

'Had the delivery been made?'

'Yes.'

'So what where you doing in Täby then?'

'I had to pick up the key to the cellar. She had it.'

'Anette?'

'That's it. The wife.'

'Sounds inconvenient, the only key to a cellar being on the other side of Stockholm.'

Savolainen fiddles with the bag of speed, opening it carefully before sprinkling a little pinch of the white powder onto the table. He shapes it into a thin line and pulls out a little metal tube, which he puts to his nostril and then bends over the table, hoovering the powder up his nose. He licks his index finger and dabs up the tiny remainder from the tabletop before rubbing it into his gums.

'The key in Täby was a spare. I had to go and get it to make sure it didn't go walkabout.'

'On whose instructions?'

'Who do you think? The guy whose basement it is.'

'And who is that?'

Savolainen picks up the bag of amphetamine, folds it, and puts it in his jeans pocket.

'Öberg.'

'Jakob Öberg? Are you running errands for him?'

Savolainen rolls his eyes.

'I'll take that as a yes,' Charles says. 'What kind of goods?'

'I don't know.'

Charles raises an eyebrow.

'You don't know?'

He shakes his head.

'They were under a cover, a big tarpaulin. All I had to do was go in and have a peek under the tarp, check that they were there. They were meant to look a bit like drying cabinets, that was all I was told, and there they were, where they were meant to be.'

'And you don't know what these goods are?'

'No. That's what I'm saying.'

'I know that you've worked out what they are, and that you know how much they're worth.' He throws up his arms in frustration. 'Can't you just tell me what you actually know? Then I can get on with my stuff and you can get on with yours?'

'Well, if you know so much, then you must know what those things are, too. What do you need me for?'

'I want to hear you say it and …'

'Not going to happen.'

'… I want to avoid any unpleasantness.'

'Get out of here now.'

Charles looks at the glowing cigarette between his fingers, how the paper slowly turns to ash. When he blinks, his eyelids feel heavy.

'Don't do this.'

'Fuck off.'

Charles nods slowly and stands up.

It was never normally like this, not even when thoughts of Bruket were still raw, the misery was still burning away inside him, and he was the new boy at The Bureau. The Bureau, SEPO, the Security Police.

He remembers the early days, him and Paul sitting in armchairs in the cool foyer of the Grand Hôtel, the scent of expensive perfume and the discreet rustling coming from the men in the restaurant flipping through their newspapers, beautiful women passing them in tight-fitting skirts and plimsolls. A man with a diplomatic manner arrived by lift and shook their hands, addressing him by a name that wasn't his: *Guten Abend, Herr Möller. Wurden Sie bitte mitkommen? Wir müssen vieles besprechen.*

They were close to history, could feel the wing beats from both East and West. It was crucially important work, and he learnt quickly, got good at it. He had no choice. One way of dealing with the past was to wallow in it now. *Herr Möller, bitte, hören Sie mir zu …*

The hours of surveillance in the car. The countless nights they spent sitting and going through registers, piecing things together, making connections between various snippets of intelligence. A meeting in a train compartment, two go-betweens briefly touching and exchanging discreet phrases. Salutations the moment before being left alone again: *Grüße aus Berlin, Herr Möller.* And it was never normally like this.

'He knows that they're VAX computers,' Charles says once he's slumped into the seat next to Paul and the car turns onto Folkungagatan. It's icy, and the useless winter tyres on his Citroën are sliding around in the slush. 'But he doesn't know what they're going to be used for.'

'Are you sure about that?' Paul glances down at Charles' feet. 'You've got some on your shoes.'

'Didn't you hear us?'

'It was crackly towards the end.'

Charles turns up the collar of his coat, exposing the little microphone, undoes two buttons on his shirt and pulls off the tape that had kept the transmitter in place. Charles sees a patch of his own skin, white and pale.

'Have you turned the receiver off?' Charles asks.

'Yes.'

Charles does his shirt up again and opens the glove box. There's a packet of tissues in there, and once he's put the equipment back he grabs it, pulls out a tissue, and wipes the blood from his shoes.

'Does he know who the delivery is for?' Paul asks.

'No. You must have heard *that.*'

A heavy truck rolls along ahead of them. The exhaust fumes force their way inside the car, strong and acrid.

Charles folds the bloody tissue and puts it in his pocket. They head north in silence and slip into the tunnel. Before long, they're close to the heart of the city, in the government district, with its buildings designed to make people feel small. It works.

What they've managed to establish so far makes things feel more under control, for now. Jan Savolainen is a no-mark with amphetamine anxiety, and of late he's been running errands for Jakob Öberg. Öberg is a gangster with a penchant for drug smuggling and handling stolen goods. Known acquaintances: Sigge Cedergren, Leif Skiffer, Clark Olofsson. Known haunts: a two-bed flat close to Oxen, a gambling den, and a bedsit out in Bagarmossen with its own basement storage.

How Öberg knows Sven-Olof Håkansson is unclear. Håkansson runs an electronics company called Sunitron, and on the twenty-fourth of February a delivery was on its way to Sweden. It got stuck in Hamburg because German customs officials thought there was something odd about it: Sunitron had asked them for a temporary exemption, which indicated that Sweden was not its final destination — it was to be shipped on to another country. Which country that was, no one knew. Not only that, the consignment turned out to contain transmitters and receivers for advanced radar equipment originally from the USA. When Håkansson was hauled in for questioning the following day, it emerged that he, too, had no idea, and was under the impression that the goods were to stay in Sweden. At least that's what he said. The transmitters and receivers were being held by the customs officers in Hamburg, and had that been that, things might have turned out rather differently.

Unfortunately, a raid was carried out that day, the twenty-fifth, on the Håkanssons' home out in Täby. Four large wooden crates were found in the garage. When asked about the contents, Håkansson said that they were air-conditioning units, but when the police prised them open it was established that they in fact contained VAX computers.

That was when The Bureau was called in. VAX 11/782 has numerous civilian applications but can also have military uses. It is part of the hardware required in the production of nuclear weapons.

The problem — which had caused the Director of The Bureau to intensify his chain-smoking — was that when Charles and Paul arrived at Håkansson's address on the evening of the twenty-fifth of February to collect the VAX computers, they were gone.

Disappeared. Stolen, with some considerable panache, as though they had simply gone up in smoke.

They informed the Director, and all hell broke loose — the ashtray hit the wall and a telephone receiver cracked when the Director whacked it on the table like a hammer. The off-white walls of the meeting room closed in, until everyone was gasping for breath.

'He's going to be pleased that we've found the computers,' Paul says as he turns into Hantverkargatan. 'But if they stay in Bagarmossen, we're going to have to call off the deal. We need to get him to think that the best thing is to keep them moving, put them in new locations every now and then. First from Bagarmossen to a second location, from there to a third, perhaps even a fourth. That way they can, in a flash, just …' He holds out his clenched fist and opens it quickly, as though the palm of his hand had burnt his fingertips. 'Pfft. Disappear right before their eyes, again, but this time with our blessing.'

'Getting him to think that won't be enough. He needs to present the idea himself.'

'Exactly,' Paul says with a little smirk.

In times like these, that's the only way to get him to agree to anything.

Charles stares at his fingers, stained yellow by nicotine. He puts his head back against the headrest, closing his eyes. They're lying to so many people. It would be nice to grab some sleep. Inside his trouser pocket, his hand clenches the blood-stained tissue.

The Bureau is a hive of activity: secretaries carrying binders and papers from one room to another, their discreet heels clicking on the floor; office workers coming back from their lunch with their coats draped over their arms; the cleaner packing the vacuum cleaner back in the broom cupboard; a visitor from one of the upper floors being led through the corridors by men with polite smiles and serious brows.

The mundaneness of it makes it easier to pretend that it's not dangerous. The Director smokes Chesterfield — the only decent American cigarette — and recently his habit's got worse, if his secretary is to be believed. She probably should be. Everyone knows he's up against it.

'So we know where they are,' he says now, holding up his glass of water and studying its contents before tasting it.

'That's right,' Paul says, turning a page in the report. 'We know that they're originally from America, and that they arrived here via South Africa and Germany.'

'Do we know how they got there?'

'No. Nor do we know who it was that moved them from Täby to Bagarmossen, how, or why. If it hadn't been for Charles,' he adds, 'we wouldn't even have known where they were.'

The Director's gaze drifts over the glass and across the desk.

'Good work, Levin.' He pulls the cigarette packet from his chest pocket. 'Do we know where the VAX computers were headed?'

'We suspect,' Paul says, 'that they were intended for the same destination as the radar equipment that was impounded in Hamburg.'

'Obviously. But where was that going?'

The Director is well aware of the most likely destination. The question is either a rhetorical one, or else he wants to see if they're lying.

'There may be any number of destinations,' Charles says slowly.

'Hungary, Bulgaria, perhaps even the USSR. But we suspect it was East Germany.'

'So do I.' The Director lights his cigarette. 'Fuck.'

He stands up, walks over to the window with hands in pockets and a cigarette bobbing from the corner of his mouth. The walls in here are covered with heavy bookshelves, full of ring binders and handbooks, nameless files. His uniform is hanging in between two of the shelves. The floor is covered with an expensive-looking rug. The smell of cigarettes and aftershave mixes with the synthetic smell of air conditioning.

The Director has a great beak of a nose and only smiles when it is in his interest to do so. On the few occasions it does happen, the resulting leer is half-hearted and cool, never quite reaching his eyes. It's difficult to distinguish between his personality and his profession, the requirements of the job having worked their way into his movements, his emotions, and his heart. Apparently, his first decision after being appointed was to soundproof the walls, since he wanted to control what was heard in here. It's actually the small sounds that expose a person, and if they squirm in their chair, fix their collar, or clear their throat in agitation — in here, those sounds are amplified, sharpened.

'And Savolainen,' the Director says, preoccupied. 'It was him you saw?'

'Yes.'

'Well, in that case, Öberg's involved in this, too. If it is the GDR, then they're working with good old-fashioned Swedish crooks. Well, I never.'

'If it is the GDR, maybe they're not aware of that part,' Paul says. 'There could be a lot of links in the chain.'

'They know,' the Director says bleakly. 'They always know. But,' he goes on, 'do they know that *we* know where they are?'

'No,' says Charles.

'And you're quite sure about that?'

'Yes.'

A flock of birds streak past the window. The Director doesn't seem to notice them. Maybe he's closed his eyes. Charles' palms are slippery, and when he lifts them from the desktop his sweat has left marks on the polished wood. He wipes his arm across it, and puts his hands on his thighs instead.

'Arrange a flat and get that cellar in Bagarmossen under surveillance. I want to know if Öberg is working for Håkansson or someone else. Have you spoken to him?'

'Öberg?' says Charles. 'No.'

'What about his lackey, Savolainen? Have you spoken to him?'

'No,' Charles lies, and the lie sounds perfect, almost like a reflex. He's so used to it.

'Is that right?'

'Yes.'

'Well, let's keep it that way. Don't make contact.' He pulls on his cigarette.

The smoke forms a cloud around him. 'Observe, and document. Do not intervene until, in the unlikely event of it going that far, the computers get legs and are about to cross the border.'

'May I ask,' Paul says, 'why this caution?'

'We are being careful because ...' The Director coughs. The cigarette falls out of his mouth and onto the floor. 'Because the prime minister will be visiting the GDR in June. That was decided this morning. If that's where the computers are bound for, then there will be an almighty rumpus if we don't put a spanner in the works.'

Paul straightens out a crease in his trouser leg. It looks nonchalant, almost provocative. The Director studies the cigarette, lying there smouldering beside his left foot. He sighs, before extinguishing it with the sole of his shoe, his hands staying firmly in his pockets.

'I've been thinking,' Paul says, 'aren't we taking a risk, having

73

them sitting there in Bagarmossen? They're going to be there for at least a couple of months. Deals like this, regardless of whether they're going to the GDR or somewhere else in the Eastern Bloc, always take time.'

'We're always taking risks. It comes with the job.'

'But … can we leave electronic equipment standing there like that? Considering it's equipment that in all probability is intended to be used for military purposes, I mean?'

'What the hell are we supposed to do? Bring them here?'

'Obviously not.' Paul furrowed his brow. 'I just mean …'

'I know what you mean.' The Director interrupts. 'You mean that it would be better to keep them moving, get the crooks to move them around at irregular intervals. The way we used to do it.'

'I just want to draw attention to a potential risk in our strategy. A risk that might be avoidable.'

'Having a bunch of unreliable gangsters moving that kind of gear around, is that not risky?'

'Well, yes.' Paul throws up his hands in frustration. It looks genuine, which is surprising, and, strangely enough, impressive. 'Sure.'

The Director slumps back in silence.

'There is one good reason to get them to move the computers,' Charles says slowly.

'What might that be?'

Careful now.

'A move like that takes a lot of hands. They'd need to bring in help. We could cast the net wider, get at even more of their people. If we make a good job of it, we might even get at some of the East Germans themselves.'

The Director pulls out another cigarette, and rolls it between his fingers.

'That's a nice thought.'

He's quiet again, for a long time. Charles is dizzy and nauseous.

His mouth is watering. He swallows.

'How do we get them to move the computers?' says the Director. 'How are we going to get people who don't know that we know what they're up to, to move those things without revealing ourselves?'

Paul laughs — maybe because it's all an act, like playing games of strategy as a kid and delighting in having been able to predict the opponent's moves and lure him into a trap.

'Details always work themselves out,' he says.

'Details,' the Director repeats to himself and then gives a little giggle — an old man who, for a second, is all too reminiscent of a little boy.

JUNE 2014

I've bought a car. A beige 1978 Opel Kadett — four cylinders, two doors, and a carburettor.

I got it cheap from a dubious character in Högdalen, a man I'd had previous dealings with concerning an assault, where it took a long time to establish whether he had been the victim or the perpetrator. The car sounds like an old hoover, and no one moves out of its way in traffic. Sam hates it and Birck just rolled his eyes when he saw it, but I like it, maybe because it looks roughly how I feel.

Bruket lies a long way inland, like an overgrown clearing in an enormous forest. Pine woods line the trunk road that leads there, so tall and so dense that many of the smaller trees are brown, as the canopy above is so thick that the sun doesn't make it through to them. The warm air, dry and hot at first, has gradually become damp and close. It's the twentieth of June — Midsummer's eve.

There was a glass factory here once, I remember. That must be why the name rings a bell. As I follow the road, the forest opens up until I pass the old factory site. It's huge, much bigger than I expected, and the buildings rise up beyond the high fence like grey skeletons. The road itself is poorly maintained, and tar bleeds from the cracks and gashes.

The sight that meets you as you turn into Bruket's square is more like a gloomy recollection of a little town than an actual little town.

The contrast between the car's dark interior and the stark sunlight on the square makes me squint. It really is unnaturally hot here.

I don't know what I was expecting. That everything would come to a standstill when a stranger's car rolled into town and parked, that eyebrows would be raised, and that people might approach me with faltering steps and cautious stares? That someone might prod me in the chest with an outstretched finger and point out that I must be in the wrong place, that the best thing to do would be to chug on out of there?

None of that happens. *Nothing* happens.

Kit is in the passenger seat, in his cage. I had to bring him with me.

He wasn't my idea, but Sam insisted, and a lot of the time it's impossible to say no to the one you love.

Now, at the stage when we're getting to know each other again, Sam knows that I'm fragile and unstable; she knows that *we* are, too. The few people who know us say that we've always been an unpredictable couple, which is true. Knowing what the next day is going to be like has never been straightforward, but it's getting easier and easier.

'Do you really want kids?' she asked me one night, a little over two months back.

'Yes,' I said. It was true. I think. 'You?'

'Yes.' She hesitated. 'But I don't know if we're up to it.'

The result: a fucking cat.

So, as I was saying, not my idea.

Sam bought him from an old tattoo-artist colleague whose cat had just had kittens. Kit is a mix of something and something else; no one's sure what. He has a dark-brown coat and green eyes, is about four months old, and to put it bluntly, isn't much good at anything in particular. He seems not to hear very well, has pretty bad sight, and has absolutely no interest in doing things that cats usually do. Mostly, he just wanders around looking blankly at the world. Sam says we're alike.

Now he raises his head and blinks, slowly. Then he yawns and slumps back into his cage.

In my pocket is a list, handwritten by Sam: *how not to kill the cat while I'm away.*

I roll the window down a bit, have a cigarette, and contemplate what I'm going to say if anyone asks what I'm doing here.

The houses surrounding the square are low and old. I get out of the car, put the cig out, open the cat's cage, leave the window a little bit open for Kit, and notice how everything that would usually matter is reduced to white noise.

An unsettling quiet hangs over Bruket on Midsummer's eve. Back when the glass factory was in full swing and everyone had something to be getting on with — a *purpose* — it was a hectic day, where people struggled to get done whatever they needed to do before they could go home or go away for the weekend. At lunchtime, you could see them walking home from the plant, all in line, almost like a train. Tove used to stand by that path, the route the workers always took, and she'd wait to catch sight of her dad's face among them. Nowadays, the whole day is spent in deep hibernation, a feeling that somehow finds its way into your head, making everything sluggish.

I don't trust anyone anymore, Tove thinks to herself. Maybe that's the problem.

That occurs to her at lunchtime. She's sitting there, making phone call after phone call to people in the area to see whether they're at home, and whether she can come round and show them a picture of a car, to see if they recognise it. She crosses out the names of the handful she's managed to get hold of, marking the ones who didn't answer with a cross.

And she thinks that, for some reason, the vast majority are hiding something. We all do that sometimes; everyone has secrets. A good police officer ought to know when she can trust someone and when she can't, but in Tove's case the boundaries have become blurred.

More than twenty-four hours have passed since Charles Levin was found dead. For an accomplished perpetrator, that is a head start that will be difficult to claw back.

Out in the corridor, someone calls her name. She goes out and finds one of the clerical staff standing there with a phone in his hand.

'What is it?'

'For you.'

It's a journalist, from the tabloid *Aftonbladet*. He wants to know if reports that the man found dead yesterday was a policeman are correct.

'No, that's not correct.'

'But …'

Tove hangs up and carries on with her own calls, until something makes her look up from the list.

There's a man standing at the meeting-room door, with a knuckle poised as though ready to knock.

'Oh, er …' he says. 'Hi. I'm looking for Ola Davidsson.'

He's about Tove's age, and is wearing a pair of Converse, dark jeans, and a grey T-shirt with PRINCE printed across the chest, next to an image of the artist's face. The man's hair is dark, and he has a prominent nose, pale skin. He looks like he used to be quite good-looking, the way that some emaciated addicts might have been before they destroyed themselves.

A black wave washes over her.

The man in the doorway shot dead her brother.

According to Morovi, the investigation is being led by a man named Ola Davidsson. The door to one of the offices carries a sign with his name and the title SUPERINTENDENT. It's open, and the computer is on, but the room is missing its owner. One of the walls is covered by a notice board, featuring a poster listing frequently used nicknames for the likes of us: filth, pigs, po-po, peelers, rozzers, tyre biters, scum.

PC Plod? Not heard that one in years.

I carry on, into the meeting room, which is a long, narrow room with a light wooden table in the middle, surrounded by a dozen chairs. On the table are rows of shut laptops, piles of paper, and various belongings that I guess have come from Levin's home, all bagged up in marked paper or plastic bags.

A large whiteboard covers most of the wall at one end of the room. Someone has written CHARLES JAN LEVIN, 1947-01-25 4694 — his national ID number — as a heading in black marker pen, and there's something about that that really brings it home to me. Alongside his name, there's a picture, attached to the whiteboard with a magnet. The picture has been circled, and a line drawn from the circle leads to a question mark. The photograph is blurred and depicts a dark-coloured car.

At the table, a woman is sitting with a telephone in one hand and a pen in the other. She seems to be filling in a form of some kind. Her forehead is shiny, and she's pale for the time of year. Her rye-blonde hair is up in a lazy bun. She's scrawny in that way that only people who have lost weight much too fast can be.

'Oh, er …' I say. 'Hi. I'm looking for Ola Davidsson.'

Against the bright light pouring in from outside, her eyes look almost black.

She puts the pen down.

'About what?'

Her voice is rough and muffled. She must smoke more than I do. I glance at the whiteboard, then at the telephone in her hand. She's gripping it so hard that her knuckles are white.

I take a step into the room, and it's like walking into a stifling wall of heat.

'Charles Levin.'

She's studying me, squinting.

'I thought you were on Stockholm's Violent Crime Unit?'

'Have we met before?'

'No. Are you from the Violent Crime Unit?'

'No.'

Strictly speaking, it's not a lie. I'm not here on their orders.

'Are you from National Crime?' she continues.

'Yes.'

The word drops out of my mouth before I have time to change my mind.

'I thought you'd be arriving the day after tomorrow, or even Monday.'

'I see. Yes. But I'm here now.'

I want to say something else, but I don't know what. There's something familiar about her.

'I'm Leo.'

'I know.'

'You do?'

She looks down at her hand, which is clasping her phone. Her ears are red, as is her neck. Slowly, she unclenches her hand and places the phone on the table.

'So we have met before?' I say.

'Davidsson said you were coming.'

I walk over to the table with my hand outstretched.

'Leo Junker.'

She places her right hand in mine. It is small and hard.

'Tove.'

She doesn't blink. Pretty unsettling. She lets go of my hand. I wonder what she's thinking, what exactly is wrong with her, or whether it's me. I'm not good at making people feel at ease. I squint at the whiteboard.

'Who's that there?'

'In the picture?'

'Yes, the man in the car. Is it him?'

'What do you mean, him?'

'The perpetrat—'

Tove gets up from her chair, which slides backwards from the force of her sudden movement, scraping on the floor. She walks quickly out of the room, leaving me standing there, halfway through a sentence, watching her go.

The world is a strange place.

I walk over to the whiteboard and the picture that someone's stuck there with a little magnet. It's a blurred photograph, an out-of-focus man in an indistinct, expensive-looking car. He seems to be leaning forwards. I squint. The face is more of a grey smudge than features and lines.

Photographs of the crime scene and piles of paper are spread across the meeting-room table. It's just a skeleton, but then, of course, you have to start somewhere. I examine the contents of the bags: a few clothes, ring binders and books, a laptop charger.

In combination, these items reveal just why they're here — those at the scene didn't know what they were looking for.

I take a Halcion. There's a constant strange flickering just behind my eyeballs.

From the corner of my eye: I see photographs of Levin's dead body.

They're treating it as suspicious. That's all Morovi said.

I pick up one of the pictures. Levin is lying on the floor, and blood has poured from a hole, at around head-height. A lot of blood. At first, that's all I see. It has a hypnotic effect.

I drop the picture. It lands next to a photograph taken by what must be the kitchen door: the body and the blood are visible — but, at a distance, that's easier to deal with — along with the sink and the fridge, and, at the edge of the picture, two chairs and a table. There are two coffee cups on the table. The position of the chairs could be significant.

A third picture captures the cloud of blood splattered on the kitchen wall. It takes a minute before I get my bearings myself and realise what I'm looking at. Levin must have been sitting on the chair when he was shot.

The fourth picture I pick up from the table is a picture of the rubbish bin under the sink. It is a small blue bucket, and there isn't even a bag in it.

I start going through the rest of the material on the table but the suffocating heat is distracting. I leave the papers and go over to the window, place my hands on the sill. Burning hot. The streets are just as empty as these offices.

Where the hell *is* everyone?

I look up towards the sky.

There's something about this place. Everything is quiet, but unpredictable; we could be swept away by an enormous wave at any moment. That's how it feels.

What the hell was Levin doing here?

Footsteps, footsteps behind me. Tove comes back, sits down again, and examines the piece of paper — some kind of list. She pulls out her phone.

'Where is everyone?' I say.

'What do you mean?'

'Well, there's no one here.'

'There aren't that many of us,' she says, without looking up, 'and the few that we have … It's Midsummer's eve.'

'But it's *lunchtime*. It's only one o'clock.'

'They're in a strategy meeting. Out the door, turn left, then it's the big room at the end.'

'Is Davidsson there?' I ask.

'No.'

'Where is he then?'

'I don't know.'

'Have you got his number?'

'Of course I have. He's my boss.'

'I'd like to speak to him.'

No response. I consider taking the phone off her, before realising that that is probably a very bad idea.

'Is that him?' I ask instead, and sit down opposite her. 'The perpetrator?'

'Do you mean in the car in that picture?'

'I never got an answer earlier, you … you just left.'

She activates the screen-lock on her phone, and puts it to one side before making eye contact.

'We believe that it is him.' At first, that answer seems to be as much as she can manage, but then she continues: 'It was taken by a witness. He sees a man walking away from the house towards the car. The man then gets into the car and it drives off.'

'And you have no idea who the driver is?'

'No.'

This time, that's all I get. I'd feel better for a glass of water.

The Halcion pill has started working, I can feel that gentle buzz around my temples, and the vibrations in my chest ease off. My eyes become comfortably fuzzy.

'What do you think happened?' I ask.

'You want me to guess?'

'I'm asking you what you think.'

Are they *all* like her?

'The suspect arrives in the Volvo, and parks up at around nine thirty.' She is scraping the tabletop with her thumbnail, as though she was trying to get rid of a mark or something. 'Levin lets him in, which suggests that it was someone he knew, or at least knew of. They end up in the kitchen, and Levin presumably makes coffee. Levin drinks some, the suspect doesn't. They talk to each other, we have to assume, perhaps for as long as forty-five minutes. The suspect then stands up, and shoots Levin in the head.' Tove folds her arms across her narrow chest. 'Something like that.'

'And then?'

'He takes a few things from the desk in the bedroom — I'm thinking computer, printer, mobile. Then he makes off in the Volvo.' Tove chews her bottom lip. 'Along those lines.'

'I … This witness.' I look for the notes. 'Fredrik Oskarsson, who sees a man walking along the path in the woods behind the house.'

'What about him?'

'Well …' I wonder if this could be construed as an insult. 'It might be the perpetrator he sees.'

Tove shakes her head. 'We have a witness who sees the car park up outside Alvavägen 10. Why would the driver head off into the woods?'

'I know,' I say. 'But …' When our eyes meet and I see her icy stare, I realise that we're not going to get anywhere, and that whatever it is that's wrong with her doesn't have anything to do with me.

'You're right.'

'I'll see if I can get hold of Davidsson,' she mumbles, fiddling with her phone.

'How did you know my name was Leo?'

'I told you.' She puts the phone to her ear. 'Davidsson mentioned it.'

'But …'

'It's me,' she says when the call is answered. 'I've got a guy here from NCS. He's wondering … Yes, I know, but one of them is already here. Are you going to call Stock— … Okay. Yes, we've started. He's had a look at the pictures and some of the … I'm sitting here with a list of people in the area who might have seen the car. I'm about to go and speak to them.'

I can hear their voices, Tove's next to me and his at the other end of the line, a rough, ugly voice, but I stop listening to the words because I spot a polaroid photo sticking out from underneath one of the binders.

I pull it out and hold it between my index finger and thumb. A man, a woman, a small child. All smiling.

I turn it over, and on the back, Levin's handwriting, written long ago:

Me, Marika, and Eva, spring '78.

Tove hangs up.

'If you wait here, Davidsson will be here in half an hour or so.'

'Good,' I say, studying the picture again. 'Nineteen seventy-eight. Do we know where the picture was taken?'

Tove looks through the prints of the crime-scene photos.

'Here.'

I compare the two pictures. On the newly taken one, it looks like a combined study-bedroom.

'Same house?'

'Same room.' She gets up from her chair, gathers her things. 'I'm going now. Davidsson will be here in a bit. Wait here.'

I look at the whiteboard again — the photo of the man in the dark-coloured Volvo.

'Have you done a search on the vehicle?'

'Of course. But given the circumstances, it's not likely to tell us much.'

'What circumstances?'

'False plates. Didn't I tell you that?'

'No.'

She shrugs and walks out.

I've started looking at the little biography while I'm waiting for Davidsson, and I wish I hadn't.

I know about his marriage to Elsa Wiklander, and that she died a few years ago, but when Levin talked about her, and on the few occasions I saw them together, I always assumed that they'd been childhood sweethearts.

Eva Levin, née Alderin.

The idea that he had been married to someone other than Elsa is at first so unexpected that I'm convinced they've got his details mixed up with someone else. But they haven't.

Eva Levin. Killed in a road accident, winter 1980. A police investigation got underway — there's a light-brown file lying on the table next to the biography, containing a handful of old documents. I flip through them. There don't appear to be any suspicious circumstances; she was on her way home after collecting their daughter, Marika, from a friend's house. The mother died, the girl survived. Photos show a clump of trees, the car that hit one of them head-on, and the blackened wreck that was left when the flames had died down. It was an old car, according to the notes, and it needed a new fuel tank. The impact caused a fracture in the tank. That, and a spark, was all it took.

A sharp pang in my heart, maybe the pain you feel when you realise that someone close has experienced losing the one he loved.

A pang in my heart, perhaps for *Marika Levin.*

He has a daughter.

I stare at the name, trying to understand its significance. Why did he never tell me? Did he keep her a secret? If so, why?

I leave the brick building. A kit-car with two young men inside rolls along the road. The spluttering din of its engine mixes with the doo-wop music blaring from the stereo, something about the book of love.

I watch the car drive off, and that's when I remember.

I've heard her name before — not Marika Levin but Marika *Alderin*.

Less than twenty-four hours ago, in fact, when two of the staff on reception at St Göran's were going through the patients' medication and I was waiting to sign Grim's visit list. Marika Alderin was one of the people they mentioned, I'm sure of it.

It must be the same person.

This realisation is so absurd that I can't help but laugh. An incredible twist of fate: Levin's daughter is on the same ward as my best friend.

Standing next to my car on the square, I'm fairly sure that there isn't an awful lot to do here. There's a bar, Brukets Bar; a convenience store; outfitters, Hannes Fashion; a newsstand; some sort of all-round service shop for photocopying, parcel collection, and P.O. boxes; the state-run alcohol store; and a boarded-up old hotel. That's pretty much everything I can see, but then again, that might be everything you actually need.

I put out my cigarette and fumble with my car keys. Kit is lying in the shade of the passenger footwell, and when I open the driver's door he lifts a sleepy head and blinks, before he realises who it is and looks annoyed.

'It's probably not good, you lying here.' I pick him up, struggle out of the Opel and close the door. 'It's so bloody hot.'

I then go back into the police station with the cat in my arms. He looks around, wide-eyed, and seems to be asking himself where the hell he has ended up.

Still no sign of Davidsson. I put Kit down on the floor of the meeting room, close the door, and fiddle with the windows to put them on the catch. I slip, cut myself on something, don't know what, and the palm of my hand is bleeding. When I finally manage to pull the windows to, they're smeared with blood.

Kit is sitting on the floor next to me and looks faintly amused.

I go to the toilet to rinse my hand, wrap paper around it, and on my way out I pull up Gabriel Birck's number on my phone.

The ringtone is slow and oscillating, sounds in some weird way almost as though it's about to take off. One, two, three rings before a sharp crackle.

'And where the fuck are you?'

'I'm on leave.'

'You're not on leave. You're on *call*.'

'I applied for leave two days ago.'

In the background, there's the sound of tapping on a keyboard. A television on low volume, some kind of news bulletin. And, beyond that, the sound of Kungsholmen, the hum from the open window in Birck's room.

'And you got it approved? Just before Midsummer?'

'Yes. What are you doing?'

'I'm on an attempted murder in Observatorielunden Park.'

'And?'

'Oh yes,' Birck says, tapping away. The sound is aggressive and sharp. 'DNA match, according to forensics. What are you doing, if you're not here somewhere?'

'I'm in Bruket.'

'Bruket? Is that outside Uppsala?'

'On the border between Halland County and Småland, somewhere. I couldn't tell you exactly.'

'Halla— ... Jesus, that's fucking miles away. What are you doing there?'

'Have you heard about Levin?'

The tapping stops.

'Yes,' Birck says, softer now, his voice heavier. 'I heard. My condolences.'

'He just moved down here in spring. I think I ... I just wanted to see him, I think.'

'How did he die?'

'Shot in the head.'

Silence. The newsreader announces that Midsummer will be a rainy affair in the main cities.

'Not much to see, in that case,' Birck says. 'Is that why you changed your leave? So you could go there?'

'Yes.'

'You do know that this isn't good for you?'

Another silence between us. The news makes way for television commercials, and an excitable male voice tells us about some place where we can buy a set of garden furniture for only 399 crowns. The heat in the room is making me dizzy; I'm blinking.

'Was that all you wanted?' Birck asks.

'I would like to ask you a favour, or two. Firstly ... don't tell Morovi about this.'

'That depends what *this* is.'

'Gabriel,' I plead.

'What do I say if she asks?'

'She knows I'm on leave. I just don't want her to know that I'm here.'

Birck sighs.

'Okay.'

'And then …' I close my eyes. 'I need to ask you to sort out a phone charger for Grim. I'll give you the money …'

'What?' He sounds genuinely shocked. 'What the fuck, Leo … ?'

'Wait. In exchange, I want him to tell you about Levin's visits to St Göran's. I think he used to visit one of the residents, possibly a woman named Marika Alderin.'

Birck is silent for some time.

'You've been making deals with him.'

'That's the nature of our relationship nowadays.'

'He tried to kill you. He tried to kill Sam.'

'I know.'

'How can … ?'

'I know, okay? It's fucked up, but I really want to know.'

'The bastard has got a phone, apparently. You call him.'

'I can't do this by phone.'

Birck sighs again. I can see him, his tired eyes, in front of me. *Rustling:* he's tearing a page from a notepad. A pen clicks once, twice.

'What did you say her name was?'

'Marika Alderin.' I spell it out. 'But it might not have been her he was visiting, that's just … a hunch. Don't give Grim the name to begin with, because then he'll definitely say yes, whether it's true or not. See if he comes up with it himself.'

'What if he doesn't?'

'Try and improvise.'

'I'm not about to go and improvise with John Grimberg.'

I can't say I blame him.

Birck clicks the pen again. He might be spinning it in his hand, because he soon drops it and swears.

'Who is this woman?' he asks.

'Levin's daughter.'

92

A long pause.

'Whoa.'

'I know.'

'Did you know?' he asks. 'That he had a daughter?'

'No,' I say. 'I don't think anyone did. They found a photo of her down here, that's how people found out. And it's *that* — the fact he kept her a secret — that might be significant.'

'I'm not an idiot. I get that.'

I give him the phone's make and model. Birck says nothing, but makes a note of it. The sound of pen on paper somehow makes me homesick.

Kit jumps up onto the table and paws the crime scene photos, studying them as if they hold some secret.

'Happy Midsummer, then, I suppose,' says Birck.

In my memories, I feel older than I do now. There, as though veiled in smoke, I can see myself one late autumn many years ago, doing my first shifts on the Violent Crime Unit and meeting Levin for the first time.

I've been given a desk in the corner of the open-plan office, and I'm sitting there feeling lost when he appears beside me: tall, gangly, head shaved even back then, and round, black-rimmed glasses on his beak of a nose, which projects out over his narrow mouth.

'The rookie.' He pulls his hand out of his trouser pocket. Big smile. 'Charles Levin.'

'Leo Junker.'

'We never met during the recruitment process, I prefer not to get involved. At least, not formally.'

He looks around, spots a stool by one of the nearby desks, and sits down, crossing one leg over the other.

'You're from Violent Crime, right?'

'Yes.'

'Before that?'

'Vice. I was only there a few months though after coming off the beat.'

'Did you like it there?'

'On the beat? Not especially.'

This makes him laugh.

'I remember that I enjoyed my time in uniform. I was at District One, as it was back then.'

His presence. I noticed straightaway that there was something about his presence. The room moved in time with Levin and could make him invisible on his say so, just putting him in the spotlight as and when it was necessary.

'How old are you, Leo?'

'Twenty-eight.'

'And I'm over sixty,' he says pensively. 'That's old, isn't it?'

'Well it's older than twenty-eight, yes.'

He laughs again, loud and harsh.

'You're right, there. I couldn't help noticing a slight smell of cigarettes around you. What brand do you smoke?'

'Chesterfield.'

He raises an eyebrow.

'Really?'

I pull the pack from my inside pocket and show it to him.

'My old boss used to smoke Chesterfields,' Levin says, his eyes following the packet. 'Officially, I am no longer a smoker, since it's deemed unsuitable for someone in a leading role within the force to be one. They say our capacity to lead by example would be undermined. Whatever that means.'

I open the packet, pull out a cigarette, and hold it out towards him, hiding it under my hand.

'This cigarette reminds me of a joke my old boss used to tell,' Levin says, as we both stand huddled by one of the neighbouring buildings, each with a cigarette between our fingers.

'Go on.'

'It's not a funny joke.'

'Now you have to tell it.'

He takes a last drag.

'Do you know who Erich Honecker was?'

'A politician in the old East Germany?'

'He was East German leader throughout the Seventies and Eighties. One morning, Honecker is on the balcony doing his exercises, when all of a sudden the sun starts talking to him, "Good morning, Herr Honecker!" Honecker, shocked, tells his comrades about this in a meeting a few hours later. He takes a few comrades home with him at lunch, and when they are all there, on his balcony, the sun talks to him again: "Good day, Herr Honecker!" For the rest of the day, they're all stunned, and can't stop talking about the miracle they have witnessed. When Honecker arrives home that evening, the sun is about to slip beneath the horizon, yet this time is as mute as a fish. "Sun," Honecker shouts, "you greeted me this morning, and at lunchtime, why are you silent now it's evening?" He soon hears a mocking laugh coming from the sun. "You can kiss my arse, Honecker. I'm in the West now."'

He goes quiet and looks at me.

'Was it funny back then?' I ask.

'For some, like my old boss, it probably was.'

'He can't have had many friends.'

'Oh, he did. But that wasn't down to his sense of humour.'

As we get closer to the entrance, he asks if I want to hear another.

'It's shorter,' he adds.

'I suppose so.'

'There are three types of people. People that tell jokes, people that collect jokes, and people who work at SEPO, who collect people that tell jokes.'

I sit down on one of the chairs in the meeting room, wipe the sweat from my forehead again, and wonder how long it will be before they realise that I'm not from NCS. Strictly speaking, I'm committing a serious crime.

Out in the corridor, someone is sneezing angrily, and then a fat man comes into the meeting room, belly first, and with a handkerchief in one hand. He wipes his nose before using it to wipe his brow.

'Leo Junker.' I stand up. 'Down from Stockholm.'

'Ola Davidsson,' he grunts, before noticing something behind me. 'Jesus.'

The cat is busy investigating one of the sealed bags. My cheeks turn bright red.

'I had to bring him with me.' I lift him down from the table, and close the door.

'I would have had to wait otherwise.'

'What's its name?'

'Kit.'

'Like the car in *Knight Rider*?'

'Erm, yeah. If you like. Or as in Kit … Kat.'

Davidsson bends down, puts his hands on his knees, and summons something that looks a bit like a smile.

'Hello, Kit.'

The cat stares at him, expressionless, before stroking up against his fat calves, which makes him chuckle. Davidsson then stands up straight and waves his chubby hand at me.

'Sit down somewhere.'

We each slump into a chair.

'You must hate Midsummer,' Davidsson says. 'Coming down today, I mean.'

'I don't really have anything to celebrate.'

'Come down to the sportsground later, if you get sick of the case notes. That's where the party is.' Davidsson pulls a packet of

Tic Tacs from his pocket, shakes four into his hand, and pops them on his tongue. 'There aren't that many of us here. Just me; Tove, who you've met; and a few lads on the beat. We have requested reinforcements, too, another fifteen people from the big cities. They're the ones who are going to do the heavy lifting on the investigation, along with you. I should think they've gone home by now. It's the absolute worst time of year for this sort of thing, worse than New Year's Eve or Christmas.'

'Yes,' I say, looking at the whiteboard. 'I know. What do you think he was doing down here?'

'Levin? Well, obviously we don't know, but at a guess he was probably working on old cases.'

'Cases? Which cases?'

Davidsson's surprise makes him look like a real policeman for the first time.

'The unsolved investigations. Didn't Tove mention them?'

'No, she didn't.'

Davidsson furrows his brow and coughs. Then he sneezes. Then he coughs again.

He leans over the table, looking through papers that are lying in a messy pile, but perhaps there is some kind of system, because before long he pulls out a folder.

'Here they are. They were in files, at the bottom of a packing box, along with books and photographs.'

I flip through the paperwork, police documents from old investigations: a fatal stabbing on one of the capital-deprived estates from 1997, a rape in Enskede from 2001, an attempted murder in central Stockholm from 2005, and the murder on John Ericssonsgatan on Kungsholmen from 2010. The only one I recall is the last one, since I was working on the Violent Crime Unit under Levin.

'This attempted murder in town,' I say, turning towards Davidsson, who is attempting to type something into his phone, with some difficulty. 'Where are the rest of the documents? These are just the notes.'

'That's right.' Davidsson looks up. 'That's what's so strange about it. There was nothing else.'

'Serious violent crime, unsolved cases. That's what he was working on?'

'Perhaps. We don't actually know what he was doing here. We were sort of hoping you might help us work that out.'

I put the papers down, and think about Levin's memoirs. I want to know what was in them.

'Of course,' I mumble. 'I don't understand why she didn't mention this. Your colleague.'

'She's a tricky one, Waltersson.'

'What did you say?'

'That she's a tricky one.'

'Not that — what's her surname?'

'Waltersson.' Davidsson raises an eyebrow and folds his arms. 'Why?'

I strain to keep my hands steady.

'I recognise the name.'

'She's from around here — I think her mum lives here in Bruket. I don't know anything about her dad. I think maybe he worked at the plant, but where he went after it shut down I couldn't tell you. And then she had a brother …'

Markus.

'Markus,' Davidsson continues. 'He was in the force, too. Weird, isn't it, stuff like that between siblings?'

'He died,' I say, weakly.

'He worked in Stockholm. He got shot by a colleague, on Gotland.'

I get up from the chair and go over to the window. The room is starting to tilt, and I have to hold onto the table so as not to lose my balance.

I knew he had a sister, didn't I?

My hands are shaking, and I fish out the tube of Halcion. Only one left. *One.* Oh shit.

It's May, one year ago. I'm standing in the harbour in Visby. A little boat comes gliding through the darkness, loaded with what we believe is a consignment of weapons. They are going to change hands. Something goes wrong. I blink. With my burning-hot pistol in my hands, I approach the darkness between two heavy shipping containers. He's lying there, Markus Waltersson, and he's bleeding to death.

'Is that everything?' Davidsson asks from behind me.

He doesn't know that it was me. Despite the acres of coverage the Gotland affair was given in the weeks after Waltersson's death, Davidsson doesn't know me from Adam. Maybe it's the same for most people I meet. Maybe I'm just imagining everyone looking at me, and that they're talking about me behind my back.

'Yes. That's everything.'

'Happy Midsummer,' he says, before standing up and walking out.

MARCH 1971

The first of March 1971. The second time Charles met Eva, he went home with her. He called the number she'd written down for him. Before he did, though, he spent a long time in one of the telephone cubicles at the conference centre, studying the angular, uneven digits on the note, numbers written by someone who'd spent their school days doing more important things than homework.

It struck him that she didn't seem surprised. Maybe women like Eva cease to be surprised by men, even by the age of twenty-one.

'Are you going to skive off?' was the only thing she asked him, and Charles felt his cheeks getting warm.

That's something he remembers about Eva, the way she could make *that'll be eighteen fifty, please* sound so suggestive that it sent blushing teenagers rushing home to wash their ears — before coming back to the convenience store to hear her say it again.

'Yes,' he said. 'For once.'

'When was the last time you did something like this?' she asked.

'I don't remember,' Charles said. 'Don't remember when I last had reason to.'

The line went quiet, a silence that made Charles worry that he'd said too much.

'See you later then,' she said.

He sneaked out of the conference during a coffee break. He

took his own car, and he saw Bruket in daylight for the first time. Towering chimneys on the horizon and white-grey pillars of smoke reaching for the sky.

The car park by the square was quite small. He headed for the shop, which occupied the bottom floor of an old dark-brown wooden building. It had a handful of trolleys parked in a bay, and a simple till. The door opened, and Eva smiled at Charles as she came out.

'So where do you want to go?' she asked.

He looked around.

'Where is there to go?'

She laughed, and pushed a strand of hair back behind her ear.

'Good question. There's a little bakery not far away. It's quite nice, if you don't mind stewed coffee.'

'I'm a policeman,' Charles said. 'I'm used to it.'

That was something people were always asking him about — being a policeman. And he wasn't the only one. Most of his colleagues, and indeed Charles himself, would often try to make the most of it in the bars and clubs down Birger Jarlsgatan. It often worked, because they didn't know what being a policeman actually involved.

Eva didn't ask about that at all. She wanted to know what music Charles listened to, whether he took sugar in his coffee, whether he preferred paintings or photographs on his walls, when he fell in love for the first time and if he was an only child or had siblings, whether he was the type of person who liked rugs around the house.

'Type of person?' Charles said, taking a gulp of the stewed coffee. 'What do you mean?'

'Whether you use rugs or not,' she said, 'it says something about you. A certain kind of people have rugs.'

'And what are they like?'

She looked down at her cup as she tried to find the right word.

'They're sort of … organised. Proper, you know, tidy and well groomed. If you've got the time and money to buy rugs, then you must be. I imagine they are the same people that go into shoe shops and ask for sensible shoes.'

She said the word *sensible* as though it came from some foreign culture.

'I don't have any rugs,' said Charles.

'That's what I thought.' She smiled. 'Me neither.'

Dusk arrived, and the colours inside the bakery changed hue in a way that was quite pleasant. She lived on Alvavägen, five minutes from Bruket's little centre. Eva didn't have a car — she preferred to walk or ride her bike, even in the winter, so they went in his car.

He pulled up alongside a low light-coloured fence. Behind it was a little path of paving stones leading up to the steps and the front door. She had bought the place a year before, she explained. That was the first thing she'd decided to do after leaving school: to save up to buy her own home.

She asked if he would like to share a bottle of wine with her. Charles nodded towards the window, and the car that was just visible on the street outside.

'I'm driving.'

'Tonight?'

As she smiled, a warmth spread over him.

They sat on the sofa, in front of her television. Eva curled up with her legs tucked under her body, pushed that hair behind her ear again. She had done this many times that day, and Charles wished that he'd counted. It would've been a nice thing to remember, a specific number.

'Have you ever thought about moving away from here?' he asked.

She had not.

'I grew up here, I enjoy living here, and I've got everything I need here. Well,' she corrected herself, 'almost everything.'

Charles drank some wine, red and heavy.

'Is that normal, for people not to? I mean, do people usually stay here?'

'I think so. I don't know. Why shouldn't they?'

She reached over and stroked his forearm, gently dragging her nails across his skin. Charles saw the hairs on his arm stand up, and she saw that he'd seen.

When he kissed her, she responded hungrily and forcefully. She had been waiting for him.

MARCH 1984

The East German Embassy is located in a district of Stockholm called Lärkstaden, on Bragevägen — in the quiet gap between the busy thoroughfares of Karlavägen and Valhallavägen. It is an embassy that never sleeps, always waiting, always watching. The lights are on throughout the building, shadows lurk behind the curtains, and cars glide down the street at all hours of the day and night.

Alienation. You can't miss it.

'This is risky,' Charles says, and notices how he sinks down into his seat as they drive past the compound.

'I know. But apparently, he's done his leg in, so he can't walk that far.'

The car is a phantom, a cool, quiet Mercedes, with numberplates produced to The Bureau's specifications. According to the digital clock on the dashboard, there's exactly two hours left till midnight.

Paul stops the car at the little T-junction where Engelbrekts Kyrkogata meets Östermalmsgatan. He keeps his hand on the key in the ignition, and a close eye on the rear-view mirror. Charles is planning to go with the flow, out of here, and wonders how long the babysitter will put up with Marika this time.

'Hello?' says Paul. 'Have you gone deaf?'

'I … No. What did you say?'

'I said that I heard the factory is in danger of going bust.'

'You mean the glass factory?'

'Yes. Which could threaten the whole town eventually. They're struggling with the competition from other factories, apparently. It's all connected, nowadays. They're all in different parts of the same big net.' Then he's quiet for a moment. 'When were you last there?'

'In Bruket? I haven't been back since we moved.'

'You might feel better if you did.'

Charles looks out through the window. A lone jogger passes by, turning orange under the sodium street lamps. The slush splashes up as his feet hit the ground.

'I don't want to talk about that,' says Charles.

'I need to be able to trust you. I need to know that I can count on you.'

'Have I ever done anything to make you doubt that?'

'Not yet,' Paul says. 'I've known you for over three years. This thing has ...'

'Stop.'

'... torn away at you every day and ...'

'Stop talking about it,' Charles says, louder.

'... and it's getting worse, too.'

He turns to face Paul, strains to relax his jaw but doesn't succeed.

'Shut up.'

'This is precisely what I'm ...'

Charles should have taken his belt off — his sudden movement causes the belt to lock as it would in a crash, and his punch changes direction. Suddenly Paul is groaning and coughing.

'You punched me in the throat, you bastard.'

Charles puts his head against the headrest. His knuckles are pulsating. Paul is massaging his throat. They're panting, out of sync.

A limping silhouette, propped up by a thin cane, swings out onto Engelbrekts Kyrkogata.

'Here he comes,' says Charles.

Paul opens his mouth, has a go at talking.

'Fuck, that hurt. How do I sound?'

'Like you've got a cold.'

'That'll have to do.'

Paul straightens himself and follows the approaching silhouette in the rear-view mirror. When it is a few steps away, Paul turns the key and the engine starts, discreetly and satisfyingly.

The door behind Paul opens, and the interior light comes on. The evening seeps in, damp and cold, along with a man who places his cane onto the seat with care, before easing himself down next to it.

'Good evening, Mr Kraus,' Paul says in English.

'Mr Goffman,' says the Resident Minister. 'It's good to see you again.'

The Residency is a position granted from the other side of the wall in Berlin by HVA, the East German intelligence agency responsible for foreign affairs. The East German Embassy is referred to internally as *Residentur 227* and is a sham, nothing more than an intelligence station with some diplomatic capacity — and the person responsible for the operation is the Resident. The ambassador is merely the public face. The Resident, for the past three years, has been Johann Kraus, and during his time in the post this capricious man has become almost as notorious as his boss, Markus 'Mischa' Wolf.

The walls of Kraus' office are adorned with framed photographs: Kraus standing in the background as Sten Wickbom shakes hands with the ambassador, yet, while both men in the foreground are smiling, Kraus' expression gives nothing away. Another picture: Kraus and Gunnar Fredriksson, politics editor at *Aftonbladet*, dining together at Operakällaren; Kraus is smiling broadly and holding up a chubby thumb, while Fredriksson looks somewhat nervous, as though the picture was being taken to send to the Kremlin. Next: Kraus sitting next to the managing director of the Royal Dramatic Theatre, in one of the comfortable seats in the largest auditorium. A fourth shows Kraus and the ambassador inside Government House. Kraus has a briefcase in one hand, and a cup of coffee in the other. They are close to Prime Minister Palme's room. The door is visible in the background, and is slightly ajar.

The photographs are more like trophies than memories.

'Mr Levin,' he says. 'It's nice to see you, too.'

'Thank you. Yes.'

'How is your leg?' Paul asks, switching to Swedish.

'Getting better all the time.' Kraus puts his hand on his cane and looks out of the window. 'Swedish health care is almost as reassuring as German.' He furrows his brow just as the interior light turns off again. 'Your throat is terribly red, Mr Goffman.'

'It's eczema.' Paul pulls out onto Östermalmsgatan. 'I always get it when it's cold.'

Smoothly, quietly, with neither a plan nor a destination, the journey continues towards Birger Jarlsgatan.

Facing the street, Kraus looks like a man discovering a new city for the first time. His thick hair is flecked with grey, and — judging by the fringe peeking out from under his black trilby — is neatly combed. He wears thick glasses, framing eyes that are as black as deep wells. He speaks German, Swedish, English, and Russian, but prefers English since it is dispassionate and reserved, the language of capitalism and the bourgeoisie: it helps him to keep emotions at bay and his thoughts in order.

He hears everything, sees everything, and is old enough to not let anything surprise him. He's Stasi through and through, and has been working for them as far back as the intelligence files on him have managed to establish.

'I had lunch with one of your government ministers today,' he says. 'You'll never guess what we talked about.'

'Money?' Paul suggests.

Kraus laughs.

'So banal. No — morality. I once heard somebody, I can't remember who, say that morality is reflected in the methods you use, or don't use, in pursuit of your ends. Would you agree with that?' Silence. 'Probably not. Presumably, you would claim, as the minister did, that the morality *is* the ends, would you not? It's just rather difficult to know what one's ends are. Particularly if one is Swedish.'

They pass the area by Roslagstull and Sveaplan, drive up towards Odenplan via the backstreets. This — meeting in person, in a car sweeping through the centre of the city — is not how these exchanges normally take place. Almost without exception, information, money, and goods change hands without those involved ever actually meeting. That is how Charles, Paul, and everyone else in the business keep themselves below the surface and between the lines, but the acute nature of the situation has forced a change in methods.

'I almost enjoy it,' says the Resident now, 'the sheer audacity of our meeting like this.' He laughs. 'Two corrupt Swedish security policemen and a simple embassy bureaucrat. A *fuck you* to Western imperialism and Swedish neutrality.'

'And no one saw us?' says Charles.

'Of course not. I chose the time and location of our meeting with great care.' Kraus leans forward. 'Now, to the matter in hand. I understand that there is … a problem with the consignment.'

'Yes,' says Paul. 'But we've got it.'

'You have the consignment?'

'We know its whereabouts, and it isn't going anywhere.'

'And you're quite sure about that?'

'You are working with criminals,' says Charles. 'You should have told us. It makes our job that bit riskier. That is, unless,' Charles continues, despite Paul's stare urging him to stop, 'you were planning to sort it out yourselves this time.'

'I'm not sure I understand what you mean,' Kraus says.

'I think you do,' says Charles.

Kraus and his friends plan to get rid of them, and then use other, cheaper middlemen. The likes of Savolainen and Öberg, who cost less because they don't have as much to lose.

Kraus pushes his glasses up his nose a touch, sighs, selecting his words.

They're behind, on the other side of the Wall, everyone knows that. There's even a joke about them: a slice of bread makes a useful compass; simply place it on the Berlin Wall. The side where someone quickly takes a bite is pointing east. Or, how do you know if the Stasi are bugging your home? Easy: suddenly there's a buzzing cupboard in the hallway and a ten-year-old trailer and a generator outside. In terms of developing technology and electronics, the USA, Sweden, and all the other countries on this side of the Wall are miles ahead. They have lots of money and far greater resources. The Eastern Bloc states do their best to hide the fact, but no one believes them anymore.

'We do not wish,' Kraus says, with a subtle but effective emphasis, 'to jeopardise either our arrangement or the consignment.'

'Well, then you will understand the necessity of renegotiation,' Charles says as Paul pulls up at a red light close to Odenplan.

The church tower, rising sharp and cold towards the heavens, looks more like a spear than anything else.

'That is what I was afraid of,' says Kraus.

'Thirty per cent instead of fifteen.'

'Not a chance. Twenty.'

'Twenty-five,' says Charles.

A Saab stops in the lane alongside them. In a child seat in the back, there's a child with soft cheeks and a round face, wearing a brown or dark-red woolly hat. The child smiles at Kraus, who raises a hand, waves, and smiles back.

'Okay,' he says. 'Twenty-five.'

Twenty-five per cent. Two million crowns — one each. The lights change. The Saab sweeps off towards Sveavägen, and the Mercedes glides smoothly and quietly out onto Odengatan.

'You will have to give me time though,' Kraus continues. 'I need to clear it with Berlin. A month, at least,' he continues, pre-empting Paul's question. 'Maybe more.'

'And,' says Charles, 'with everything that we need to take into account here, we won't be done before the summer, perhaps not until early in the autumn.'

Saying it out loud, how drawn-out this is all getting, fills him with a sense of hopelessness. A never-ending story.

'That sounds reasonable,' says Kraus. 'And?'

'The only way to make them disappear is to keep moving them, at irregular intervals, between three or four sites, and then they happen to go up in smoke somewhere along the line.'

'And how could you avoid such a disappearance coming to the attention of your Director?'

'Well, we can't,' says Paul. 'We'll have to lie.'

'And given his current condition, if I am correctly informed,' Kraus says, 'that may be reasonably straightforward. Is it correct that he is now chain-smoking?'

'Yes,' says Charles.

'Chesterfield?'

'That's right.'

'Chesterfield may be the only tasteful thing ever to have come out of America,' Kraus says. 'With the exception of the atom bomb.'

When they arrive back in Lärkstaden, there's an hour to go until midnight. Charles wants to get home, worried that the babysitter might have fallen asleep or simply given up and left, leaving Marika alone in her bed, alone if she wakes up from a nightmare.

'Our man in Stockholm will contact you in due course,' Kraus says, with his hand ready on the car door handle. 'It may be a while, but when he does, I suggest you show him rather more hospitality than you have shown me tonight.'

'We will,' Paul says. 'I do apologise.'

'Excuse me,' says Charles, 'but was that a threat?'

Kraus smiles and opens the door.

'We are socialists, not bandits.' He puts the tip of his cane on the tarmac. 'Good evening, gentlemen.'

He really ought to get rid of the babysitter. Every time she looks at him, it's with a look that says he should be spending more time with his daughter. He suspects it might have got her sacked before. Her name is Pauline, she's nineteen years old, and each time she comes she brings a new, thick book, which she reads whenever Marika is busy with something.

She is sitting on a chair in the hall, boots on and coat in hand, when Charles enters.

'Is she asleep?'

'Yes.' She stands up. 'I couldn't be bothered with the washing up.'

'Don't worry.'

There it is — that look. Charles gets his wallet out and starts counting notes to avoid seeing it.

'Was everything okay today?'

'Not exactly.'

'What, did something happen?'

Pauline puts her coat on, one arm first, then the other, slowly, deliberately drawing it out, as a punishment. He has the urge to slam her against the wall.

'She was violent towards a kid in her class.'

'Why?'

'What do you mean *why*?'

'Marika isn't wicked. If she was violent towards someone, they must have done something to her.'

Pauline sighs.

'Right. This time at least, according to the teacher, it was unprovoked.'

'Who was this kid?'

'Patrik.'

Charles tries to recall the name.

'Is he ...' he says with the notes in his fist, 'a bit of a handful?'

'No.' Pauline takes the money. 'No, he isn't.' She looks in the mirror, straightens her hair. 'There's a note on the kitchen table.'

'What kind of note?'

'From the school. She threatened him with a knife.'

Then she leaves.

A twelve-year-old girl shouldn't need a babysitter, but he isn't at home enough, and when she's on her own she doesn't eat, doesn't wash, doesn't clean. Marika doesn't follow any instructions unless she knows you're watching. It's always been like that. The mother passes her dark side to the daughter.

Charles gently pushes the door to her room open. She's lying flat on her back, exhausted, and is sleeping with her mouth half open.

Out in the kitchen, the ceiling lamp casts a warm light over the kitchen table and the two dirty plates left on it. Sausages. Again. Is that all Pauline can cook? Charles really should get rid of her.

At first, he had suspected that she was a spy, despite the detailed background checks he had carried out before employing her. He's not really worried about that anymore. She's not clever enough, and what she lacks in intelligence she makes up for with ethics and integrity, two characteristics that are positively unhelpful for an intelligence operative.

Between the plates is a note, from Marika's school, on which someone has, for some reason, written the heading INCIDENT REPORT 01-03-1984. It is from head teacher Roland Rasmussen, and the contents inform Charles that at lunchtime Marika Levin first threatened, and then attempted to injure, one of her classmates with a knife. It happened in the dinner queue, and didn't last long. Patrik managed to parry the knife and Marika quickly calmed down.

INCIDENT REPORT. Like they were police or something.

Charles folds the paper twice, and leaves the washing up. The great thing about Pauline is that she'll always do what needs to be done, no matter how much she wants, out of principle or malice, to leave it undone. If it's too messy, she'll clean. If there are no clean plates or cutlery, she'll wash up. She'll take the bin out if it stinks too much.

Charles goes to the living room and pours a glass of whisky, no ice, stands by the window, and gazes at the student flats opposite.

Marika loves reading; her shelves are heaving under the weight of her well-thumbed books. She's recently started pinching his cigarettes — several times lately he's come home and noticed how her coat sleeves smell of smoke. She's useless in the mornings, and she prefers jeans to a skirt or a dress.

These are the sorts of things he knows about his daughter, but he didn't know she was violent. If she really has been, that is. He persuades himself that he has doubts, that Marika would never do something like that.

He takes the note out of his trouser pocket again. At the bottom, Roland Rasmussen has written Patrik Olsson's parents' telephone number. Per and Agnetha.

Charles paces around the flat with the glass in his hand, gulping too much whisky at a time. It stings and shreds his throat. Names, exchanges — things people said to him then and now repeatedly pop up to bounce around inside his head in no particular order: Paul, Kraus, Eva, Paul again.

Showtime.

It's just rather difficult to know what one's ends are. Particularly if one is Swedish.

Do you have rugs or not?

He stops for a moment, looks at his hand. He's holding the phone and has only two digits left to dial when he realises that there's less than half an hour to go till midnight, and that Per, Agnetha, and Patrik Olsson are probably asleep by now, and that he ought to go to bed himself.

Pfft.

He drains the glass. Everything is spinning, and outside the world is glittering.

MARCH 1971

He was always being told that he threw himself into situations and events without thinking. As he was growing up on Södermalm, his parents had constantly struggled to deal with it. Charles' father used to say that every day he came home from work without being confronted by a note from one of the teachers, telling him about his youngest son's latest misdemeanour, was a day he'd need one less beer to calm his nerves.

Charles wasn't sure whether that was true, but it probably was. After a while, and without anything significant having taken place, Charles started telling himself that he had matured, grown out of it — yet, strangely, that was often the point at which something new would happen.

That's what happened, for example, that time he had, at the age of twelve, borrowed Mark's moped without asking him, due to a sudden impulse to head over the water to Gamla Stan, and the best ice-cream stand in Stockholm. Mark wasn't home, and Charles thought he was with his girlfriend. In actual fact, he was out buying brake pads for his moped. Charles skidded and came off. He sprained his ankle, broke a rib, and was left with concussion. His right leg was badly burned by the hot engine. He also had to spend the summer earning the money to buy Mark a new moped.

Perhaps that rashness, the impulsive streak, was still lurking inside him.

Stockholm. Charles was home again, and Mark was the first person he told. Despite being siblings, they had always kept their distance from one another, maybe because they were so alike. The older they got, the closer they became. Now Mark knew more about Charles than anyone else did. Mark was in his first year as a doctor at Sabbatsberg Hospital, and they would meet up in the canteen and nurse a coffee each, since apparently that was the only form of family time that a junior doctor could squeeze in.

'You sound excited,' Mark said. 'What have you done now?'

Charles told him about Eva, and Mark smiled, and asked whether he could tell their parents. Charles laughed, shook his head — said he wanted to wait, see how things felt.

'That's probably not a bad idea,' Mark said. 'Try that, for once. You know what they're like — tell them you're going to study medicine, and the next thing they want to know is which hospital you want to work at when you've finished. Tell them you've met a girl and they want to know when you're moving in together.'

'You're not wrong there.'

'You really like her.'

He couldn't stop thinking about her.

Outside the window, rain was falling.

'See you soon, bro,' Mark said a while later as they stood up to leave, putting his hand on Charles' shoulder. It felt like a tender gesture. 'Take care.'

Charles walked home afterwards, despite the rain. At a building site nearby, someone turned on a pneumatic drill, which began scraping and juddering angrily. It was never quiet in the city; there was always something to disturb you. The tower blocks and the rumble of the underground, the exhaust fumes rising over the long streets and the claustrophobia you'd get in all the queues the congestion caused: in the space of a couple of days, what had once meant security and freedom now made him feel contained, stifled. So far away from Eva.

He thought about her skin, the feel of her lips when he touched them, how her rapid breathing hit his chest. That night, they'd both been insatiable. With her, Charles had done everything he'd ever fantasised about; things he'd dreamt about but never dared attempt with anyone else.

She counted her climaxes when they had sex, she told him; she had done since she was a girl — *girl* was the word she used — when she'd first discovered what her body was capable of. It was automatic, like a subconscious ticking. Something about the way she said it made him feel invincible.

In the darkness, Charles had laid there on his back, listening to her breathing in between words. He felt her fingers stroke him around his navel until he was so hard that something deep inside him took over. When he grabbed Eva, she giggled and laughed until he pushed inside her again, making her tremble and then release a prolonged moan as she clung onto his shoulders.

When he got home that afternoon, he lay down on the sofa and closed his eyes. Her body and her house appeared in front of him, one merging into the other.

The phone rang out in the hall. Charles got up and answered it.

'Hi, it's me,' she said.

Eva's voice made him feel warm. He asked her how her day had been, she asked about his. Then a brief silence.

'It's a bit empty here without you,' she said. 'I miss you.'

Charles leaned against the wall. Strange: the same questions and conversations as any relationship, but with the physical element reduced to a voice in your ear.

'I miss you, too.'

'Describe your home for me,' she said.

'Eh?'

'Well, you know what my house looks like. Not least the bedroom,' she added, giggling. 'I don't know anything about yours.'

'You can come and see it for yourself.'

'But until then,' she said. 'I want to know now.'

Charles looked around the hall, at his own reflection in the mirror, at the floor.

'I don't have any rugs, anyway.'

She laughed.

'You told me you lived in a flat,' she said, realising that she'd have to help him out.

'On the fourth floor, in a one-bed flat on Kungsholmen.'

'Whereabouts is Kungsholmen?'

'It's central, near the Town Hall and the new Police HQ.'

'Do you walk to work then?'

'Yes, or take my bike.'

'Okay. Where are you now?'

'At home.'

'Duh — where in the flat?'

He liked her playful tone.

'I'm standing in the hall,' he said. 'That's where the phone is.'

'Is that the only phone?'

'No, I've got one in the bedroom, too.'

'So you're standing right inside the door?'

'Yes, pretty much.'

'What's the first thing you see when you come in to your place?'

During the call, he went into the bedroom, swapped phones. When he put the receiver back on the cradle, it was after eight in the evening, and the darkness had settled onto the rooftops outside his window. His ear was warm, and the glossy phone had become slippery in his hand from the sweat. He lay on the bed, naked and hot. His ejaculate — thick and white, long strands that seemed to have come from somewhere deep inside him and then pulsed out with violent contractions — spread across his stomach, and on his chest it had dried, making his skin tight.

He longed to be with Eva, but also to be in Bruket. He could smell the scent of the little town, as he listened to her voice taking his thoughts to the old buildings. How detached the place seemed from the rest of the world, and how liberating that sensation was.

I'm falling, he thought to himself.

This time, I'm really falling.

MARCH 1984

Charles looks at the letterbox. Just a few minutes have passed since they emptied it; nearly half an hour to go until the next time they'll need to go out. This might be all there is to life — pointless tasks, in endless, miserable cycles.

For a while now, an unknown criminal has been engaging in extortion in the form of elaborate bomb threats against state authorities and various companies. The sums involved add up to over one billion crowns. The threats arrive in brown A5 envelopes, and the police, including Charles and his colleagues at SEPO, have made no progress. Now though, some bright spark reckons that the suspect is posting his threats in the last-minute postbox by Central Station. The police have had it under round-the-clock surveillance since January: from an apartment across the road, they film and photograph everyone who posts anything in that box. They then empty it every half an hour, go through the letters, and then put them back.

This photographic work is normally done by the Surveillance Unit, but for some reason most of them are on a course today. Since SEPO are in charge of the investigation, they are also ultimately responsible, which is why he and Paul are sitting there.

Unfortunately, they are not alone.

'Marika,' says Charles. 'Where are you?'

There's a sofa in the corner, and on one of the cushions is an unaccompanied copy of *Goodnight, Mister Tom*, open at a page somewhere near the middle.

'She went to the toilet,' says Paul. 'Didn't you hear her say that?'

'No.' Charles lowers his voice. 'I'm sorry I brought her along. I couldn't call the babysitter again.'

Paul squints at the postbox.

'Here comes another one.'

On the other side of the road, a man is walking towards the postbox with his hands in his pockets and a thick white letter under his arm. He stops in front of the postbox, and Paul adjusts one of the rings on the stills camera, puts his eye to the viewfinder, and clicks the shutter. The man posts his letter and carries on, untroubled and innocent.

'Charlie.' Paul lowers the camera. 'You need to be a lot more diplomatic in the company of people like Kraus. I'm serious. You need to obey my commands and follow my instructions. Don't forget what this relationship is actually about.'

It doesn't sound like a threat, but it is one, a little reminder that Paul once advised Charles that their relationship was not grounded on friendship or common interests, but something else entirely. Strange, really, that you can teach yourself to live and work under such circumstances.

'I know,' says Charles. 'I will.'

'Good.'

And with that, the chill is gone from his voice.

The toilet flushes and the pipes in the old apartment creak audibly. Marika emerges and steps out of her Converse shoes, sits down cross-legged on the sofa, and goes back to reading her book without saying a word.

They really are alike. Marika has dark hair, she's got that from

Charles, and her nose is pronounced and hooked, a beak passed down to her from him. Everything else, though, is Eva's.

'Listen,' Paul says quietly. 'Sit down with her for a bit, until we've got to empty the box. Do it while you've got the chance.'

'It's alright. There's no need.'

'Er, yes, there is.'

Charles gets up from the chair, heads for the sofa, and slumps down next to Marika. He can feel her go stiff.

'You don't have to,' she mumbles, staring at the book.

'But I want to.' Tentatively, he puts his hand on her back. 'Why didn't you want to go to school today?'

Marika turns a page in *Goodnight, Mister Tom*, and tucks a stray strand of hair behind her ear. She has a ring on her middle finger, a thin, neat, silver one. Charles studies it, tries to work out who she might have got it from, or whether she's bought it herself, and in that case, where the money came from.

'What happened yesterday?' Charles says. 'With …' It takes a while for him to remember the name. 'Patrik?'

Not a flicker. He moves his hand about in front of Marika. Over by the window, Paul puts the camera to his face, clicks the shutter, checks that the film camera is rolling.

'Marika. Could you put the book down? Marika.'

She turns another page.

'Could you please put the book down and talk to me?'

Nothing. Charles pulls the book out of her hands and slams it shut. Marika doesn't even seem surprised, just folds her arms across her chest.

When she does finally look at her dad, it's with Eva's eyes, sparkling and clear, and he looks away.

'Can you tell me about what happened yesterday, with Patrik?'

'Haven't you spoken to Pauline?'

'I want to hear your version.'

'My *version?*'

'Yes?' says Charles. 'Your version.'

She sighs.

'I've spoken to Pauline already.'

'You must speak to me as well.'

'*Must?*'

'Yes.' He undoes a button on his shirt; he's getting a bit warm. 'Did Patrik say anything to you? Did he do something?'

'Like what?'

'I don't know. He might have said or done something silly when you were standing in the dinner queue.'

'He didn't do anything.'

'What did you do to him, then?'

She doesn't respond. Instead, she looks over at Charles' left hand, and the book, then stretches over him to reach it. He moves it further away, as if it were a game.

'Did you threaten him with a knife, Marika?'

'Yes.'

'Why did you do that?'

'I don't know. Maybe I thought he was too loud.'

'You thought he was too loud? You mean he was being noisy?'

'Yes. Maybe.'

Maybe. Paul's camera clicks again. Charles looks at his watch. Quarter-to ten.

'You can't say *maybe*, Marika. Threatening someone is extremely serious.'

'Okay,' she says, mechanically. 'I did it because he was being too loud.'

'If he was being too loud, why didn't you just ask him to be a bit quieter?'

No answer.

'Marika.'

'I don't know, alright?' she hisses. 'I don't know why I did it, I just did. It might be something to do with my upbringing.'

'I have never threatened you,' Charles says, in a strangely thin voice. 'I have never hurt you.'

'No, you have never hurt *me*.'

Charles looks down at the floor. Paul takes yet another picture.

Marika gets up from the sofa and pulls the book from her father's hands.

JUNE 2014

It's Midsummer's eve, and the streets are deserted. Everyone is somewhere else, with people they really like. Maybe that's why Gabriel Birck steps out onto the balcony and lights a cigarette, despite the fact that he no longer smokes.

Below him, Lützengatan is silent and warm, and he can just make out the hum from Karlaplan. He finishes the cigarette and heads back inside, puts on his shoes and a thin jacket. He then leaves the flat and drives towards Kungsholmen, with the window down and the radio off. As he pulls into St Göran's, he suddenly feels weighed down by an unexpected burden.

John Grimberg is a sick bastard, and it's best not to think about just how deep his relationship with Leo might be. They grew up together in Salem, Birck knows that much, and Leo fell for Grimberg's sister, Julia. She died when they were teenagers, and, according to John, that was Leo's fault.

'Was it?' Birck asked when Leo told him.

'I don't even know anymore,' he answered. 'It was so long ago, and everything is so … complicated. But Grim thinks it was, and maybe that's what counts.'

Apparently, their split from one another happened in Salem, over fifteen years ago. Last year, though, their paths crossed again, resulting in an act of vengeance of the kind you would only expect to see in bad crime novels: for some inexplicable reason,

Grimberg had decided to seek the revenge he felt entitled to exact. To get close to Leo, he used Sam. His attempt failed, and he's been sectioned here ever since.

Birck glances at the phone charger lying on the dashboard. He's known about Leo visiting Grim for ages, but this — he's bargaining with him. Fucking hell.

He ought to tell Martin, who he'd done his national service with, and who, back then, was a real beer monster. He still is. For the last four months though, Martin Sanchez-Jankowski has also been the clinical director of the ward where Grim is resident, putting him in charge of much of what goes on in there. He and Birck still meet up now and then, but less and less often.

Leo doesn't know that, indeed he's not even aware that they know each other. At times, Birck has come close to telling him, but just as often he's been seconds away from picking up the phone to ask Martin about Grimberg's status, how many visits he's getting, and how often the visitor is Leo. This has to stop, and maybe Martin might be able to help him. But is it really anything to do with him? What is the right thing to do? Leo is being hurt by the grip Grimberg has on him. At work, there aren't many people Birck can put up with, but Leo has gradually become one of them, and Birck might be in a position to help him.

It's unusual to get an application for a visitor's permit for Midsummer's eve approved. That doesn't have much to do with legal formalities, but rather more to do with the fact that the staff would prefer to have as little as possible to do, and would rather be sitting in their offices and bemoaning the fact that they're spending Midsummer's eve in a loony bin. The only highlight probably consists of a slice of dark bread with pickled herring in the staff room, if there's anyone left in there.

'Thanks for this,' Birck says when he meets one of St Göran's middle managers, a gloomy bloke called Westin. 'It can't wait, I'm afraid. I did try to get hold of Martin, but he didn't answer.'

'He's probably at a party somewhere,' Westin says flatly. 'What is it about?'

'I'm not entirely sure myself,' Birck says with his lips pursed thin, because nothing gives a liar away like a smile. 'But it concerns the policeman who died.'

'I understand,' Westin says. 'I'm sorry, but I am going to have to search you.'

Once Westin's finished, he pulls out a great big bunch of keys, chooses one, and slides it into the lock. He then holds a card up against the reader on the wall and punches in a code that allows them to enter.

'John Grimberg really ought to be on maximum security. Unfortunately, he's far too well behaved for us to get that approved.'

'You mean he's not on maximum security now?'

Westin shakes his head.

'Not since the first of June. But there isn't an awful lot he is allowed to do.'

Beyond the door, a small corridor leads them to another door, identical to the first. Then they are on the ward where John Grimberg now lives his life. It is quiet and still here, yet there is a tension in the air that makes you want to turn back immediately.

'Grab a seat in the first visiting room,' Westin says. 'And I'll get John.'

Birck sits down on one of the chairs, examines his right hand. Had he expected it to be so steady? He's spent nearly twenty years with the force, and in that time he has been afraid on a number of occasions. On three of them, he has had to discharge his firearm. He never did so with John Grimberg, but Grimberg remains the one person who has scared Birck more than any other.

'*You,*' Grimberg says, shocked, when he sees Birck from the doorway. He then turns to Westin. 'I'm not talking to him.'

'I'm not here because I've missed you.'

'John, stop it now,' says Westin.

'I want to go to my room. Give me my pills.'

'Talk first,' Westin smiles. 'Then you can have your tablets.'

'This is not allowed,' says Grimberg. 'I could report you.'

'And who would believe you?'

Westin is still smiling. Birck is examining his own shoes. Grimberg is standing, hesitating in the doorway before he allows himself to be led into the room.

'I'll let Johanna know that you're sitting here,' Westin says. 'She'll only be a minute or so.'

'No worries.'

Westin looks at his watch and checks Grimberg's handcuffs before leaving the room, closing the door behind him.

'You've got used to them,' Birck says, looking at the cuffs.

'It's not something you ever get used to. You adapt.'

Birck bends down, pulls up one trouser leg over his calf, revealing the little charger that had been hidden by his sock. It was sheer good luck. Westin's search had been haphazard and clumsy.

Birck puts it on the bare tabletop, just far enough away from Grimberg for him not to be able to reach it.

'Make your mind up quickly, John. Anyone could look through the glass in that door. You give me the name. You'll get this in return.'

Grimberg looks at the charger with all the interest you might show when studying a bit of tarmac.

'What name?'

'The name of whoever Charles Levin was visiting here.'

He lifts up his hands.

'You'll have to stick that inside my jumper. My hands are, well, otherwise engaged.'

'Name first.'

Grimberg shakes his head. Birck stares at him before eventually grabbing the charger, getting up, and walking around the table, ending up behind him. He's expecting Grimberg to try and keep watching him, but he doesn't. He just sits there and waits.

I could kill him, Birck thinks to himself. Might be just as well, before he kills me.

He grabs Grimberg's hair, drilling his fingers into the short quiff and pulling, forcing him to throw his head back and gasp to catch his breath. Birck quickly pushes the charger down the front of his jumper, and sees it get stuck under his chest. When he sits back down, he puts one hand inside the other, to hide just how much they're shaking.

'Did you have to do it like that? You've given me a crick in the neck now.' Grimberg scowls before tugging at the jumper with two fingers. 'Can you see it?'

'No, the jumper's baggy enough. Now tell me.'

'Haven't you got better things to do, on Midsummer's eve?'

'John.'

'Answer my question first.'

Birck rolls his eyes.

'This is a favour.'

'I see. How is he?'

'Who?'

'You know who I mean.'

Suddenly Grimberg brings his hands up to his face, and the movement makes Birck stiffen up. Grimberg smiles and scratches his cheek. It's a clear, rasping sound.

'You seem a bit het-up,' he says.

Birck blinks. He should just stand up and leave, and give Grimberg a punch on his cheek or nose on the way out.

'Who was Charles Levin visiting when he came here?'

Johanna arrives outside the door and peers through the glazed pane. Sirens wail somewhere close by, sudden and sharp. Outside, the colours of evening descend. Rain on the way.

It's gone nine p.m. when Birck calls. I'm working to avoid thinking. I've gone through page after page from the crime scene. It's hard, but not as hard as I feared. When it comes to looking at documents, photographs, or files, my approach is cool and scientific.

'The woman Levin came to see was Marika Alderin,' says Birck. 'She'd been there a long time, according to Grimberg, somewhere between five and ten years. Apparently she can barely talk, and whenever she does say anything it's just nonsense. That's if he is to be believed, I mean. And I don't think he is.'

Not normally. But this time, perhaps.

He rounds off with a 'Happy now?'

'So he doesn't know that she's Levin's daughter?'

'He didn't seem to. But I never asked, because I didn't want to risk giving that away.'

'Did you speak to her, too?'

'She was asleep. They wouldn't let me.'

'Are you going to have another go tomorrow?'

'On Midsummer's day?' Birck says.

'I've got a feeling this could be important.'

'A *feeling*?'

'Why did he keep his daughter a secret?' I say, thinking aloud more than talking to him. 'It must mean something.'

'Yes. Maybe.'

130

'Gabriel ...'

'Okay. I'll talk to her tomorrow.'

My phone has received a picture from Sam during the time we were talking: she's standing by the Thames, wearing shades, denim shorts, and an unbleached white woolly jumper. *Miss you*, reads the message. And then: *cat still alive?*

Kit is lying on one of the chairs, asleep. I don't know where the others are. Outside the meeting room, it's quiet. From time to time, I can hear the emergency line ringing on the floor below, then a voice answering, but I can't make out the words.

As soon as I relax, Markus Waltersson is back. I found a list of the reinforcements assigned to the investigation on the table, and the names of the local group were also listed. *Tove Waltersson*. I made a note of her mobile number, and I've nearly called her several times, but always thought better of it.

She might be avoiding me. Might be staying away. My restlessness takes over. I need to talk to someone. The ringing is slow and monotone, and, when he answers, the shouting and bustle of a noisy party can be heard in the background.

'This is Leo Junker.'

'Changed your mind did you?' Davidsson slurs his reply, barely audible above the din.

'His house keys,' I say. 'I'd like to ...'

'In my desk, bottom drawer,' he roars. 'Happy Midsummer.'

I'm about to return the greeting, but Davidsson hangs up before I get the chance.

Driving around an unfamiliar place is a strange experience, above all in twilight, when the world seems to be shedding its skin and changing its form.

Loneliness. Loneliness is the way moving through a town you've never been to before can make you feel so alone. Free too, perhaps, but freedom terrifies me, always has. I don't trust myself, what I'm capable of doing, if no one else is around to make sure I stay in one piece.

I follow the trunk road and think about Eva and Charles Levin, about the car crash that took Eva's life in the winter of 1980, about Fredrik Oskarsson's witness statement. There's a little plastic bag in my trouser pocket containing Levin's house key. It's on a little key ring, and it was found in the study. According to their inventory, it was the only key that forensics had found, yet both the front and back doors were locked. Levin must have had a copy, which the perpetrator took with him.

The cordon ought to have extended right out to the main road. Instead, the first sign of blue-and-white tape flapping gently in the summer-evening breeze is at the end of Alvavägen. I stop the Opel, which coughs in surprise before quietening down to silence. It's a warm evening, and the air is light, almost hopeful. From a distance, I can hear a lonely dog barking, over and over again. There's a squad car parked next to the blue-and-white tape, but it's empty and all the lights are off.

I get past the incident tape and amble down the little street. A hunched figure appears from the shadows, the glowing tip of a cigarette moving around just in front of it. The figure stops and then goes stiff at the sight of me, and that's how I know that it's her.

'What are you doing here?' she says.

'I thought I'd find out what his house was like.'

'Haven't you seen the pictures?'

'It's not the same. What are you doing here yourself?'

'I wanted to see the area behind the house, in the woods.'

'And?'

She pulls on the cigarette. Then she lets it drop to the ground, despite the fact that we're inside the cordon.

'Nothing. I didn't find anything.'

She's now wearing a short leather jacket over her T-shirt,

and has one hand in a jacket pocket. Tove Waltersson looks like someone who might play bass in an inner-city garage band.

'Where's your car?' I ask.

'I walked. It's not far.'

She looks around, over at the house. Maybe now she knows I've realised; maybe she can tell.

'Shall we go in?' she asks.

'I can do this alone.'

'No, you cannot.'

The garden is small and overgrown, and there's only one explanation for that: Levin never had the chance to start sorting it out. He would never have let a property look like this if he'd had time to do anything about it. My chest tightens, and I clear my throat, blink several times. Tove is next to me, looking puzzled.

I retrieve a pair of latex gloves from my pocket, and after a brief struggle I manage to get them on. There are little traces of the forensic work here and there: someone's forgotten a glove; a torch with POLICE written down the side is perched on the steps.

Inside, it smells like an antique shop, and the ceiling hangs low overhead. The only trace of Levin's body is a large pool of dried blood on the kitchen's wooden floor. It all feels so unreal. Forty-eight hours ago, he was here, alive, drinking coffee with the perpetrator.

I can almost feel it with my tongue, and yes, there it is, suddenly he feels so close. He's there in the doorway, just out of my line of sight, observing me. I can hear his voice saying my name through the silence. It sounds warm, welcoming, as if he were glad to see me.

I investigate the kitchen, the living room, and the hall. I look at the area around the door that leads out to the lawn at the back of the house. There are those tiny traces of rubber scraped from the soles of shoes. I open the back door and take a step out onto the grass, and kneel down.

'What are you looking at?' she asks.

'If there are prints in the grass, they're probably only visible in daylight.' I look over at the woods. 'You didn't find anything.'

'Is that a question?'

'Yes.'

'I didn't find anything.'

'Good.'

Something about the damp gloom scares me; I don't know quite what.

'This witness,' I say. 'The one who was out getting his parasol down. He saw someone.'

'We're looking into that.'

That'll do, I think to myself, and head back into the house.

'Where is his study?'

She goes first, stands just inside the door with her arms folded, and lets me in, keeping an eye on me throughout.

I think about my own big brother, who I only see a few times a year, despite him being one of the best people I know. What would I have done if someone had taken him away from me? What would I do in Tove's situation?

I'm afraid I might well have walked over, put my firearm to the nape of their neck, and beaten the person unconscious.

She just stands there.

'You're from here, aren't you?' I say. 'Originally?'

'What do you mean *originally?*'

I run my hand along the wall, the bed, the little desk, sit down on the chair where Levin might have sat. Or perhaps he preferred to work elsewhere. Whatever it was he was working on.

'Your accent,' I say.

'What about it?'

'It's almost disappeared.'

'Accents don't disappear — they change.'

'Same difference, isn't it?' I say.

The desk has no drawers; it's just a heavy wooden tabletop on low, thick legs. I stroke my hand across it, feeling the dust on my skin, before doing the same on the underside.

My hand touches something.

I get down on my knees, turn on my phone's little torch, and shine it underneath the desktop. Unlike the top surface, the underside is not polished or painted, just dark and matt. And there it is, secured with a little strip of tape.

'What is it?' Tove says from behind me.

I point the phone's camera under the table and take a photo. The flash comes on and for a second everything disappears to white. Then I carefully remove the tape and hold it up between my fingers, show it to her.

'A key,' I say. 'It was stuck to the tape, hanging like a pendulum. Haven't forensics been here?'

'Yes, they have.'

I stand up and hold the tape up to the window, and take another photo.

'We need to put this in something.'

Tove pulls a stiff little envelope out of her leather jacket and holds it out for me to drop the key and the tape into it.

'Do you always carry that around with you?'

She doesn't answer, just closes the envelope and puts it in her inside pocket.

'The logical explanation would have been if it was for a desk drawer or a locked cabinet somewhere in the house,' I say. 'It looks like that kind of key. But the desk has no drawers, and I haven't seen any cabinets. Have you?'

'No.'

Tove puts her hands in her pockets. I take my gloves off.

Soon, I think to myself; it's going to happen soon.

Outdoors. Dry air, the sky streaked with purple-pink stripes, like the aftermath of a fireworks display that has only just finished.

'Where are you going now?' I ask.

'There's no Midsummer party waiting for me. So home, I should think.'

'I can drive you home if you like. But I do have a cat in the car.'

Tove looks for something in her pocket, pulls out a cigarette and a lighter.

'Yes. Alright.'

She lights the cigarette and takes a deep drag, then blows the smoke out in front of us.

'Which of your colleagues are going to be working on this?' she asks.

'You mean here, on site?'

'Yes.'

'I, er, don't know. Do you know people at the National Crime Squad?'

'No.' She takes another drag. 'And neither do you.'

'What?'

'What the fuck are you playing at?'

'What do you mean?'

'What are you doing here? Is this a fucking joke or what? How did you imagine it was going to end?'

'A joke?'

'I checked you out. You have no idea which of your colleagues from NCS are coming here, because you don't have any. It's one big lie, all of it. You're on the Violent Crime Unit in Stockholm, and you're on *leave* as of yesterday.' She spits the word out. 'The reason for that is that you're popping some sort of pills and

136

generally behaving badly.'

Ahead of us, the incident tape is fluttering gently and neatly. Despite fully expecting it, being exposed is embarrassing and shameful.

'I knew him,' I say. 'We were … I want …'

'He spent his whole life as a policeman,' she interrupts. 'Of course he had colleagues who were also friends. But do you see any of them here? Did anyone else come down sticking their oar in and carrying on like this? No, because that would be serious misconduct. I'm going to make sure you get sacked, you fucking moron.'

She steps over the tape and walks over to my Opel, which is parked next to it. Kit is on the passenger seat, tense, his eyes constantly darting back and forth.

'I let you in his house one last time, to say goodbye. Do you understand? Unlike you, I have a heart.'

We're standing right next to each other, so close that I can smell her hair. It smells familiar, in a weird way.

'Is this about Mar—'

Tove drops her cigarette and then, so fast that I have no chance of defending myself, she knees me in the guts.

The pain radiates out, up into my chest and down into my groin, and I bend double. She grabs my hair and pulls my head up, and I see the knee coming towards me again, towards my face this time, and I shield myself with my arms, but I'm too slow, I still get hit in the forehead. I groan, I think, because some sound escapes from my throat before my eyes fill with tears. I lose my balance and collapse in a heap on the warm tarmac.

She sits astride my chest and grabs my hair again. The punch that lands on my cheek sets bells ringing.

It feels cathartic, almost welcoming. I relax to avoid breaking anything, I don't resist, and I close my eyes to the pain.

She hits me again, somewhere near my right ear I think,

because it pops and everything sounds muffled. Her clenched fist comes again, and I hear a plop when my lip splits open.

Hot, hot blood in my mouth, down my throat. She's banging my head on the tarmac.

I take another blow somewhere — around the temple, I think. Everything is swaying too much, and I'm nauseous, yet the swaying is quite pleasant, the kind that might get you off to sleep. The pain that is pounding across my face sails slowly away, and I'm just about to drift off when she drags my face up and leans over me.

'Look at me,' she hisses, but I can't. *'Look at me.'*

I open my eyes. So bright, everything is so bright, and it hurts. Stings my eyes. My neck hurts; so does my nose.

Her stare is dark and glazed.

'Get out of here and stay away. Got that?'

She lets go of my hair, and the back of my head hits the tarmac. I see the sky above, treetops at one edge of my field of vision, my car tyre on the other. She rubs her hands on me. Blood, I think to myself. She's wiping the blood off.

'If I see you again, I will beat you to death.'

My chest hurts. The last I see of Tove is her walking briskly away, and being swept into the shadows until she disappears, and I think that I've finally got what I've deserved all along.

SEPTEMBER 1984

The clerical assistant is a small, slight man with thick glasses and short stubbly hair, the type who would surely have ended up a conscript dogsbody if it hadn't been for his talent for gathering intelligence.

'Telephone,' he says, standing in the doorway.

'Who is it?'

'She didn't say. Just that she wanted to talk to someone. It was important.'

'Get someone else to take it. I'm busy.'

'But …' He hesitates. 'She called your room. The direct number,' he explains.

Up here, officially at least, all calls must be routed via the switchboard, a severe group of female voices who allow themselves neither to be intimidated nor impressed, though there are exceptions made for unofficial colleagues and informants of various kinds.

Charles has been sitting in one of the numerous offices, going through documents relating to Palme's visit to the GDR in June, and they make for bizarre reading. The prime minister sought peace in the mornings and sold weapons in the afternoons.

'Why did *you* answer then?' Charles stands up and goes out into the corridor. 'And what were you doing in my room?'

'Looking for a file.'

Charles goes into his room. As he closes the door, the intense noise of the open-plan office quietens to a low, muffled murmur. It's nearly possible to catch your breath.

There's a telephone on the desk, and one of its buttons is pushed in and lit up. He stays standing and presses the button, connecting the call.

In the background: a hum of voices, a phone ringing.

'Hi,' says a high female voice. 'Hello, who am I speaking to?'

'Who are you looking for?'

'It's the police, isn't it?'

'Why do you ask?'

'Which department?'

Beyond her voice, the phone is still ringing.

'What's your name?' she asks.

This doesn't feel right. Someone picks up the receiver, making the ringing phone go silent. The person answering, a male voice, says *Swedish Television, Fredrik.*

'Are you a journalist?'

Click.

It's been a hard summer. He started drinking so he could get to sleep, and promised himself he'd stop, but he hasn't yet succeeded. In the evenings, he followed the media reports about the murder of Catrine da Costa and felt strange ripples emanating from the past.

Transporting banned materials to a state subject to embargoes means taking diversions. The only chance of successfully getting the VAX computers out of Sweden is by synchronising all parties — those in the country of origin, the necessary people in the transit zones, and those responsible in the destination country — which is what takes time. The synchronisation needs to take place via messages and signals, the sending and receiving of which is a highly clandestine process.

It *always* takes time, but never this long. For the time being, the computers are being moved around from one address to another at irregular intervals by Öberg and his underlings.

Paul spoke to Resident Kraus towards the end of the summer, a cryptic conversation that had to take place over the phone, and Kraus reassured them that the cogs were in motion: the deal was on. That it was almost time.

Our man in Stockholm will contact you.

Neither Charles nor Paul know who this man is, or indeed whether he even exists.

And as if that is not enough: Charles suspects that Marika has started nicking his alcohol.

He sits down, phone in hand. He then presses the switch-hook to get the internal dialling tone, dials the number, and lights a cigarette while he waits for the call to be answered.

'Yes?' says Paul's voice on the other end, four rooms down.

'We need to meet.'

We are now in a new era, tense and insecure. No one knows who is a friend and who is an enemy anymore. They look the same, speak the same language, and have the same warm handshakes.

When we lie to each other, we do it because we have to.

Even before Charles' existence became centred on the work carried out at The Bureau, he had already found himself in deep, deep water, and perhaps he should have had an idea of what lurked behind Paul's mask even then. It started with small things, just after he'd arrived at The Bureau, almost four years ago: details in cases and investigations that were altered by Paul. He had the ability to divert a sum of money, a weapon, or a shipment of heroin away from SEPO's vaults and into his desk drawer.

Paul was no collector, and the confiscated items — that's what he called them — were not simply stacked in piles. Money, weapons, drugs, and other booty had the cumulative function of capital, which was then reintroduced into the black economy, leading in turn to new successes.

A sum of money that disappearezd from a raid on a communist sect in Sollentuna was used to bribe an official at the social-welfare office a month later.

A weapon that Paul pocketed, after a policeman with links to underground groups on the far right took his own life, found its way into the hands of a former Soviet spy, now living in Stockholm and fearing for his life after defecting to the West.

Seized drugs that Paul managed to secrete somewhere were used to recruit informants and attract people who found intoxication difficult to resist, like Savolainen.

It wasn't *just* a nice little earner. It also became an element of Paul's official role, and, at times, the Director would look the other way, choose to nod quietly at the successful results, rather than asking questions about the methods used. By now, no hands that had held anything of significance were clean — that illusion had been well and truly shattered by the so-called 'IB affair', and that was many years ago now.

The fact that Paul's hands were busily working away under the table wasn't immediately obvious to Charles. It wasn't until 1982, late one night at a petrol station near Bergshamra, where they'd stopped after a raid on a suspected terror group outside Uppsala, that he finally understood.

The petrol station was deserted, but as he and Paul stepped out of the car, a man revealed himself, emerging from the darkness just beyond the light cast by the street lamps. He was older than them and wore glasses that looked thick and heavy, their weight causing his nose to turn a strained shade of red.

'Have you got something for me?' he asked in a broad southern accent.

'That's right.' Paul handed the little packet over. 'I've taken my cut.'

The man weighed it in his hand.

'Quite right.'

'You'll have to trust me — that, as usual, I've only taken my fair share.'

'Who is that?' the man said.

'My colleague.'

He inspected Charles.

'Is he with us?'

'Yes,' said Paul.

'What's your name?'

'Charles.'

The man nodded, adjusted his glasses, and disappeared back into the shadows.

'This thing isn't completely ... kosher,' Charles said in the car a few minutes later, as the university campus in Frescati whizzed past the windscreen. 'Is it?'

'Not many things are, nowadays,' Paul said. 'Open the glove box.'

Charles did as he was told. Inside was a thin but dense wedge of notes, dry and rustling against Charles' fingers.

'What is this?'

'Your share.'

Charles tried counting it. When he got to thirty thousand, he lost count.

'We nabbed eighty in total,' Paul said. 'These terror muppets have plenty of money. Makes you think, eh? You can only imagine how they might have got hold of it. Anyway, that's forty. I gave him twenty, and I keep twenty myself.'

'Forty?' The notes got warm in Charles' hands. 'Why so much?'

'We split the original sum in half. Then I give half of my share to people like Gert.'

'What do you do that for?'

'Because ...' Paul shifted down a gear, slowed for the red light.

'I needed help once. Like I helped you. The only ones who came to my aid were the likes of Gert.'

'What was it?'

'That I needed help with?'

'Yes.'

Paul stopped, put the car in neutral.

'I really shouldn't talk about it.'

'But do you want to talk about it?'

'No.' The lights changed. 'Not that either.'

Charles fingered the notes one last time.

He would later discover that Paul's parents had lost the custody of their son, but not why. He was put in a foster home, a farm outside Uppsala, and that's where he met Gert.

It would be a while before he understood who Gert was, or rather what Gert was *a part of*. Paul diverted money to an extremist right-wing movement comprising police, servicemen, and private citizens who used to meet in an apartment in Gamla Stan. He did so not because of deeply held ideological convictions, but because he got to keep half for himself. Charles never knew what Paul did with his share. The movement, though, used theirs in various schemes to exert pressure wherever they saw fit. They hated Palme, and, above all else, they wanted him dead. They still do.

'I don't want it,' Charles said on the way back from Bergshamra. 'I don't want to get involved in this.'

Paul stared at him, his expression giving nothing away. Charles dropped the money into Paul's lap.

'Pick that up.'

'No.'

'Do you really think you have a choice?' Paul's voice was cold. 'You know what I've got on you. You know what I can do.' He picked up the wedge of notes. 'I need you,' he went on, gentler. 'I need you for this. You know what I did for you. I saved your arse, for fuck's sake. I saved you *both*.'

'But I can't.'

'I'm not your enemy, Charlie. I'm your friend.'

Charles looked out the windscreen, avoiding eye contact with Paul. He'd already lost, he knew that; he'd lost long ago.

He let Paul place the notes in his hand.

It's late. Music pounds through Marika's closed bedroom door, crunching guitars and bashing, echoing synths, a voice singing *just like the old days* again and again, broken, almost panting, as though the singer had just been stabbed.

She can't get to sleep without listening to music. Every night, Charles has to go in and turn the stereo off. At first, it irritated him, but it soon became one of the most precious moments of the day: Charles goes in, turns the music off, and stands there in the darkness, glass in hand, and looks at his daughter lying there, always on her back and with the duvet pulled up round her cheeks, her hair fanned out across the pillow and her mouth half-open.

He sits down on the sofa and takes a swig from the glass, looks at the little dark-red book on the table in the knowledge that he's going to open it. Yet still he tries to resist.

She's left it there for him. She wants him to read it.

It's lighter than it looks. He takes another sip from the glass, then puts it to one side. A severe headache rumbles away at his temples, making it impossible to relax. The book is a kind of notebook, not a diary or a journal, but Marika has dated the entries, or the texts or whatever they are. The first is entitled 8/3/1984, and from that point she writes every or every other day, up to today's date, 25/9/1984. He's surprised at how well she writes, how gifted she is with words. It must be all the books she reads, he thinks to himself, and his chest swells with pride at first, but that gives way to shame before long.

I don't even know what my daughter is good at.

He doesn't want to read it. Yet he still does. Just the last entry. That's as much as he can bear. After running his fingers over the page, feeling the words against his skin, letting them trace the lines left by Marika's pen, he puts the book down.

His hands — he can't stop them shaking.

Marika's state of mind was unpredictable even four years ago, and it was impossible to know how she had dealt with what happened then. He can tell that she remembers, but not how much.

Charles has never asked, never dared. He knows that memory is at its least reliable in the aftermath of experiences like the one Marika had been through, thanks to the brain's own suppression mechanisms. But he has also read somewhere that young people tend to remember traumatic events with more clarity than others, precisely because of the intensity of the experience.

And now he knows. He stares at the book.

She really does remember.

With quiet steps, he goes into the bathroom and sits down on the floor, and then sits there, crying silently, perhaps out of grief.

OCTOBER 1965

Years ago, there was a farm on the outskirts of Uppsala. One late-October evening, the area around it was so still that it could easily have been abandoned, the young man walking up the gravel track no more than a shadow.

The bag that had been so heavy and awkward on the journey up now felt strangely light. As he made his way over the fence and across the meadow, into the farmyard, there was a vibrating in his chest. Despite it only being a matter of hours since he was last here, it felt like a homecoming. His thoughts were already somewhere else.

He stopped in front of the house, had an unsettling feeling of being watched. Looking around, he saw nothing, just more darkness.

This must be the moment, he thought to himself; the moment that fills me with doubt.

He dropped the bag to the ground and crouched down, opened it and carefully lifted the shotgun out, placed it to one side and pulled out the hunting knife. It was heavy but the grip was intuitive, the skin on the palm of his hand responsive, and his fingers willing.

Their voices echoed around his head. For four years, he'd had to keep them in check. They did it because they could. Because no one stopped them. Because people had never been good and they never would be.

As he entered the house, his heart stayed in its normal place in his chest, not racing or pounding, just a calm, rhythmic beat urging him on.

When he came out again, he wasn't finished, but had to catch his breath. A pause for effect, that was all. It had been worse, bloodier, than he had feared. It was on his hands, his cheeks, his face, in his mouth, everywhere.

He wiped the knife on his trousers, dried it, and spat.

'I can help you.' The voice reached him through the gloom of the farmyard.

It was quiet, composed, and had a strange accent, but it passed through him like an electric charge.

'No,' he whispered.

'Is there cash in there?' said the man.

'Yes.'

'Valuables?'

'I think so.'

'Do you know whereabouts?'

The young man nodded. The knife was warm and heavy in his hand.

'Go in and get them. Put them in the bag.'

'But …'

'I know what you're doing,' he interrupted, 'and I understand why. But if I'm going to be able to help you, you're going to have to stop now.'

'I can't,' he whispered. 'Not yet.' He turned towards the house. 'I've still got the children left.'

OCTOBER 1984

I know what you're up to. Ring 08 180614 at 1.30pm.

That's what it says on the little note that arrived at The Bureau today, inside an envelope that was addressed to a telephone number rather than a name.

Charles' telephone number.

Paul is sitting opposite him, examining the envelope. Charles is smoking. The drags are greedy, the way nervous people smoke, but he can't even manage an attempt at hiding it.

'What should we make of this?' Paul asks.

'A threat?'

'I mean the fact that it's addressed to your telephone number, not your name.'

'That she doesn't know my name, at a guess.'

'How do you know that it's a woman?'

'I'm just assuming that it's the same person who called me a few weeks back. The one I told you about, the journalist.'

Charles chews on his bottom lip, taps the cigarette so forcefully that the glowing tip falls off.

'I've got a really fucking bad feeling about this.'

'It will pass,' says Paul. 'We're basically finished now. We just need to talk to the Resident, so that everything is in order at his end too. Just focus on the money. Don't think about the risks.'

'She had a high voice, the journalist,' says Charles. 'Sounded young.'

Paul puts the envelope down and examines the handwritten note.

'Scrawled handwriting, like a child's. And the number goes to a phone box?'

'Central Station, on the ground level.'

'So … practical,' he says, smiling weakly.

Charles lights the remains of the cigarette and blows out smoke, watches it rising towards the ceiling.

He leans forward, placing his forearms on the desk.

'What do we do if she does actually know?'

Paul folds the note and puts it in his inside pocket.

'We don't even know if it is her. We'll start by calling the number.'

The door behind Paul is wrenched open and the noise from the corridor — clattering typewriters, hurried steps from one place to another, a voice asking if anyone knows the best place to buy cigarettes in East Berlin — rushes in. In the doorway, the Director, who looks like he's just been asleep and has his sleeves rolled up, with several buttons undone under his chin.

'Levin and Goffman. My office, now.'

'I've got word that the VAX computers have been moved again, from one of the storage units out near the Royal Institute of Technology down to a garage in Skärmarbrink.'

He slumps into his chair, leans back, and puts his feet on the desk. There's a cigarette butt stuck to the sole of one of his shoes. Neither of them mention it.

'Okay?' says Paul. 'That's good, isn't it?'

'It's making me nervous. I want this sorted as soon as possible. It's been going on for over six months now.' He feels for cigarettes in the chest pocket of his shirt. When he doesn't find them, he looks around, confused, until Paul gets to his feet and offers him one from his own packet. 'Thanks.' He lights it. 'So, sort this out.'

'We've got them under round-the-clock surveillance,' says Charles. 'But we still haven't seen any sign of anyone other than Öberg and Savolainen. We are trying to identify their whole network.'

'It's not worth it.' The Director slams the tabletop with his hand. A pen falls to the floor. He's red in the face. 'This has got to stop,' he barks, the saliva flying from his mouth. 'Now.'

'It's not that simple,' says Paul.

'Don't use that tone with me.'

'Of course. I apologise. But given the nature of the goods in question, we have put significant resources into this. It would be unfortunate, against that background, if we were not able to present any results. And we will soon be in a position to do so. We just need a little more time.'

The Director grunts, breathless from the exertion that his sudden outburst seems to have entailed. He isn't far off a heart attack.

'A week,' says the Director. 'You have one week.' He opens his mouth again but pauses, looks at the elegantly framed calendar on the wall, before eventually adding, 'You've got until the eleventh of October.'

'I think it'll be over before then,' says Paul.

'I want shot of them. They annoy me.'

'They annoy us, too.'

'Good. Now get out of here.'

Charles wraps his coat around him and goes in via the entrance from Klarabergsviadukten to avoid being down on street level. As he approaches the main hall, the hubbub gets louder. One voice lists departure times, another announces delays. He keeps his hands in his pockets and avoids all eye contact.

There's a row of three telephone booths down there. Up here, there's just one. Charles goes in, pretends to dial a number, but keeps his eyes on the ground level. He has a good view, which calms him down, temporarily.

He exits the telephone booth and checks the time on his watch, squints at the board showing arrivals and departures hanging on the wall, and then studies the long rows of seating.

13:27.

Marika. Since reading that text in her book, Charles has wanted to go through the other pages too, but each time he approaches it a force field goes up between him and the little dark red book. It's the key to another time, another life that will never return.

13:28.

She never brings friends home, almost never goes to anyone else's place after school. He thinks. He needs to ask Pauline; he might have asked her before, but he can't remember right now.

13:29.

Charles takes the coins from his trouser pocket, and rubs his fingers across them. They're cold and slippery. Women and men walk past the small cabins down there, but none of them look to be stopping or hanging around.

13:30.

Charles inserts the coins, dials the number. The ringtone sounds in the receiver, and far away, through the noise of the main hall, one of the phones down there starts ringing. Out of the corner of his eye: Paul, aimlessly wandering around the hall, plastic coffee cup in hand.

Charles adjusts his glasses and sees a woman walking hurriedly between the benches. She has a little round nose, an angular profile, and light brown hair, parted in the middle. It falls around her shoulders but not much beyond that. She's wearing jeans and trainers, a dark-green jacket that reaches her thighs and looks a bit like a rain coat.

She goes into the middle kiosk and lifts the receiver. Paul watches her from a distance.

In Charles' ear, the ringtone stops.

'Hello?' he says.

'I know what you're up to, and I want to talk.'

'What's your name?'

'Don't even bother.'

'If we're going to talk, I need to know what your name is.'

'Likewise.'

'My name is Frank Möller,' says Charles.

'Is that your real name?'

'What about you?'

'I have a number of details that I would like you to comment on.'

'You are a journalist.'

'And you work at SEPO.'

She speaks without hesitation, and has prepared what she was going to say in advance. Paul passes the phone booth and glances at her back. When Charles blinks, he's gone.

'Is that correct?' she asks.

He hesitates. The name Frank Möller belongs to an operative of theirs, a registered employee with correct personal details and genuine documents, even a little biography, but he doesn't exist. He is mere data and bureaucratic paperwork, nothing more. They create and use decoys for missions like this.

'Yes,' says Charles. 'That's correct.'

'Is it right that you currently have a consignment of VAX computers destined for East Germany under surveillance?'

'If we arrange a time when we can meet face to face instead ...'

'It is true, then?'

'No. But I would like to meet you and discuss the origins of those details.'

'Well, that can wait.'

She is not handling this well at all. Charles squints down at the phone booth. She moves and holds herself like a young person, can't be particularly experienced.

A departure time is announced. Charles can hear it on the concourse around him, straight from the loudspeakers, and through the telephone receiver. In the booth below, she is suddenly stiff.

She knows that I am in the vicinity.

'How do you know Sunitron's managing director, Sven-Olof Håkansson?' she says, attempting, but failing, to sound composed.

A cold wave rushes over him. *She knows.*

He slams the receiver back on the hook and stares at the telephone, then at the woman down in the booth. She looks surprised, then carefully replaces the receiver and opens the door, looking around before she sets off.

13:32.

In the blink of an eye, Paul has appeared a few paces behind her, still carrying the plastic cup, and he follows the woman out of Central Station.

SEPTEMBER 1971–AUGUST 1972

I love her, he thought to himself. I really do.

He knew that, but it wasn't until after he'd moved that he understood the implications of what he'd done. Sivertsson, his boss in Stockholm, muttered something inaudible when Charles told him about it.

'It's always the smart ones that leave my unit,' he said. 'But this has to be the first time someone's left to go to some village in the back of beyond. You haven't gone and become a bloody hippy have you?'

'No.'

'Well, it's still a crying shame — I hope you know that.'

'I am sorry.'

Sivertsson responded with a harsh, barking laugh.

'Course you're fucking not. Good luck anyway.'

Charles was glad to see the back of most of his colleagues, but the Fox from Högdalen was one he was going to miss.

His parents were clearly shocked at the news, but tried to give the appearance of being merely surprised. He did his best to calm them down, even introducing them to Eva, who had travelled up to Stockholm that summer to spend a very peculiar evening with them. Mark just smiled at them, or perhaps at the situation, and sat there slowly shaking his head.

'I like Mark,' Eva said when it was all over. 'But I really don't know what to make of your parents.'

During dinner, they seemed to be straining to understand what she was saying; the Bruket accent seemed almost to be like a different language to them. Whatever they did understand, they took no notice of.

'You are not even married,' Charles' mother mumbled. 'It's unfathomable.'

'We haven't got married yet,' Charles said. 'We are planning to.'

'That would ...' his father began. 'Moving in together before getting married, it's ...' He laughed. 'It was a bit ... It is drastic.'

'Drastic,' Charles repeated.

'Yes? Drastic.'

Mark laughed at them. Charles sighed. Eva seemed to be unsure what to do with her hands.

'You haven't thought about ...' Charles' father said, hesitantly. 'You have a good life here, Charles. Good job, nice flat. *You* work in, what was it, a shop?'

'In a supermarket,' Charles said, and noticed how bitterly he pronounced the words. 'Like she just said.'

'I can speak for myself, darling.' Eva put her hand on Charles' shoulder, and made eye contact before looking over at his father. 'That's right. I work at the supermarket.'

'Nothing wrong with that — it's a good job,' said his father. 'But you could ... you could live here.' He cleared his throat, peered across at the woman who had been his wife for twenty-nine years. 'Isn't that right?'

'Yes,' she replied, and took a deep breath.

Then it came. A long explanation of just how easy everything would be if *Eva* were to move *here* instead. How they wouldn't need a car, how Eva could move in with Charles to begin with and his parents could help them find a bigger flat, and how there were plenty of job opportunities for Eva here — how there were two supermarkets in the very neighbourhood they were about to spend the night in and …

'But Mum,' Charles said. 'We don't want to. *I* don't want to. I'm twenty-four years old, not a child.'

'Yes, so you keep saying,' she said as she stood up, quickly collecting the coffee cups, several of which were still half-full of coffee, and went out to the kitchen. 'But this idea is silly enough to have come from a child.'

Mark rolled his eyes. Eva squeezed Charles' hand. Charles sighed. This is where we lose each other, he thought, my parents and I.

He dragged Eva into the bathroom, next to the kitchen where his mother was clattering the dishes, and pushed her against the wall. Eva was wearing a long navy-blue skirt, and when she lifted the hem above her hips there were no knickers to be seen, just the thick triangle of dark hair and her pale, smooth thighs.

She smiled. Which made him feel like he was mad. Then she turned serious.

'They are very strange. But I think they just want to still have you around.'

'Yes.'

'That's not unusual. You're their child after all.'

'I know.'

She stroked his cheek. Then she turned her back to him.

'Hard,' she said, as if she knew exactly what he needed. 'As hard as you can.'

So he threw himself into a new life, just as he threw himself into most things that would, in the end, turn out to matter. But he was young when he made that decision, he *felt* young, and he had nothing valuable to leave behind when he went.

If this wasn't actually the beginning of real life, then at least it was a nice way to spend the time waiting for real life to start.

In an aerial photograph, the glass factory resembled a small town in its own right, with car parks and little roads skirting around the heavy buildings. In the mornings, on the journey away from Bruket as he headed for his new job with Halland's police force, Charles drove past the large car parks and saw the men climb out of their cars and walk, almost in a column, towards the main building. Their backs were straight and their hands held lunchboxes or rucksacks. Sometimes, if he finished early, he could see them streaming out again, only now more stooped, as if each step was weighed down with something heavier than the day's work they'd just put in.

Charles arrived in Bruket as an outsider and he always remained one. He did make the odd acquaintance, and one of the foremen at the glass factory, Lars-Erik Sunesson, had even had him round for coffee on a few occasions, after Charles had helped reunite him with his stolen car. He was friendly, yet there was something slightly uncomfortable about their relationship. Sunesson behaved like a man who was forever indebted. Charles got to know another Bruket resident, Petter Aspgren, in the queue at the supermarket one afternoon. Aspgren was in charge of Bruket's considerable volume of internal mail and was a bloke you could trust, slightly built but robust in character.

For the first few years, Charles tried to get a job at Bruket's police station, but it had only a small workforce, and whenever a vacancy did come up, they would fill it with one of their friends or acquaintances. That was just the way it was. He contemplated leaving the force, even getting a job at the glass factory, but Eva managed to persuade him not to.

'You'd never be able to be anything other than a policeman,' she said, and Charles knew she was right.

The house he moved into soon became a part of him. For Charles, the house was like his shell. Eva Alderin became Eva Levin. The ceremony was a short one, with few guests besides the couple themselves.

'Perfect,' Eva whispered to him that night. 'This has been an absolutely perfect day.'

Eva liked changing her name, she said. It felt like shedding a skin. Her belly started growing, and when Charles put his hand on it he could feel a slight but definite flutter, just under the surface.

And then, as if in the blink of an eye, Charles was driving the long miles to the hospital and Eva sat in the front alongside him, squeezing his hand with each contraction. When their daughter saw the light of day a few hours later, the world did a somersault and everything was perfectly quiet. A very beautiful little girl. She had her mother's eyes and her father's dark hair ...

... so when he realised what was happening, they had already bonded with each other. The next morning, Eva was sleeping and Marika was lying at her breast when Charles left; and when he returned, nine hours later, they were still there.

'Have you been lying here all day?'

'Uh-huh.' Eva's voice sounded mechanical, vacant. 'She needs changing.'

The little girl wasn't crying, wasn't screaming, wasn't doing anything in particular, besides discovering her own hands and gurgling.

'Haven't you changed her?'

'Once,' Eva said, blinking. 'I didn't have the energy after that.'

'Is everything okay?' Charles sat on the edge of the bed and picked Marika up. 'Are you ill?'

'I don't think so.' Eva looked down at her hands. 'I'm just ... I just feel so tired.'

He'd heard about post-natal depression, and he was worried

that the woman he loved might have fallen victim. But the next day, weirdly, she was smiling and laughing, had got her energy back, and when Charles gave her a kiss she reciprocated hungrily.

It would remain one of life's mysteries. Some days Eva was just tuned half-a-note lower than others. She sank into herself, became absent, almost apathetic. It would carry on for a day or two, three at the most, and then she would be back to normal.

He tried to handle it as light-heartedly as possible. They both did.

'Are you my little darkness today?' he would ask in a playful voice, standing by the sofa, where she lay staring into space, with their little treasure asleep on her chest.

'Uh-huh,' she mumbled, with a little laugh.

It takes a long time, getting to know someone else, and, what is worse, even longer to get to know yourself.

Little darkness. It soon became an in-joke, the kind all couples have, something that only they understood.

'I love you,' he said, and when she smiled in response he knew that he, too, for the first time ever, was truly loved by someone else.

Charles was twenty-five, Eva twenty-three. So young, he thought to himself whenever he allowed himself to look at the photographs.

JUNE 2014

Blood, Tove thinks when the old man greets her at the door. Shit! I've still got his blood under my nails.

He doesn't notice the rusty-brown patches. He just smiles weakly, but with a pained look in his eyes.

'It's a shame he's gone,' he says. 'He was a nice chap.'

The handshake comes to an end, and she stuffs her hands into her trouser pockets.

On Midsummer's day, just after half-nine in the morning, they're the only ones there, apart from a man asleep in his car on the square.

The company is run by a man named Petter Aspgren, and his whole business is really just a leftover from the glass factory's heyday in the Seventies. Back then, his office was situated within the grounds of the factory, and his job entailed dealing with the huge volume of internal mail that circulated within the site. Gradually, he developed his business idea, and once the factory closed down he had made himself an indispensable part of the local infrastructure — so he bought premises on the square and has been there ever since.

When Sweden's post offices disappeared and the handling of letters and parcels was outsourced, Aspgren started offering his customers cheap photocopying and printing, parcel collections, and post-office boxes to rent. He's the sort of person people remember from their childhoods, a warm man who Mum would visit to pick up her mail-order purchases.

One of the walls inside is covered with plain metal P.O. boxes, another with examples of Aspgren's handiwork in the field of copying and printing: posters, paintings, placards, and a flyer from 2005 for a demonstration against the decision to close the town's hotel. In one corner stands a large, silent photocopier and printer; in another, a little counter, behind which an open door leads to a small office.

Aspgren takes off his dark-blue cap and wipes his hand through the remaining strands of hair on his head before replacing it. He's a short, spindly chap with a big silver-grey moustache and rectangular glasses.

'The reason I called you was this: I really ought to have made contact sooner, but it didn't occur to me, simple as that. But then I woke up last night, couldn't sleep — it was that bloody hot — I lay there tossing and turning and then all of a sudden something clicked up in the old noggin.' He taps his head. 'What the hell am I going to do with his box now that he's dead?'

'Charles Levin's box?'

'That's the one.' Aspgren holds his fingertip in the air, close to the box marked 382. 'I've started renting these out, to keep afloat. These are tough times. Anyway, this one was his.'

'He rented it from you, is that right?'

'He did. My problem is that I can't open the box without breaking into it. There's only one key.'

It's in her inside pocket, after Leo found it during the visit to the house yesterday. *Before I smashed his face in.* Her knuckles are buzzing at the thought of it. It felt good. She'd waited so long. It was right.

Leo had tricked her. She thought that maybe he'd been temporarily assigned to NCS from the Violent Crime Unit, precisely because he was close to, and knew a lot about, Levin. He could potentially have been an asset. It was only later that she realised that NCS would never allow someone with such a relationship to the victim onto the case, and it was then she picked up the phone and called Stockholm.

She wonders whether she could be in the shit for having allowed an unauthorised person access to a murder inquiry. That thought causes her fists to clench.

Whatever happens, she can't get as much shit for it as *he* is going to.

That thought makes everything feel a tiny, tiny bit better.

She looks at the box's shiny lock. With any luck, the key won't fit. The fact that it was Leo that found it, that they had missed it, was a real annoyance. Worse still if it turned out that his discovery was significant.

'Do you know what he kept in there? The box doesn't look very big.'

'All of these are the size of an ordinary letterbox. But I have no idea what he might have kept in his. That's part of my recipe for success — not sticking my nose in.'

'Has anyone been here asking about him or his box since he died?'

'No. No one.'

'And you're the only one who works here?'

'That's right. We are a one-man band.'

'Do you know how long he had been renting it?'

'I can tell you that,' says the old man, apparently delighted at being able to help out for once, and goes into his office. 'It might take a while, that's all.'

In the meantime, Tove goes out into the sunshine and gets two latex gloves from the car's glove box. They hide her nails, at least. When she returns, Aspgren is standing there with a gnarled finger deep in a large, open ring binder.

'He started out renting box 382 on the twenty-first of May, and hired the same box until now.' He runs his finger across the page. 'I haven't written anything in *miscellaneous*, so there was nothing unusual about him or the transaction itself.'

'Good. Thanks.'

Twenty-first of May, right after Levin moved here.

'Did he come here a lot?'

'Oh yes,' says Aspgren. 'Every morning, every afternoon he was here.'

'Did he come last Wednesday, too?'

'Yes, twice.'

She pushes the little envelope from her pocket, opens it, and shakes it carefully until the little key, wrapped in its piece of tape, falls out.

'This sort of key?'

Aspgren's eyes become wide with surprise.

'Yes.'

Tove gently removes the piece of tape. Then she puts the key in the lock and turns it. Damn. It works.

'I would like to do this undisturbed.'

'Of course. I've got some bookkeeping that I'm a bit behind with — I'll get on with that. Let me know if I can help with anything.'

With light steps, Aspgren walks away. Tove looks inside the box. Empty.

Then she squints. No, not completely empty. She carefully squeezes her hand inside, and her fingers touch a small, rectangular object.

She opens the window in the meeting room. It ought to be open all the time, so that the night air would have time to cool the room down, but when the custody officer finishes the evening shift, one of his duties is to do a final check of cabinets, doors, and windows. Tove has considered bribing him.

She starts up one of the laptops, enters the password, and, while she's waiting for it to get going, pulls out the object that was at the back of Charles Levin's post-office box.

A red USB memory stick, with a black lid. It's smaller than a cigarette lighter. When the computer is ready, she pushes the stick into the little socket.

It contains a folder called *text*, which in turn contains files named *77*, *80*, *81*, *82*, *83*, and *84*. Must be years. Next to the primary folder is a sound file, and when she spots it, her stomach turns.

It is called *leo*.

The sound file is less than fifteen minutes long. She listens to it twice, hoping to be able to distinguish between the two voices, bring some kind of order to what she hears; she makes a note of which voice says what.

One of them belongs to Levin; another to someone called Paul. A third person, also male, is present but is never addressed by name.

Tove opens a new text document and plays the sound file again, transcribing the conversation as best she can. This takes almost an hour, but she has a feeling that it is important.

She prints a copy and locks the computer, puts the USB stick back in her pocket, and goes out the back to smoke a cigarette and work out what the hell she should do next.

She doesn't understand everything they're talking about, but she understands enough to rule something out. The file carries his name: Does Leo know about its contents? Does he know it exists? Would he hear something in what Levin says that she doesn't?

And who is this Paul?

She scrapes some of the blood from her nails. Shit. She really ought to wash her hands.

Midsummer morning in Bruket is slowly burgeoning. After driving through the centre, she passes the small houses around Alvavägen. People have their doors open and are eating breakfast in the sun. You can smell the coffee and the grass; you can hear children shouting and adults laughing. Neither Leo nor the old car are still there on Alvavägen, only the blue-and-white incident tape.

She glides along Bruket's backstreets, past dead ends, the wide grassy meadows, and the dense little woodlands, through the streets in the centre, and out towards the ruins of the glass factory, looking for the faded Opel. She should have got his mobile number, should have made a note of the car's registration. Her pulse rises around her temples as the anxiety mounts: What does she do if she finds him? What does she do if she *doesn't* find him?

The glass-factory site covers a vast expanse. Shortly after it closed, the area was searched, and a number of inhabitants were discovered, including the odd fox and a number of feral cats, but also a few humans. There weren't that many homeless people around then, but the few there were had already moved in, until both they and the wildlife were chased away by the police.

She turns left, following the line of the high fence, and then it appears.

The Opel is parked with the passenger side closest to the fence, as though the driver had stopped for a rest under one of the thick trees lining the road. Half-hidden by the sparse leaf coverage on one of the branches, the car looks more like a leftover from the glass factory's days than anything else.

Tove parks by the roadside, slings her bag over her shoulder, and walks in under the tree, up to the driver's side of the car. It looks empty from here, but soon she can make out small, shadowy movements.

The cat. It's meowing and pawing him on the chest. Tove leans forward, getting so close that the tip of her nose touches the glass.

Leo's right hand, rusty brown from the dried blood, trying

without success to bat it off. Either he's too weak or the cat is too nimble.

He's reclined the seat, as far back as it goes in the little car. Great streams of blood have run down his chin and across his throat from the split in his lip, and the whole upper-half of his T-shirt is discoloured.

I did this. I'm the one who left him looking like this.

The driver's door is locked, and Tove puts her knuckle to the glass instead, and knocks twice.

He lifts his head and grimaces. He soon finds the little wheel to wind the seat-back up. This takes time.

Once he's sitting up, direct sunshine hits his face, and he closes his eyes with a groan. It sounds distant and muffled through the glass.

'The cat,' he croaks, blood seeping from his lip as he opens the door. 'He needs water.'

Tove doesn't know exactly what the feeling is when she sees him, but whatever it is makes her want to light another cigarette.

'Can you move the car?'

Leo draws his hand across his chin, wiping away the fresh blood.

'Umm?'

'Can you roll it forward a bit so that I can get in the other side?'

His eyes can't focus. They glide past Tove's eyes, her shoulder, to her face, without landing anywhere.

'Why?'

'So that I can sit next to you?'

'What for?'

'Can you do as I say?'

'I'm so dizzy.'

Tove closes the door for him while he starts the engine and

167

slowly turns the wheel. She takes a step back as the car lurches forward in three jolts, leaving the front end pointing out towards the road. Tove walks around the car and opens the unlocked passenger door, lifts up the cat, and sits down, closing the door behind her.

The air inside the car is stuffy and stale; the smell of sweat mixes with the smell of old polyester and metal. The cat is small and warm in her hands, limp when she drops it to the floor.

'No, hold him,' he says, his voice thick.

She picks the cat up again, and Leo opens the driver's door, holding onto the steering wheel as he leans out. A gurgling noise comes from deep inside him before the vomit slaps onto the gravel.

She looks at the cat, and he looks inscrutably back at her. Leo groans. Then he closes the door again, gingerly leans back against the headrest, and breathes out.

'I feel so sick.' He looks at the cat in her lap. 'In the back, there's a little bowl, and a little container of water.' He makes eye contact, and this time his stare is clearer, more balanced. 'Could you …'

After finding it and pouring some water into the bowl, she puts it down next to the bag between her feet. The cat jumps down and laps it up, noisily and greedily.

'What's his name?'

'Kit.' Silence. 'Are you here,' he says — and takes another breath — 'to beat me to death?'

'Eh?'

'That's what you said yesterday. That if you saw me again, you'd …'

He doesn't finish the sentence.

'No, that's not why I'm here.'

He adjusts the rear-view mirror and examines his face, the great purple-blue swellings across his forehead and down his cheek.

'I have, believe it or not, looked worse,' he says.

Tove resists the urge sweeping through her again: she *wants* to hurt him.

He moves a hand up to the inside pocket of his jacket and removes a little tube, flips off the lid and establishes that it is empty.

'Why are you here then?'

'I ...' she says, but that's as far as she gets.

Did she really say that, that she would kill him? Or is he lying?

Kit stops drinking, and settles down at her feet.

'I had a phone call this morning,' Tove says, and while she tells him about the USB stick that was in Levin's P.O. box, Leo winds the window down.

'What was on it?'

'Just two things. A folder called *text*, which contains a load of documents, and a sound file. Which is called *leo*.'

'Is it?'

'So you didn't know about it?'

'No.'

She opens her bag, pulls out the laptop, and starts it up. In the quiet of the car, the whirring of its fan sounds noisy.

'I've transcribed it, but it might be easier for you to listen.'

'The key.'

'What about it?'

'Is that what it was for? The post-office box?'

'Yes.'

She fumbles to get the USB stick out of her pocket, and accidentally pokes Kit with her foot. The cat raises its head, cocks it to one side, and looks rather put out, before slumping back down again.

[Crackling, scraping. A door opening]

CHARLES: Hi. Sorry I'm late. I was in [Inaudible, rustling].

PAUL: Hi, Charlie.

CHARLES: I thought it was going to be just the two of us. That's what we said wasn't it?

169

MAN: Yes. [Clears throat] I know that's what we said, but then I gave it some thought and decided to ask Paul to sit in. I think it might be a good idea under the circumstances.

CHARLES: Uh-huh.

[Crackling, scraping. Levin sitting down?]

PAUL: It's good to see you again, Charlie. It's been a while. How are things?

CHARLES: Good. A bit confused, that's all.

PAUL: [Laughter] I understand that things are getting chilly down at Internal Affairs.

MAN: Maybe you'd like some coffee? Shall I ask my secre—

CHARLES: No, thank you.

MAN: Down to business, then, perhaps. What can I do for you, Levin?

[Silence]

CHARLES: I [Clears throat] know that this sounds a bit rude, but I would really like this conversation to take place just between [Crackling] of us.

MAN: I understand. But I would very much like Paul to be present, if you do not object.

CHARLES: Why, if you don't mind me asking?

MAN: I think that will become clear during the course of our conversation.

CHARLES: No offence, Paul.

PAUL: None taken. This is a weird situation for all of us.

MAN: Right, let's get started.

CHARLES: Yes, I'd ... I would like us to go through this one more time.

MAN: And by 'this' you mean?

CHARLES: This latest recruitment to Internal Affairs. I'm struggling to understand it. In order to be able to answer any questions my staff might have, not least if something were to go wrong, for the Police Federation and for the press it wou—

MAN: Naturally.

CHARLES: It would be good if I did.

MAN: No disagreements from me there.

CHARLES: Right. [Silence] You want us to take on Leo Junker.

MAN: That's right. The reason being [Short crackling, scraping] and I trust that our conversation will not leave this room.

PAUL: Whatever is said here, stays here.

CHARLES: Okay.

MAN: Good. I've received orders from above — and when I say that, I think you know what I mean — to take steps to deal with the situation at Internal Affairs. For starters, it was against that backdrop that the board decided that you were a suitable candidate for the leadership, and I was clear about that at the time. Wasn't I?

CHARLES: Yes, you were.

MAN: Well, since we have intensified our work with informants and infiltrators, the risks — the risks to us, I mean — have also increased. We —

CHARLES: That is, excuse me interrupting, but that's where my first question comes in. You mentioned it last time, too. I would just like some clarification from you, about exactly what that means, that the risks to us have increased.

[Silence]

PAUL: [Clears throat]

CHARLES: If you can, that is.

MAN: Of course, of course. I just want to articulate this in a way that is sufficiently clear without being misleading. But it is self-evident really. A leadership that approves of police activities that are perched right on the boundaries of what the law allows — on the boundaries, admittedly, but those boundaries are very, very fuzzy in practice — is a leadership that is politically sensitive. We are putting our own positions and reputations at stake if something were to happen. All of us, not least you, would be in a difficult position.

CHARLES: I am, as I have said before, acutely aware of my own position.

MAN: Nevertheless, we cannot possibly achieve the demands made of us in terms of organised crime if we do not work this way. Our increased resources need to bring results. There may be a wiser, safer, more effective, whatever, method for achieving the results we're getting from our informants and infiltrators, but right now I can't see it.

CHARLES: Which also says something about the unreasonable nature of the political demands.

MAN: What can we do about them? Nothing. We are civil servants. Bureaucrats. That's all we are. And, given these conditions, this is the only solution.

CHARLES: And this solution ... That's where I require my second clarification from you. As I understand it, and you'll have to excuse me if I express this rather bluntly, but the impression I got from our last conversation was that you wanted to deploy a fall guy? Someone to take the blame if any of the operations or raids were to go wrong.

MAN: It is [Silence] a rather blunt way of putting it. But, and this is important, Levin, I want to underline the fact that neither I nor anyone else in the leadership seriously believe it will ever come to that. This is clearly anything but a standard solution to possible complications.

CHARLES: In the memo, it said 'in the event that one of our operations should be compromised'. That is pretty vague, to say the least.

MAN: And that is a very unfortunate choice of words, because it is not actually true. It ought to have read 'in the event that one of our operations turns into a complete disaster'. And, do not forget that we run, what, one, max two, high-risk operations per year? Since your organisation is now always involved in all operations against this kind of criminality, it is appropriate for the person

172

concerned to be connected to you.

CHARLES: But if something were to go wrong, and we were forced to use this scapegoat, it would emerge that he was with us. That undermines the whole unit's credibility.

MAN: We start with the assumption that all attention will be focused on the individual concerned, not the unit he belongs to. Which, of course, is precisely the point. In the event, we will have to make sure that the debate and the spotlight are pointing in the right direction. In other words, crisis management and PR.

CHARLES: That is not terribly reassuring.

MAN: No, I know. And at the end of the day, Levin, we're all up against it. No one wants to be standing closest to the flames if things start burning, because they don't want to catch fire themselves, but some part of the organisation will have to. This is the solution we have, and the man we have proposed will be perfect for the purpose.

CHARLES: The purpose that also risks ruining his life altogether.

PAUL: May I ask, [Short crackle] excuse me butting in but —

MAN: No problem at all.

PAUL: Thank you. Why don't you just take any old crook?

MAN: Too untrustworthy. It would never work.

PAUL: Well, what about one of the informants or infiltrators?

MAN: They — and I do realise that this might sound bad — are too important.

PAUL: I see. [Silence] Leo Junker, was that his name?

MAN: Yes.

PAUL: What is it that makes him so suitable?

MAN: He's worked closely with Levin for years, at the Violent Crime Unit. That means he trusts you, Levin. Trust is probably the most important factor here. He needs to be convinced that you have his best interests at heart. Not only that, but your relationship makes it very likely that he will agree to the transfer from the Violent Crime Unit. And he's young, too, just over thirty. He has, to put it mildly, a troubled past, including personal tragedies. As far as I can see, he is a good detective, but he isn't altogether stable. If, once again, Levin, if we, against all the odds, were forced to deploy such a drastic strategy, he is an ideal person for the purpose.

[Silence]

PAUL: I must say, he sounds like a very good candidate.

CHARLES: But how is this supposed to work in practice? That's what I don't understand. The whole thing is built upon the idea that not only is Leo going to be present on the operation in question, but also involved in it going wrong, which is also a bit of a leap. Leo is, for all his flaws, a very competent officer. Let's say that the operation goes wrong, but then Junker is completely innocent of any wrongdoing. How can he be the fall guy then?

MAN: That side of things can always be dealt with, Levin. You know that.

CHARLES: But if I'm going to launch this thing, I obviously need to know what steps I should take if it comes to it.

MAN: You have, naturally, several alternatives. One, you persuade him to take the flak to protect the unit and, by extension, the force as a whole. It is not inconceivable that he —

CHARLES: In Leo's case, that is an absolutely absurd idea. He would never agree to it. Believe me.

MAN: The second choice, would, of course, be to smear him, present him in an unflattering light. In other words, despite him not being a scapegoat in the strict sense of the word, we would make him one.

CHARLES: That would require some monumental lies from us. And when Leo can prove that he has nothing to do with whatever has happened, what happens then?

MAN: This is getting extremely hypothetical, Levin. You can't talk about things in concrete terms when these are merely possibilities, conceivable scenarios. However, if such a situation was to present itself then we would present evidence to the contrary. Exactly what kind of evidence depends, of course, on the actual events. We have done this sort of thing before, when it came down to it. The operation in Danderyd in 2010, for example, the raid in Gothenburg in 2002, or the one in Råcksta in 2004.

CHARLES: The officer in the Gothenburg case killed himself six months later. The one who carried the can after the mess in Råcksta is now living on benefits.

MAN: These are the directives under which we operate. These, therefore, are the solutions available. Like it or lump it. If you'll excuse my directness.

CHARLES: That brings me to my final, most important question. You have made your position quite clear. What I want to know is, what happens if I refuse to follow it?

[Silence]

MAN: Isn't that where you come in?

PAUL: I'm afraid it is.

CHARLES: I can't say I'm surprised.

PAUL: Your background is messy, to say the least. As is mine and — [Laughter] well, everyone else's — those of us who are still around. You know what I've got on you. And, since everything blew up in 1986, so does our dear superior here, or at least some of it. Not everything, but quite a lot.

MAN: I should add that I have no desire to find out any more. The more you know about those years, the worse your headache. That was what Holmér was always saying.

PAUL: And quite right he was, too. You know what you've got to lose, Charlie.

CHARLES: If I lose, you'll be dragged in, too, no two ways about it.

PAUL: And not just me, large parts of our operation and our organisation would be closely scrutinised. Once again, just like 1986. That is precisely why I am so keen to sort this out to everyone's satisfaction. And ...

[Silence]

CHARLES: What?

PAUL: Could you pop out for a second?

MAN: Me?

PAUL: Yes.

MAN: From my own room?

PAUL: You did just say you didn't want to find out any more.

MAN: I see. Yes. I'll nip to the gents. [Footsteps, a door opening then closing]

PAUL: Funny chap, that one. Isn't he?

CHARLES: I was just thinking the same thing.

PAUL: What kind of person frames their law-degree certificate? And then hangs it up on the wall?

CHARLES: Not the kind of person who ought to be in a leadership position.

PAUL: [Laughter] Touché. Like some kind of [Crackling] trophy.

CHARLES: What's this about, Paul? What is it you want?

PAUL: Well, Charlie, it's like this. I'm guessing you get it already, but I want to be absolutely sure that you understand the consequences for you if you fail to go along with his, and the rest of the leadership's line. If you don't, and they are forced to ... If your background has to be revealed. They wouldn't be able to leave Marika out of it. She's there, right at the back with all the rest of it. I know that you want to protect her, and I, all of us in fact, would of course do whatever we could, but ... it wouldn't work. [Long silence] Do you understand?

CHARLES: Yes.

[Crackling, rustling. Levin stands up. Footsteps]

PAUL: Charlie, what —

[Loud thud]

PAUL: [Groans]

[Silence]

PAUL: I guess I deserve —

CHARLES: Don't make it sound like you care about her. You've

176

never cared about anyone other than yourself.

[Silence]

CHARLES: I just don't understand how you [Footsteps, rustling, crackling. Levin sits down again?] You're putting so much on the line, Paul. Everything from the Lichter case onwards.

PAUL: I don't have as much at stake as you. And you know as well as I do that the one with the most to lose is always the one to back down.

[Long silence]

CHARLES: I have started [Inaudible, too quiet] her everything.

PAUL: What? Marika?

CHARLES: I tell her a bit every week, when I visit.

[Scraping, movement. Paul stands up? A few footsteps]

PAUL: Why? Why are you doing that?

CHARLES: Partly because she's all I've got left. Because even if she doesn't register a word I say, she still deserves to know the background to all this. But, above all, perhaps, because I'm selfish. Because it all gets a tiny, tiny bit easier to bear if you say it out loud.

PAUL: How do you know she's not taking in what you're saying?

CHARLES: You've met her once, haven't you? Since ... since she ended up in there.

PAUL: Yes.

CHARLES: Well, then you know, too.

PAUL: But still ... she ... she was there.

CHARLES: Even if she did understand what I was saying, even if she did decide to start telling people, who would believe a mentally ill woman locked up for attempted murder?

[Long silence]

PAUL: So I take it we're agreed then? On the matter in hand, I mean.

CHARLES: Yes.

PAUL: Good.

[Another long silence]

CHARLES: Sooner or later, this will catch up with you.

PAUL: That day —

[Knock at the door]

PAUL: Yes?

MAN: [Muffled] Have the gentlemen finished?

[Short silence]

PAUL: Yes.

[Door opens and closes, footsteps]

PAUL: And I think we're agreed.

CHARLES: I'll get in touch with Leo tomorrow.

MAN: Excellent. Paul, what the hell happened?

PAUL: What are you talking about?

MAN: Your cheek is all red.

PAUL: Oh, that. It's … eczema. I get it sometimes.

[The man says goodbye. The door opens and closes again. They seem to go in different directions. Levin, now alone, stops. A click and a beep. A buzzing noise followed by an electronic voice: 'Seventh Floor.' Levin enters the lift. The doors close. Loud crackling and rustling]

CHARLES: Twentieth of August 2012.

[Clip ends]

The voices fall silent.

'You haven't got a cigarette have you?' Leo says. 'Mine are in the back.'

Tove gives him one from her packet, and he looks at Kit, who's lying between her feet, asleep, before carefully opening the door and lighting the cigarette. For the first time, Tove notices that he's not using his left arm. It's lying there, limp and still, next to his torso, with the palm resting on his thigh.

He looks over at Tove's hands, her nails, the dried blood.

'Is that mine?'

'Yes.'

'Maybe you should wash your hands?'

'I'm going to.'

He smokes the cigarette. The filter is speckled with blood.

'I have some questions,' she says.

'Me, too.'

'Did you know about this?'

'What?'

'The reason you ended up with Internal Affairs? You seem remarkably composed, given that you've just found out you were betrayed.'

'Levin had hinted that there was something bigger behind me being on Gotland, but not that it was connected to me ending up in the unit in the first place. I ... I didn't realise I was such a big deal.' He blinks. 'I think maybe I'm a bit shocked. It's a lot to take in.'

'Levin obeyed them, anyway.'

'Partly, at least.'

'What does that mean?'

'Internal Affairs served as an alibi for other departments. Officially, the post that Levin gave me was purely administrative, but, unofficially, my role was to investigate the unit itself, from the inside. Then, where possible, to close down flawed internal investigations. So I truly was a rat.' As he speaks, he carefully turns his head, testing out his neck. 'That might have been the only resistance I could manage.'

'The other man is named as Paul,' Tove says. 'But the third voice?'

'I think I know who that is. It's not the director of the National Police Authority, but it is someone very close to him. Or rather was. His name is Einar Wallensten, and he died from prostate cancer about a year ago. I think Levin went to his funeral.'

'Bit ironic.'

'The other one's, Paul's, surname is Goffman. He works at SEPO, counter-subversion.'

'SEPO. Whaddya know.'

'For what it's worth, they're probably investigating Levin's death, too, but up in Stockholm. That'd be my guess anyway — I can't imagine they wouldn't be.'

'I haven't heard anything about them being involved.'

'Exactly,' says Leo, as if that proved his assumption.

'Do you know Goffman?'

'Not really.'

Leo has smoked his cigarette right down to the filter. As he throws it onto the gravel, he looks disappointed that the fun is already over.

'Did you know that he and Levin knew each other? Judging by their conversation, they had a long history.'

'I know that they knew of each other. But that they'd had such … No. And that case, what was it he mentioned at the end there?'

Tove pulls the transcript from her bag, flips through to the right page.

'The Lichter case.'

'That rings a bell, but I just can't place it.'

'Same here. It does sound familiar.'

He blinks. His eyes are bloodshot, tired.

Tove pulls out her phone and types *Lichter case* into the browser's search bar. The first hit is an article from *Svenska Dagbladet*, published just a few days earlier. It's about the still unsolved murder of Catrine da Costa, and points out that, this summer, it will be thirty years since someone took her life. Alongside the article is a list of famous killings where the victims had been dismembered.

'One of them is the murder of Ted Lichter,' she says. 'It doesn't say much about him, if it's even the same Lichter. An addict, from here, who was butchered by a fellow junkie in spring 1980.'

'Hmm,' Leo says, and furrows his brow.

'What?'

'I'm too close.' His voice sinks to a whisper. 'Everything looks blurred up close. I can't ... see what I can normally see.'

He remembers something, pulls his phone out from his jacket pocket, and starts looking through his contacts, then puts the phone to his ear.

'Hello,' Leo says. 'Did I wake you up? Okay, sorry. Shall I call back later or ... Okay. I was just thinking, if you've already been there, but in case you haven't ... No, I understand. Give me a ring when you've ... Good ... No, I ... No, it's nothing — think I've just picked up a bit of a cold overnight. When you do speak to her, ask what she and Levin used to talk about when he was there. Okay, yes, bye.'

He hangs up.

'Who was that?'

'No one. That was nothing.'

'You come down here, get stuck in to an investigation which you have absolutely fuck all to do with, and then you refuse to tell me — and I'm actually on the case, remember — what you're up to?'

Leo sits still in the seat, blinking, breathing, grimacing in pain, blinking, and trying to breathe again.

'If you don't tell me what you're playing at,' Tove says, 'I'm going to report you for gross misdemeanour.'

As she's saying the words, her enjoyment is increasing: at the fact that *she*, finally, has power over *him*. Leo turns his head slowly, and raises an eyebrow.

'Haven't you done that already?'

She stares at him.

'I understand,' he says then, and suddenly he looks remarkably tiny.

She ought to get out of the car and drive, drive off and leave Leo here. But at the same time, she needs him. The case belongs to her and Davidsson, for another twenty-four hours at least, and despite the clock ticking and the conclusion to the case being about to slip from their grasp, they are closer now. Leo might know things that she doesn't know about Levin, things you wouldn't give a second thought to because they seem pretty mundane, but then turn out to be absolutely crucial when seen in a new light.

The problem is, she might lose it.

The problem is, she might attack him again.

'I asked my colleague in Stockholm to go to St Göran's,' he says. 'Marika Alderin is a resident, sectioned years ago. I know that Levin used to visit her.' He looks at the phone, swipes a finger across the screen. 'My colleague hadn't been there yet.'

'If it's right, what they say in the sound file, she doesn't even seem aware.'

A car passes by, one that she doesn't recognise. Tove watches it into the distance, and he notices.

'What's that?'

'Journalists. They've started gathering outside the station. Speaking of which.' She looks at her phone. 'I should get down there.'

'Where's Davidsson?'

'Last I heard, he was going to go and talk to an old acquaintance who apparently knew something about Eva Levin. I'd say he'd be done by now.'

She shuts the computer, pulls out the USB stick, and puts it in her pocket, slides the laptop into her bag.

'What was in the text files?' he asks.

'I haven't had time to have a good look at it yet, but it looks like a mixture of things, some seemed to be scans of old documents, and photographs. I'm going to go through it now, after the meeting. I didn't have time to ...' She hesitates. 'I wanted to talk to you first, about the sound file.'

'I understand,' Leo says.

'You'll have to leave your car. If you can make your way over to mine then you can come along.' She opens the passenger door. 'Don't expect any help.'

As they roll down the trunk road past the petrol station, they end up behind a spluttering tractor, driven by an old man with a cap on his head and the sun on his back. The sweat glimmers on his neck.

'They were lucky,' says Tove, 'that you did actually fuck things up on Gotland.'

'I know.'

'They could just seize on it and ride on the wave.'

'I know.'

'The stuff in the recording,' she says slowly. 'That you were supposed to be their scapegoat — it doesn't change anything for me. You do get that, right? You're still the one who shot him. If it wasn't for you, he'd still be alive.'

'I thought you were going to kill me.'

The words hit Tove harder than she'd expected.

'So did I, to begin with.' I need to know, she thinks. I need to find out. 'Do you ever even think about it?'

'What do you mean?'

'About Markus.'

'Almost every day.'

'Don't lie.'

'I didn't think it would be possible to live with it. I mean, I never thought I'd be able to function like an ordinary human being, doing everyday things like going to work and talking to people about the weather and where they're going on holiday and all that shit. I never thought I'd be able to. And for about nine months, I couldn't. After that, it started becoming manageable. But I haven't … I'm not quite standing on my own two feet.'

'You mean you're popping pills?'

'Yes.'

'Because?'

'Because they allow me to function.'

They approach the square.

'I suggest that you resist, next time — If I hit you again, that you defend yourself. Otherwise, I don't know what might happen.'

He is silent for a long time.

'I don't know if I want to.'

'If you want to do what? Resist?'

'Yes.'

'You really are sick in the head.'

'You know that I didn't … It was a mistake. I panicked.'

'I don't want to hear any fucking excuses.'

'That's not what I meant. I was sent to Visby a few days before the bust. We suspected that the sellers would be arriving in the harbour by boat, and that the buyers would be in cars. I investigated the area, memorised the routes in and out of the harbour, for cars and for pedestrians. I started feeling shaken and unsure, I didn't know why, but something was wrong. When we got word that things weren't right, I got even more disorientated and … My life at the time was such a mess. I'd split up with my girlfriend, we had … Life was fucking hard. On the night of the bust, I was standing pressed up against one of the buildings in the harbour to give myself a good view. A motorboat arrived, no lights. The boat moored, and shadows started rushing around it, stressed. They unloaded crates. A big jeep pulled up, someone opened the boot. The buyers met the sellers. The buyers wanted to see the contents of the cargo …'

'I know all this. I've read about it.'

The buyers were one of the estate gangs from Stockholm. The sellers were one of the major crime syndicates. The cargo did not contain any weapons, just old newspapers and plastic toys.

'Who was planning to rip who off was never really established,' Leo went on, slowly. 'Lots of people thought that Stockholm police had teamed up with one of the men in the syndicate and persuaded him to switch the contents. There were, according to Levin, things that pointed to that. But it was never cleared up. At that exact moment, when the buyers realised they were going to get ripped off, an enormous searchlight came on. The SWAT team,' he adds, and looks at Tove.

She stops by the square.

'I don't know who fired the first shot, but it wasn't the police,' he says. 'Probably the buyers. Suddenly everyone had a weapon in their hands. It's the only time I've ever seen anything like it. Several people were injured, including police, and I remember ... I remember coming out of the shadows where I'd been hiding. Like I said, I must have panicked. I fired a shot at what I thought was one of the sellers who had just tried to hit, maybe even *succeeded* in hitting, one of the SWAT team. I couldn't just stand there. I had to do something. But I was in no fit state. I was too unstable.'

He stops talking. Tove has her hands on the wheel. The engine is ticking over. The cat's cage is visible in a corner of the rear-view mirror. The sun overhead is strong.

'I know that you didn't do it deliberately,' she says. 'I know that it wasn't just black and white, what happened. Do you think I'm that stupid, that I wouldn't understand that?'

'No, but ...'

'Let me finish.' Her voice is trembling from the strain. 'I know it's not that simple, but I need to believe that it is. Do you see? I need to see my brother's death in those terms, because otherwise I haven't got a fucking clue how I'm supposed to keep functioning. Alright? Drinking doesn't help, working doesn't help, and I've got nothing, no friends or anything. All I've got ... The only thing I can do is tell myself that my brother died because somebody wanted to harm him, not that it was just a fucking *mistake*.'

I'm exposing myself, she thinks. Way too much. God, I could really do with a large whisky. A large whisky in a dark room — a quiet, cool room. In the silence, she can hear her mother's voice, and within that, her grief. It's been a hell of a long year without Markus.

'I understand,' Leo says.

Tove turns off the engine, but they stay sitting there next to each other, in silence, staring at the pale wall in front of them.

'I'm going to have to go up,' Tove says. 'Davidsson's waiting.'

Leo pushes his tongue across his lip, licking blood from the wound.

'He mentioned you and Markus, what had happened,' he says then. 'Davidsson, when I met him yesterday. I don't think he knows it was me that did it, though. He didn't seem to recognise me, or even place my name.'

'Davidsson has the good taste not to give a shit about anything other than what's going on in Bruket. That'll be why. Are you coming up?'

'I, er ... I don't think I can walk on my own. I'll probably faint.'

'What the *fuck?*'

Davidsson's jaw drops when he sees me.

'It's okay,' I say. 'I just need to sit down.'

We head into the meeting room. I collapse into a chair and put Kit's cage down.

'But what happened to you? As if it wasn't bad enough that the journalists are onto what's happened, do I have to deal with this as well?'

'Sorry.'

'And by the way, who's leaked Levin's name?'

'Do they know it was him?' Tove asks when no one answers.

'Well, if they don't, they must be bloody good at guessing,' Davidsson growls.

'It isn't that hard to find out who was living in the house,' I say, but Davidsson's not listening, he's busy shouting at Åhlund in a hoarse voice, asking him to bring the first-aid kit.

If possible, Davidsson's cold sounds even worse than yesterday.

'I fell over and banged my head,' I manage.

'Where?'

'Up at the old glass-factory buildings. I was there having a look — I'd only been told about them. I went onto the site and then got into one of the buildings, up a staircase that I should've stayed well away from.'

Davidsson squints.

'And you landed on your face?'

'Not the first time that's happened.'

I try to smile at the absurdity of it all, and shake my head, but that makes something black appear in my peripheral vision, so I stop.

My mouth won't stop bleeding. I've stopped wiping the blood away; now I'm swallowing it instead. Soon I'll have had so much that I'm going to get nauseous.

Levin's voice. Hearing it through the little laptop speakers, so familiar yet so different, has shaken me up. I was right. I was placed in Visby, and it was down to him. I played right into their hands, though, and allowed them to get away with it. Otherwise, the strategy would have failed, sooner or later.

I've wondered about it for so long, and managed to convince myself that whatever the truth of it, just knowing would be a relief, perhaps even a help.

I don't feel anything like that.

I don't feel anything at all.

Or do I? I don't know — the physical pain makes thinking about anything else difficult. Maybe I really don't feel anything, but then again maybe this could be the beginning of the end of it.

Åhlund arrives with a big green bag emblazoned with a white cross.

'Bandage him up,' Davidsson says. 'Then he needs to get to a hospital.'

Åhlund looks hesitantly back and forth between me and Davidsson.

'I'm not a nurse.'

'I can do it myself,' I say.

Davidsson scoffs.

'You can't even move your left arm.'

'It's because of my ribs. My arm is okay.'

'Just *do* it,' Davidsson tells Åhlund. 'We're in a hurry.'

Tove, who's sat down on a chair and has been quietly studying Kit's movements inside his cage, looks surprised.

'Are we?'

'Needless to say, I appreciate your assistance in the inquiry, and I am grateful for the esteemed visit from the capital. I'm sure it's great that there'll be more of them here tomorrow or on Monday, but this is more than likely to have been solved by then.'

'Solved?'

Åhlund examines me in silence. He has experienced hands.

'I trained to be an ambulance driver,' he mumbles. 'Two terms, until I got into the police training programme in Växjö. So I don't really know what I'm doing, but almost.'

This feels reassuring.

'Solved,' Davidsson affirms with a cough. 'More than likely. We have gathered new information this morning. Information that has led us to a suspect.'

He closes the meeting room door.

OCTOBER 1984

'There. There she is. See that?'

Paul turns off the radio, forcing Fleetwood Mac into silence. The sound of the rain on the windscreen grows louder.

'I see her.'

The woman in the dark-green jacket emerges from the supermarket entrance. She is huddled against the rain, and zips the jacket up before continuing.

'She lives over here, Barnängsgatan 40. This is where she came yesterday, after she'd talked to you at Central Station.'

He turns the ignition, starts the engine.

'I don't know if this is such a good idea,' says Charles.

'Me neither.' Paul indicates left, looks over his shoulder. 'But it would be nice to know what she knows, and, more importantly, *how* she knows.'

Being shaken isn't part of Paul's character, but something's up. There's an awful lot at stake: the consignment is ready. The payoff is within reach. Now Charles can feel the cash's throbbing pulse; it's influencing them. Being so close to it changes their perception. Paul's eyes betray both a greed and a fear that everything might mess up — that they will be exposed.

A fucking journalist. Damn it.

'This will work itself out,' says Paul.

'I think she knows,' Charles whispers.

'What did you say?'

Charles closes his eyes, just for a second.

'Nothing.'

I am not really here.

They roll down Nackagatan, at Södermalm's eastern edge. The smell is the same as anywhere else in Stockholm, exhaust fumes and cooking fat. A boy peddling for all he's worth zips past on a BMX, and Charles watches him, wonders where he's heading, whether he's skiving.

The boy turns southwards, onto Barnängsgatan. Paul and Charles turn right, northbound towards the apartment blocks. She disappears behind a porch marked with a four and a zero.

'Maureen Cathryn Harriet Falck,' says Paul. 'Her given name is Cathryn, but apparently people call her Cats — thirty-one years old, born in Enskede on the eleventh of July 1953. She works at SVT as a reporter for the *Rapport* news bulletin. That sounds impressive, and I'm sure she'd like to present herself as an investigative journalist, but from what I understand she's more of a dogsbody, does little snippets here and there. She's recently moved from being a production assistant to being a reporter. So she's not exactly a hotshot. No husband, no kids — lives alone.'

They pass the address and park up outside a shop, a bit further up Barnängsgatan.

'She lives on the fourth floor.' He looks at Charles. 'Do you want an umbrella?'

Charles shakes his head and opens the door.

'Hey,' Paul says, and puts his hand on Charles' arm.

'Yes?'

'Careful now.'

The steps echo around the stairwell behind him. He looks at her door, at the letterbox with her name and NO JUNK MAIL PLEASE handwritten on a bit of lined paper. The doorbell is dark brown and old, and before he puts his thumb to the button he puts on his gloves.

The sound of the bell is sharp and grating, and Charles takes a step back so as to be visible through the spyhole, waits.

'Who is it?' comes her voice from inside.

'It's me,' says Charles. 'Frank. We spoke on the phone.' Silence. 'I thought we could talk.'

'How do you know where I live?'

'We could help each other out.'

He looks around. Her door is just one of four on this landing.

Nothing. Charles sighs and turns to leave, not really intending to do so, but it probably looks convincing, and that's when the lock clicks.

The flat is small, with low ceilings. Two chairs and a table are squeezed into a narrow kitchen; straight ahead is a combined bed-sitting room. That, and a toilet, is it.

She hesitates. She's tanned, has recently been abroad.

'Would you like some coffee?' she asks.

The very thought of it makes Charles' stomach turn. He has no recollection of when he last ate.

He forces a smile.

'Coffee would be great.'

'Right,' he says, and drinks some of the strong coffee. The mug is white, with SVERIGES TELEVISION written on it in dark blue. 'What would you like to know?'

'Your name is Frank Möller,' she says, and lets go of the mug's handle, straightens out the little tablecloth.

'Yes.'

'And you work at SEPO.'

'Yes.'

'Operations Department.'

'Is that a question?'

'I just want to know if I've got it right.'

'So far, so good.' Charles gulps down some more coffee. *I can't drink anymore — I'll be sick.* He smiles and puts the mug to one side. 'How do you know who I am?'

'I didn't, until yesterday.'

'But the letter,' he says. 'The phone number.'

'I didn't know who it belonged to, just where it went.'

'How did you find that out?'

She shakes her head.

'I protect my sources.'

'You can't give me a name, or anything that might lead me to one. But it's not a name I'm after.'

'Well then, what are you after?'

Careful now.

'When we spoke yesterday you mentioned computers.'

'VAX computers.'

'What do you know about them?'

'That they have lots of different uses, including several civilian ones, but they also have military applications.' She hesitates, as though she needs to decide whether or not he can be trusted. 'They can be used in the development and production of nuclear weapons. And,' she goes on, 'I know that these particular ones are heading for East Germany, in breach of the embargo. They're going to be smuggled over. For the moment, they're being moved back and forth between a number of addresses in Stockholm. East Germany is using parts of Stockholm's underworld to do it.' She strokes her mug with one finger. 'That's true. Isn't it?'

'Don't you already know that?'

'Just say whether it's true or not.'

Charles nods carefully.

'I know that the VAX computers arrived in Sweden from America via Håkansson's company, Sunitron,' she continues, 'and that's where you came in.'

Someone must have leaked. Someone at their place, who knew that The Bureau got involved at that point, and that Charles and Paul are primarily responsible. Someone who doesn't know about their unofficial role, that they've been doing it for ages. Or else it's someone who knows very well what their actual involvement is but is withholding that information from the journalist, since the informant might lose out by telling her that.

One of the bandits? Öberg himself?

No. Savolainen?

Savolainen.

'What was it you wanted from us?'

'Confirmation.'

'Of what?'

'That this is true.' She looks him straight in the eye, calm and cool. 'East German intelligence is in cahoots with known Swedish criminals. You do realise what a story this is?'

That's her scoop, Charles thinks. She mustn't know about my and Paul's involvement.

'Haven't I already given you confirmation that it is correct?'

'I want names.'

'Whose names?'

'The Swedish criminals, the East German agents. As many as possible.'

She leans back in her chair and looks out the window.

'We haven't managed to implicate the East Germans. Up to now, we have only been able to tie the Swedes to the computers. I can give you their names.'

'On the record?'

194

He laughs, since he's expected to.

'Absolutely not. I can give you them, but you'll have to confirm them with someone else.'

'And what do you want from me?'

'Two things. First of all, I want to know how you got hold of the telephone number you contacted me on. And secondly, you show me the data you've got. This is going to look huge in the headlines, which it is. It's important for us to safeguard our international relations, not least for the prime minister. In his view, the GDR is just like any other trading partner.'

She stands up, grabs a notebook and pen from the worktop, and sits down again.

'You first.'

'Jan Savolainen,' says Charles. 'And Jakob Öberg.'

She writes it down, asks Charles to spell Savolainen, asks if it's Jakob with a K or a C, but it's just a game, it's obvious that she already knew of them. She'd never get a word out of Öberg, but Savolainen is less of a challenge.

That's who she's been in touch with. That's dangerous. Savolainen knows about his and Paul's true role in the whole thing — Savolainen *knows*, but he must have not mentioned it to her. The question is, why not?

Or perhaps he *has* revealed it to her. *Maybe she knows, too.* She might be trying to get him to paint himself into a corner.

Charles blinks.

Everything's spinning.

'Any more?' she says.

'That's what we've managed to tie to the case. That's what we've got.'

She can't hide her disappointment; even her shoulders give it away, as they sink downwards. Charles drinks some coffee.

'Your turn,' he says. 'How did you get hold of my telephone number?'

'I got hold of some of Håkansson's paperwork. He'd written it down.'

'Sven-Olof Håkansson?'

'Yes.'

'Strange.'

'That's what I thought,' she says with a slight smile.

In early February, before the goods got stuck at West German customs, Charles had had direct contact with Håkansson. He gave Håkansson his number, but insisted that he was to memorise it and not write it down under any circumstances. Håkansson sighed and said that Charles was paranoid, but still did as he'd been asked.

He said.

Shit.

'It might become clear, eventually,' says Charles. 'And then the second thing — that you show me your info before publication. I won't be asking you to change anything, suppress any information or details. That's usually the way of things, but I'm not going to ask you to agree to that. I just want you to give me some advance warning, so that my colleagues and I know what's coming. That's all. And,' Charles adds, 'that you don't hold anything back. How far off publication are you?'

'I've got other stuff to do at work — this is basically something I'm doing on my own time. So it will probably be a while yet.'

They sit in silence. She seems to have run out of questions, and he really just wants to get out of there. *Something's not right.*

He leans forward, resting his forearms on the edge of the table.

'Next time you contact me, do it in the normal way. It makes things easier, for you, and for us.'

'I had to be careful.' She folds her arms. 'I didn't know what your role was.'

She still doesn't, but she *suspects.*

Beyond the kitchen window, the rain is still falling. And in

here, at the little table, the air has gone thin. It feels like a noose
being put round Charles' neck.

At the heart of Kungsholmen, just a stone's throw from HQ,
there's an old motel. It once had a neon sign, which, when it worked,
informed you that you were standing outside PONTONJÄRENS
MOTELL.

The motel occupies the basement, half a flight of stairs down
from street level. The enormous space is divided into rooms, each
with a small, narrow window up near the ceiling. Each room
contains a single bed, a bedside table, a lamp, and a wardrobe. That's
it. On the edge of the bed in Room 2, sitting in front of Paul and
Charles, is a severe-looking man with pale skin, square features,
low, droopy eyebrows, and eyes so deep-set that he always looks
drawn and ashen. A dark-brown overcoat is slung over the bed.

Our man in Stockholm.

His handshake is cool and noncommittal; he's wearing a pair of
light-blue jeans and a white T-shirt, like Bruce Springsteen on the
cover of *Born in the USA*. That might be the look he's going for, in
keeping with the East German intelligence service's famous sense
of irony.

'Heffler,' he introduces himself. 'Good evening. As I understand
it, you are both fluent German speakers?'

'That's correct,' Paul replies in German.

Heffler is just the alias the Stasi gave him the first time he found
himself inside The Firm's four walls ... IA Heffler. Just like there
are supposed to be people employed by IKEA whose only task is
to give names to the company's products, the Stasi, it is said, have
a working group whose sole socialist endeavour is to create aliases
for the Informal Associates that their operatives recruit. Charles
has got one, *Wächter*, as does Paul, *Meister*.

There's no way of knowing how long Heffler has been tailing them. Days? Weeks? According to Paul, he didn't make himself known until today, when he walked past the car on Barnängsgatan while Charles was at Cats Falck's kitchen table trying to keep his nerves under control.

Heffler carried on for another block, crossed the street, and then went back the way he'd come — and once he was alongside the passenger door, he opened it and slipped onto the seat next to Paul. He then forced Paul to drive around the block, and named a time and place — here and now — before opening the door and getting out again.

It's not quite as elegant as you might imagine.

'We're ready,' Heffler says. 'Monday. There's a morning ferry from Malmö just before six. From Denmark, we take them to Ghent.'

'Why Belgium?' says Charles.

'That's the route we've managed to piece together. If we hadn't been waiting for everything to align for all those involved, we would have done it some time ago. A week ago they were to reach us via Spain. The week before, we were expecting them via Switzerland. But these are tough times. One of our …'

A packet of cigarettes is lying on the bedside table. He pulls one out, puts it in his mouth and then pats his trouser pocket for a lighter.

'One of our colleagues in Ghent gave us the opening, after having recruited a marvellous woman with connections at one of the courier companies that delivers goods around Belgium. She …'

When he can't find one, he moves on to his coat, rooting around the pockets. That's when it peeks out, the varnished revolver, black and heavy.

'Of course, we had to check her out a number of times.'

He manages to produce a box of matches from somewhere. The tobacco catches and hisses in the quiet room, sounds almost like walking through dead leaves. He looks at the two men, then up at the little window that affords a view only of the shoes and trousers of passing pedestrians.

'Fascinating, isn't it? Just seeing people's feet.' He holds out the cigarette packet towards them. 'Perhaps you'd like one?'

'No, thanks,' says Charles.

This is the way the Stasi always work. Heffler is the hub in a network of several players who have synchronised to enable the shipment. The Stasi never have direct contact with the goods or the people concerned; they always use middlemen and lackeys who never know more than is strictly necessary. That's what makes the Stasi invisible, what gives them power.

'You must've been scared,' Heffler says now, 'back at the end of February, when the computers just disappeared. My Resident has explained to me that you were rather upset by our being helped by the city's more unsavoury elements.'

'Upset is the wrong word,' says Paul. 'Concerned, more like. They are unreliable. And we know,' he went on, 'that one of them has been spouting off.'

'Really?' He raises an eyebrow, but they're so low that it makes no difference. That must cause a person problems, not ever being able to look surprised. 'He has, has he?'

'You know who it is,' says Charles.

'I have my suspicions. That was a miscalculation from our side. We thought Savolainen was with us. Who has he leaked to?'

'A reporter, at Swedish Television.'

'And what, more specifically, has he leaked?'

'That's what we don't know,' says Charles, before recounting his conversation with Cats.

'Unfortunate,' is Heffler's only comment.

'We suspect,' Charles continues, 'that she may be rather more interested in us than she let on. She claims that her story is about your dealings with Swedish criminals, but we believe that she may have played down her interest in our possible involvement.'

'Of course,' Heffler says, thoughtfully. 'Who wouldn't? What's the journalist's name?'

'Cats Falck.'

'Unfortunate, to say the least. But this will sort itself out. Just make sure that the lorry delivering the goods from Stockholm on Monday doesn't have company.'

That is more difficult than it might seem. The Bureau has its watchful eyes on the goods twenty-four hours a day, eyes that never blink, and a car ready to follow them whenever they move around. Charles and Paul can't sit in the one that's going to follow the lorry — that's too risky, too *close*. Distance is everything.

The ceiling above them hangs claustrophobically low. Heffler stubs his cigarette out on the bedside table. An ugly, rough scar forms on the surface, and the smell of burnt wood fills the room.

When the October sun is low in the sky, the Sofia church tower casts a heavy shadow over one of Södermalm's decrepit blocks, one due for imminent redevelopment. One of the side streets is narrow and dark, an ideal place to kill someone, if you weren't able to do so inside.

The second floor of one of the buildings is home to Jan Savolainen. There's no name on the door, just a subtle message to the postman and any other visitors: GO AWAY.

'We ought to punish him,' Paul says on the way up the stairs. 'We ought to neutralise him.'

'But he already knows too much. It's better to make sure he has something to lose by talking to Falck.'

The face that peers round the door stinks of beer and cigarettes. It's been more than six months, but the signs of Savolainen's previous run-in with Charles are obvious: a horrible tear runs along his lip, almost the entire width of his mouth.

'We want to talk.' Charles holds up a bag of amphetamine in front of him. 'It's worth it.'

'I don't want that stuff. I'm going to give up, get clean.'

That makes Charles laugh.

'Open up now.'

'I don't know what you want.' Savolainen lights a cigarette and leans against the work surface. 'Me and Öberg have done exactly what you told us to.'

'That's good.' Charles pulls up a chair, sits down at his kitchen table. 'That's good, Jan.'

'Fucking weird orders, I'll tell you that,' he says, blowing out smoke. 'Move them there, move them back again. They're fucking heavy and all.'

Charles places the bag of amphetamine on the table. He pulls out the cash from the inside pocket of his coat, counts eleven, twelve, thirteen, fourteen, and fifteen thousand crowns.

'That should pay your rent for a while,' says Paul. 'And any Christmas presents. It's nearly that time, you know.'

'Fuck off. You know where that money'll end up.'

'How much do you owe Öberg?'

'Fifteen thousand.'

He's exaggerating, of course, but probably not by that much. Charles lays another five thousand-crown notes on the table.

'It's yours, on two conditions. Firstly, we ask the questions and you answer, without lying. We'll come back to the second thing — that will take a bit more work.'

'Work? What the hell is that supposed to mean?' Savolainen's eyes fix on the bag. 'Chuck it here.'

'As I was saying, we'll come back to that.' Charles gives him the bag and then crosses one leg over the other. 'First of all. Cats Falck.'

'Who is that?'

'I know that you two have spoken.'

'I don't know what you're on about.'

'Jan,' says Paul. 'Come off it.'

Savolainen drops the cigarette into the sink. It hisses as it lands. He opens the bag, puts his finger in his mouth, and then pushes it down into the white stuff before he polishes his gums with it.

'All I want to know is the nature of your relationship, what she asked you, and what you answered.'

His eyes flit back and forth between Charles and Paul, and then settle on Charles again.

'I didn't mention you. Not a word.'

'Take it easy now. How did you meet?'

Savolainen pushes his finger into the bag again, then brings it to his mouth, this time licking it like a kid with a lollipop.

'She called me.'

'How had she got hold of your number?'

'She said that she'd spoken to Håkansson's wife, Anita.'

'Anette,' says Paul. 'And that's what led Falck to you?'

'I guess so.'

'And what did you talk about?'

'She just asked loads of questions about the stuff, about Öberg, about the East Germans, about you.'

A slight tremor runs through Charles. He can feel it in his fingertips. Savolainen looks down at the notes and licks his lips.

'She asked how you were involved,' he says. 'But I didn't say anything. Seriously, that's what happened.'

This goes on for a couple of minutes, Charles and Paul asking and Savolainen denying.

'I think he's telling the truth,' says Charles.

'Damn right I am.'

'That's good, Jan,' says Paul. 'And if she gets back to you, what do you say then?'

'I'm not a fucking kid,' he hisses. 'I know what to say.'

'Good,' says Charles. 'So, onto the second part of this. The bit that's going to take a bit of work.' He takes a little notebook and pen from his coat pocket, writes down the car's registration. 'This car,' he says, pushing the note across the table, 'is going to be parked near the goods' location tomorrow, in the car park at Skärmarbrink.'

Savolainen leans forward, reads the number, and looks at him, puzzled.

'And?'

'Smash four or five bottles in advance. Take them with you in a thick blanket or a jumper and spread the splinters out around the car park, but not too close to the car. Make it look like a fight. Slash one of the car's tyres. But make two holes, one tiny little one close to the rim, so that you can be sure that the air will escape, then you do a rougher one, the old-fashioned way, you know, in the tread itself. It's one of our cars, but it's on standard tyres, so it shouldn't be too difficult.'

'It's better to get the car leaking coolant or something. Less complicated, more effective.'

'That, and other, similar methods are better in that regard,' says Charles. 'But they also look a lot more like sabotage, which absolutely must be avoided.'

'What am I going to do the tyres with then? I'm not about to use my own fucking knife.'

'No, you won't.' Paul slides his hand into his trouser pocket and produces a little knife. 'Use this.'

'You're going to have to get there half an hour earlier,' says Charles. 'And then wait for your opening when no one's around.'

'I get five thousand for that?'

'Five thousand now, another five thousand afterwards. Deal?'

Savolainen licks his lips and holds out his hand, and Paul puts the knife in it. Savolainen tests the weapon, expertly folds out the blade and pushes it carefully against his forearm. A little drop of blood squeezes through the skin.

Savolainen puts the knife away. Paul smiles. Savolainen's index finger heads back into the bag.

MAY–JULY 1980

'She's not well, Charles,' said Eva. 'You can see that, surely?'

'I don't see what the problem is. She's just a bit cranky, that's all.'

'She's not like the others — haven't you noticed? She's much quieter, until she gets angry. Then she gets furious.'

Marika was quieter than others, until the tantrums came. They weren't longer than a few moments, always followed by her falling into a bubble where she would remain for an hour or two before pulling herself up. That was all there was to it.

They sat in the kitchen, staring at the shards of shattered porcelain on the floor. A short while later, when they stood outside her room and opened the door slightly, she was sitting staring blankly at the wall, with her knees under her chin and her arms wrapped around her legs.

'It's okay,' Charles said.

'That doesn't become any truer just because you keep repeating it,' Eva said and then left.

Something's changed, he thought to himself as he watched his wife heading for the kitchen to cook dinner. She never touches me anymore. I don't touch her, either.

He spent a little while trying to work out when it had started and why it had happened. A little while, no longer, because things were different now.

Charles had turned thirty-three, and a murder investigation had landed on his desk: a man had disappeared in suspicious circumstances, and when his body was recovered it was a couple of teenagers who had found it.

Or, strictly speaking, *part* of it.

They had been drinking beer by the little river that runs through the outskirts of town. Old oak trees rose high above the water, and their heavy branches leant over to touch its shining surface. When one of the teenagers went off for a piss, he noticed something odd about the network of branches, then realised what it was. He was pissing on a human arm.

It belonged to a man, but to begin with that was all they could say for sure. It wasn't possible to say whether the murderer had dismembered the body, or whether it had had a run-in with the sharp propeller of a motorboat. Before long, his other remains surfaced close to the site of the first find: a thigh, a leg, a ribcage, and a head. It wasn't until then, when they saw the bullet hole in his forehead, that they were able to determine the cause of death, as well as the victim's identity. His name was Ted Lichter, and the case became known as the Lichter case.

It was a tough investigation. They found no trace of the perpetrator; they were understaffed, lacked experience in investigating this type of crime, and were also forced to grapple with countless leaks to the media.

The case was opened on that balmy evening in May when the boys found one of Lichter's arms. At that point, the victim had been reported missing for ten days. He was thirty-two years old and lived in a condemned apartment block near the town centre. They found nothing in the flat that could lead them to whoever had taken his life — all Charles took with him was a sense of just how far a person can sink without even reaching the bottom.

Lichter was a heroin addict and made a living selling sex, primarily to men.

May turned into June. Reinforcements were sent down from Stockholm. Charles' desk was gradually filled with documents from the preliminary investigation, until they overflowed and ended up on the floor. Somewhere, under all that, his typewriter was waiting, but he hadn't seen it in days, maybe even weeks. He stopped watching the clock, didn't make a note of what time he got in or when he went home. The more listless and demoralised the Lichter investigation became, the more determined he was not to let go of it.

The central point in his life had shifted. From having been the home, with Eva and Marika, it was now split between his office and the car journeys to and from his parking space outside the police station. This dislocation, much as he didn't want to admit it, brought a sense of relief.

Charles dropped his daughter off at school every morning, and the car journey between their home and the low-slung buildings near the sports ground gave them a little time together. He would try and talk to her, but she never said more than the odd word, for the most part just sitting, staring out of the windscreen and watching the world go by with an indecipherable expression.

She had turned eight just after the Lichter investigation got underway, and had had a party, a party which Charles had managed to make it home for only by the skin of his teeth, and even then it was thanks to his colleague who disturbed his reading of the case notes by asking if today wasn't the day he was supposed to finish early to buy balloons and a chocolate cake.

'I made it,' Charles said when he saw Marika sitting in the living room surrounded by her classmates. 'Daddy made it.'

Marika looked at her hands. Eva smiled, but it never made it to her eyes.

A lot of the time, he would get home so late that Marika had gone to bed and Eva would be sitting waiting on the sofa — she always stayed up until he came home, no matter how tired she was. As soon as he came through the door, she would stand up, say hello, give him a hug, and then go straight to the bathroom and get ready for bed.

Charles would sit in the darkness, alone in front of the telly, with a beer, waiting for the alcohol to make him so dozy that he could no longer keep his head upright. He often woke up on the sofa the following morning, woken by the sound of Eva stacking crockery in the kitchen. Charles had started to think that she did it on purpose, that it was supposed to wake him up.

They still had sex. He needed it, and convinced himself that she did, too.

They would often do it in the morning, before Marika woke up — in the kitchen, or on the sofa or the bathroom floor. These were silent agreements: she would move closer to him or vice versa, and it didn't take more than for her to close her hand or her lips around him, or to guide his face to her neck or breasts, to get him rock hard. He thought it surprising that Eva still had that effect on him. It was always over far more quickly than either of them wanted.

'It's the only time you're really here,' she said.

'I know,' he replied.

Eight years, he thought. We had eight good years. Will we get any more?

He wanted to say sorry, but couldn't.

He had heard all about them, policemen who had been consumed by their jobs and then watched as everything else fell apart, without doing anything about it, and Charles had promised himself and Eva that it would never happen to them. He also recalled how the question — *is it happening now?* — had popped into his mind one sunny morning in July, the first day of his summer leave, yet he still got in the car to go and take a new witness statement about Lichter.

Charles laughed at that, firstly because *is it happening now?* was an absurd question, and then, when he realised that the answer was *yes*, because he could do nothing about it.

OCTOBER 1984

It was a day to remember.

The car tailing the lorry heading south with the goods has to stop, close to Södertälje. The reason: puncture, rear left tyre. Operatives Larsson and Johansson are inside, and they make a forlorn call-out on the radio before changing the tyre. In the meantime, the lorry disappears into the autumn gloom.

They have repeatedly described the vehicle's appearance and registration to their colleagues, which is completely futile since the car is deliberately nondescript and the driver switches the numberplates at a service area en route to Malmö.

When a deflated Larsson and Johansson return northwards and are summoned to the Director, they are unsure of what might have caused the puncture, although both seem to remember seeing shards of glass in the car park.

'It is lucky,' the Director hisses across his desk at Charles and Paul, 'that this has been an invisible operation from the start. Otherwise I would have been forced to fire the whole Bureau staff, myself included.' He has a glass of brandy in his hand. It's eleven a.m. 'Is that even possible? Can you fire yourself? I've never fucking known anything like it. So much money. So many resources. Larsson and Johansson, like Kristiansson and fucking Kvant.'

'We know that the lorry was heading south,' Paul says. 'We're guessing that they went to Gothenburg, to get the boat over …'

'I know.' The Director's voice is trembling. 'I know. Maybe England, right? Maybe even Norway. Or perhaps the lorry drove down to Malmö, onto a ferry, and then through Denmark. Or West Germany. Whichever it is, we've lost them.'

Paul blinks.

'That's correct.'

The Director examines his glass.

He flings it at the wall. The shards fall to the floor and the brandy splatters. One drop lands on Charles' lip; another hits his cheek.

'Gentlemen,' the Resident says with a smile. 'Comrades. I must congratulate you. Berlin sends her warmest regards.'

With Johann Kraus, it's never *East* Berlin. That would be tacit recognition of West Berlin as a city, which in turn would give legitimacy to the forces on the other side of the wall. The East German way is always to operate in denial. In times like these, this might be more important than ever.

This time, he's sitting in the front seat, next to Paul. He's clutching a briefcase. Charles is sitting behind them with a headache and a blue holdall. He could do with a stiff drink, but has to wait so that it doesn't get out of control.

'Everything went swimmingly, I understand,' says Kraus.

'That would be our assessment,' says Paul.

They roll off slowly, leaving Lärkstaden. Kraus hands the briefcase over to Charles, who opens it and runs his fingertips over the notes. Everything is so familiar, as though it's only been a matter of days since the last deal was concluded. In fact, it's been over a year.

'Half now,' Kraus says without looking at Charles. 'Half in just over a month's time.'

Charles opens the holdall.

'There was one snag, was there not?' Kraus says, staring straight out of the windscreen. 'Heffler mentioned a journalist.' When neither of them respond, he goes on: 'I am rather hurt, I must say, by the fact that I have to be the one to bring this up.'

'The reason being that we still aren't sure exactly what it is she knows,' says Paul.

'That is what I am afraid of.'

'We are in the process of finding out.'

'That is all I ask, as you are aware. That, and then that you take appropriate measures once you have concluded your investigations.' In the darkness, Kraus's profile is as sharp as the cutting edge of a knife. 'The rabbit warren is deep, far deeper than you think. You know the intended purpose of our VAX machines, and you know about The Firm's long fingers. Dear ASEA — the electrical-engineering giant — have been supplying us with isostatic presses for four years now. We manage the deals separately, but, since they depend upon each other, there are still some common elements. If you find yourself standing far down enough in the rabbit warren, the links become apparent. This journalist is in danger, in the most inappropriate way, of searching far too deep. There are *names* down there. Anyone who finds their way down there cannot return to the surface.'

None of them say anything. The cool, dry notes rustle in Charles' hands as he transfers them to the bag.

'I understand,' says Paul.

'I am not, of course, asking you to do anything drastic. Such a thing would never occur to me.'

'Of course not.'

'*If,* however …'

'I understand,' says Paul, again.

JULY 1980

The breakthrough in the Lichter investigation came in the shape of a witness who had been too scared to contact them earlier. He called the station late one Saturday in July and insisted on talking to Charles. The constable who'd taken the call then contacted Charles and passed on the telephone number, which Charles then rang from home. The man did not say who he was but claimed to have information about Ted Lichter. He just gave a time and place where he wanted to meet, and hung up.

So Charles was left standing with the receiver in his hand and a fluttering in his chest, the sort you get when you know that something's about to happen.

When Monday came around, the first day of his summer leave, Charles went and got into his car, despite having promised Marika that they were going to eat breakfast and watch telly together. Eva walked to the door with him, didn't say a word.

'You,' Charles said when they met. 'I wasn't expecting this.'

They sat in Charles' car, up on the hill from where you could see the houses, the church tower, even the bridge over the little river that wound its way down towards the coast.

The man sitting next to him was a councillor, married with two children, and was a pretty well-known figure in the town.

'I've been thinking this over for a long time,' he said. 'Ever since I realised that it was him.'

'That it was Lichter?'

'Yes. But I haven't … I'm putting so much on the line.'

'I'm not going to force you to make an official statement. It might not even be necessary. If you give me information that helps me get on — that might be enough.'

'I feel like I have to. It isn't right, going around knowing, or at least suspecting, what might be behind something like this, and not saying anything.'

He looked at Charles with an expression that seemed to be looking for reassurance.

'I agree.'

'I've read about you in the papers,' he went on. 'You seem like a decent bloke.'

'I do my best,' said Charles.

The councillor laughed.

'Same here, in the end. Maybe that's all you can ask of yourself.'

About two years earlier, he had dared, for the first time, to do something about the urges that were tormenting him. That wasn't Ted Lichter, but since then he had met several men, including Ted Lichter. *Met* was the word he used.

At first his relationship with Lichter had been impersonal, or at least as impersonal as things can be when it's a matter of having sex in return for payment.

'The last time we met was just a few days before he disappeared. By then, we'd moved on to a bit of small talk, both before and after, however you might put it. He'd seen me in the newspaper, he said, when I'd been at the opening of the new swimming pool. That's what I'd been afraid of all along, that something like that might happen. He could see that in my face, which wasn't difficult — in

214

fact, I think it was pretty obvious, if you know what I mean? He calmed me down though, laughed, told me he was used to these kinds of situations. I asked what he meant, which is when ...' He shook his head. 'Ted told me a very strange story.'

'A true story?'

'I have no evidence of that. It might be out there if anyone goes looking for it, but I didn't want to get involved. I can't see why he would lie about it. There was no point.'

Charles waited, wanted to smoke a cigarette, but the councillor was no smoker, he knew that, so he abstained.

'He told me that he'd met a man — a politician who had been here on a visit alongside a former government minister — who requested his services. That was the beginning of March, and it all took place in the same hotel where he and I used to go, but in one of the more luxurious rooms.'

'Who was the politician?'

The man stayed quiet for a long time.

'I'm guessing that you will work it out, and so I am merely saving you a bit of time by telling you, wouldn't you say?'

'Yes.'

The councillor took a deep breath, and held it, for ages.

'Ulrik Bondesson. It's not a name that rings bells with the man in the street, granted, but during Palme's time in office he was at Defence, as one of Foreign Minister Paulsson's closest aides.'

Bondesson. Paulsson. Palme.

Unexpected names.

'After the act itself, the phone rang in Bondesson's room. At this point, Lichter was in the shower — Bondesson could hardly shoo him out before answering. What came next was a conversation in German. Since Lichter was in the shower, he only heard half of it and, oh yes, Lichter was Swedish of course, but his

215

grandparents came from Hamburg, so he could speak German, or at least understand it. That was one part of his brain not yet addled by the drugs.'

As he said the words, a sadness fell over the councillor's face. Charles wrote Bondesson's name in his notebook and waited.

'Bondesson asked if he could call back later, that he had a visitor and the caller was ringing at a very bad time, but it must still have been urgent because after all that they still spoke for some time. And Bondesson mentioned a name,' the councillor added, quietly, before slowly allowing the name to fall from his lips.

Charles made a note of that, too.

'I recognise it,' he said.

'He's been managing director at ASEA for the last few years.'

'How do you know it was him?'

'It must have been him, or at least it is certainly reasonable to assume that it was. Bondesson has been working closely with him to seal a new contract between ASEA and West Germany. They couldn't agree on a price last time around, you might remember?'

'Vaguely,' said Charles.

'Lichter also heard *The Firm* and *those bastards in Berlin*. Then the call ended. When Lichter came out of the shower, the first thing that happened was that Bondesson screamed at him. If Lichter ever breathed a word of what he'd heard to anyone, he wouldn't see the sunrise the next day.'

'Blimey,' said Charles.

The man adjusted his position in the seat next to him, then felt around for the wheel that adjusts the seat back. Having found it, he reclined the seat a few notches, put his head against the headrest, and closed his eyes.

'Of course, I asked whether he had done so, whether he'd said anything to anyone. He hadn't. But he was pretty fearless, Lichter, although he wasn't stupid. Rather than spouting off, he did a little research. I have no idea of the details, but someone in his position has unexpected contacts, as you might imagine, often rather powerful ones. He told me that *The Firm* almost certainly referred to the Stasi, and the man he had sold sex to, Bondesson, was one of their agents.'

'Blimey,' said Charles, again.

'I know.' He cleared his throat. 'That was all. A few days later, Lichter was reported missing.'

Charles looked out over the city that spread out beneath them, its many houses with their small windows. He could see the roof of his workplace. Being on leave seemed odd.

He reviewed his notes, trying to tie them together, trying to see a story.

'You mentioned that you could see no reason for Lichter to lie. I can see several.'

The man opened his eyes.

'Such as?'

'Boasting, seeming important, for example. As though he knew things.'

The politician shakes his head.

'He wasn't that sort of person.'

'What does that mean?'

'Ted never drew attention to himself. That was one of the things I liked about him. He was who he was. But yes, he could have been lying.'

Charles looked at him, then at his notes again.

'Thank you for this. It might not lead anywhere, but I will check these details.'

'Things like this usually lead all the way to the end,' the councillor said as he opened the car door. 'The question is whether we really want to find out what's waiting there.'

JUNE 2014

The air inside the meeting room is still. Davidsson gasps, grimaces, and sneezes so powerfully that his face shifts from pallid pink to red. Åhlund smirks in front of me.

'That tear in your lip,' he says. 'I think that needs stitches.'

'Can't we tape it?'

'We can try.'

'And something for my ribs.' I swallow another little gulp of blood. 'Preferably morphine.'

Åhlund hesitates before he returns to the first-aid kit.

'So, we have a suspect,' Tove says, looking at Davidsson. 'Can you tell us anything about the circumstances?'

'Well, I told you that I was going to talk to my friend Dan, who knows everything about everyone. One nosy bastard, but otherwise a good bloke. He's been a big help before, and had it not been for his occasional habit of driving a car despite not having a driving licence, he would probably have been more of a blessing than a curse around here. Anyway.' He stands by the whiteboard, where Levin's name and ID number are visible alongside the photograph of the unknown man in the car. 'What we knew yesterday was that the victim is from Stockholm, but that he lived here for a little over nine years, from 1971 to 1980. At that time, he lives on Alvavägen with Eva Alderin, who soon becomes Eva Levin, and they have a daughter together, in spring 1972.'

He draws a horizontal line, originating from Levin's name, then writes *Eva Levin (Alderin)*. From the middle of the line, he draws another, vertical, and writes *Marika Levin*.

'What my friend Dan tells me is that there's a fourth person in the picture. We just don't know how exactly.' Above the Levin family, Davidsson draws a diagonal line, and writes the name *Daniel Bredström*. 'Who, then, is Daniel Bredström? A little biography might be in order, for our recently arrived colleague.'

'Much appreciated,' I say.

Åhlund finds a pill bottle, reads the label before shaking out one of the pills. It's small, oval, like an ordinary painkiller.

'These are really prescription only,' he says. 'Would you like some water?'

'Just give it here.'

'Don't you want to know what's in it?'

I shake my head. My neck is killing me. I put the pill in my mouth. It's slippery, and glides down easily.

'Daniel Bredström, born October 1950, which makes him sixty-three. Raised here in Bruket. After military service, he got a metalwork apprenticeship with Erkensjö's, which used to be over by the junkyard. After two years, they take him on, and he works there until 1975, when he starts his own business. The company repairs and repaints cars, and goes straight onto the scrapheap in 1980 when we notice that his bookkeeping isn't up to scratch, that he's had occasional dealings with the shady characters of the day, and that he's been handling stolen goods. In early 1981, he's convicted for the fencing and gets a huge tax bill, declares himself bankrupt. He starts drinking, and gets done for assault in 1982 after a scuffle down at Brukets Bar, and he's then sentenced to a year's imprisonment. It's all downhill from there. He goes into rehab a few times, but it seems to be mainly for the sake of appearances, and to make sure he keeps his benefits. Over the years, he's been cautioned for possession, of both drugs and illegally acquired firearms — including a musket and a revolver — buying sex, two further assault charges, one aggravated, carrying an offensive weapon, and assaulting a police officer.'

Davidsson clears his throat. Åhlund dabs my lip with surgical spirit, making my eyes water. It feels like it's burning. Tove pulls a notebook from her bag, starts writing in it.

'By now, Bredström is probably too old to cause too much trouble and is living a relatively law-abiding life. He's been medically retired for a few years now. The booze has remained his best friend, and there's not much left of his liver. He lives up in the woods down one of the gravel tracks by Vårmyntan, is only ever seen at the alcohol store — and once that's gone, we'll probably never see him round here again.'

Åhlund is carefully taping my split lip. I don't know if it's going to help, but straightaway everything feels pretty good, until I realise that it's actually just the morphine beginning to take effect.

'At the end of May, Levin shows up in Bruket again, after thirty-four years,' Davidsson goes on. 'And when it comes to our victim, there are a number of troubling indicators that would seem to point to Bredström.'

Davidsson writes a 1 alongside Bredström's name on the whiteboard.

'First of all, and this is Dan's own witness statement, Levin ended up behind Bredström in the queue at the alcohol store three days ago, on Wednesday the eighteenth. The day he died.' Davidsson explains. 'With less than twelve hours left to live, Levin is buying a half-bottle of scotch, while Bredström is getting himself a crate of beer. Levin, presumably, is treating himself to a little midsummer tipple, while Bredström is probably just buying his daily dose. Dan knows this, since he was also standing in the same queue, behind Levin.' Davidsson takes a deep breath, and looks like he could do with a glass of water. 'Neither Levin nor Bredström notice who they're standing next to, until Bredström puts down the little *next customer* bar on the till belt. That's when the men notice each other, and, according to Dan, their exchange was not a long one, and what was said was anything but warm.'

He writes 18/6 alongside the 1, and adds, *L&B meet.*

'Then comes Dan's turn to pay, so he doesn't know what happened for the subsequent minute or so. But when he comes out of the shop, he sees Levin and Bredström standing on the corner by Aspgren's service store. They're talking to each other — or rather, Bredström is talking at Levin. Agitated and intense, that was how Dan described it. Bredström even went as far as poking Levin in the chest with his finger. Bredström then turns on his heels and walks off, quickly. Levin goes into Aspgren's and Dan cycles home.'

Davidsson studies his own notes and adds a word.

1 18/6 L&B meet. Threat?

Åhlund has finished on my lip, and he closes the green bag.

'Those pills you had in there,' I say. 'Can I have the bottle?'

'No, but you can have a few.' He shakes five of them out. 'You ought to see a doctor,' he continues, before standing up and turning to Davidsson. 'You want me to stay?'

'No, go down to the cells and check out the drunks. Most of them should have sobered up by now.'

I put the pills in my jacket pocket, and notice the blood on my Prince T-shirt. I need to change tops.

Åhlund leaves the room. Davidsson sneezes again.

'Okay,' Davidsson continues, his voice thick. 'That was the first thing.' He adds a 2 underneath the 1. 'Secondly.' He places the photo of the man in the car next to the number. 'The car. Its most recent known keeper is Bredström.'

'What?' I say, causing strain across my lip. 'This is a man living on benefits, spending his money on crates of beer, yet he can afford a car like that?'

'We suspect that it is stolen, and that he's been keeping it in his garage in order to sell it later. The fact that it has false plates would point to that. Anyway,' he says, 'Bredström leads a *relatively* law-abiding life. His nearest neighbour lives a couple of hundred metres further down the same gravel track, and he's seen Bredström with the car on at least two occasions. I spoke to the neighbour, Ylva Larsson, myself, and she didn't hesitate at all when shown the photograph. "You can tell there," she said,' Davidsson says, tapping the photo. '"If you squint, you can even see that it's him." Which brings me onto my third point.'

He adds a *3* underneath the *2* and pauses for a second before writing *appearance*.

I glance over at Tove and wonder if she's thinking what I'm thinking: that Davidsson is avoiding the word *description* because he's not sure how to spell it.

'If we assume that the person in the picture is our suspect, he and Bredström certainly look alike.'

'But that picture,' Tove says. 'It's extremely blurred. It's impossible to make out any features in it.'

'By a process of elimination, it is possible to get somewhere at least. The man in the picture certainly doesn't have dark hair, and neither does Bredström. Even if his age is difficult to establish, he doesn't look particularly young, and Bredström is sixty-three.' Davidsson throws his hands up. 'And the man in the picture is sitting in a car that Bredström had access to, according to Ylva Larsson.'

'I'm guessing that Ylva Larsson didn't notice the car's registration, though?'

'She didn't. So we can't be completely sure that it is the same vehicle, not least because this car,' he nods towards the picture on the whiteboard, 'has false plates. What we do know is that we haven't yet found the car in the picture.'

'It's not at Bredström's, then?' I say.

'Not right now. The garage is empty.'

'How do you know?'

'Because I've been there. I went to see him.'

'You didn't mention that,' says Tove, surprised.

'I asked him where it was, and, of course, at first he had no idea what I meant, what car I was talking about, or anything else. He'd never owned a car like that. But in the end, he crumbled.' Davidsson half smirks. 'He claimed to have owned the car, but that someone had stolen it. Presumably, he had parked it somewhere after the murder, set light to it, and got rid of it that way — what do I know? There was also a yellow sack truck in the garage. Naturally, we need the proper paperwork in order to examine it more closely, and it probably won't be significant, given how common they are, but make a note of it. There might have been a trolley like it at Levin's place.'

'No computer, though, or phone, or printer?' Tove asks.

'Not in the garage. Either they're somewhere else in the house or he's already sold them. Who knows what he's had time to do since the eighteenth of June? That ties in with my fourth point.' Davidsson now adds a 4 under the 3, writes *Alibi*. 'Bredström hasn't got an alibi for the time Levin was shot. He claims to have been down to the alcohol store and then afterwards to have just been sitting at home watching telly and drinking beer for the rest of the day as well as the evening, which no one can corroborate. He didn't call anyone, meet anyone — nothing. Not only that,' Davidsson says as he writes a 5, 'he probably has access to firearms. Finally, he has a history of blacking out when he gets seriously angry, and when he does, he seems to not really know what's going on. His most recent conviction for assault is only a couple of years old. Safe to say that he has a violent nature and that he doesn't really know when to stop.'

Davidsson now adds the 6 and writes *violent nature*, before pressing the top onto the pen and putting it on the table, then studying the board and admiring his handiwork.

'So,' Tove says. 'You've already spoken to him.'

'I let him think that the stolen car itself was the main focus of our inquiries, and that I just wanted to kill two birds with one stone by establishing his whereabouts on the evening of the eighteenth.' He turns to me. 'We often work like that here. We start by checking in with the usual suspects. So it's not the first time he's had a visit like that from us. I've put Brandén on surveillance duties — he's in an unmarked car on the gravel track between Bredström's place and Ylva Larsson's, so he's not going anywhere unnoticed.'

'Had he heard about Levin's death?' Tove asks.

'He had. He didn't exactly seem to be in mourning either.'

I study the names on the board: Levin, Eva, Daniel Bredström. There's some unnamed connection between them, something *more*. The names are nothing more than waymarkers in a missing story.

'Could it be that Eva and this Daniel —' Tove says, but is interrupted by a knock at the door.

Without waiting for a response, Åhlund opens the door and pokes his head in.

'This car,' he says. 'What was the registration?'

'FOR 528,' says Tove.

'We just had a call.' Åhlund looks down at the note in his hand. 'It's been found in the woods behind the graveyard.'

Davidsson smiles broadly.

'What did I tell you?'

'Torched,' Åhlund adds, unsure whether that detail has any bearing on the matter.

Last year, Gabriel Birck had spent Midsummer's day pleasantly hung-over in bed, with only *Last Exit to Brooklyn* for company. It's a book whose characters' life stories are far from cheerful, yet they still pale in comparison to the life that Marika Alderin has lived.

She is forty-two years old and was taken into care on numerous occasions before finally being sentenced to secure psychiatric treatment, following a failed murder attempt in central Stockholm some nine years ago.

Sitting at his computer in his office, Birck alternates between gulping down juice to get his vitamins and coffee to combat his tiredness, as he clicks through the various open registers.

She was born Marika Levin, but in 1990 she became Marika Alderin, according to the tax authority's records. She took her mother's name. In several of the registers, that is the name you have to start from in order to find what you're looking for, and even then you find only splinters of a life: an address here, a tax return there — no more.

He leaves his office, heads for St Göran's.

'I don't know if you remember what psychiatric care was like in the Eighties,' Plit says, standing shoulder-to-shoulder with Birck in one of the rooms at St Göran's, reading Marika's notes. 'I was barely born myself.'

'They dished out pills all over the place, thinking that was the solution to all young people's problems, and that it didn't have any unforeseen consequences.'

'Exactly,' Plit says. 'This part of the record is always just an outline, and for people like her it always will be. There are unexplained gaps in her life that won't ever be filled.'

In spring 1985, Marika Levin started taking anti-anxiety medication to treat panic attacks. *From a very young age*, the journal continues, *she has been a psychiatrically unstable child. Her father is now of the opinion that the situation has become untenable.*

In 1990, after five years of anti-anxiety tablets, she changed her name whilst also having developed a regular drug habit, which soon lead to her being put in custody under young-offender legislation. Afterwards, she was released again and seems to flit between various towns in central Sweden: Norrköping, Uppsala, Enköping, Sala, Västerås.

In the year 2000, at the age of twenty-eight, Marika Alderin walked into the social-services office in Nyköping and told them how she had started hearing voices. *She says that amongst other things, she hears her mother's voice. Mother has been dead for twenty years (LEVIN, EVA).*

What happened next isn't clear, but she didn't get any help, and nor did she show any significant improvement. In autumn 2002, Stockholm's drug squad cleared a drug den in Bandhagen where they found Marika Alderin and others. She was convicted of possession and sent to a rehab centre. She was soon out, but within months she was once again in custody.

So it goes on, until 2005, when something happened: she absconded from a rehab centre at the end of April, took an overdose, and fell into the psychosis in which she remains to this day.

That was her condition when she attempted murder in central

Stockholm, leading to her being sectioned that autumn. She was so heavily sedated on the drive up to Säter that she was all but unconscious.

'She's been with us about five years,' says Plit. 'You can see there, up at the top, when we took over her care from Säter. Twenty-fourth of August 2009.'

'Does she know that her father is dead?'

'Yes. We told her as soon as we found out.'

'And what did she say?'

'Nothing.'

'Did she react at all?'

'Well, maybe she did,' says Plit. 'But not so we noticed.'

Marika Alderin has her legs crossed, and her hands in her lap, her neck and head hanging like a vulture's. She was once dark-haired, but now her shoulder-length hair is streaked with grey. A limp centre-parting hangs over her forehead, fringe uneven, the hairstyle that young children end up with when their parents cut their hair. Her face was probably beautiful, but someone has twisted all her features, made her eyes too big for her nose, her mouth too wide for her chin. She looks funny, yet not funny at all. She moves her mouth mechanically, like someone chewing gum, and stares at Birck, who is sitting in the chair opposite her.

It feels as though he's trespassing, entering a place where he really shouldn't be.

'Marika. My name is Gabriel. I would like to talk to you.'

Her voice is deep and dark, and as rough as sawdust.

'The child is the father of the man.'

She looks from the tabletop to Birck, raises an eyebrow.

'Yes,' Birck says gingerly.

'Yes.' She folds her arms as best she can and rocks from side to side in her chair. 'Yes. Yes. Yes.'

'If you don't want to talk to me, just say so. Then I'll go away.'

'Uh-huh. Uh-huh. Uh-huh.'

'I think somebody has been coming here to see you. A man.'

She cocks her head to one side, blinks once, and smiles weakly.

'It burned up. Soot and ash were all that was left.'

'Marika, I want to ask you about the man who was here. I'm going to show you a picture of him. You can just say yes or no, that's plenty. Do you understand?'

Her face shifts form again, to something approaching anticipation.

'Yes.'

He clicks through to the picture of Charles Levin, and holds the phone up towards her. She leans forward.

'Has he been here to visit you?'

'Younger, eh?'

'Was he younger, the man who visited you?'

She shakes her head.

'Is he younger in the picture than he was in reality?'

'You are much younger.'

This makes Birck laugh, a resigned chuckle.

'It's true.'

He leaves the phone on the table in front of her.

'It burned up. Soot and ash were all that was left.'

'What burned up, Marika?'

'The car. It burned up.'

'There was a car that burned up?'

'Uh-huh. The car. Burned up.'

She looks down. Ribbons of grey and dark hair fall across her cheeks. The phone's key lock kicks in, and the screen goes black.

'Could you look at the picture again, Marika?'

'If you like.'

'I would like you to.'

Birck opens the picture again.

'Pain,' she says.

'Are you in pain?'

'Uh-huh. Pain from looking.'

'So you do recognise him?'

'Oh, yes.' She starts rocking on the chair again. 'Oh, yes. Never forget him.'

'So he is the one that visited you?'

'The child is the father of the man.'

'Marika ...'

'Soot and ash were all that was left.'

Something bubbles up inside her, as if something's waking up: a giggle. The giggle is intense, and it grows and grows until it escapes from her mouth and she flings herself from side to side in her chair, an invisible hand grabbing hold of her, and the giggle becomes a laugh that violently bounces back and forth from one wall to the other.

Bloody Leo, sending him here, to one of the saddest places on earth, for no good reason.

'Thank you, Marika. I'll leave you in peace.'

She goes quiet, stops, and looks at him. Her eyes reveal an emptiness so discomfiting that he shivers.

'You can sleep with me if you like,' she whispers.

Birck gets up from the chair and makes for the door. He's embarrassed.

He'd like to have a stiff drink to dull his emotions, or smoke a cigarette to keep his hands busy, just something to *do*. He doesn't do either; instead, he stands there in the car park and concentrates on his lungs, filling them with air and then letting it out again. Control, he thinks to himself. I must keep control of this.

Then he goes in again, past the security check and along the corridor that leads back there. When Birck returns, Plit raises an eyebrow.

'I wondered where you'd got to.'

'I just needed to go out for a little while.'

Plit looks like he understands. It might be something that everyone in here needs to do from time to time, just to get through it.

'Lunch.' Plit looks at the clock. 'You hungry?'

'No.'

'Me neither. But we should go somewhere anyway.'

'So yeah.' Plit scratches his beard and takes a bite of his sandwich. The smell of roast beef and fried egg smothered in a surprising volume of curry mayonnaise is a strong one. 'Talking to Marika Alderin isn't that straightforward.'

'She did recognise Levin, though — I could tell.'

The little canteen at the far end of St Göran's is calm and quiet; the air is light and pleasant. A good place for Plit, now busy with another bite of his sandwich, to talk about the kind of things he really should be keeping quiet about. Birck pokes a carrot stick into the little plastic tub of hummus.

'The problem is that there's this invisible wall between her and the outside world,' Plit says.

'But she's no cabbage. She does register things.'

'Yes,' says Plit. 'Sometimes, some days, like today. We know that music helps — she likes listening to music. She did have an MP3 player for a while, but we had to take it off her a week or so ago. She's only allowed to have it in her room, but she'd taken it out with her.'

'But if music helps …'

'I know. But rules is rules — what am I supposed to do? The only time I've ever heard her saying anything coherent, in the whole time she's been here, she was talking to another client. We think they must be old acquaintances, that their paths must have crossed at some point, and that Marika used to enjoy his company. It seemed to activate something inside her. That made us look again at our assessment of her condition. We believe that —'

'Who?' Birck interrupts.

'Eh?'

'Who,' Birck continues slowly, 'is the client?'

NOVEMBER 1984

Charles and Paul meet up with the Resident to receive the remainder of their share of the money from the VAX computers. The Resident calls it their *remuneration*. They arrive in Paul's car and then drive round the block.

As they climb out of the car, there's a bright flash in Charles' peripheral vision, like one from a camera. He turns his head. There's some kind of party, a banquet or reception, going on in the building over there. It might have been that.

The Resident doesn't notice it, but Charles, still standing by the car, about to close the passenger door, goes stiff.

Shadows. Shadows in the darkness.

A man calls Paul's direct number. He's upset and angry. He works as a secretary at one of the companies set up by The Bureau's Operations Department for use in their undercover missions. Setting up companies in the first place had been the Director's idea, but now, years later, he seems to regret it. They're hard to control. The man on the phone says that something weird happened an hour ago.

'There was a woman here asking whether a black Citroën with registration SOM 364 is registered to this company.'

SOM 364. Paul's car.

'I said yes,' said the secretary. 'What the hell was I supposed to say? "Has it been stolen?" she asked. "No," I said, "not as far as I know." Then she asked if we were an ordinary firm of accountants. "Yes, sure," I said, "we are indeed." Then she asked how come, since the car is registered to us, and it hasn't been stolen, it's being used by two SEPO employees.'

'Now I don't follow,' Paul says into the receiver, and Charles is sitting right next to him.

It feels like a cold grasping hand, going straight for the heart.

'She showed me a photograph,' the secretary says. 'A picture taken close to the East German Embassy. Your face and your colleague's face are clearly visible. Worse still, the East German Resident Minister in Sweden is also visible.' The secretary is quieter now, sounds more curious than upset. 'What kind of contact have you had with him?'

'What's the journalist's name?'

'Cats Falck.'

Paul ends the call. Charles is still there in his room. They discuss it at length: How could she get that close to them? What have they missed? Could she have seen the car and made a note of its numberplate? If so, when?

'For fuck's sake, Paul. She's got photographic evidence.'

Paul is chain-smoking. Charles opens the window. Paul goes and closes it. Charles sees the paranoia in his eyes, and it's getting worse.

Time. Time is the only thing in life that can't be frozen, the only thing in constant motion, at the same speed, regardless of whether or not you try to resist. Certain phenomena are much greater than man.

The digital clock is ticking away in front of Charles: 22:14:55, 22:14:56, 22:14:57. Next to it, the cassette is in place in the recorder, still and silent, activated only when the receiver at the other end picks up a sound.

22:15:00. Forty-five minutes remaining until Paul arrives.

A cold evening rain is falling.

The city is closing in around him, allowing the shadows to form and the countless alleys to become even deeper. Whatever you're looking for in this city, you can find it on one of its backstreets. To enter one is tempting — to allow yourself to disappear down its throat.

The apartment is opposite Barnängsgatan 40, and the kitchen is the only place where the static crackle isn't unbearable. This is also where the shadows are longest.

22:19:42.

He adjusts the headphones. They're scratchy, and as soon as you touch them the connection scrapes and crackles so loud that it could be coming from inside your own head.

Charles has started reacting every time he hears sirens, imagines that they've found him out and that they're coming to take him away.

Paul planted the mic yesterday, once she'd left the flat for the day. Charles recalls a small living room, and yes, it should be in there somewhere, perhaps in a vase or inside a lampshade. The receiver is supposed to activate only in response to human voices, but it's old equipment and can also react to radio or television or creaking doors and windows.

Crackling. Charles swears.

22:47:11.

22:47:12.

Now.

She arrives home, gets off her bike, and disappears into the entrance. The lights in the stairwell flicker.

22:48:09. The light in her hall comes on.

22:48:50. Clicking in the headphones. Charles holds his breath.

The tape starts rolling, misses the opening words.

'… Cats. Is Lena there? Thanks.'

Her phone, shit, they should've tapped the phone, too.

'Hi, it's me. Sorry for calling so late, but I've only just got in … No, at work … Listen, Lena, you don't get it, I've been hanging around the embassy all afternoon. I've got a fucking huge thing in the works. They're going to give me a Pulitzer for this.'

She laughs.

Charles is nauseous.

'We will, tomorrow when we meet up. That's what I wanted to double check. I'm coming round to yours and then we'll clean up. Later on, in the evening, how about drinks at Öhrns Hörn? … Ring your brother then, and make sure we get a table. Then we can go to Café Opera afterwards … Good. Okay … Yep, I'll call Ulla as well. How nice. It'll be really fun. See you tomorrow … Bye.'

She hangs up, but there's a thirty-second delay before the microphone deactivates, so Charles can hear her dial another number. The conversation that follows between her and Ulla — who is *that?* — is shorter than the last one, they only mention tomorrow.

He's sweating. It's running down over his temples, and the headphones are getting wet, the sound even noisier. He adjusts them again, wipes his ears with his T-shirt.

Half a minute goes by. The noise stops, and the microphone shuts down. The lights in the flat stay on. She sallies past, a little way away from the window.

22:54:31. Another click in the headphones. The radio's on, that's why. He can hear her footsteps; hear her brushing her teeth, running the tap. He hears Bob Dylan singing about fate, hears her getting undressed. It's an intimate moment, one that makes him feel ashamed.

22:58:50. Out in the hall, the barrel of the lock turns. Paul arrives.

'Everything okay?' he asks.

'She's got something on the go, something she thinks will win her a Pulitzer prize.'

Paul laughs.

'Pride comes before a fall.'

Charles leaves the room, goes out into the hall, and picks up the phone. The receiver is heavy and red.

Marika is at Jenny's. That much he remembers, but not the telephone number of their house out in Danderyd. Charles sighs and calls Pauline. It's a while before she answers, and when she does she giggles out her name. There's loud music in the background, and shouting. Once he's got the number out of her, he says thanks. Pauline hangs up without saying anything. Maybe she is a spy after all, he thinks to himself.

'Hi,' Charles says when Marika comes to the phone. 'What are you doing?'

'What do you want?'

'Have you eaten?'

'Yes.'

'What are you up to?'

'Watching a film.'

'Which one?'

'Dad, what do you want?'

'I just want to know what you're doing.'

'Why?'

Charles has only met Jenny once, but he doesn't like her. She was wearing worn-out, patched-up jeans and a shameful amount of make-up, and had the sweet smell of perfume and cigarettes. There was something in her eyes that worried him.

'What are Jenny's mum and dad doing?'

'They're away.'

'You didn't tell me that.'

'I did actually, but you weren't listening.'

'Marika, are you drunk?'

She slams the receiver down so hard that it rebounds off the hook and the line stays open. Charles hears her walking away, hears Jenny ask, 'What the fuck was that about?' and Marika answering, 'Nothing. No one.' Then, Marika again: 'Top me up?'

They are twelve. *Twelve.*

There's a song playing in the background, perhaps on the telly, and it's a song he's heard before, but it's never hit him like this before. He's standing there in the darkness with the receiver in his hand listening to 'Dancing in the Dark' and his daughter getting a top-up, giggling, saying, 'Not too much, you're spilling it, you're spilling it,' until the track fades out.

Charles returns to the kitchen and starts to say something, but Paul hushes him while staring without blinking, his jaws clenching tightly as he listens.

Charles sits down on the far side of the table. The tape is rolling. The time: 23:14:02. There's a burning sensation behind his eyes. He needs a night of undisturbed sleep. He can't remember when he last managed to grab more than two or three hours in a row. Every night he's woken by sweat, paranoia, fear.

The sound leaks from the headphones: Cats Falck's voice. Has she got visitors? Is she on the phone again? He glances at the window. The curtains are dark green and look a bit like a fringe.

The headphones go quiet. The seconds tick away.

What will he do if something happens to Marika? What if she gets too drunk?

The tape stops. Paul takes off the headphones.

'What?' says Charles. 'What is it?'

Paul stares out the window.

'We should've bugged the phone.'

'That occurred to me, too.'

He rewinds the tape a bit.

'She called someone, I don't know who. Put the headphones on.'

Charles listens to the recording's background noise. Then, the voice: 'Hello? ... Hi, it's me, is this a bad time?' Short silence. 'Okay, great. Yes, listen, I'd like to talk to you again. I just came back from ... My phone, at home. Why? ... Aha, no, no worries. I'm starting to understand how it all adds up now. What I'd like to ask is ... Yes, sure, but all I want you to do is confirm something, if it's true, of course. You don't need to mention any names ... No, yours won't be mentioned. You're my background, that's all. Right, so ...'

The sound of rustling paper. She's flipping through a notebook.

'The Swedish company Sunitron are smuggling electronic equipment to East Germany, circumventing and breaching the embargo, and this has been going on for years. Is it correct that a number of VAX computers, model 11/782, were smuggled out of Sweden in early October this year?'

You can hear the tension in her voice.

'Good. Is it correct that the National Police Authority's security division kept the computers under surveillance while they were in Sweden?' Another pause. 'Okay.' She takes a deep breath. 'Is it correct that employees of the Security Police were involved in the deal?' Silence. 'Okay, do you know what I mean by invol— What was that? You don't know *how*, but you know that they *were* involved, that ... Good.'

She doesn't sound surprised. Charles presses the headphones to his ears, straining to hear.

'Can you tell me which of them you have ... No, okay. Of course. I understand. One final question. East Germany's Resident Minister in Sweden, Johann Kraus, do he and the Swedish operatives ... You don't know. Are you sure? No, I … Yes, certainly.'

They end the call.

'Yes, Jesus Christ,' is the last thing she says, to no one in particular in the empty apartment.

Thirty seconds pass. The headphones click off.

'Savolainen,' says Charles. 'I'll bet you anything that it's him, again. There aren't many other candidates, since whoever it is doesn't know about the connection to Kraus.'

'If the source was telling Falck the truth, that is.'

'He was telling the truth about everything else. What the source confirmed for Falck was what Savolainen knows. And he's the only one who knows that. It has to be him.'

Paul scratches his cheek thoughtfully.

'Maybe we'll have to do something about him.'

'But if she splashes the scoop, has used Savolainen as her source, and he then disappears, it's not going to look good at all.'

'The alternative is that we let him carry on roaming the streets with that slack junkie mouth of his.'

They've been doing it for so long. They're lying to so many people.

'What the fuck are we going to do?' says Charles.

'Stop her.'

'How?'

Paul's gaze returns to the street outside.

Charles thinks about Marika again, and about how, sooner or later, he's going to lose her.

JULY 1980

The Lichter case. In 1980, Charles spent the first days of his summer leave doing searches and rummaging around where he shouldn't have. A systematic approach and a process of elimination led him forward, took him upwards to where he saw *ASEA, The Social Democratic Party*, and ultimately *Ulrik Bondesson*. He double-checked the information: who was where, and when?

After a week, he had managed to get a fairly clear picture of what had happened. The core was the councillor's witness account, a core he augmented with — and the details of which he was able to verify through — existing registers. In spite of this, he only had access to a carefully chosen selection of documents and entries, often coming up against confidentiality blocks.

Towards the end of Palme's premiership, the defence minister had had an aide by the name of Leif Paulsson. One of his closest associates, Ulrik Bondesson, was recruited by the East German intelligence services. He, in turn, was the political link between Sweden and East Germany, the one who helped electronics firm ASEA sell equipment to the Eastern Block, in breach of the embargo. Charles had telephone records indicating direct conversations between Bondesson, ASEA, and the East German Embassy's Resident.

Christ.

The story was explosive, but sitting there in his room on the floor that housed the unit, the office almost empty during the summer holiday season, he didn't know what to do with it. It still didn't include the name of Ted Lichter's assailant, a detail that was hidden beyond the confines of that story.

'Where's your mum?' he asked, when he saw Marika sitting on the old bench by the living-room table. She was busy drawing something.

'I don't know,' she said.

'Is she working today?'

'She said she was going out.'

Charles checked the time.

'When was that?'

'Don't remember.'

'Did she just go off, leave you on your own?'

'She said she'd be home soon.'

He walked over and sat down next to her.

'What are you drawing?'

She shrugged. There were two trees, drawn in brown and green chalk in the background. In front of them was a mass of moving water. A man standing in the waves. His legs were too long for his body, but other than that he was in proportion. Marika had drawn a big smile on the man's face, and one hand was holding up a severed head.

Charles felt his vision going black.

'What's that, Marika?'

'I found a magazine.'

'There are no magazines with pictures like that in this house.'

'I know he didn't have a head,' said Marika. 'I read that.'

'In the magazine?'

'Yes.'

'Where is it?'

She looked around.

'It was here before.'

'I don't want you to read magazines,' Charles said. 'And I really don't want you drawing pictures of …'

The words got stuck.

'But I …'

'No, Marika.' It wasn't until his daughter recoiled that he realised how angry his voice sounded. 'Darling,' he said, gentler, his guilt growing as the pain around his temples intensified. 'Can't you draw some horses instead? Or princes and princesses?'

She didn't answer. She put the chalk away. Charles took the drawing off her.

'You and Mummy,' Marika said, her eyes blank. 'Aren't you happy?'

'Eh?'

'You don't seem very happy.'

'We are very happy,' he said, smiling, struggling to keep his voice steady. 'I promise. And you must never forget that both Mummy and me love you very, very much.'

She looked at him.

'Give me a hug,' he said.

As Marika did as he'd asked, he breathed in the scent of her hair — like Eva's, only sweeter — and felt the lump in his throat tighten.

If that man hadn't rung the doorbell that afternoon, it probably wouldn't have been long before Charles started to wonder where Eva was. But ring the bell he did, an hour or so after Charles had stood in the bathroom and ripped up Marika's drawing, then flushed it down the toilet.

'Hello,' he said, standing in the doorway.

His car, a dark-blue Citroën, was parked next to the little

fence that ran alongside the road.

'Hello.'

'This is a bit strange, a bit sudden, but ...' The man hesitated. 'I don't suppose I could come in?'

'What is this about?'

'Sorry.' He stretched out his hand. 'My name is Paul. Paul Goffman.'

Charles took it, hesitantly. Paul wasn't from around here. His hand was cool, and dry.

'Charles.'

'I know. We are colleagues.'

'Are we?'

The man pulled out his badge.

'From Stockholm,' Charles read aloud.

'Can I come in?'

'What is this about?' he repeated.

'Ted Lichter.'

He said it mournfully, as though what would follow would cause both of them grief.

Paul Goffman was about the same age as Charles and was dressed in dark jeans, a light shirt, and matching blazer. He was slim, with broad shoulders, like a swimmer's, and had a square face with distinct eyebrows and ice-blue eyes.

'What a beautiful daughter you have,' he said, as they sat by the kitchen window, each with a cup of coffee in front of them.

'Yes, she is quite something.'

Paul drank some coffee.

'When I was searching for your address, I noted that there was also an Eva Levin registered here, too.'

'That's my wife.' Charles looked at his hands. 'She's at work.' He looked up. 'Right. Ted Lichter.'

'Ted Lichter,' Paul repeated. 'That's right. I understand …' He changed his mind. 'Perhaps you understand where I come from?'

'I'm guessing the National Police Authority's security division.'

'Operations Department. We have had an interest in Ted Lichter, or rather those strands that tie together around him. I believe,' he went on, 'that our view matches the one that you, judging by your searches and investigations, have begun to form. ASEA, Bondesson, all that. Your theory, in other words, is correct.'

'I don't care whether I'm right or not. All I care about is getting hold of whoever did it.'

'And that's where I think I may be able to help.'

'How?'

Paul took a deep breath.

'I can give you a name.'

'A name?'

'That's right.'

'Of the person who did it?'

'Of the person who held the weapon, at least. All I ask of you is that it stops there, with him, and that you don't start pulling any of the threads that the Lichter case contains. That is our job, not yours.'

'Sure.'

'Good,' Paul said, somewhat surprised. 'Then we have an agreement?'

'Yes.'

'We will be checking to make sure you follow it.'

'Right then. You can go back to Stockholm now.'

Paul laughed.

'Okay. Manfred Lundin.'

'Manfred Lundin?'

'That's who did it.'

'I find that very difficult to believe.'

Manfred Lundin was one of their most notorious junkies, a

man in his forties who had spent half of his life in custody or in treatment. He was named in their inquiries but simply as one of the victim's associates.

'Lichter knew too much. One hand hires a second, who hires a third, who hired Manfred Lundin. Two men on the same low rung in society had a falling out. At least, that's what it was supposed to look like.'

'Did he dismember him, too?'

'You'd be surprised,' Paul said, 'what addicts are prepared to do to make sure they get their fix. They are often used by organisations like this.'

'What organisations are you talking about now?'

Paul smiled and looked out of the window.

'It's a funny little place, Bruket. How did you end up here?'

Something about Paul, possibly his tone of voice, revealed the fact that he already knew.

'I was at a conference nearby, and happened to meet Eva by chance.'

'Aha. Of course. Women.' He blinked, and drank another gulp of coffee. 'That was quite thorough handiwork there, Charles. I took the liberty — now I hope this doesn't make you feel uncomfortable — but I took the liberty of looking up your old test scores and results from the training courses you've done, and the cases you've handled. Your CV is outstanding. Not only that, you're young, like me, and you seem to understand the politics of things. You would be very valuable to us.'

Charles was surprised by his directness.

'Another time, perhaps.'

'You did used to work in Stockholm, didn't you? Under Sivertsson?'

'Yes.'

'There's a real policeman for you. Don't you miss the big city?'

'Sometimes I do. But it's not the city itself that I miss, more the way that life was back then. Anything else?'

'No.' He stood up. 'I won't keep you any longer. Have a think about my offer, and give your charming daughter my regards.'

Charles stood at the window and watched him drive away. He'll find his way around here, he thought. He didn't need to decide which route was best; he already knew that. Charles noted the car's registration number and the strange feeling that he was going to see him again.

Half an hour after Paul's car disappeared down Alvavägen, Eva came home. As she passed Charles in the hall, she had a scent, or rather an air, that he didn't recognise.

'Where've you been?'

'Out,' she said.

'Is everything alright?'

'Yes. Everything's alright.'

'Good.'

Charles slunk off.

Two weeks later, a search of Manfred Lundin's flat was carried out. Under a floorboard, they found a set of seven knives, knives that could have been used to dismember Ted Lichter's body. A forensic analysis revealed that four of them still carried traces of human blood.

Lundin was remanded in custody at the beginning of August, and Charles remembers that it was an extremely hot day, and that Marika was at the summer camp a little way north of Bruket — but, by then, so much else had gone wrong that he didn't care anymore.

NOVEMBER 1984

Resident Kraus' man in Stockholm, Informal Associate Heffler, is dejected when they meet up with him in his apartment.

'It's my sleep,' he explains, in English. 'If I don't sleep, I get cranky.'

'Who doesn't?' Paul ventures, in German.

Heffler yawns.

'Apologies,' Charles says, 'but we really had no choice. I know that you prefer to conduct meetings at the motel.'

Heffler's home is large, bright, and has tall ceilings. It smells of paint and new electronic gadgets, and if you stand by the window you have your back to the water and can see Götgatan running between the houses.

The clock above Heffler's head is showing twenty-six minutes past four a.m.

'We have a problem,' says Paul.

'You said it.' Heffler pulls his coffee mug across the table. 'With the journalist, I believe.'

'How much Swedish do you understand?'

'Enough.' He swallows a gulp of coffee, then winces. 'Fucking Swedish coffee.'

Paul pulls open the heavy bag of recording equipment.

'You can have a listen yourself,' he says, unwinding the cable, looking for a plug socket. 'That's probably easiest.' He switches on the heavy tape recorder and picks up the headphones. 'This was recorded a little over six hours ago.'

Heffler isn't used to the headphones, and mutters as he puts them on and presses PLAY. The tape clicks and starts rolling. Paul blinks. His eyes are red.

Heffler had been making coffee and watching television while waiting for them to arrive — a taped episode of the East German children's programme *Unser Sandmännchen*. Charles has seen it before: it all starts with little events in the daily life of the main character, Sandmann. Sometimes he travels to other parts of East Germany, to the Soviet Union, or even into space.

Now Sandmann is travelling with two friends, visiting the East German army. The leader of the East German armed forces gives them a guided tour of a military installation. Sandmann and his comrades applaud.

Heffler removes the headphones.

'*Blöde Fotze.*'

'There's a photograph,' says Charles, 'of Kraus getting out of Paul's Citroën.'

'And you can see that it's him?'

''Fraid so,' says Paul.

'This is bad.' Heffler shakes his head. 'Really bad.' He chews his bottom lip. 'I need to talk to the Resident. Do you know what she's doing over the next few days? When is she going to release this?'

'We don't know exactly how close to an exposé she actually is. We don't have access to that information.' Charles lights a cigarette without asking. 'But *the risk* is ...'

'Yes.' Heffler drinks some more coffee. 'It certainly is. Where does she live?'

'Barnängsgatan 40.'

Paul goes out into the kitchen and opens one of the cupboards. Clinking crockery, followed by the sound of a coffee cup being filled.

'We do know,' he says when he returns, 'that she's going to help a friend, Lena Gräns, to clean her flat today. At seven tonight, they, along with another woman, named Ulla Jones, are meeting at Öhrns Hörn, at the junction of Folkungagatan and Borgmästaregatan. Gräns' brother works there. They're planning to go to Café Opera later on in the evening.'

'That will be our first chance — we can't get to them at home. I think we'd be wise to take it, despite us not having anything like the time we'd need to do this neatly. Does she have a car?'

Paul shakes his head.

'Her friend Lena Gräns has a white Renault TS. Registration number HSG 771.'

'Can we bank on her using it tonight?'

'Possibly, to get to the restaurant. She'll probably leave it if she's drinking.'

'That's a good start, considering what we have in mind.'

On the telly, Sandmann and his friends return home and are welcomed by a happy, hopeful little gang. Sandmann recounts all that he's seen on his visit to the East German military installation. They all celebrate.

Paul yawns.

Heffler picks up the remote control and presses a button to mute the television.

'How far is it from this restaurant to Hammarby harbour?' he asks.

JULY–AUGUST 1980

I am not even surprised.

Charles stood there in their bedroom doorway one July afternoon. He didn't know the name of the man in the bed, but he recognised him. He ran the little car mechanic's in Bruket. The air was heavy and warm. The man was wearing pants, but they were pulled down at the front. She had been busy taking them off, and he was hard, *big*, yet it contracted with each pulse until it ended up looking a bit puny.

Charles' eyes met Eva's. Her chest was flushed red with arousal. She said something, he could see her lips moving, but he didn't register any words.

He remembered how he'd felt young when he moved down here, how he had plenty of time to find his way to that moment when he would actually start his proper life.

Somewhere along the way, he had turned thirty, soon thirty-three, and become an adult. His age was really the wrong place to start. What actually defined where he'd got to, more than the number of years he'd been alive, was his everyday life, with its attendant obligations and responsibilities: what he talked to his wife about, his daughter and their relationship, how much he had to do with his neighbours, how many of his colleagues he also considered friends, how many white envelopes the postman brought, and the sum recorded on his payslip.

And which decisions he took at critical moments, whether to split up and run off or to stick around.

In order to understand one's life, it's necessary to examine the details, and when he did so he realised that he'd become somebody he no longer recognised.

He should break it off.

He booked into a hotel in the city nearby and stayed for several nights, grateful for the fact that he was on leave and could visit the alcohol store whenever he felt like it. Nevertheless, he went only once, bought a bottle that he drained, and then regretted doing so. It felt like another defeat, and he didn't have anywhere left to go.

When he returned to Bruket, he was convinced that Eva wouldn't be there, that the house would be locked, with the lights off. It wasn't: the lights were on and the door was open.

She had tears in her eyes when she met him in the hall.

Charles looked past her. He wanted to hit her in the face, but didn't.

He really should break it off.

They sat there on the sofa, an arm's length apart. He wasn't sure how long they'd been sitting like that — half an hour? An hour? Maybe half the night. Apart from Eva, no one could hear him, so he screamed until he was hoarse. Eva sobbed silently, without looking at him, until he insisted. When she did so, Charles clenched his fists.

He looked away. He launched a beer bottle against the wall.

'I have to go to the toilet,' Eva said.

She stood up slowly and walked away. When she'd locked the door behind her, Charles crawled over to the shards covering the floor close to the wall and gathered them all up.

He asked about details — how long it had been going on, where and when they would normally meet, what they would do. He asked whether the man had any tattoos. Charles asked her if she'd let him come inside her, in her mouth.

Eva looked at him as though he was sick. Maybe he was. He didn't want to know, but could see how she was tormented by answering the questions, how ashamed she was, and he did want that. She deserved to be punished.

'Do you plan to keep seeing him?'

'No.'

'You're lying.'

'No.' Tears pushed their way out into her eyes again. 'No, I am not lying. I am not going to see him.'

'Why did you do it then? Would you rather be with him?'

'No.'

'Well, then why did you do it?'

'I don't know. I don't know. I just feel so …'

'What?'

'I don't know,' she whispered.

'I can never trust you again. You do realise that? This can't be fixed.'

She looked him in the eye. He reciprocated with a blank stare.

'What does that mean?'

'I don't know.'

Charles left the house and went and got in the car.

In the evenings, he would say goodnight to Marika and push his lips to her forehead. It was always warm, smooth, and so soft. Then he'd get in the car and drive off.

He'd spend the short hours of summer darkness at the wheel, sleeplessly gliding up and down Bruket's streets and byways. He'd have the radio on, and the music struck something deep inside him, close to the void where he still told himself that he kept his soul.

July had become August, and the end was getting closer.

NOVEMBER 1984

Stockholm: despite the cold, the air is suffocatingly damp at lunchtime on the eighteenth of November 1984. The sky hangs heavy, like sheet metal, *close.*

He stays in the background at Paul's, who is on the phone. He lives in Gärdet, two streets down from Charles and Marika. On the table is a Russian doll that seems to be observing you regardless of where you are standing in the room.

'I'll put the speaker on,' Paul says. 'There's only the two of us here.' He perches on the edge of the desk, and gestures to Charles to come over.

'Herr Levin,' the Resident's muffled voice crackles through the speaker.

'Herr Kraus,' says Charles. 'Good day.'

'Hardly.'

The Resident coughs sharply. More crackling.

'What is this about?' says Paul.

'An unfortunate coincidence.'

Kraus pauses for effect.

'Let's hear it,' Paul says, weakly.

'I have been in contact with Berlin. They are asking me to withdraw Heffler.'

Charles and Paul look at each other. *No.*

'Asking you?' Paul manages.

'That was how they put it. But I happen to know, gentlemen, that when Berlin ask, they do so with a noose in their hands and a roof beam in their mind's eye. The Master himself was in the room, in the background — I could hear him.'

The Resident says it as though he has had a close encounter with a supernatural being. Perhaps he has. Erich Mielke sits on the top floor of the Stasi's tower, and has done so since 1957. Presidents and prime ministers arrive, stay a while, and then move on, but no one dares touch Mielke.

'Why ...' Charles' voice doesn't make it, and he has to clear his throat and start again. 'Why are they pulling Heffler now?'

'That, I'm afraid, is something that I do not have a view on,' Kraus says. 'The most immediate consequence, as far as we are concerned, is that it puts this evening's operation in rather a different perspective.'

'Yes,' Paul says slowly.

'It does need to be carried out, as you will understand.'

'Yes,' Paul repeats.

'I fail to see any candidates other than you two.'

Paul blinks. Charles walks over to the window, holding his breath. He strains to see his own reflection in the windowpane but can't make out anything except the grey sky, the cold buildings, and the colourless trees.

'We don't know,' Paul says in a surprisingly steady voice, 'exactly what Heffler's plan was.'

'Of course not. I assume that he kept that to himself.'

'And then we do not have the necessary experience. We don't have the resources required.'

'Now I think you are selling yourselves short.'

'Herr Kraus ...'

'I do not wish to patronise you,' he interrupts again, 'but one naïve journalist versus two clearly competent operatives ... I don't see the problem.'

'The problem,' Paul insists, running his fingers through his hair. 'The problem …'

He runs out of steam. Suddenly, he seems remarkably small.

'You know the consequences that will await if you do not solve this problem, and I am not alluding to the journalist's so-called scoop.'

Church bells chime in the distance.

Paul stares at the speaker.

'Is that a threat?'

A click. The line goes dead. Morality is a strange concept, rather a robust word for such a capricious phenomenon.

Paul stares at the telephone. Then he grabs hold of it and hurls it with some force, leaving an ugly crater in the wall.

'Shit,' he screams. 'Fucking bollocks! Fuck!'

The veins on Paul's neck, and those around his temples are clearly visible. He's red in the face and his lips are glossy with saliva. He slams his clenched fist onto the tabletop.

'Damned fucking shit,' he roars.

Charles moves away from the window, examines the telephone. The plastic on the receiver is cracked. Paul is shouting himself hoarse.

Charles slumps to the floor, leans his head against the wall, and shuts his eyes. The bells ring.

Sometimes it's as if he isn't even there.

'You *know*,' Paul says, his arms hanging limp by his sides and his voice strained, 'what I have done for you.' He takes a deep breath. 'You *know* what you owe me.'

'I know.'

'If this blows up … It's going to be huge, Charlie.'

'I know.'

A little part of him wants to see it happen. A part of Charles wants to witness it all exploding.

'Think about Marika.'

It's Paul's last resort, and that's how Charles knows just how desperate he really is.

'That's what I'm doing.'

'So …' Paul swallows hard. 'It's on?'

Paul waits.

Charles wonders how long it'll be before the bells start ringing again.

JUNE 2014

The real effect of the morphine comes when I'm sitting in the meeting room, after the constables at the scene have found the chassis number on the burned-out car and reported that the car in question was stolen from a Helsingborg address in February. Its actual registration is XJP 396, and the owner is a Lars Ingvar Rönnerud.

'So,' Tove says, 'what do you reckon? After shooting Levin, Bredström leaves Alvavägen and heads off to get shot of the car?'

'Yes. Maybe.'

And that's when the morphine kicks in, wrapping not just my body, but also my soul — if I possess anything worthy of the name — in warm wool. Everything gets calmer, warmer. Softer, somehow.

I've been given a top that someone has dug out from one of the old lockers. It's a washed-out T-shirt featuring Garfield's surly face and torso. He has his paws crossed in front of his chest, next to the words *You've cat to be kitten me right meow.*

'If Bredström's our man,' says Tove, 'how does he get home from the spot where he torches the car?'

'Bike?' I suggest.

'What, that he's put there in advance?' she shakes her head. 'No, that's not it. He must have walked, and that's a fair old trek.'

'And what do you think the connection between Levin and Bredström is?'

'Easy. Bredström and Eva Levin have a fling in summer 1980.'

My phone rings, and Birck's name flashes up.

'My colleague.' I look at the time. 'I have to take this. He might have spoken to Marika Alderin by now.'

'Put it on speaker,' she says.

'Wait a sec.'

'For what?'

'Just hold on. Hey, Gabriel. How did it go?'

'Depends what you mean. I've spoken to Marika Alderin. She basically doesn't say anything, and the few words you do get are pretty incoherent.'

'I thought that might be the case.'

'Well, why the fuck didn't you say so then?' He sighs. 'I showed her a picture of Levin. She recognised him, you could tell. But, apart from that, nothing. The only thing she talks about is a car, which apparently burned up leaving only soot and ash.'

'And here they've just found a burnt-out car.'

'You're kidding?'

'No.'

'What kind of car?'

'A Volvo. Could be the perpetrator's car — it was used around the murder, anyway. In which case, we might have the guilty party.'

'Must be two different cars,' Birck says. 'She's been here since August 2009, and she's been sectioned since 2005, and as I said is anything but lucid. She cannot possibly know about a car fire down there. According to the staff, she's been like this all along. That's what I'm calling about. According to Plit, she's only ever made sense on a handful of occasions, and that was during their association hour, talking to another resident. You'll never guess who.'

It takes a second for Birck's words to land at my end.

No.

'John Grimberg,' says Birck.

No. I close my eyes.

Everything's a circle. Everything's standing still.

'Okay. Talk to him.'

'Again?' I hear Birck's voice, disconsolate, over the static.

'Yes, and check Marika's visiting history. They keep lists of visitors.'

'I've got no right to demand to see them.'

'I know,' I say. 'Do your best.'

'But I don't know what to ask him,' Birck says.

'All I know is that Levin visited her on countless occasions and that he told her things.'

'What kind of things?'

'I don't know.'

'I'll call again soon.'

We finish the call and I open my eyes. Everything is a circle.

'I'm not interested in talking to you again,' Grimberg says.

'The feeling's mutual. But this is how it is.'

'This is for his sake, too. Am I right?'

'Something like that.'

'And it's about Levin's death?' Grimberg raises an eyebrow. 'Well, whaddya know. You want information. And what's in it for me?'

'Nothing.'

'A monthly day-release,' Grimberg says. 'Twelve hours at a time.'

'Okay,' says Birck, without giving it any thought.

Grimberg nods slowly. Then he turns towards the door, and shouts for Plit. The man opens the door and peers in.

'Plit,' Grimberg says. 'Would you be so kind and show this friendly officer out?'

Plit gives Birck a puzzled look.

'Eh?' says Birck. 'No, not yet. I said yes, didn't I? We'll arrange it. Close the door, please.'

A black veil has fallen over Grimberg's face.

'You're going to trick me.'

'No, I am not.'

'Don't lie to me. *"Okay"*? Do you think I'm thick, or what? You should never say something like that, because you don't have any say in what day-release I might get. And you know that *I* know.

You should've said, "I don't have the authority to arrange that, but I'll do my best" or "I'll have a word with the clinical director." Thinking I'm going to swallow a simple "okay" is an insult.'

Plit stands there next to Grimberg, powerless. They don't wear gloves here, Birck thinks to himself. They really should. What the hell do they do if Grimberg bites them?

'It's up to you, John,' Plit says gently. 'You don't have to talk to him.'

'Five minutes,' Birck says to Plit. Then to Grimberg: 'Believe me, I don't want to talk to you for a second longer than is necessary.'

'It must be important, this mission of yours, if you're prepared to lie about it.' Grimberg squints. 'It's unusual for you to lie, isn't it?'

'Normal people do tell the truth most of the time.'

Grimberg looks at his hands.

'No, they do not.'

Plit waits there for a second, before he slowly leaves the room. Birck can hear his own pulse, feel his heart beating against his ribcage.

'Okay, John, one more time. It's about Marika Alderin, a name that you're rather more familiar with than you wanted to let on when we were sitting here yesterday.'

'If I answer your questions now, considering that you just tried to trick me, how will you know I'm not lying?'

'I don't know,' says Birck. 'I suppose I'll just have to trust you. When did you first meet Marika Alderin?'

'Do you mean, in here?'

'No. I mean *ever.*'

Grimberg looks off to one side. Either he's straining to recall it or he's pretending to.

'You're asking about my dark years.' He gives a crooked smile. 'I haven't … I don't have very clear memories of that time. I think it was 2002. It was after the World Trade Centre, but before Anna Lindh.'

'And how did you meet?'

'Oh, you know, the usual.'

'Drugs?'

'Yes. We ended up in the same flat for a while.'

'Which flat?'

'Somewhere in Bandhagen. I can't remember exactly.'

'Was it just the two of you there?'

'No, this was a place lots of people went to, to get loaded and have a good time, if you know what I mean. Forget everything for a while. I think it must have been autumn, September in fact, because I remember hearing a thing on the radio about Ground Zero in New York, one year on.'

'And Marika Alderin was there then, too?'

'I think so.'

'John. Was she or wasn't she?'

'She was there. She was doing speed, I was on smack. I think there were about fifteen people there by the end, like some kind of fucking commune. Then the Drug Squad raided the flat, and the ones that happened to be there got done. I was lucky.'

Bandhagen. 2002. The Drug Squad's clearing of the flat. That bit matches the records at least.

'If we go back to the time before the Drug Squad emptied the place. Were you a couple, you and Marika?'

'What?'

'Were you together?'

'Where have you got that from?'

'I haven't. I'm just asking.'

'We most definitely were not.'

'You must have made an impression on her, anyway.'

'What do you mean?'

'Well, you're the only person she talks to in here.'

'Aha.' Grimberg smiles. 'Well, maybe, yeah.'

In my memories, I feel older than I do now.

The last time I meet Levin is at the end of April, in the canteen. I'm sitting at one of the tables by the windows in the corner. The sun's shining in, making the tabletop warm, and I drink my coffee, and look at the cinnamon bun on the little saucer in front of me. The sky outside seems more hopeful than it has for a long time. It's going to be a good summer.

He walks over with a cup of tea and a sandwich, tall and gangly as ever, with the round specs and his shaved head, the nose that shoots out over his lip, and his narrow mouth. He reminds me of a scarecrow.

I avoid eye contact. It's been nearly a year since the Gotland affair.

'Leo?'

I look up.

'Alright if I sit down?'

'Yes.'

He takes his blazer off and sits down, drinks some tea. Levin uses a cool, fresh deodorant, a discreet scent. He has done as long as I've known him.

'How are things up there?' I say.

'Stormy.' He smiles and peels the cling film off his sandwich. 'How are things down at yours?'

'Noisy.'

He laughs, loudly and heartily.

'I miss the Violent Crime Unit,' he says.

You don't notice at first, but now it's obvious: the creases in his skin are deeper than usual, and dark rings frame his eyes, which are slightly bloodshot. The shaved head has a few days' worth of silvery stubble.

'You look tired.'

He takes a hungry bite.

'I've turned things upside-down recently. Up all night, sleeping in the day. It's not like me at all, but unfortunately it was unavoidable.'

'How come?'

'You know,' he says between bites. 'Paperwork.'

'Paperwork,' I repeat. 'What kind of thing?'

'The kind you have to do when you're alone.'

I understand, without *understanding*. Levin's role as a superintendent at the National Police Authority means that he works on cases and issues that no one else is allowed anywhere near. A lot of the time, you don't know what the colleague in the room next-door is working on.

I wait for a continuation, but none comes. It's always like this: Levin, who one minute is remarkably direct and straightforward, clams up again the next.

My coffee's getting cold. The nausea mounts when I think about the cinnamon bun.

'Will there be a party?' I ask.

'What did you say?'

'In May, your retirement. Will there be a party?'

'Aha.' He laughs again, not as heartily. 'No.'

'Why not?'

'A white-collar retirement is no cause for celebration, Leo. Retiring is a very …' He takes a new bite of his sandwich while he

265

searches for the word, 'troubling rubicon. It's sort of final.'

'So is that what you're doing? The paperwork?' I ask.

'Something like that.' Long silence. He takes the last bite of his sandwich. 'Are you not eating your bun?'

'You can have it if you like.'

'You need to eat, Leo. You're looking thin.'

I slide the saucer over.

'So are you.'

He drinks some more tea and takes a bite of the bun.

'All well with Sam? With the two of you?'

'We're thinking about getting a cat.'

'*Cat?*'

Levin is seldom surprised, or at least he almost never reveals it, but this is one of the few occasions when the mask slips.

I squirm in my seat.

'Wasn't exactly my idea.'

'I've always thought of you more as a person who needs a dog.'

'Why?'

'Cats are self-sufficient, proud creatures. They don't need anyone to look after them, they're fine on their own. However, you leave a dog on its own for fifteen minutes and you can bet your bottom dollar that it's either got depressed or is about to eat something poisonous or valuable. Dogs need looking after.'

'And I need someone to look after?'

'Routines and responsibilities, more like.'

'Yes,' I say. 'Maybe.'

'Sam's working again now, isn't she? At the art gallery on Rosenlundsgatan?'

'Yes. Someone she studied art history with years ago got in touch and asked if she'd be interested.'

'I had some errands in the area a few days ago. It's a fantastic gallery. Have you been?'

'I haven't managed to get there. But I will.'

'Good.' Levin smiles. 'Sam looked well. That cheered me up.'

'She's certainly getting better.'

We stay there for a while without saying anything. He polishes off the cinnamon bun, looks at his watch, and puts on his blazer.

'This might be the last time we see each other for a while, Leo,' he says. 'I'm not quite sure what's going to happen. But whatever happens, I'm going to be a long way away.'

'What do you mean?'

'I can't really talk about it.' He looks out of the window. 'But I will be back.'

'Will you?'

'Yes,' he says, smiling, but I can tell that he doesn't know, that he might even be lying, and just being able to read Levin that easily makes me realise that he's shaken, and that this must be serious.

One evening in May, I arrive at the block in Gamla Stan where Levin lives with a present in my hand. It was Sam who persuaded me: he has just retired after all. I take the lift up and step out, walk to his door, and notice a sign decorated with ornate lettering and smiling faces under words explaining that the property is being sold by the real-estate agents, Stockholmsmäklarna.

The letterbox no longer bears his name.

He disappeared just as I imagine he once appeared, quietly and when no one was looking, just a shadow of a figure who appeared at the moment when the light was just right: now you see him, now you don't.

Waiting. Always this waiting.

In the corner of the computer monitor, the clock ticks along: 14:21, 14:30, 14:55.

'Why are they taking so fucking long?' Tove says to Davidsson on the phone. 'Are they? That's good.' She glances at me. 'I'll let him know.' Tove ends the call. 'The prosecutor is reviewing the evidence against Bredström now,' she says. 'And Davidsson asked me to tell you that your colleagues from NCS set off an hour ago. We're expecting them to arrive at some point this evening.'

'Hmm,' I say, distracted by the computer display. 'Good.'

'Good?'

'I'll probably be gone by then.'

'How do you know that?'

'Just a hunch.'

'The shit's going to hit the fan anyway. Davidsson's going to realise that you're not one of them. I shouldn't think NCS themselves will be too pleased either.'

'You're right, there.'

'You don't seem to care?'

'I do.' I tear my eyes away from the screen. 'I do care. I just don't know what to make of all this.'

Tove turns towards the computer.

The text folder on Levin's memory stick contains sub-folders called *77*, *80*, *81*, *82*, *83*, and *84*, and each of them contains date-marked photographs and documents from the year in question.

There are lots of individual files, and I have tried to print them off several times, to make it easier to sort through them, but every time I do the computer answers with a hiss that continues until the machine freezes and has to restart.

In the folder marked *77*, there's a memorandum from 1977, sent to the director of the Security Police's Operations Department. If I'm interpreting Levin's comment correctly, it's a summary of a successful recruitment attempt, the subject being a man named Jonathan Ekblom. That's it.

The *80* folder contains several more files. The first is a memo written by Detective Constable Charles Levin on the fifth of July 1980, concerning the murder of Ted Lichter. Levin summarises a conversation with a witness who is not named, referred to only as *The witness* or *He*, perhaps because the conversation includes an admission of having paid Lichter for sex.

What comes next is more than 300 scanned pages and photographs, and, in the corner of each one, someone — I assume it was Levin — has written a short explanation of what the reader is looking at.

'That's what he was up to down here,' says Tove.

'Well, he wasn't trying to solve any old crimes,' I say, and feel my pulse climb, which in turn gives me another headache. 'He must have had far more documents with him than the ones found at the house.' I look at her. 'There were no more, besides those in the files?'

'I can check the technician's notes, just to be on the safe side.'

She stands up from her chair, and shuffles through the papers spread across the oblong table.

I think about the voices I heard in the car, the conversation taped just before I was recruited to Internal Affairs. Levin's manipulation put me there, tricked me into going to Gotland. He had to. That's why I was there, and why my life changed direction and ended up on such a destructive trajectory.

Now though, finally, at least I know about it. The file was called *leo*. He wanted me to know. He knew that it would end up in my hands. I look down at them, my hands. The morphine is keeping them still.

Goffman. They were friends — perhaps he knows. I need to talk to him.

'No,' Tove says, reading the thick pile of notes from forensics. 'I can't find anything about any other boxes containing similar stuff. Clothes and shoes, crockery, books, kitchen utensils, and so on. That's it.' She carries on flipping through, until she shakes her head. 'Nothing. So if they were here, the perpetrator took them with him. If that's part of the motive, then it would surely make Bredström a pretty unlikely suspect?'

'There might be something about him in here, too. The question is whether Levin had got that far. They seem to be arranged in chronological order.'

'Open that last file.'

I click on the 84 folder and scroll down to the file at the bottom of the list, a text document. At the top is a striking stamp, STRICTLY CONFIDENTIAL. Next to that, someone has written FOR YOUR EYES ONLY. DESTROY UPON READING in angular block capitals. I don't know who the sender is, but just like the first memorandum it is addressed to the then director for the Security Police's Operations Department.

10/10/1984

It is with great regret that I have received your update
on the — due to the failure of your operatives — missing
VAX computers. While I have no desire to tell you how to

manage your bureau and staff, I assume that you will take appropriate measures when dealing with the operatives in question. Based on our mutual past, and my knowledge of your capacity and skill, I am confident that you will.

Intelligence collected by our operatives agrees with your suspicion: the most likely recipients are our treacherous neighbours. We will, of course, do our best to locate them. Please await further instructions.

'So do you think he finished it?' Tove asks. 'Is this actually the last one or just the last thing he entered?'

'I don't know,' I say. 'VAX computer. What the hell is that?'

'No idea.'

We sit there quietly for a moment, just staring at the screen, before I start clicking away in the hope of finding something that relates to Daniel Bredström.

'Well, maybe it was a scanner after all,' Tove says suddenly.

'Eh?'

'We weren't sure whether it was a printer or a scanner that had been sitting on the desk.'

I carry on clicking, and stumble across a photo of an older man who I don't recognise. In the photo's white border, Levin's handwriting: *J. Kraus, 1984.*

'He felt that this content was important enough to keep secure in a post-office box,' Tove says. 'Content that is missing in hard copy along with his computer, mobile phone, and scanner.'

'He told me that he was doing some paperwork.'

'What?'

'He said it in the spring, the last time we met. The sort of thing you need to do when you're alone in the office.' I look at the screen again. 'It must have been all this. That hadn't occurred to me until now. And yes, I think that his assailant took the computer, the phone, and the scanner, if that's what it was. And the paper documents themselves, one or maybe more boxes. That's why he needed the trolley.'

The door to the meeting room swings open. Over in the corner, Kit stops eating and turns his head sullenly.

'We haven't had it approved yet,' says Davidsson, red-faced and excitable. 'But we're not waiting any longer. We're bringing Bredström in for questioning now.'

'I didn't know you smoked,' Grimberg says.

'I don't,' says Birck.

'Your clothes smell of cigarette smoke.'

'In that flat, 2002, during the time you … hung out, you and Marika. What did you talk about?'

Grimberg sighs, visibly bored.

'Junkies don't talk much. And she was quite a lot older than me, almost ten years older, I think. It took a while before we started talking. And she was … Well, she's very ill now, as you know, but it had already started. She said she was hearing voices.'

'What did the voices say?'

'I don't know.'

'What else did you talk about?'

'The sort of things junkies usually talk about, I suppose. Who'd got done for what, which dealers were good, and which ones to give a wide berth.'

'Did she say anything about herself? About her background?'

Grimberg's hesitation is just perceptible.

'That …' he begins. 'I thought it was a joke. She told me her dad was a copper.'

'When did you realise that it wasn't a joke?'

'I asked her if it was true. She said yes.'

'And you believed that?'

'I could tell she wasn't lying.'

'Did she say anything else about that? About him?'

'That he had ruined her life. That he had ruined her mum's life.'

Birck waits.

'Nothing else?'

'No.'

'When did you realise that she was Charles Levin's daughter?'

'Not until I ended up in here, and saw them together — last winter.'

'If we go back to 2002, did she say anything more about herself then?'

'Like what?'

'Anything.'

'Most of the people who end up in flats like that are not that keen to talk about themselves. It's easier to talk about other people.'

'She didn't say anything else about the voices she'd started hearing?'

'Just that it ended up as it always did.' Grimberg looks out the window with an expression verging on disgust. 'She had tried to get help for it. They had ignored her, told her it was down to the drugs and that they were the real problem.'

'Do you think they were right?'

'Very often, it is the drugs that ruin things. But there was something deeper here. Something else, like a kind of darkness. I think you can only really see it in others if you're like that yourself.'

'And you were?'

'Yes.' Grimberg looks Birck in the eye again. 'I'm afraid I was.'

That must have been why they became close back then, thinks Birck, and perhaps that's why she lets him get close to her now, all these years later. Old sorrows bring people together.

'Did you tell her? About your background?'

'Gabriel,' says Grimberg, using his name for the first time. It sparks fear in Birck's chest.

Grimberg notices.

Grimberg smiles.

'Yes?'

'You are boring me. I don't want to talk anymore. If we're going to carry on, you're going to have to give me something in exchange.'

'Like what?'

Grimberg doesn't stop smiling.

EXCERPT FROM INTERVIEW TRANSCRIPT (REF 0500-K1754-08)

INTERVIEWEE: Bredström, DANIEL

ID NUMBER: 19501024-4674

ROLE: Accused

SUSPECTED CRIME: Suspicion of murder: Charles Jan Levin 140618, at victim's home address: Alvavägen 10, Bruket.

INTERVIEWER: Ola Davidsson

DATE OF INTERVIEW: 20140621

INTERVIEW START: ca 16:10

INTERVIEW END: ca 17:00

LOCATION: Interview room, Bruket Police Station

INTERVIEW TYPE: RB23:6

TRANSCRIBED BY: R. Å.

— — — — — — —

DAVIDSSON: How did you find out that Charles Levin was dead?

BREDSTRÖM: I don't remember exactly. I think someone told me.

DAVIDSSON: Who was that?

BREDSTRÖM: Don't remember.

DAVIDSSON: When did you find out? Can you remember that?

BREDSTRÖM: No.

DAVIDSSON: When did you last see Levin?

BREDSTRÖM: It, when was it, Wednesday. The eighteenth, in the alcohol store. He was behind me in the queue. That was the first time we'd seen each other in thirty years. Mad, that was.

DAVIDSSON: Did you speak to each other then?

BREDSTRÖM: Not really. I said something along the lines of: 'Oh, look who's here,' or something. He just said, 'Yes.' That was the end of it.

DAVIDSSON: Nothing more? You can't just shake your head, the video camera's not working so you need to say it so that this microphone picks it up.

BREDSTRÖM: Aha. No. No. Nothing more.

DAVIDSSON: So a brief exchange in the queue, and that was it?

BREDSTRÖM: That's right.

DAVIDSSON: After not having seen each other in thirty years?

BREDSTRÖM: That's right.

DAVIDSSON: You didn't say anything to each other outside, on the street?

BREDSTRÖM: No.

DAVIDSSON: We have solid intelligence that says that you spoke to each other standing outside the alcohol store. Why are you lying?

BREDSTRÖM: What difference does it make if I did?

DAVIDSSON: It might make a huge difference, Daniel. Answer now.

BREDSTRÖM: [long pause] Okay. We talked.

DAVIDSSON: Why didn't you say that to begin with?

BREDSTRÖM: I know he's dead. I get brought in by Kling and Klang, sirens blazing, and you sit me down in here and ask me when I last saw him. I'm not daft, I have done this before you know.

DAVIDSSON: So, one more time. Tell me about when you met him.

BREDSTRÖM: [sighs] Nothing much happened inside the store. I paid for my stuff and went outside. Then I had a chat with him.

DAVIDSSON: Go on.

BREDSTRÖM: Well, I suppose I just went up to him and asked him what the fuck he was doing here after all these years, whether he'd come back to ruin even more people's lives. I told him to keep out of my way. That he should watch it if we bumped into each other again.

DAVIDSSON: And then you did? Bump into each other?

BREDSTRÖM: No.

DAVIDSSON: We'll come back to that. How did Levin respond to your threat?

BREDSTRÖM: It wasn't a threat, more of a useful tip.

DAVIDSSON: It could be interpreted as a threat, I would say. I asked you how he reacted?

BREDSTRÖM: Nothing special. He just gave me a look.

DAVIDSSON: And then what happened?

BREDSTRÖM: Nothing. I took my crate of beer and went home.

DAVIDSSON: Tell me about your relationship to Charles Levin. How did you get to know each other?

BREDSTRÖM: I didn't get to know him. I got to know his wife. If you know what I mean.

DAVIDSSON: You'll have to expand.

BREDSTRÖM: She, Eva, worked on the till in the shop. I thought, well all of us thought, she was fucking gorgeous, I'll tell you that. But she wasn't the least bit interested in anyone or anything. Then she married that cop and had a kid, and it must've been when the marriage got a bit shaky, a few years down the line, that she was unsatisfied and started looking for something. Then we started seeing each other.

DAVIDSSON: When was this?

BREDSTRÖM: Summer 1980. I don't remember when exactly.

DAVIDSSON: Charles Levin. When did you first meet him?

BREDSTRÖM: Let me see. Later that summer, at some point. I think he was on leave, but he went into work anyway. So Eva rang me, and I went round. Their kid was away at summer camp or something, so she was there on her own. But then, of course, he came home in the middle of it, during the actual ... into the bedroom.

DAVIDSSON: And then what happened?

BREDSTRÖM: He just stood there staring at us, didn't even blink. I remember that clearly. Then he turned around and left. That's how it ended, I think. Eva came down to my workshop a week or so later, said that things at home were a mess, that the kid was getting really down, and that she had to try and keep the family together. We couldn't carry on.

DAVIDSSON: And how did you take that?

BREDSTRÖM: I was pretty upset, I think. I was young, you know, hadn't found my feet yet. I thought that maybe she was the one. I liked the daughter, Marika, too. She was a sweet little girl. Maybe a bit difficult, but all kids are at that age. So yeah, I took it badly. But you know, I picked myself up after a while. I suppose it was then, that autumn, that I realised what that guy was capable of.

DAVIDSSON: What does that mean?

BREDSTRÖM: When my company was driven to the wall.

DAVIDSSON: You were arrested on the seventeenth of October of 1980, a week before your thirtieth birthday. Convicted the following February. Bankruptcy —

BREDSTRÖM: March eighty-one.

DAVIDSSON: That's right.

BREDSTRÖM: And that was him. I know you lot talked about how much you'd checked it all out and how it was nothing to do with him, but I know that's what happened.

DAVIDSSON: You do, do you?

BREDSTRÖM: He was at me the whole time, sat there photographing people coming in and out of my workshop, that kind of thing. An acquaintance saw him doing it. Fine, I wasn't whiter than white. It was me in those pictures, and the stuff that I was getting in and selling on was stolen, right. I'll admit that. But I couldn't have kept the business going otherwise.

DAVIDSSON: When was this, him photographing you?

BREDSTRÖM: I don't know. I didn't find out until afterwards, when the verdict came. And I know that's what happened, but I can't prove it. By then, Eva was dead and buried, and Levin had moved on, as luck would have it.

DAVIDSSON: Are you insinuating something about her death?

BREDSTRÖM: I don't know any more than the next man. She had a car accident. At least, that's what everyone's always assumed. And that's all I know. But it was all hushed up, if you ask me. I reckon that, one way or another, he did it.

DAVIDSSON: [long pause] So Charles Levin killed his wife.

BREDSTRÖM: I've got no evidence for that. Everything to do with that fucking man was hushed up. He had friends in high places. Considering everything else that has to do with Charles Levin, it just felt like a very strange coincidence that she happened to be killed in an accident just a few months after she'd been unfaithful. Now, Eva did have a licence, but she almost never drove anywhere. She preferred to go on her bike or walk, even in winter. That she just got in her car that night, I don't buy it. Did you even check whether anyone saw her in the car that night?

DAVIDSSON: Of course we did.

BREDSTRÖM: Who saw her, then?

DAVIDSSON: It was over thirty years ago. I don't remember right now, Daniel. But we checked.

BREDSTRÖM: I'll bet you anything that if you go back and check the details, you won't find a single witness saying that they saw her in the car. The official version, your explanation, isn't true.

DAVIDSSON: That seems to upset you, Daniel. Did you mention this when you saw him on Wednesday? Did you talk to him about Eva?

BREDSTRÖM: No.

DAVIDSSON: But perhaps it crossed your mind? You remembered it?

BREDSTRÖM: Course I did.

DAVIDSSON: Perhaps you were still thinking about it when you drove round to Levin's that evening?

BREDSTRÖM: You're not hearing what I'm saying, are you? I wasn't there.

DAVIDSSON: Well, in that case, there are a few things that I don't quite understand, if what you're telling me now is that you're not the one we're looking for in connection with Levin's death.

BREDSTRÖM: I'm not the one you're looking for.

DAVIDSSON: No, so you keep saying, but we don't altogether believe you. The reason being that you had a stolen car in your garage. The car is no longer there, as you showed me. It's burnt out, in the forest on the other side of the graveyard, and was last seen on the evening of the murder. We know that the car was parked outside the victim's house at the time Levin died, a time you cannot account for beyond the fact that you had had a lot to drink, and we both know how you have a tendency to behave when you're drunk and upset. You get blackouts, and you don't know what you're doing. Just a few hours earlier, you met Levin and behaved in a threatening manner towards him. Not only that, you suspect that he was somehow involved in Eva's death, many years ago, a suspicion that has now resurfaced in your mind.

BREDSTRÖM: [long pause] I —

DAVIDSSON: It doesn't look good, Daniel. Surely you can see that.

BREDSTRÖM: Someone bust the padlock on my garage. Someone stole the car. I didn't drive the car that night. And it wasn't me. I was at home.

DAVIDSSON: What was the registration number of the car that was parked in your garage?

BREDSTRÖM: I don't know. It had false plates.

DAVIDSSON: It's the false plates I'm interested in.

BREDSTRÖM: FOR 528.

DAVIDSSON: Take a look at this. This is you, isn't it? And for the tape, I will point out that I am showing a photograph taken by a witness close to Alvavägen 10 on the evening of the eighteenth of June. A photograph where a Volvo, registration FOR 528, is clearly shown, as is a man sitting inside. That man is Daniel Bredström.

BREDSTRÖM: That isn't me. It can't be me. I was at home.

DAVIDSSON: Try and see this from my perspective, Daniel.

BREDSTRÖM: You can't even tell whether that's a man or a woman. The picture is as blurred as anything.

DAVIDSSON: I'm not even going to ask you one last time, Daniel. I'm going to go outside and get some fresh air instead, and let you sit here and think this through in peace and quiet.

BREDSTRÖM: Fuck you.

Birck looks down at his notepad, and for a second his own handwriting looks unfamiliar, as though the words have been written by another man's hand. Must be the room, the whole of St Göran's. Everything is slightly distorted. Nothing in here is quite like it is out there.

The door in the corner is opened, by Plit, and, when Birck spots him, it's like he's finally being led out to the fresh air again after having been confined for a long time.

Plit is holding a single sheet of paper.

'I've got that list for you.'

Grimberg looks curious.

'A list?'

'Thank you,' Birck says, and exits the visiting room with Plit, closing the door behind him, leaving Grimberg alone in there.

'From May, up to now,' Plit says. 'As you can see, she doesn't get an awful lot of visitors. If I'm going to go any further back, I need to go into the archive, and that's on another server.'

'I think this should do it,' says Birck.

At the top of the page, Marika Alderin's name and ID number, and then four columns: NAME, ID CHECKED, DATE/TIME, and RELATIONSHIP TO CLIENT. Her visiting history is recorded in them.

'It looks like we're a bit slack filling in the second and fourth columns,' Plit says. 'But if there's no tick or *yes* in the ID CHECKED column, it means that the visitor has shown ID on a previous visit and that the person responsible recognises them. Same thing with RELATIONSHIP TO CLIENT.'

'Thanks.'

'If anyone sees that,' Plit adds, 'it didn't come from me.'

Grimberg is just visible through the glazed part of the door. He is sitting very, very still.

'He's got another half an hour,' says Plit. 'Then he's got his first hour of therapy.'

'We'll be done before then.'

Birck studies the columns. Marika Alderin's first visitor in May is Charles Levin: he arrives on the seventh at eleven thirty-five and stays for forty-five minutes. On the tenth, twelfth, and fifteenth, he visits her again, but in the afternoon. Apart from that, May seems to have been a rather lean month for Marika Alderin in terms of visitors. Occasional visits from external therapists and some poor officer from the Drug Squad who probably doesn't know what he's letting himself in for when he arrives to interview Marika Alderin, apparently about a ten-year-old drug ring that was never cleared up. The case number is written in the margin.

Charles Levin made his last visit to St Göran's on the nineteenth of May, between four thirty and quarter-to five, and although it doesn't say so, it doesn't have to: he was saying goodbye.

So far, she has had only six visitors in June, and even if there are a few days left of this cursed month, she's unlikely to have many more. Another external therapist, a social worker, and a woman from the social-security department who has been here for some reason. Then there's a man who has visited her three times, a man whose name confuses Birck. There are no entries in the ID CHECKED or RELATIONSHIP TO CLIENT columns; just the name and date are recorded.

On each of the three occasions, he has arrived shortly after four p.m. Each time, he has left after forty-five minutes.

Birck reads the name over and over again.

Him. What the hell was he doing here?

'If we carry on,' says Birck. 'When you got here, how long before you realised that Marika Alderin is also a resident?'

'So as I was saying, I'm bored.' Grimberg examines him. 'But you're not. You are … shaken. What does it say on that list?'

Birck weighs up his options. What the fuck is he actually supposed to do? He takes a deep breath.

'If you give me information that leads to us arresting Levin's murderer, I will do whatever I can to get your application for day-release approved.'

Grimberg smiles.

'How?'

'Martin Sanchez-Jankowski is a friend of mine.'

'You're lying.'

'Well, for once, you've got that wrong,' says Birck. 'Me and the clinical director, believe it or not, we did our military service together.'

He gets out his phone and scrolls through the text messages until he finds the conversation. Then he reads the most recent messages, sent just a few days earlier, to make sure they don't contain any sensitive material.

Grimberg looks at the screen.

'Does Leo know about this? That you know him?'

'No.'

'I'm going to tell him.'

'You do that.'

'When's his birthday?' he asks. 'Martin Sanchez-Jankowski. What date?'

'Why do you ask?'

'If you do know him, then you ought to know when his birthday is.'

'Do *you* know when his birthday is?'

Grimberg smirks.

'Course I do.'

The temperature under his shirt collar is rising. His tie's become a noose, and loosening it, just a tiny bit, would be so nice, but he doesn't want to give Grimberg the satisfaction.

'March. Fifth of March.'

'That might still be bollocks.'

This time, Birck is the one smiling.

'I suppose you'll just have to trust me.'

'When you arrived here, last autumn,' Birck says, 'how long was it before you realised that Marika Alderin was also a resident?'

'A few weeks.'

The memory starts playing in Grimberg's head — Birck can see it. When he blinks, it's gone. Seems like it appears on demand and disappears at will. If it was even there in the first place.

'In the beginning, they kept me locked up for twenty-three hours a day, while they were doing all the tests and observations. So I didn't see much beyond the four walls of the cell, or *the room*, which they call them here for some strange reason. When I did see her, it was during association. I said hello and she didn't even react. It really was a sad sight, seeing how far down into the shit she had sunk, so I didn't want to give it any more thought.'

'When did you start talking to each other?'

'We've just exchanged a few pleasantries, that's all.'

'That's not what I'm asking.'

'November, maybe early December. She was sitting there in front of the telly in the common room, and I happened to end up next to her. She recognised me.'

'What did she say?'

'My name. Well, not my name, but the name she thought was

mine. That was it. Since then, she always says something every time, but never more than a sentence or two.'

'Like what?'

'She asked if I could get her another chair so that she could use it as a footrest. I said, "I can't, I'm afraid," that I had certain … impediments.' He smiles weakly. 'It's tough being bound at the hands and feet. "Oh, okay," she said, "of course." So one of the staff had to do it. Then she was gone again.'

'I'm starting to feel a bit stressed,' says Birck. 'And I'm a bit disappointed.'

'Why's that?'

'What you're telling me are meaningless anecdotes. They don't lead anywhere. I thought, quite honestly, that you knew more than that. This isn't worth a day-release.'

Grimberg's hands are still, but Birck checks them to make sure, and although it's barely discernable, he thrusts his shoulders upwards and doesn't blink.

'Maybe you're asking the wrong questions.'

'What should I be asking you, then?'

'I'm guessing that when you and Plit were talking about Marika Alderin, he told you about a stereo. A stereo that was taken off her about a week ago.'

'What's your point?'

'Why do you think it was taken away?'

Maybe he's lying. He could well be.

'Why was Marika Alderin's stereo taken away from her?'

'Fourteenth of June,' says Grimberg, 'during association, after lunch, Marika leant over to me and said that she was scared. I asked her why. She said that she was expecting a man to come and visit her the following day. A man who wanted to hurt her.'

'And?'

'I told her to do something about it.'

'Which was?'

'I told her to record the visit.'

'Are you sure it was the fourteenth?'

'Well, she certainly had a visitor the next day, the fifteenth.'

'And did she?' Birck asks. 'Did she record it?'

Without thinking, he gets out the list and studies it in front of Grimberg. On the fifteenth of June, Marika Alderin had only one visit.

Grimberg leans forward.

'Interesting,' he says, reading the page. 'I recognise that name.'

'I'm pretty damn sure it's him.'

Davidsson is red in the face with excitement.

'I was right, anyway,' Tove says, standing behind him. 'Eva Levin and Daniel Bredström were getting it on behind Levin's back.'

I look at the man sitting there, think about the pain it must have caused Levin, the rage he must have felt. Pain and rage are not good for a man.

'It's just a matter of time before he cracks,' Davidsson goes on.

'Yes,' says Tove. 'But he won't necessarily be cracking because he did it.'

'What do you mean?'

'That,' she says, nodding towards Bredström, who's sitting and staring at his hands without blinking, 'is a profoundly confused individual. Could he really have done it? I don't think so.'

Davidsson looks at Tove, then me, then back to Tove again, stunned.

'Everything stacks up.'

'Everything *could* stack up,' I say.

'So you're ...' Davidsson begins, but then goes quiet and grimaces. Then he sneezes, loudly and angrily. 'You agree with her?'

'Yes. And I'm not convinced about the motive.'

'The motive,' Davidsson spits. 'The motive is something

people and the media speculate about to kill time. What matters are the *facts*.'

'All we've got is circumstantial evidence.'

'A confession is all we need for it to stand up.'

'A confession that you haven't yet managed to get,' says Tove.

'I'm telling you, it's just a matter of time. I mean *look* at him.'

'That's what I'm doing,' I say. 'And I agree with Tove. He's …' I don't know what to say. 'Charles Levin's assailant acted calmly and collectedly, focused on the task in hand. He didn't touch his coffee, shot Levin from point-blank range, and seemed to be aware that he had plenty of time. Not only that, he took Levin's computer, mobile phone, and printer. Or scanner. What the hell would Bredström want with them?'

'Sell them,' says Davidsson. 'Why not? He's probably already done it. I'll ask him, but I'd say he saw a chance to get something in his empty coffers once he'd done away with Levin.'

'I really doubt that,' Tove says. 'But yeah, it's a thought.'

An unlikely one, verging on the stupid considering it's coming from someone who's supposed to be a policeman. When men of Bredström's ilk bump people off, they are not generally sufficiently composed to process that kind of arithmetic.

'One thing I don't believe,' Tove adds. 'I don't believe that that's Bredström sitting in that car either.'

'I …' Davidsson says, but he's cut short again, this time by a ringing mobile phone in his pocket. 'Yes, Davidsson … That's correct … Okay, already? … Well, I never. Yes, we're glad to have you here, of course … Good. Ring when you get here … No problem, I'll make sure your colleague stays here and waits for you … Eh? Yes, him, what's …' He turns to me. 'What's your name again?'

Tove looks at me, and it's impossible to know what she's thinking.

'Leo Junker,' I say slowly.

'Leo Junker,' Davidsson repeats.

I open the door and walk out into the corridor with hasty, jerky steps. The pain in my ribs and my head comes in jolts, and while Davidsson's voice tails off behind me I pull one of the morphine tablets out of my pocket.

I put it in my mouth and stop outside the meeting room. The pain is getting worse, makes me groan.

'What the fuck?' I hear Davidsson scream.

About time I got out of here.

SEPTEMBER–OCTOBER 1980

'All I ask of you, Charles, is that you actually consider the advantages and don't just see the drawbacks. You may, of course, bring your family.'

Charles clamped his office phone between his shoulder and his ear while he looked for a new ream of typing paper.

'I am flattered. But this isn't the best time to call.'

'What's a poor civil servant to do to get you to reconsider?' said Paul.

Charles laughed.

'Nothing.'

'Real police work is all about doing favours and calling them in, even between colleagues. I am grateful to you for balancing the various delicate elements of the Lichter case so well.'

'That was what we agreed on,' said Charles, lowering his voice despite being distracted.

'That's right.' Paul cleared his throat. 'Let me know if there's anything I can do to make your daily grind easier.'

It was the fourth time Paul had made Charles the offer by phone. At first, Charles had been embarrassed, then flattered, and by the third time he felt a bit perplexed. Now the circle was complete and he felt embarrassed again, but for another reason this time. Charles took a deep breath.

'I've stumbled across something a bit odd in Bruket. I think the guy who owns the mechanic's there, a man named Daniel Bredström, is a fence.'

'And what makes you think that?' says Paul.

'I have a few photos of the activities that go on round his workshop. In some of them, a lorry arrives and delivers goods to Bredström, who takes them into his premises. I have good reason to believe that those goods are stolen. I also have photographs of him with the goods, when they are leaving his workshop in the hands of a new buyer.'

'Well, there you go,' said Paul. 'Awful. What do you need me for?'

'I work over in the city, not at the station out there. The local talent need a tip-off that doesn't come from here. Bruket is a small place, and this station isn't much bigger. Everyone knows everyone. If someone put their mind to it, then it could be traced back to me.'

'I understand,' Paul said, and something, perhaps his tone of voice, indicated that he actually did. 'Just send me the pictures. But,' he added, 'one day you have to tell me what it's really all about.'

'Maybe.'

Paul laughed.

'Speak soon, Charles.'

His heart was beating dangerously fast as he hung up.

Only now was he beginning to realise just how much it hurt. Over a month had passed. On one occasion, she'd tried to touch him, but he'd backed away. He slept on the living-room sofa. They never said it, not in so many words. It was easier not to.

Somehow, Charles knew that he would be staying.

He didn't even know whether or not he wanted to, just that the family had to be held together. It felt so old-fashioned — so stale and so full of the maxims that his parents lived by — yet it was everything he clung on to.

How many people in Bruket knew? Eva could be discreet, but Bredström? He wasn't a quiet kind of guy. Quite the opposite, in fact: he was the type of guy who loved to boast. Charles avoided going down to the square, but, on those occasions when he had to, he convinced himself that people's looks contained silent messages, that they were whispering behind his back, that they were laughing at him.

The rage grew inside him, but he did nothing with it.

Eva did everything at Charles' pace. He felt grateful for that at times, because nothing was expected of him. Other times, he hated it, and he wanted to scream at her to stop. It made him feel like a child.

He didn't say anything to his parents, not a word to his brother, nor his colleagues. He carried that shame — and it was shame — alone, hoping that it wouldn't always feel as heavy as it did now.

One chilly day in October, Daniel Bredström was remanded into custody, charged with receiving stolen goods.

In the mirror: Charles, paler than before.

NOVEMBER 1984

'Wasn't there supposed to be three of them?' says Paul.

'Yes.'

'Have we missed one of them?'

'No. Calm down.'

They have a good view of the bar — Öhrns Hörn — in the rear-view mirror. The women have arrived in Gräns' white Renault. They look chirpy: Gräns' gait self-assured and agile, Falck's comfortable and relaxed. They choose a table near the window and share a bottle of wine. Talking, laughing. Gräns has a necklace that flashes occasionally as it catches the warm lighting.

'What was the third one's name?' Paul asks.

'Ulla Jones. She might have had to cancel.'

'Yes. Shit.'

The vehicle: an old Ford, waiting to be scrapped and de-registered. It belongs somewhere near Sätra, and was missing for six months before it turned up in one of Södermalm's underground car parks a month ago. No one knows how it got there, and no one seems to want anything to do with it.

It was the best they could find. Paul's Citroën was out — Falck might recognise it. The news comes on the radio: the murder of Indira Gandhi has led to rioting among Hindus, which is thought to have left thousands of Sikhs dead. Palme makes a statement, expressing his consternation at the events. Sweden now, and

Bofors: The controversy surrounding the complaint made to police by the Swedish Peace and Arbitration Society in May continues. Leading executives are now demanding that those responsible for leaking the details of Bofors' arms deals with Dubai and Bahrain step forward and explain their actions.

Charles turns the radio off.

There's nothing to do but wait.

They've been in hot water before, essentially ever since 1980 when he sent the photos of Daniel Bredström's misdemeanours to Paul, who did as Charles asked him. A favour. That was all. Things were never the same again.

How much can a person take before they fall apart? He has never felt like he knew the answer to that question, but he'd never thought it could ever be this much.

That might be why this feels like entering the lion's den with blood on his hands.

'What's on your mind?' Paul asks.

'Why do you ask?'

'Just wondered.' He puts his hands in his overcoat pockets. 'Jesus it's cold.'

In the backseat behind them is the gadget that Paul dragged out of his wardrobe after the conversation with Kraus. It is small, dark grey in colour, and made of metal. It looks a bit like an air compressor, but with an extra tank for water. In one corner is a stamp revealing that it belongs to MFS HAUPTABTEILUNG IX.

'That thing scares me,' says Charles.

'It was given to me as a present by Kraus' predecessor.'

The road in front of them, Folkungagatan, glistens with frost. The damp cold finds its way into the car and down their collars; it settles around their necks and backs.

'Wind the window down a bit,' says Charles.

'Are you mental?'

'The windows are steaming up. We have to be able to see them.'

Paul winds down the driver's side window just enough that you would be able to stick a finger out through the gap.

'You do know,' Charles says without looking at him, 'that after this … there can be no more. This is heavier than anything else. This is … The risks … This is the last thing we do.'

'I know.'

'I'm going to ask for a transfer.'

'Where to?'

'I don't know. Violent Crime Unit, maybe. Or the Surveillance Unit. I liked it there back in the early Seventies.'

'Just don't forget, Charles, that there are certain things that have happened in our world, but not in theirs.'

'I'm not a child.'

Paul opens his mouth and takes a breath as if he was about to say something, but then seems to think better of it and breathes out again, heavily.

'She remembers,' Charles says instead.

'Who remembers what?'

'Marika. She remembers that night.'

'How much?'

'Quite a lot. She wrote about it in her diary at the end of September.'

'Have you read it?'

'Just that entry.'

Paul nods, says nothing.

There are no more words.

The stream of people along the Folkungagatan's pavements never ends; it just increases or decreases in intensity. The clock ticks, first half-past seven, half-past eight, slowly passes nine o'clock, crawls up to quarter-past.

'They've just asked for the bill.' Paul checks his firearm is in place, under his left armpit. 'Wish me luck.'

'No.'

He laughs, a joyless laugh.

Paul goes and stands outside Öhrns Hörn. Inside the restaurant, Cats Falck and Lena Gräns are putting their coats and scarves on. Gräns says something to Falck, who concurs and laughs. They emerge onto the pavement. Paul approaches them. Falck freezes, and a bewildered Gräns looks at Paul, then her friend, then back to Paul again.

Paul unbuttons his coat as he talks. The exact moment — *there* — when they realise he's armed is plain to see.

Charles watches Cats' mouth: *What do you want?*

Paul: *To talk.*

She shakes her head, then looks at her watch. Paul smiles. Gräns looks over her shoulder.

I wonder how he chooses his words, if he's choosing them at all.

Paul gestures gently towards Gräns' white Renault. Gräns shakes her head: *I've been drinking wine.*

Falck's stare is fixed on the gun under Paul's armpit. She puts a hand on Gräns' arm, to get her to be quiet.

Paul and the women walk towards Gräns' car. Charles slides over to the driver's seat in the Ford and watches Gräns' car back out of the tight parking space. Then he follows them through the darkness of the November evening.

Hammarby's docks are deserted; the shadows are almost close enough to touch. Across the water lies Lugnet, with its faltering industries and dark dank sheds.

The white Renault turns left by the quay marked *301*, drives past the neighbouring wharves, slows down by *309*, and then stops far too abruptly by *310*.

Charles can't brake in time, and has to swerve out behind them

— the right-hand side of the Ford scrapes against the Renault's left flank. Chips of paint fly into the air.

Fuck.

Falck and Gräns climb out of the car, with Paul behind them.

'So,' Paul says, looking around.

'My car,' Gräns says as she bends down to run her fingers over the paintwork.

Charles shuts the driver's door of the Ford behind him.

'I didn't have time to avoid you. You stopped so suddenly.'

'You!'

Falck takes one, two, three steps forward, and her heels make them sound more determined than they actually are. She's so close that he could reach out and touch her now.

'I knew it,' she says. 'This is completely absurd.'

'What's this about?' Gräns asks.

'You wanted to talk,' says Falck. 'Talk away, *Charles*. That is your name isn't it?'

He can smell the scent of her perfume. She's standing with her back to the water, its dark depths waiting beyond the edge of the quay.

Water.

Good.

Charles takes a deep breath.

It's called a tiger claw, a strike with the heel of the hand. Charles aims for Falck's nose. She has time to open her mouth as if to say something, and one of her teeth scratches his glove.

The blow connects, and, when Falck's nose cracks, the noise mixes with a muffled thud behind Charles: Paul has neutralised Gräns.

Falck screams, staggers backwards, reeling. Charles catches her when she faints, and lays her gently on the ground. Behind him, Paul is standing over Gräns, who is now lying on her side, still and silent. Charles pulls out the little cloth from his overcoat pocket.

'The bottle,' he says.

'Wait.'

Paul gets out his own cloth and opens the bottle, pours chloroform over it, and presses it to Gräns' face.

The effects of the chloroform are much slower than the impression you'd get from seeing it used on film. The long seconds tick away slowly, and when Paul throws the bottle over to Charles, Falck has started moaning and moving around in front of him, as though she was dreaming.

He screws the cap off the bottle and puts the cloth down on the ground by his feet, then soaks it in chloroform before holding it to Falcks' nose and mouth. Her breathing is rasping and hoarse, her body is twitching, and Charles has to put his knee on her chest.

He closes his eyes, counts the seconds, thinks about everything that Cats Falck will never get to experience, thinks *I am not really here.*

Time — this is taking such an incredibly long *time.* Charles gets the hoses, attaches them to the compressor-like contraption. He turns the key, and somewhere inside the machine the battery comes to life: the light under STANDBY flashes red one, two, three times before becoming a solid green. Paul wrenches Falck's jaw open, and in the darkness his eyes are glossy black puddles.

'Give me the first one.'

Charles complies, and Paul forces the tube down Falcks' throat, down into her lungs. She gurgles, and Paul grimaces. Charles stares at her face, expecting her to come to at any second, to start coughing and retching.

'Give me the other one.'

Paul carefully pushes the second tube down alongside the first.

'Now.'

Paul puts his hand on her chest, and Charles turns one of the machine's two dials. It hums briefly, like the sound of a vacuum cleaner being turned on and then immediately off again.

Falcks' chest collapses as her lungs are slowly emptied of air.

'The other one.'

'Oh Christ.'

'*The other one,* Charlie.'

Charlie turns the other dial on the machine. The water edges down the transparent tube, moving through it like a snake, and as her lungs are emptied of air, they are filled with fluid. It is hypnotising.

'Stop.'

He turns both of them off. Charles looks around. They are alone under the low sky. Paul carefully removes the tubes.

'She's done,' Paul says. 'Can you do the other one?'

'No.'

Charles is on the verge of throwing up, and has to move away, has to get some air. He can't do this. He wishes that the chloroform was enough, that they hadn't had to go this far, that Cats Falck had never tried to make contact with him.

'Focus, Charlie,' Paul hisses behind him.

Charles turns around. Paul's voice is pleading:

'Help me.'

He sits down on his haunches by the machine once more and waits while Paul inserts the tubes into Gräns; and once more he turns the controls on Paul's command. He avoids looking at the machine.

Paul pulls the tubes out and inspects them carefully. The necklace is gone from Gräns neck. Paul must have taken it.

'I think I scraped one of them in the throat,' Paul mutters.

After coiling up the tubes and lifting the machine into the back seat of the Ford, they help each other to place the women in Gräns' car. Their bodies are limp and unnaturally heavy. Charles puts his thumb on Falck's wrist, looking for a pulse. When he finds it, the ticking is weak and irregular.

Paul pulls the gearstick into neutral, and turns the wheel until the tyres are pointing straight ahead. They close the doors. The interior light turns off. Then they start to push the car away from the quayside.

'This is enough,' Charles says after a while, out of breath. 'Surely this is enough.'

'The windows,' Paul says. 'We need to take them out. It'll sink quicker that way.'

'Well smash them, then.'

'That would hardly look like an accident.'

'But driving round the quays with no windows in November, *that* would look like an accident would it?'

'But …'

'We need to get out of here, Paul.'

Paul opens the driver's door and puts it into first, then his eyes scan across the port and its many shadows.

They put their weight against the boot, and Charles' soles struggle for traction on the slippery ground. They move a metre, two, three. Picking up speed. Charles isn't walking anymore, he's running, with the palms of his hands pushing against the boot, and his arms straight.

Charles charges forward, as fast as he can.

'Shit,' Paul pants. 'They're sitting wrong.'

'Eh?'

'This is Gräns' car.'

And Falcks is sitting in the driving seat. How the fuck could we miss that — this is not going to look credible, *this is not going to work*.

His shoulders are now in searing pain, and Charles is panting from the exertion. The air is coming out like puffs of white smoke, and this is as fast as they're going to be able to get the car to roll, and they're close to the edge of the quay now, Charles sees it rushing towards them, and it's all too late, *I'm not really here*, and ...

'Now.'

They stop, let go of it. The car carries on. It reaches the quay's edge, tips forwards — *there* — and the front end hits the water, a sound so loud that it echoes, and as the car slowly rotates and sinks to the bottom, roof first, Charles' racing pulse remains constant.

NOVEMBER–DECEMBER 1980

The winter was as bitingly cold and white as the summer had been lush, warm, and green. The weather was never as extreme as it was in Bruket, the contrasts were never as powerful anywhere else.

One morning in late November, Manfred Lundin was convicted of the murder of Ted Lichter and the subsequent mutilation of his body.

'I cannot emphasise enough,' Paul said in a phone call a few days after the verdict had been delivered, 'how important it is that you stick to our agreement.'

'I wasn't planning on anything else.'

'I would feel much more secure if you were working for me, Charlie.'

'Don't you trust me?'

'It's not about trust.'

He had started calling him Charlie. At first, Charles had hated it, because it made him feel like a child. Recently he had started to like it.

'I understand,' Charles said, unsure whether he did or not.

'As it happens, I'll be passing through Bruket in a few days' time.'

'Will you now.'

'Almost, anyway. I will be meeting colleagues in Malmö, but for once my schedule has plenty of air in it. We could meet up.'

'Are you trying to recruit me?'

He laughed.

'Not as anything other than my drinking buddy for an evening. I've given up hoping for anything else.'

Charles and Eva did the pre-Christmas clean-up together, changing tablecloths and curtains. Getting out candelabras. It felt good.

'There we go,' he said, admiring the newly decorated rooms. 'Everything's okay, then.'

She took two steps towards him, looking at his shoulders. Maybe she was considering touching them.

'Is it?'

'Getting there, at least.'

'I love you,' she said.

He didn't answer, despite the certain knowledge that she meant it.

When the Lichter case was closed once and for all, he started winding down: working less, spending more time at home. Eva had explicitly asked him to.

'I want to be with you, but for this to work you need to be at home.'

'That's what I want. I want to be with you.'

'Is that true?'

'Yes.'

And it was.

On the evening of the fourth of December, Eva worked in the shop until closing. Marika was going to sleep over at the house of a classmate, Josefine, who lived over on the other side of Bruket, so Eva was home alone. At least that's what Charles assumed. He didn't know, because he wasn't there. He was sitting at one of the corner tables in Brukets Bar, with Paul.

'How did you get here?' Paul said as he was getting out of the car to meet Charles on the square.

'In the car. But I always park a little way away.'

'Why?'

'I like walking.'

The truth was that he didn't want the car to be seen parked outside the bar. It wouldn't look good, he thought. Whenever he went to Brukets Bar, he would always park in a clearing tucked away in the woods a little way from the square.

'Well, how are you planning to drink then?'

'I'm not planning to drink.'

'What a great drinking buddy I've found,' he muttered as he locked his car.

'How were you planning to drink? You're in a car yourself.'

'I've got a room at the hotel.'

Paul ordered a beer from the man behind the bar, the same man who'd stood there when Charles visited Bruket, and met Eva, for the first time.

'He's not very talkative,' Paul observed when they sat down.

'He's been standing there for many years and will more than likely be standing there until the day he dies.'

'You mean that one might not be that keen on talking, if one has that past and those prospects?'

'Something like that.'

They laughed. He enjoyed Paul's company, and Paul seemed to enjoy his. They had only met once before, but they might just as well have had countless nights like this behind them.

He used to tell himself that it was the sign of a nascent friendship, but friendship can be confusingly like the bond that forms between two people forced to keep a secret.

'You look better, Charlie. With the greatest respect, a lot better than the last time I saw you.'

'I am. The summer was … strange.'

Paul drank some of his beer and waited for him to go on, but Charles didn't feel like doing so. He sipped his lukewarm water.

'Same here,' Paul said. 'As you know.'

'No, I don't, but I can imagine.'

'You'd like it at ours,' said Paul. 'Not least because these are interesting times we're living in. Your skills would be very useful.'

'You're flattering me,' said Charles.

'Are you quite sure you're not going to have a beer? You can walk home from here can't you?'

'In this weather?'

Paul drank some more beer.

'I see what you mean. Winter down here isn't like winter in Stockholm. Somehow it's more like winter up north.'

When Paul asked the question a little later on, he did so as innocently as if he'd been asking where the gents' was.

'So how come you were so keen to see Daniel Bredström get done? I was happy to help — that's not what I mean. Favours given and returned and all that. I'm just curious about the underlying motive.'

'Isn't handling stolen goods enough?'

'I'll rephrase the question. Why were you so determined that it wouldn't be possible to trace it back to you?'

'I told you that then.'

'No.' Paul smiled. 'You never did. That's why I'm asking.'

'Why didn't you ask me then, three months ago?'

'I didn't need to know then.'

'But you do now?'

'I'm just curious.'

Charles could feel the suffocating feeling from that summer — and the darkness of the early autumn — returning, enveloping him.

'Anyway, are you really not having a beer?' said Paul.

Thinking about it now, he's struck by how that was just typical of him — what a narrow perspective he'd had. He's seduced by the versions concocted in hindsight, the ones shaped by what he now knows about what went on. Signs and pointers only become signs and pointers in the here and now, when he *knows*. At the time, they were nothing of the sort.

Time. Time can change everything.

If there's one thing he has already learned, it is that.

Sweden. He had his suspicions back then, almost thirty-five years ago, that something wasn't right.

His suspicions were correct, but not in the way he thought.

Sweden. The great betrayal had its roots in the little one.

Charles had a beer. He had two. He had a third. Paul started going a bit blurred round the edges.

Meanwhile, the phone rang on Alvavägen. Eva answered, and it was Marika, who didn't want to stay over at Josefine's place anymore. Josefine's parents couldn't drive her home — they'd had a bottle of wine between them while the girls were watching *Close Encounters of the Third Kind*.

Marika really wanted to sleep at home.

Eva said she'd come and get her.

Charles sat behind the wheel of his car, in the clearing in the woods not far from the square. He couldn't put his seatbelt on. How had he got so drunk?

'Maybe you shouldn't be driving home, Charlie,' Paul said as he looked at him. 'Why don't you get a cab?'

'There aren't any out here.'

'I'll drive you.'

'Sod that.'

Paul put a hand on Charles' shoulder.

'But Charlie ...'

'Let me go,' he slurred. 'I'm going home.'

He drove through the darkness. The dashboard clock showed 01:35. The road was completely deserted, its surface glittering with frost. His head spun, and he veered into the middle of the road, saw the central line disappear underneath him, steered to the right to get back in lane. He could smell smoke. Somewhere — it could've been close by or miles away, he had no idea — someone had a fire going.

He found himself on one of the unnamed roads, which had taken him a long time to find and an even longer time to actually dare to follow. The road was lined with tall, frozen grass. The speedo hovered around seventy, climbed to a hundred, then down to eighty, up to one-ten. His foot alternated between feeling far too light and way too heavy. There was a strange prickling sensation in his fingertips.

How much had he had to drink? He couldn't remember. Was it five beers? It must've been more.

Out of nowhere, a person on the road, in thick winter clothes, leading a pushbike.

Charles slammed on the brakes. The wheel became light in his hands, steering easy with no resistance, but nothing happened. He *glided* across the tarmac, off to the right, heading off the carriageway.

The car's nose flattened the tall grass nearest the road. It made a harsh, loud rustling sound. That's the last thing his ears remember. From that point onwards, all that remains is touch and the information his eyes registered:

The front of the car struck the cyclist's thigh, and their head smashed into the bonnet. The bike's frame was crushed.

Charles wanted to close his eyes but couldn't. His foot stayed stuck on the pedal, pushing on the brake until his toes went numb.

He blinked. He thought he recognised the thick winter coat.

The world stopped, until it was frozen, silent.

Blood. So much blood, everywhere: in her hair, on his hands, on the coat, the bonnet, and the ground. What had happened? What was she doing here? He couldn't make sense of anything.

Someone must have followed him with their lights off, because he saw a car slow down and then stop. A door opened, then slammed shut, footsteps rushed towards him.

Charles saw his mouth move: *Charlie, what have you done?*

'I …' he began, but when he saw Paul's face above him, he didn't know how to carry on. 'I think her neck is broken.'

He didn't ask what Paul was doing there, how he'd been able to drive. Charles didn't ask anything, because he couldn't.

Paul's eyes slid over towards the side of the road, to the girl standing there with her mouth half-open, her glossy eyes glistening in the darkness.

Marika. Charlie, my God, what have you …

'Eva needs to get to hospital,' Charles whispered. 'She can … It …'

Charlie. Paul put a hand on his shoulder. *It's okay. Everything's okay. I'm going to help you, but you need to do exactly as I say, do you understand?*

Charles was looking for eye contact, but couldn't focus. Everything sloped off to the left, and his hands were shaking so violently. His body realised that he'd lost her long before his soul did.

Just over there is a traffic patrol car. I heard them on the radio, and I followed you to try and warn you. Now listen, Charlie. You have to do exactly as I say.

You see that tree over there?

Charles turned his head.

'Yes.'

Get back in the car.

'I can't.'

Charlie. You have to. It's the only way. Otherwise, I can't help you.

'But I can't. I can't move.'

Charlie!

JUNE 2014

I got myself out of there. It worked.

The feeling was the same as ever when Tove approached the sign telling you that you are now leaving Bruket.

The road ahead of her narrowed and then disappeared, as it does on the horizon, only *nearer*. She'd drive over a cliff if she carried on, and the trees came towards her, becoming walls that threatened to fall, to fall and crush her. The steering wheel was burning hot in her hands and her seat started to breathe, or at least got a pulse — it was *alive*, and now the seat grew and closed in around her shoulders, started to grip her thighs.

She stopped the car, then forced herself to get out. She wanted to throw up but didn't. Leo witnessed it, and the fact that it was him made it all feel that much worse. When she got back into the driver's seat, she did so in order to turn around, as she always did, but she didn't do that. Instead, she carried on, forwards, and with her heart in her mouth she got the car past the sign, and out of Bruket.

It felt like she was betraying someone.

Maybe she was.

The world is a strange place.

I must've nodded off somewhere south of Jönköping, because I'm woken by a clenched fist banging on my shoulder, and when I gasp I feel a sharp pain in my ribs.

'Stay awake.'

'I wasn't asleep.'

'People who are snoring aren't usually awake.'

I massage my shoulder.

'It's the morphine.'

'Keep reading.'

I flip open the laptop that's resting on my lap.

'It's not that easy to interpret these documents. By the way, what happened back there, when you stopped the car as we were leaving?'

'Nothing.'

'It looked like a panic attack.'

'Shut up and read, will you.'

We overtake a heavy goods vehicle with foreign numberplates. I keep my eyes fixed on it to see where it's from. The Netherlands.

I'm worried about what kind of measures Davidsson might deploy now he knows that an unauthorised policeman has been rummaging around in the investigation for over twenty-four hours, and what Sam's going to say when she finds out what I've done, that I'm suspended. When she sees the state of me.

'Did you know about this?' Davidsson had screamed in Tove's ear, loud enough that I could hear him, when he called her half an hour ago.

'No.'

'This is absolutely beyond fucking belief.'

'I know.'

'And a disaster for the inquiry.'

'I know,' she repeated.

'Where the fuck are you?'

'I'm driving him back to Stockholm.'

'Why the hell are you doing that?'

'So that we know he won't come back.'

Davidsson was far from convinced, but went along with it — he had no choice. The interview with Bredström had been due to continue, but he'd asked for food and drink and to speak to a lawyer. Not only that, Davidsson had had to get hold of the prosecutor again.

'It'll be hours before I get to question that bastard again,' he sighed. 'I hope I make it, before it gets too late.'

Before NCS get there and steal your thunder.

I don't know what made her drive me up. It might not have had anything to do with me. Maybe she shares my hunch that the answers to the questions surrounding Levin's death are not going to be found in Bruket. Or perhaps she doesn't want me to disappear from her orbit.

Maybe she hasn't yet decided what she wants to do with me.

I study the documents on the screen. Almost all of them are in chronological order, evidence of Levin's fastidiousness. He departs from the stringent succession on only a few occasions: a memo from October 1981 appears before one from March of that year;

the same thing happens with some from the years 1982 and 1983; and an incident report from early-December 1984. It informs the reader that a known addict and petty criminal, Jan Savolainen, has died after an accident. It says that he fell from a rooftop in central Stockholm. The report's author is Charles Levin.

'I don't get what this is,' I say. 'Who the fuck is Jan Savolainen?'

'It might not be the individual parts that are important.'

'Well, what is, then?'

'The whole. The combined picture that those documents give of … someone. Or something.'

'Yes. Yes, maybe.'

I turn carefully in my seat and open the basket in the back, let Kit out. He peers out as if checking the coast is clear before he emerges, hesitantly, from the cage.

I pause. In the 84 folder, there's a file named *contact*.

It's a text document comprising only three lines.

Gabriella Halvardsson, prosecutor, 0732 87 78 08
Joakim Sturup, journalist, 0708 19 05 40
JO, 0737 28 88 47

I read them aloud for Tove.

'JO? As in the Justice Ombudsman, in Parliament?'

'I guess so,' I say.

'Is that his private number there?'

'It could be.'

'Do you recognise any of the names?'

'No.'

'Not even the prosecutor?'

I shake my head, carefully.

'Call them,' says Tove.

I fish up my phone and dial JO's number. It rings, for ages, the ringing tone oscillating and scraping in the poor reception.

'No answer.'

'Well, call the next one, then.'

I call the journalist's number. No answer. Finally, I dial the third number and put the phone to my ear.

Outside: detached homes on the outskirts of Jönköping. The houses are made of wood, and are beautiful. The flora seems less green than in Bruket, the sun more forgiving.

There's a click in my ear.

'Gabriella.'

'Hi,' I say, with no idea how to carry on from there. 'My name is Leo Junker. I have ... Is this Gabriella Halvardsson?'

'Yes.'

'You're a prosecutor?'

'What did you say your name was?'

Her voice is alert and coarse, apprehensive.

'My name is Leo Junker. I'm a policeman,' I say. 'I'm sitting in a car on the way to Stockholm, from Bruket. I'm with ... I have a computer in front of me, with a large folder, that belonged to Charles Levin. You are aware that he is dead?'

'I know that they suspect a crime, nothing more.'

'The folder is full of scanned documents and photographs. One of them contains your name and telephone number.'

'Right?' she says, puzzled.

'I know this is a strange question. But do you know why he had written down your name?'

'No.'

'Did you know each other?'

'Are you in charge of the investigation?'

'The National Crime Squad are in charge now,' I say, glancing at Tove. 'But I'm sitting in the car with a colleague, Tove Waltersson, who was on the case down in Bruket. That was where he was found.'

The balance of the conversation shifts, and, before long,

Gabriella Halvardsson is the one asking me the questions, asking for my ID number, my police badge number, where I'm stationed, and why someone from Stockholm's Violent Crime Unit is involved.

'I knew him,' I say. 'He was my boss, first at the Violent Crime Unit and then at Internal Affairs.'

She goes quiet, for a long time.

'Now ... I ... with her ...'

'The line keeps cutting out,' I say. 'Sorry, what was that?'

'He talked about you,' she says, louder. 'You were the one who ended up on Gotland.'

'So you did know each other.'

Gabriella Halvardsson takes a deep breath.

'Not exactly.'

'They were acquaintances,' I say.

I turn the dial that controls the aircon on my side. I wonder how bad my condition actually is, what might happen when the morphine wears off.

'They were acquaintances, according to her, nothing more. Their paths crossed six months ago on some investigation that had to do with the police force, I'm not quite sure how exactly, and she had been moved from her post because she refused to be influenced by the National Police Board during the investigation. They tried to bribe her, apparently. She didn't go into detail, but presumably her response had precluded her from further participation at the very highest level. At that point, she and Levin went for dinner a few times. She respected him, because he wasn't like the others up there.'

'And he trusted her,' Tove says, 'because she wouldn't be cowed?'

'Something along those lines, I think.'

The laptop is resting on my knees, with one of the files open. It shines brightly and clearly in the grey-blue gloom inside the car.

'Did she know about that?'

'No. But when I mentioned a few examples from it, she sounded very interested.'

'Did she know of this journalist — Sturup — then?'

'Only that he's one of the investigative journalists at *Dagens Nyheter*. She wasn't exactly fond of him, but then I wouldn't really expect her to have a positive view of journalists.'

'So,' she says, running a hand through her hair, 'he prepares this document to give to people he thinks are going to do the right thing. Or, if something were to happen to him, to make sure that the information still reaches the right people? Is that how to look at this?'

'Maybe. I don't know. She asked me to get back to her tomorrow.'

My phone rings, Birck's name flashing on the display.

'Where are you?' he asks.

'On my way home.'

'When will you be there?'

'I don't know. We just passed Jönköping, so maybe three hours? Just before eleven?'

'I won't be able to be here then, I've just been called in. Some madman on Observatoriegatan has just stabbed three-quarters of his family to death. So you'll have to deal with this on your own, I guess.'

'Birck,' I say. 'What's up?'

'Speaker,' says Tove. 'Put it on speaker.'

I reluctantly activate the speakerphone, and Birck's voice fills the car, sounding scratchier and sharper than it did in my ear.

'Paul Goffman,' he says.

'Yes?'

'You don't sound surprised.'

'He and Levin were friends. That's why I'm going home. I need to talk to him.'

'I'd be very careful about that if I were you.'

'Eh? Why?'

'I haven't got time right now. But I spoke to Grimberg and looked at Marika Alderin's visitor log. Goffman has been to see her three times in June.'

Tove raises her eyebrows.

'Fucking hell,' she says.

'And,' Birck goes on, 'she … it, the … visit.'

'I can't hear you,' I say. 'The line's breaking up. Repeat that last bit.'

'She recorded his last visit.'

'How did she manage that?'

'It was your friend's idea.'

'Grim,' I say, doubtful.

'She had told him that a man was coming to visit her. A … who … hurt her. Sh—'

'It's breaking up again.'

'A man who wanted to hurt her,' Birck says. 'She was allowed to have an MP3 player in her room, but she wasn't allowed to take it out of there. This … she did though, app—tly. They took if off her after the visit, when the warden … she'd … on her and felt they had no choice but to follow the rules.'

'Hang on,' I say. 'I lost you there.'

'The player ended up in a drawer where they store clients' … and that's where it was … I picked it up just now. Grimberg didn't know whether she had foll— his suggestion but … had.'

'And?' I say.

'I don't know if I follow … I hear. Better if you have … yourself. I am not … the player away from here. I have a copy of the file and … on a USB stick. I could go past yours on the way to Observatoriegatan, and leave it with Sam.'

'Sam's in London,' I say.

'Well, your letterbox, then. What's the code for the entrance?'

I give it to him.

'One more time,' Birck says. 'It keeps cutting out.'

I repeat it, more slowly.

'I take it you know what she's in there for?' Birck says then. 'Marika Alderin, why she's at St Göran's in the first place?'

'No.'

'An attempted murder in the city centre, nine years ago.'

'An attempted murder,' I repeat. 'So, 2005.'

'That's right.'

'On Vasagatan? In May?'

'So you did know,' says Birck. 'Why didn't you say so?'

The case that Levin took with him to Bruket. The case that consists of a single memo.

'I didn't know it was her.'

The world really is a strange place.

Tove puts her foot down.

Stockholm: every time I leave, even if it's only for a day or two, the city changes.

I recognise the roads and the architecture, but something about the city's form is constantly changing. Unpredictable, unreliable, the city that is and always has been my home, and perhaps I am the person I am today thanks to the people it raises.

We approach from the south, ripping through Södertälje at around ten thirty. Ragged grey clouds fly across the sky, but the summer evening is still light.

From the corner of my eye, I spot the exit for Salem. I can see the water tower through the trees, away in the distance.

I retrieve one of the morphine tablets from my pocket, pop it in my mouth, and carefully tilt my head back to swallow it. I feel around to see how many I've got left. Two. Fuck.

This time, Stockholm's figure is soft and tender, the shadows more comforting than threatening. Then I realise that it could deceive me, might want to betray me, or make me feel secure when I'm actually seconds away from disaster. I can feel it now, the morphine distorting not only my experience of my own body but my awareness and perception, too.

Tove says something, but I don't catch the words. 'Eh?'

'What's on your mind?'

'Why do you ask?'

'You look like you could break down at any moment.'

I blink as I look through the windscreen. Yes, there is something. Something's wrong.

'Fredrik Oskarsson, the man who was out putting his parasol away on the evening of the eighteenth. I'm wondering who it was that he saw in the forest.'

'Probably someone who has nothing whatsoever to do with any of this.'

'Yes. Could be.'

The phone rings again.

'Hello?'

'Hi, it's me.'

'Hi,' I say. 'How's it going?'

'I met the Queen today. She's her usual self, but she didn't say very much.'

'Eh?'

Sam laughs. I turn in my seat, away from Tove. This feels too private. Maybe she notices, because she turns the radio on and adjusts the volume. An empty voice reads the news headlines.

'We've been to Madame Tussauds,' Sam says.

'Oh, right.'

'What are you up to? How's it going?'

'I'm on my way home. Just passing Skärholmen now.'

'So you … Everything's okay?'

'I think so, yes.'

'What had happened then?'

'You mean with Levin?'

'Yes.'

'I'm not sure. But I think that whatever it was that happened, the solution isn't down there in Bruket. It's here in Stockholm.'

'And the cat?'

'He's sitting in the back.'

'And he's alive?'

'Of course he is.'

She mutters something I can't hear. I close my eyes and imagine that Sam isn't in London, that she'll be there waiting for me when I get home. I think that's my only wish right now.

'You sound weird,' she says then.

'Do I?'

'A bit sort of … strained.'

'Might be the connection.'

'Yes,' she says, and I can tell she doesn't believe me. 'Might be. We're coming home tomorrow, quarter-past nine. Will you meet me at the airport?'

'Of course.'

'I love you. Listen, Leo.'

'Yes?'

'Whatever it is you're up to, do be careful.'

'I'm not the one getting on an aeroplane for three hours tomorrow evening.'

Sam laughs.

'You and your ludicrous fear of flying. We need to talk about that when I get home. It's not healthy. Don't forget to feed the cat.'

I examine my face in the wing mirror on the passenger's side and establish that I look even worse than when we left Bruket, if that's possible. The swellings slowly change hue: from having been a burning bright purple and pink they are now assuming the colour of red wine. The only thing that doesn't look too bad is my lip. Åhlund's handiwork was better than I thought. It strains when I talk, but the tape keeps the split together.

Tove stops outside my front door on Chapmansgatan.

'I haven't had a piss since we left Bruket,' she says.

'Come up then.'

When I carefully nudge Kit into his basket, he gives a little meow of resignation. He might be dehydrated; I can't remember when he last had anything to drink.

I get out of the car, open the back door, and lift out the carry cage, and his effects in the little bag. Tove follows me up the stairs, carrying the laptop.

My phone vibrates.

are you home yet Leo?

I open the door to the flat, and put the cage down.

'The toilet's in there on the right,' I mumble.

It's lying there on the doormat, Birck's little dark-blue USB stick. I pick it up and put it in my pocket, look again at the text message on my phone.

yes, I reply.

With the phone in my hand, I head into the kitchen, fill a bowl up with water, and put it over by the balcony door where Kit usually sits.

be careful

It stops me in my tracks.

I reply: *you do know me, right?*

I dig out the cat food, fill a bowl, and put it down next to the water.

Grim's last text is just three words:

see you soon

Everything is as I left it yesterday morning. Right down to Sam's scent hanging in the air, I convince myself. The coffee I didn't have time to finish off is still in the pot, and the empty cigarette packet is still lying on the balcony table.

Tove comes out of the toilet and looks around at her surroundings, as if trying to understand the flat's occupants. She puts the laptop down on the coffee table and opens it up. While she connects the USB stick and waits, Kit ambles over to the cat food and sniffs it.

'Would you, er, like anything?' I ask as I walk into the kitchenette. 'I've got coffee, water, and …'

'Coffee's fine.'

I empty the pot, prepare another, and go back out to Tove.

'Right then,' she says. 'Looks like the file is less than ten minutes long.'

She adjusts the volume and clicks PLAY.

MAN: Have you had … Good. Drink some water too, Marika? Water. Those tablets give you such a dry mouth. [Silence] Good. Let's go.

[Repeated scuffing sounds. A door closes. Keys turn]

MAN: Right then. Visiting Room 2 today. He's been to see you before, hasn't he? It was just few days ago, wasn't it?

[Scuffing sounds end. A door opens]

MAN: Right, Marika. I'll just come in with you, then I'll leave the two of you in peace.

[More scuffing. A chair being moved, then white noise and static]

MAN: Okay, there we go. I'll be outside. You do know … You know that she's not really with —

GOFFMAN: I know, thanks.

[A door closes with a muted click]

GOFFMAN: It's lovely to see you again, Marika. It's not that long since last time. Would you like anything? I have [Static] ... I was only allowed to bring a bottle of water in, but I thought perhaps you'd want it.

[He places it on the table. Silence]

GOFFMAN: This really is a funny place. I can see why you find it so difficult to relax in here. I think that's probably a sign you're getting better more than anything else. [Laughter]

[Silence]

GOFFMAN: I'm going ... I have to tell you that this isn't easy for me. It gives me sleepless nights. I know that you know. Do you know what I mean? I know that he talked to you, that he told you. Of course, he claimed that things were so bad that you weren't registering any of it, but he wasn't at all convincing, if you ask me. And now I think, quite honestly, that my fears were well founded.

[Long silence]

MARIKA: Hesitation.

GOFFMAN: Quite.

MARIKA: Soot and ash. All that was left.

GOFFMAN: Soot and ash.

MARIKA: The car was on fire. Soot and ash were all that was left.

GOFFMAN: I understand. You're talking about when your mother died.

MARIKA: Soot and ash were all that was left.

GOFFMAN: I understand that it changed your life in so many ways. I remember the first time we met down in Bruket — what were you then? Seven, eight maybe? And then those times we met in Stockholm, eighty-three? Eighty-four? I could tell even then that you weren't very well, even before ... But your mother's death, it must have made it worse. You must hate him for what he did, and I understand you. I am very sorry for what happened to your mother.

[Long silence]

MARIKA: Are you?

GOFFMAN: Yes.

325

MARIKA: Soot and ash.

GOFFMAN: Soot and ash.

MARIKA: Were all that was left.

GOFFMAN: Yes. [Sighs] Yes, I know. I really need to talk to him, Marika. I need to see him. I am worried that he might do something stupid. I have asked you this before, but I'm going to have to ask you again. I know that he has been here, that he has visited you several times.

MARIKA: Not again.

GOFFMAN: You don't want me to ask again?

MARIKA: Not again.

[Silence]

GOFFMAN: Do you mean that he isn't going to come here again? Did he say that?

MARIKA: Mm.

GOFFMAN: He said that to you.

[Silence]

GOFFMAN: I know why you are here, Marika. I know what you tried to do, and I can't say I blame you for it. Quite the opposite, in fact. I know that you know where he is. I know that he told you. I have been looking for him for nearly a week, but with no success. He seems to have just gone puff, up in smoke. It's typical of your dad, if you ask me. He has a habit of doing that. But he is in Sweden, I know that much. Is he in Stockholm?

[Silence]

GOFFMAN: I know that he — [Deep breath] He's there, isn't he? He went back?

[Silence]

[Goffman leaves the room without another word. The warden returns and starts helping Marika out. After a couple of steps, he discovers that she has the MP3 player on her. The file ends with it being switched off]

'Rewind it,' I say.

'All of it?'

'No, just a little bit.'

Tove clicks and drags the cursor backwards, then releases.

'I know what you tried to do ...' Goffman's voice says.

'Just there,' I say.

'... and I can't say I blame you for it,' he continues. 'Quite the opposite, in fact.'

Tove pauses the file. Sitting next to her on the sofa, I drink some coffee and carefully tilt my head back. The pain has now reduced to a muffled murmur just behind my temples.

'What does that mean?'

'I don't know,' says Tove. 'But it doesn't sound good.'

I close my eyes. The hot mug is burning my hands.

Paul Goffman.

Other than the fact that he works at SEPO, I know next to nothing about him. Our paths crossed last winter, after a sociologist was stabbed to death in Vasastan. The case, which ended up with me and Birck, was linked to far-right and far-left extremism, which piqued SEPO's interest, and Goffman emerged from the shadows to take the investigation off us. What I remember most is the impression he gave of being unshockable, impossible to surprise. Paul Goffman kept shtum when he should've been talking and talked far too much in situations where he would've been well advised to keep his mouth shut, and I think he did so on purpose. People who break with micro-norms make those around them tense and uneasy — the balance of power shifts towards the norm-breaker.

I remember that, and that he had a knack for turning up at precisely the right moment. That time last winter, he very probably saved my life, as well as Birck's.

'It would be good if we could talk to him,' says Tove.

I open my eyes. The ceiling light is painfully white.

'Yes.'

Tove reaches for her mug, still untouched next to the computer. She takes a gulp and winces.

'Not very nice.'

'I thought it might not be.'

'He scares you, doesn't he?' she says.

'Who, Goffman?'

'I can tell just looking at you.'

'Okay.' I would really like to close my eyes again. 'Yes.'

Seconds away from midnight.

When our paths crossed last winter, I did a search on Paul Goffman. Doing searches on people who cannot be linked to a live investigation is strictly prohibited. The risk of getting caught is pretty much guaranteed, since all searches are logged. I was given a ticking off, then a warning, and eventually threatened with a heavy fine if it happened again.

His details were marked confidential on the electoral roll, but that's not unusual for SEPO employees. The only detail I found was the one that flashed up when I did an internal search and saw where his wage slips are sent.

At least there was an address coupled to Paul Goffman, by the green expanse of Tessinparken, close to Gärdet. Blanchegatan 14. It's an eight-storey-high block, muted orange, that towers proudly above us as we slow down and then stop on leafy Askrikegatan, on the opposite side of the park.

'There are lights on in some of the windows,' Tove says. 'But how do we get in?'

'We wait until someone arrives or leaves, I suppose.'

'Do people do that at this time of night?'

'There's always someone who does. There's a one-way system here. Let me out and then drive round, I'll go and stand by the entrance.'

'You?' she says. 'In that state?'

'I've met him before. You don't know what he looks like.'

'That's not what I mean. Are you going to do it on your own? That's just asking for trouble.'

'We don't even know if it is him. It might not be. But if it is, I'm better off going alone.' I check the time. 'If you haven't seen or heard from me in fifteen minutes, then come up. And ring 112.'

'Maybe you ought to have something to defend yourself with, if it is him.'

She leans over the gearstick, opens the glove box in front of me. Out pour soft-drink bottles, a pair of gloves, pepper spray, *Highway 61 Revisited* on CD, and a road atlas.

'Take this.'

Right at the back is a knife, a small black one with a button that makes the blade flick out.

'You're supposed to have this on you,' I say, picking the pepper spray off the floor. 'It goes against directives, having it lying around like this.'

She puts it back in the glove box and then closes it, leaving the rest of the stuff spread across the floor.

'Says you.'

I open the door, and the night air that rushes in is cool and light.

The area around Tessinparken is quiet and still. Karlavägen hums away in the distance, and the cars roll slowly southwards along Värtavägen. The tarmac smells like it does just after a rain shower, but the ground beneath my feet is dry. I cross the park, notice that I'm limping. For some reason, that makes my ribs hurt less. I bend over and pick up one of the park's countless stones, so that I've got something to prop the door open with if I do manage to get inside. The stone is as big as a heart, and, as I stand up, the dizziness returns, makes me stumble.

I reach Blanchegatan 14, and lean against the wall for support before going up to the locked door and checking it. The stairwell inside is just straight lines and shadows, with the darkness getting progressively deeper. I light a cigarette and smoke it greedily while I wait.

Five minutes pass. Across the street, a car pulls up, then goes quiet. Tove.

Levin is dead. I will never speak to him again. I'm not sure how I'll get home, and I am so, so tired.

A man passes by, veering back and forth and slurring into his mobile phone. He's about my age, I think to myself, but then I catch sight of my reflection in the glass door and realise that I must be at least ten years older than him.

I light another cigarette. Time is passing so slowly. My car is still down in Bruket. How am I going to get it home? Is it even worth it? Everyone would probably think that I was doing them, and the car, a favour if I was just to leave it there to disintegrate on its own.

Inside, from the stairwell, there's a click. The lights come on. Hard heels echo down and then the door opens from the inside.

I let go of the cigarette, grab the handle and hold the door open.

'Hello,' I say.

'Oh, hello,' the woman says, wafting away the cigarette smoke with obvious irritation, then walking past without looking at me, too busy adjusting the shawl around her neck.

I'm in. Finally. I place the stone in the doorway and make sure that the door doesn't shut behind me.

I find a list of residents on the wall, and, according to that, there's a P. Goffman on the third floor. I get in the lift and wait as it climbs up the shaft. Around the temples, my pulse is increasing, and the dizziness makes me unsteady, but the buzzing in my fingertips is quite a pleasant sensation. Must be the morphine.

On the third floor, a pale, cold light enters through the stairwell window. I find his door, a thick, heavy one, and if someone was moving on the other side I'm not at all sure it would be audible.

The doorbell sits at the same height as the door handle. I push it with my thumb and hear it echoing around on the other side of the door.

Something tells me that he already knows.

The lock clicks and the door handle turns in front of me. I clench the knife in my pocket.

'Leo,' he says. 'I thought it might be you.'

DECEMBER 1980

That memory would always remain too clear to be distorted by time, or space: it was a winter night in Bruket, 1980. Eva's heart was no longer beating, had been still for several minutes, when Charles got back behind the wheel.

Are you sure that no one saw you, that no one saw the car, Charlie? Are you sure that no one saw you?

He wasn't. He avoided looking at his wife lying still and cold on the ground, her legs splayed strangely. The idling engine puffed out exhaust fumes from the little round pipe.

As fast as you can, Charlie. As fast as you dare.

Next to him, Paul stood holding a jerry can full of petrol. In spite of the chaos, there was something methodical, rational, and well thought-out about what was happening.

It was an accident. I understand that, an accident that should never have involved you at all.

Behind them, Marika stood and stared.

Listen to me, Charlie. You are innocent. You couldn't ... Doing this will just put things in order.

As he closed the car door, Charles felt no rage, no gratitude, no grief, not even fear.

He revved the engine and could sense the vibration in his feet, saw the clump of trees rushing towards him, much faster than he had imagined, and felt nothing.

JUNE 2014

EXCERPT FROM INTERVIEW TRANSCRIPT (REF 0500-K1754-08)

INTERVIEWEE: Bredström, DANIEL

ID NUMBER: 19501024-4674

ROLE: Accused

SUSPECTED CRIME: Suspicion of murder: Charles Jan Levin 140618, at victim's home address: Alvavägen 10, Bruket.

INTERVIEWER: Ola Davidsson

DATE OF INTERVIEW: 20140621

INTERVIEW START: ca 22:15

INTERVIEW END: ca 22:30

LOCATION: Interview room, Bruket Police Station

INTERVIEW TYPE: RB23:6

TRANSCRIBED BY: R. Å.

– – – – – – –

DAVIDSSON: Right then, Daniel. Now you've eaten, drunk, pissed, shat, and anything else you can think of. So let's try again.

BREDSTRÖM: Alright, alright. That was me sitting in the car in that picture.

DAVIDSSON: We knew that much already. Tell us what you're doing in the picture instead.

BREDSTRÖM: Well, I'm leaving, aren't I.

DAVIDSSON: You get in the car to leave Alvavägen 10.

333

BREDSTRÖM: Yes.

DAVIDSSON: The time is?

BREDSTRÖM: I don't really know. Somewhere between half-ten, eleven.

DAVIDSSON: And how long have you been there?

BREDSTRÖM: Not sure. An hour, maybe.

DAVIDSSON: So you get there sometime between, what, nine and half-past?

BREDSTRÖM: Something like that.

DAVIDSSON: So you've been at Levin's house for nearly an hour. What did you do in there?

BREDSTRÖM: No. I never went in.

DAVIDSSON: What do you mean?

BREDSTRÖM: What it sounds like, that I never went in.

DAVIDSSON: You're confusing me, Daniel.

BREDSTRÖM: [long pause] I was sitting at home, that evening, having a beer or two. And then, I don't know, I just felt a bit uneasy, right, fucking irked, you know, after seeing him down by the square earlier on. I sat and mulled it over, back and forth, all the shit that'd happened since 1980, and I know I haven't got long left, eh. I'm not daft. If you've lived a life like I have, it takes its toll on your body. So I wanted to put it to bed, to talk to him. I wanted him to admit that he'd stitched me up that time, because I know it was him. One way or another, it was him.

DAVIDSSON: You went to talk to him.

BREDSTRÖM: Yes.

DAVIDSSON: In a stolen car.

BREDSTRÖM: I had to — mine wouldn't start. It's played up before, and I couldn't get it going — I was there on the drive for half an hour before I gave up. And once I'd decided to go and confront him, I had to do it. For my own sake. It was worth the risk. And fuck it — it was late, the area around Alvavägen is always dead, the risk of someone seeing me wasn't very big.

DAVIDSSON: And what do you do when you get there?

BREDSTRÖM: The lights were on in there, so I knew he was in, but I couldn't see him. And I dunno, maybe it was the beer making me a bit edgy, but I felt like I had to [long pause] pull myself together before I rang the bell. You see?

DAVIDSSON: No.

BREDSTRÖM: I don't know what it was, but standing there, looking in, you know, it was the same fucking house, right? He was living in the same fucking house that him and Eva lived in. I had to pull myself together. And I know that there's a path that goes round the woods at the back of Alvavägen. It's a fair old way, an hour's walk, give or take, and I thought it'd do me good. I'd sober up a bit, too. So I went off.

DAVIDSSON: You did.

BREDSTRÖM: Yes.

DAVIDSSON: Leaving a stolen car on the road in the meantime.

BREDSTRÖM: I wasn't thinking straight, was I? You don't, do you, when you're a bit edgy, and I'd had a bit to drink, too. Anyway, then I came back — you come back out onto Alvavägen if you follow the path around the edge of the woods for long enough, so I came out a couple of houses further down. It was a cracking walk, I tell you, I mean, I felt a lot cooler in my thinking afterwards.

DAVIDSSON: Did something happen during the walk?

BREDSTRÖM: No, nothing special. Well, actually, there's a clearing in the woods, and when I'd gone past it, and I was a bit further on, I heard a car. I saw a car driving in and parking up there. It —

DAVIDSSON: What kind of car?

BREDSTRÖM: No idea. A normal car. Fucked if I know. I only saw it from a distance, must've been at least thirty metres, because I'd gone a little way. It was just a pair of headlights. I guess it was someone out walking their dog.

DAVIDSSON: At that time of night?

BREDSTRÖM: I don't fucking know. You asked if anything had happened, and that was the only thing that happened — I saw a car in the clearing. Then there was someone in one of the houses further down, someone out fiddling with their garden furniture. I think he was taking down one of those, what do you call it, not an umbrella but a ... What do you call it?

DAVIDSSON: I know what you mean. When you come out of the woods again, what do you do next?

BREDSTRÖM: I went to his house, and I was just thinking I'd knock on the door. The lights were on, I could see that as I was walking towards it, and when I got there I looked in the kitchen window to see if he was in there. And then, I don't know what it was, but you get a fucking funny feeling sometimes, don't you? Like there's something going on that you're best off staying out of?

DAVIDSSON: Maybe. What do you mean? What did you see?

BREDSTRÖM: Someone else was already there.

DAVIDSSON: What?

BREDSTRÖM: There was already someone else in the house.

DAVIDSSON: And it wasn't Levin?

BREDSTRÖM: No.

DAVIDSSON: What was he wearing?

BREDSTRÖM: Some kind of light shirt, grey, I think it was. I just saw him from the waist up. [long pause] He was all bloody.

DAVIDSSON: What did you just say?

BREDSTRÖM: He had blood on him, on his sleeve and his face. Like it had splashed onto him.

DAVIDSSON: And what was he doing?

BREDSTRÖM: He had one of those, what do you call them, a little trolley for moving packing boxes around.

DAVIDSSON: A sack truck?

BREDSTRÖM: That's it. That's what you call them. He had a box on it.

DAVIDSSON: In the kitchen?

BREDSTRÖM: No, the living room.

DAVIDSSON: Could you see what was in the box?

BREDSTRÖM: No.

DAVIDSSON: And no sign of Levin?

BREDSTRÖM: No.

DAVIDSSON: What else did you see?

BREDSTRÖM: That was it. I could see that there was something going on in there that I should keep well out of. Even being seen in the area, in a stolen car, when I'd bumped into him earlier that day — it wouldn't look good. Considering where I am now, I was obviously right about that. So I sat in the car and got out of there.

DAVIDSSON: Let's say that this is true, Daniel. Why then did we find the car in question burned out near the graveyard?

BREDSTRÖM: I wanted to get shot of it. It'd already been up at my place for far too long, and the longer a car is in your vicinity, the more difficult it is to slip away. No one wanted to buy the thing, and even less so when it had been close to all that. I could see that myself, right. And the car was the only thing putting me on Alvavägen, so I thought I'd be just as well getting rid of it. I've got no plans to do any more time, especially not for something I haven't done.

DAVIDSSON: Well, if that was so important to you, why did you leave the false plates on the car?

BREDSTRÖM: I didn't think of it until I torched the car, and then it was too late, wasn't it?

DAVIDSSON: If this is true —

BREDSTRÖM: It is true.

DAVIDSSON: Yes, I realise you're going to insist that it is. But why the hell didn't you mention this to begin with, Daniel? [long pause] Is it not the case that someone beat you to it, Daniel? Weren't you planning to do exactly the same thing as the man in there, if I'm going to believe you, had done?

BREDSTRÖM: [long pause] I don't know.

337

DAVIDSSON: You don't know?

BREDSTRÖM: I don't know what would've happened if he'd been there on his own and I'd gone in. It would've depended on him, not me, put it that way.

DAVIDSSON: This man that you claim to have seen, wou—

BREDSTRÖM: I'm not just saying it. I saw him, clear as day. If you showed me a picture, I'd recognise him. And let me tell you, if I do ever see him again, I'll give him a pat on the back and buy him a beer for what he did.

Tove has never liked it, this city. Something about it makes you feel small and insignificant. She remembers it from her time as a trainee, how you could never be yourself here. Markus could, but not her.

She checks the time: she's got eight minutes left to wait. Itchy fingers. Eight minutes — not going to happen.

She still hasn't decided how she's going to allow this, her meeting with Leo Junker, to end. She thinks about her mum, who right now has no idea that they are separated by more than 500 kilometres, who doesn't even know that Leo's been in Bruket. Tove should've called her.

Seven minutes left. She checks her weapon, gets out of the car, and crosses the street. She stands by the entrance and checks that the stone is still there and that the door hasn't closed, smokes a cigarette.

Her phone rings. Davidsson. Fuck. Not now. Tove's about to press reject, but just at that moment she's overcome by a feeling of uncertainty and she changes her mind.

'Hello?'

Davidsson sighs, loudly.

'It's probably not him. It's not Bredström. He might have been *planning* to do it, but I don't think it was him that actually did it.'

'Eh?'

A half-slurring Davidsson drawls through his account of his second interview with Bredström. Tove can see Davidsson in her mind's eye, sitting there at home in his easy chair with the footrest out, and a glass of strong brandy or whisky on the table next to him, resigned to the unfathomable stupidity of the world at large.

She smokes the cigarette to the nub and then drops it to the ground.

'Bredström says he saw Fredrik Oskarsson fiddling with his garden furniture. He actually says he saw Oskarsson folding his parasol. How the fuck would Bredström get that right unless he'd actually been there?'

'And then when he returns, he sees someone else in the house, is that right?' Tove says.

'A man with blood spattered on his sleeve, standing loading a box onto a sack truck,' says Davidsson. 'He claims. Whether it's true or not, I don't know, but I did get this funny feeling in my belly when he said that. Bredström left, so where the man in the house went from there he doesn't know. And who the fuck this guy is, I have no idea. Bredström also says that he's seen a car parked up in the clearing in the woods, but it was that far away that he's only seen the headlights. That is a car very close to the scene, at the time of the murder, but a car that we know jack shit about other than that. If Bredström is telling the truth, who the hell is that sitting inside it?'

Tove looks at her watch. Four minutes left. She can feel it in her fingers. Something is happening.

'Bredström could be lying, of course,' Davidsson slurs. 'He probably is. But I don't know. I just got the feeling that he was telling the truth.'

'I've got to go.'

'Eh?'

'I need ...'

She doesn't finish the sentence, hangs up instead.

And then, the verification: the gunshot. It rips a hole in the silence.

The air, there's something funny about the air: at first, it's full of that clinical smell that you only get in hospitals. Then it fills with something else, a warm, rich scent, like grass in summer.

'I don't mean any offence,' Goffman says with his back to me as I enter the apartment, 'but you certainly look rather haggard. Please take your shoes off. The rug you're standing on is handmade, and cost more than your flat.'

He says it with such perspicuity that I obey without a second thought and clumsily step out of my shoes.

I walk through the hall and find him in the kitchen. He's standing by the cooker, and is slowly stirring the contents of a saucepan with a beautiful, elegant spoon. That's where the funny smell is coming from.

Goffman is wearing a pair of black jeans and a grey-and-white-checked shirt with the sleeves rolled up. He's tanned and broad-shouldered, so tall that he seems to be hunched over the stove. It's the first time I've seen him in anything other than a suit.

'How did you know it was me?' I say.

'I didn't. I suspected.'

I stand in the doorway, leaning against the doorframe. It feels good, unburdening.

'How come?'

'He was your mentor and your friend, after all. And he was

my colleague and comrade once, long ago.' His gaze falls onto my T-shirt. 'Garfield.' He cocks his head to one side. 'You've cat to be kitten me right meow.' He chuckles. 'I get it. Very funny.'

'It's not my T-shirt.'

He turns around and glances out the kitchen window, which faces the street.

'Did you come alone?'

'Yes.'

'Would you like some tea?'

'No, thanks.'

'Does my joints good, apparently. At least, that's what my doctor would have me believe, but each time I see him he seems more and more like a charlatan.' He opens one of the cupboards over the sink, takes out a mug, and fills it. 'Are you sure you won't have some? You look like you could do with it.'

'I have to ask you,' I say, and wobble against the doorframe.

Goffman raises his eyebrows.

'Yes?'

I get my balance back.

'You know why I'm here. So you know what it is I want to know.'

Goffman puts the saucepan on the hob, turns off the ring, and pulls out one of the drawers, gets out a teaspoon and plops it into the mug, stirring slowly in a circular motion. My eyes follow his hands. Goffman's fingers are long and bony. I remember that about him, that he had fingers like a skilful pickpocket and that you need to keep your eyes on them.

'You want to know where I was on the evening of the eighteenth of June.'

'Between half-past nine and half-past ten.'

I hear how heavy my breathing is. Inside my pocket, I'm clutching the knife so hard that it's hurting the palm of my hand.

The ceiling light is on, but the light it casts is weak and warm, which gives Goffman bags under his eyes.

'I was with a good friend of mine. Her name is Susanna. We had dinner at Sturecompagniet, in the city centre, and we got the bill just before ten. I remember that, because I looked at the receipt and noticed the time. Then we walked down Sturegatan towards Valhallavägen, and along it for a bit. I don't recall exactly which way we walked, but we ended up here, anyway.'

'Have you still got that receipt?'

'No.'

'Does Susanna have a mobile phone?'

'Doesn't everyone?'

'I would like you to call her.'

'But of course.' He picks up the steaming teacup from the worktop with two hands, takes a cautious sip. 'Come out to the living room. That's where my phone is.'

'You first.'

'Sure.'

I back out of the kitchen, towards the hall. The room tilts under my feet. I need to keep my feet further apart, otherwise I'm going to fall over. I need to stay upright.

The morphine made me cocky, but it's leaving my system now. Fuck, what if it is him? What do I do then? The only thing I've got to defend myself with is a knife.

'You say that you just want to talk, and I'm happy to do so, but I can tell from your manner that you have your suspicions. It's not the first time someone has suspected me, and that, presumably, is why I'm not more upset. But I would still appreciate it if you could be a little more polite. You are in an innocent man's home, and, quite frankly, you have no right to behave like this. Besides,' he adds, raising one of his narrow eyebrows. 'Aren't you on leave?'

'Where have you heard that?'

Goffman chuckles as he walks past me, tea in hand.

'I'm sixty-six years old, Leo. I don't always remember who said what.'

Goffman's living room is spacious and airy, the walls covered in expensive-looking art. In one corner is a little desk with a computer on it, next to a Juliet balcony. By the desk is an old black bag, like a sports holdall but made of leather, the sort of thing that men in old films have with them when they travel. The floor is covered with a large ivory-coloured rug, and a three-piece lounge suite stands on half of it. On the coffee table — glass and dark metal — is a mobile phone. Goffman sinks into the sofa, puts the cup on the table, and picks up the phone.

'Right, let's see,' he says. 'Have a seat, Leo.'

'I'm happy standing.'

'I don't believe that,' he says with a pained expression. 'In your state. But fine, stand.' He puts the phone to his ear and checks the time on his watch. 'She's not going to be happy. I'm going to wake her up.'

'I'm sorry,' I say, the doubt gnawing away at me. I don't know where it comes from, but it's growing with every passing second. 'To have to do this,' I spell out.

He looks down at the nearest cushion. I need to sit down. Everything is spinning.

'I understand that you nee— ... Yes, hello, Susanna, it's Paul. Hello. I understand that ... Yes, I know.'

It's not him either, I think to myself. Goffman didn't do it. He's too composed, too well coordinated. Who the fuck was it then? I flop into the armchair.

Bredström. Yes, it has to be him. It's almost always about love, or retribution. I must remember to ask Goffman about him. Maybe he knows.

'I know I'm disturbing you,' he repeats, adjusting the cushion slightly, 'but I have a young man here who would very much like to talk to you. He just wants to confirm a detail. It's about Charles. No, it ... It won't take long. Here he is.'

Goffman leans over the table, holding the phone out towards me.

'Please, go ahead.'

When I stand up from the armchair, my neck is pounding and my ribcage is straining as if it were about to burst.

'Thank you,' I groan, take the phone from him, and slump back into the armchair. 'Hello?'

Silence.

'Hello?'

I wait. Look at the phone, then at Goffman.

'There's nobody there.'

His fingers. I took my eyes off his fingers. The cushion, I think to myself. It was under the cushion. In his right hand, the revolver is silent and black.

'Did you really come alone tonight, Leo?'

'Yes.'

'You're lying,' he says.

Then he shoots me in the chest.

Tove puts the phone to her ear, waits for the operator to answer. Her hand is shaking.

'My name is Tove Waltersson. I am a police officer, and someone is shooting at my colleague, at Blanchegatan 14.'

'Someone is shooting at a *police officer* — is that right?'

'At Blanchegatan 14, Östermalm.'

'Which floor, did you say?'

'I ... I don't know.'

'We have ...' The seconds ticking by are so long. '... a car five minutes away.'

The operator asks her to stay on the line until they get there. Tove hangs up and wraps her fingers around the gun's handle, hugging the wall as she slowly climbs the stairs up to the first floor, reading the surnames on the letterboxes before continuing up the stairs towards the second.

Somewhere above her, a door opens. It closes again, gently. Someone pushes in a key, and locks it.

The second floor is empty and quiet; Tove carries on to the third.

The lift doors slide shut in her peripheral vision. The lock clicks. She rushes over, holding her breath.

There. He looks at himself in the lift's mirrored wall and makes brief eye contact with Tove. An old man, she thinks to herself, older than her father, with clear eyes and sharp features.

The lift disappears into its shaft —*fuck*— and she flings herself down the steps, breathless and weak at the knees.

Below her, the lift stops with a heavy, whirring puff, and the doors open. The sound of his footsteps is drowned out by the clacking of her own, and when Tove gets her first sight of the ground floor the front door is open and then she sees him disappearing out through it with a bag in one hand, and something black and shiny in the other.

Out on the street, surrounded by long shadows and tall buildings. He walks quickly but calmly along the deserted pavement. He might have convinced himself that he has already managed to escape and now just needs to blend in.

Tove tries to see which way he is heading, and whether he has a car waiting for him. He glances over his shoulder, and Tove raises her weapon and shouts. All that does is get him to stop walking — instead, he bolts across the road, and runs in amongst the trees and shrubs on the edge of the park.

Tessinparken is a park comprising mainly open spaces, all grass, small footpaths, and cycle lanes, but with lush clumps of trees and bushes here and there, and a playground enclosed by a low fence at its northern end. It is a place that makes you feel a bit uneasy, without really knowing why.

Tove can't see him anymore, and stops and listens, but she can't hear his footsteps, just her own heavy breathing. She moves slowly between the trees at the park's edge, hugging the line of the rough old trunks and smelling the leaves in the crowns above.

She forces herself to relax, drop her shoulders, and, as she does — *there* — a rustling in front of her, and she sees him, no more than a silhouette. He has extricated himself from the shadow of the trees and is running across the grass with the bag in his hand, heading towards the playground.

Tove fires a warning shot. The sound booms across the park, bouncing off nearby buildings and activating the fear inside her.

She pauses again, a little way out on the grass, takes a deep breath, and raises her weapon. Low down, she tells herself. Hit low down.

As she squeezes the trigger, her pulse is throbbing in her fingertip, and everything instantly goes very, very quiet.

She is firing for effect.

Ahead of her, his right arm flies upwards.

The bag. Tove hit the bag.

He lets go of it, dumping it in the grass.

Tove stumbles as she chases him, hitting the ground and breaking her fall with the palms of her hands. The weapon falls from her grasp.

She gets up again. The shot is still ringing in her ears, still lingering in her arms. She runs past the bag. The bullet has torn a little round mouth in the leather, and Tove avoids thinking about what might have happened up in the flat, whether Leo has been shot, and, in that case, whether he's still alive.

He has cleared the fence around the playground, and disappears between the swings and the small wooden playhouses, which are low and colourful.

A flash in front of her, and a bang rips through the park. She reacts without thinking, ducks down, and is about to take shelter behind one of the playhouses, but it's too late.

She'd been expecting this, a punishment — her reward for having left Bruket.

What she *hadn't* expected was that touch would be faster than hearing. In the tiny ember of time that passes before the sound of the second shot, Tove feels the upper part of her left arm explode.

Blood. There's blood in my mouth.

She spits. Must've bitten herself somewhere, her lip or her tongue. She doesn't know and can't feel anything, either.

She's fallen backwards. Someone is holding glowing coals to her arm. Tove can't get any air; the pain of each breath sticks in her throat and becomes a gasp. She daren't look at it.

Panic. She's going to panic.

Everything tilts, and she can tell that her left arm is still there, that the explosion hasn't ripped it off, but when she moves the arm her vision goes black: she's going to faint.

Tove spits again — *more* blood — and slowly gets to her feet. A scratching, slicing sensation in her fingers and her neck. She can't move the arm, has to steady herself against the roof of the little playhouse so as not to collapse again. Weapon in hand, she founders through the shadows at the edge of the playground.

Up to the fence. She can see him: he's getting into a car, a low-slung Citroën parked on the cobbled street. By the time Tove has forced herself over the fence, he is far away. She must memorise the numberplate.

That's when it happens.

A horn blares and then blares again, a long blast this time, and it doesn't stop until it's too late.

At the end of Tessinparken, Askrikegatan ends abruptly, met from the right by the unexpected narrow road that had taken Tove by surprise as she drove past less than twenty minutes earlier.

Down the road, a howl comes from the heavy goods vehicle that, however desperately its driver pounds the brakes, is unable to stop — and when they collide, the silhouette inside the truck's cab is thrown forwards. In the car, the man gets flung around in his seat.

Flakes of paint and shards of metal, some the size of fingernails but others much bigger, rain down over them onto the ground.

Tove wants to run, but can't. The fingers of her left hand are tickling, and it takes a while for her to realise — it's blood that has trickled down from the hole in her arm.

Finally, the sound of sirens, growing in strength. She is, remains, alone, and her throat feels strained, like when you have just screamed. Maybe she has; she can't remember anymore. Everything is getting even darker, being erased in front of her.

The man in the car is bleeding, from his forehead. He moves his hand up to the blood and then looks at his fingers, as though he's surprised at having just discovered a shortcoming.

Tove aims the barrel at him, her finger resting on the trigger.

'Out,' she screams through the tumult. 'Get out.'

Don't get out. Please, stay where you are. Let me hurt you. I need to hurt someone.

Bright lights arrive, perhaps from a car, but Tove isn't sure. What she does know is that the lights are bright and white, illuminating the man slowly extricating himself from the Citroën. He is groggy and unsteady, has to hold himself up against the bonnet.

Before long, flashing blue lights strike the walls and the tarmac, and the man is still standing, propped up against the bonnet of the car.

Tove doesn't lower her weapon until someone takes it from her hand. She can't feel anything anymore. She's mute, inside and out, just skin and bones, and the thought that washes over her is that something might be coming to an end.

I blink.

My breathing hurts, and dead people don't breathe. That's how I know this is a halt, a short pause. The driver has stopped on the roadside. Maybe he's having a cocktail. I want one myself. My tongue is dry, so it's sticking to the roof of my mouth; my lips are peeling and tight. You should be allowed that before continuing the journey — a cocktail and a last chance to meet the one you love.

I am in a room, and the room has a door, and when it opens it does so silently. The driver is a short man with a potbelly, and he's wearing a funny white coat over his green clothes.

'Leo,' he says. 'Leo? Can you hear me?'

He picks up a torch, shines it in my eyes.

There's this bleeping in here. What is that noise? Is that sound inside my head?

My chest really hurts.

'Leo,' he says. 'Can you hear me?'

'Yes.'

He asks me if I know where I am.

I blink.

'No.'

He says that I am in Karolinska Hospital. That his name is Christopher Åström, and that he's a surgeon. It's the twenty-fourth of June 2014.

'It hurts,' I wheeze.

'Where does it hurt?'

'When I breathe.'

'Your lungs?'

'I … don't know.'

There must be something above my head because his eyes keep drifting off in that direction.

That's it. That's where the bleeping is coming from. It must be my pulse, but it sounds alien. Maybe it belongs to someone else.

He says something, I think, but I don't hear what, because the journey continues, and it's about time, I really want to get out of here and every breath surges through me like electricity, down my spine and out through my arms, and *now, finally* it all goes dark again, and in the background someone shouts something, and the bleeping suddenly becomes very, very intense and

In my memories

In my memories, I feel older than I am now.

It's autumn, long ago, my second year on the Violent Crime Unit. I walk along Norr Mälarstrand, following the shoreline of Lake Mälaren, and the air is crisp and light. All the colours are stronger than usual. Beside me, Levin is walking with his hands stuffed in the pockets of his thin, open trench coat. It feels good to be outside for a change. We have both spent the morning conducting separate interviews concerning a suspected manslaughter in a flat on Pipersgatan.

'You've met someone,' he says.

I light a cigarette, and Levin's eyes longingly follow my hand movements.

'How do you know that?'

'Your clothes. They no longer just smell of smoke and fabric softener. Can I have one?'

I take a cigarette from the packet. He puts it between his lips, and I give him a light.

'What's her name? If you don't mind me asking?'

'Sam.'

'As in …?'

'As in Sam. I don't know if it's going anywhere, but there's something captivating about her.'

A large bird passes over our heads, silently, on flaccid wings. It glides out over the water.

'Captivating women often have short names,' Levin says, his eyes following the bird's flight.

'Is that a theory you've got?'

'It's a theory I am testing. My experience supports it, thus far.'

'You mean Elsa.'

'For example.'

He rarely talks about her. I know they have been married a long time but that they don't have kids. I don't know whether that's because they couldn't, or if they simply didn't want to.

'Be careful in love,' Levin says. 'If you're only going to follow one piece of my advice, I suggest that should be the one.'

Winter, many years later. It's after the Gotland affair, after my suspension. I find myself on the fringes of a murder investigation that is nothing to do with me. It's almost Christmas, and Levin has less than six months to live. I'm standing on Kungsholmsgatan, and I spot him on the other side of the road. A car rolls onto the junction, and Levin raises his hand, gets it to stop. He climbs into the back seat, and the car disappears in the direction of St Göran's. I don't see who the driver is, and it's so cold that the air is freezing, becoming tiny sparkling pearls.

The sun is shining through the windscreen, blindingly bright, and warm. I sit in the back next to Levin, on the way to or from something — I can't remember what. I just remember an old song on the radio, and Levin singing along, *in the pines, in the pines, where the sun don't ever shine, I would shiver the whole night through.*

1984 to 2014.

Thirty years in the blink of an eye. Thirty years, almost half a life, yet no more than a single breath.

It is the eighteenth of June, and the figure at the back door is tall and curved like a bracket, the posture you assume in the face of a challenging task. Twice he has put his knuckle to the door — *knock knock* — and that is how Charles knows that it's him.

'Good evening, Charlie,' he says as he is let in. 'Were you expecting me?'

'Not really.'

Paul is carrying a black leather bag. He closes the door behind him, and asks, 'Do you have visitors?'

'No, why do you ask?'

'It looks like you're alone here, but there's a car parked outside the front.'

'Is there?'

'A dark, expensive Volvo.'

He goes into the kitchen ahead of Paul and confirms that he is right: parked alongside the low fence is a car he doesn't recognise.

'Strange.' He hesitates. 'Would you like some coffee?'

'I would love some.'

'If that's not your car out there, then where did you park?'

'There's a clearing in the woods, I parked there.'

Paul pulls out one of the chairs by the kitchen table, sits down, and undoes the top button of his shirt. He puts the bag down on the floor.

'It really is freakishly warm here,' he says. 'I'd forgotten that.'

'I know.'

'I bet it's not even something you get used to either?'

'Not really.'

They had last met at a meeting with one of the directors two years previously, the meeting that forced Charles to move Leo Junker to Internal Affairs. The meeting that he had taped and saved in case one of those rainy days finally arrived. He is glad he did.

Paul looked better then, he recalls; despite being much paler, he had still seemed healthier. He is emaciated now, his cheeks sunken and his jaws marked in a way you only see in sick people.

Charles fills the coffee pot with water, pours it into the machine, and gets out the coffee.

'How did you find me?'

'Oh, you know.' Paul folds one leg over the other, stares out of the window. 'By piecing things together.'

Charles puts a filter paper into the coffee machine and puts in five small scoops.

'You talked to Marika?'

'I don't know about talked,' Paul says. 'I tried.'

'When were you there?'

'A few days ago.'

'How was she?'

'Same as usual, I'm guessing.'

Charles turns on the coffee machine, and it starts hissing. It's a pleasant sound, and sitting there opposite Paul he's struck by the way everything goes in cycles — that time must be a loop rather than a line.

'She tried to kill you,' Paul says.

'Nearly ten years ago.'

'But still. Chilling.'

'She was psychotic.'

'You're defending her.'

'No, that's not what I'm doing.'

'What happened with the investigation?'

'Why do you ask?'

'Just curious. She was sectioned, I know that much, but I couldn't even find the name of the victim.'

'The files will be there somewhere, I should think.'

'You got them to hush it up.'

'I didn't really have much choice.'

'I can imagine. As you know, I don't have kids of my own, but I can imagine how it must have felt. Do you know why she did it?'

Charles doesn't answer. He stands up from the chair and takes two cups from the cupboard, puts them next to the spluttering coffee maker, and glances out at the car outside. He suspects that Paul is lying. The car must be his.

'Isn't it weird, being back here?'

'It sure is.'

Paul smiles weakly.

'Does he still live here?'

'Who?'

'Bredström.'

'Yes, he still lives here. Black, right?'

'Yes, please.'

He fills the cups with coffee. The pot is shaking in his hands, but it's not just the weight; there's something else that he can't put his finger on. He puts the cup down in front of Paul.

'Back in a sec,' Charles says. 'There's something I want to show you.'

He goes into the bedroom, opens the top packing box, and digs out the sheet of paper, which is folded double.

Out in the kitchen, Paul is sitting motionless, his stare fixed on his hands. Charles puts the paper down in front of him. Paul picks it up carefully, unfolds it, and then reads it. It's obvious that the content doesn't surprise him.

'Is this the original?'

'No.'

Friday the seventeenth of June 1977, more than three years before Charles met Paul Goffman for the first time, a successful recruitment was sealed in Malmö. This news was reported in by the operative responsible, with a summary of the circumstances and their potential consequences, in a document delivered to the Director of SEPO.

The subject was Jonathan Ekblom, a thirty-five-year-old man who lived in a detached house near Möllevången with his wife and two children. He worked for Swedish Customs in Malmö. Four months earlier, in February that year, he had been approached at work by a man from Stockholm who was ostensibly interested in the workings of shipments that crossed the border on the way to West Germany.

The man dropped several hints during his visit about how a potential future collaboration could be lucrative for both Ekblom and the company the man claimed to work for. Ekblom was a polite soul and thanked him for the offer, but declined it. Further attempts were made to persuade Ekblom of the benefits of cooperation, but none were successful.

Ekblom was a complicated target. He spent little money, and therefore had no debts; he had no secret affairs, had no police record, and all his papers were in order.

As a result, a drastic, and therefore complicated, solution was required.

On the evening of Wednesday the fifteenth, several witnesses told how he had spent the small hours getting drunk with a man at one of the watering holes near the harbour. After that, he was put in his car, and Ekblom headed for home. Halfway between the bar and his home was a patrol car manned by Officers Ambjörnsson and Fant. Ambjörnsson was apparently busy with a crossword at that point, so it was Fant who had to wave the car into the kerb because it was swerving markedly.

Ekblom was immediately arrested, taken to the station, and put in a cell to sleep it off. If the officers had been more alert, they might well have got someone to do a blood test on him. It would have been a wise move, because Ekblom had never before got behind the wheel after drinking alcohol, and, as far as anyone knew, there was no reason for him to have done so that evening either. A possible explanation would have been that Ekblom had been drugged, in which case the man who he had been seen drinking with might reasonably have been suspected.

That, though, is not what happened.

In their defence, there had been some confusion when Ambjörnsson and Fant had arrived at the station. The duty officer looked at the crossroads recorded under LOCATION in their incident report, and wondered what on Earth Ambjörnsson and Fant had been doing there. They replied that they had received a call on the radio and had been sent there; but when the officer in charge asked them for the name of the person who'd called them, Ambjörnsson looked quizzically at Fant, who looked back at Ambjörnsson with a look that was every bit as puzzled. And, as was so often the case, nobody really seemed to know which way was up or down.

As dawn broke, Ekblom received his first and only visitor during the twelve hours he spent in the cell: the man he had drunk himself legless with.

'This is a precarious situation,' the man said as he opened the incident report that Ambjörnsson and Fant had submitted.

After that, it went like it always did.

'This sheet, along with all the consequences it entails, could go up in smoke. All it would take is for you to agree to help us with small favours, every now and then: little errands, checking information here and there, contacting us about a certain vehicle and whether this or that person has passed through customs. It will take up hardly any of your time and will be of great benefit to our operation.'

And if Ekblom were to continue to resist?

Well …

Well, the consequences would, in that case, be unfortunate.

Paul drops the sheet of paper onto the table.

'How long have you known?' he asks.

'A while. It wasn't that easy to get hold of.'

'How long had you *guessed*?'

'A long time.' Charles folds the sheet of paper and slides it into the back pocket of his jeans. 'You were supposed to be staying at the hotel that night, but you must have got into the car to have been able to hear the police radio. Then I started wondering what that squad car was even doing there in the first place.'

It happened occasionally, that the area's local talent would stand at the roadside and wave cars in, even on the least busy roads — that was where their hit ratio was best — but in all his years in Bruket, he had never known them to be out at that time of night.

'But you shouldn't set great store by feelings and hunches.'

'Is that why you're doing this?' Paul asks. 'To punish me?'

'Doing what?'

'I saw your log-on activity in the archive. I know what you were up to this spring.'

Charles drinks some coffee.

'So that's why you're here.'

'I don't want you making a big mistake.' He throws his hands up. 'You're sixty-seven. Given your lifestyle, your diet, you've probably got another twenty years in you. Do you want to spend them in a cell? That is — excuse my saying so — stupid, Charlie.'

Charles studies Paul's hands, folded in his lap. He hasn't touched the coffee.

The collection of documents that he is scanning, one by one, onto his computer, is all that remains: the only thing he has left to show what actually happened. It's his chance to do something right.

'It's high time to put things right,' he says, concentrating in order to keep his voice steady. 'It's time for us to pay for what we did.'

'That was another age, Charlie, another life.'

'Another age, maybe, but not another life. We are the same people. And,' he adds, 'I very much doubt that your motivation for coming here is quite as noble as you're trying to make out.'

'I do not wish to present it as anything other than what it is. But if you are compiling what I think you are compiling, and you then hand it over to the wrong person … It won't just be you going down.'

'I know. You will, too.'

'But not just you and me. Others, too — many of them are still alive. Where are you going to send them?'

'Where am I going to send what?'

'You know what I mean. The papers, the documents. The pictures.'

'I haven't quite decided yet.'

'Your talent for lying has withered with time.' Paul smiles weakly. 'I am …' he continues, before changing his mind. 'I don't know what to say. I am genuinely sorry for what happened to Eva.'

Charles blinks. Even now, after all this time, a burning

sensation builds behind his eyes.

'It was never meant …' Paul says. 'I didn't know that … I was just trying to help you. I just wanted you and Marika to be okay.'

'It was supposed to be a copy of the Ekblom recruitment.'

'We stopped those kind of tactics before your time. Ekblom was one of the last — the method was too risky, involved too many external players. But that time … I had no choice, Charlie.' His voice is now just a whisper, an affectation that, if you're not careful, could easily be confused with genuine remorse. 'They forced me to do it. You knew too much, thanks to the Lichter case. It was the only way.'

'You could have used Bredström against me.'

Paul sniggers.

'Never would've worked. You've always been far too straight. But the accident … That she was walking down the road with Marika. It was never … I was only trying to help you. I called it off as soon as I saw what had happened.'

'You let me believe,' Charles says slowly, and, as the words emerge, he realises that he would really have liked to have been armed, 'that it was my fault.'

'You said yourself that you suspected it from the start. Why didn't you ask? I wouldn't have lied to you. Not then.'

He can't say it. He had no one else besides Paul then. Paul knew it, and exploited it.

'You spiked me,' says Charles.

'You're the one who drank the beer.'

'But you're the one who put something in it.'

'No.'

'Stop lying!' His roar comes as a surprise even to himself, a rage with its origins in an unknown part of him. 'Don't lie to me again, Paul!'

His breathing is heavy.

'This was … this was thirty years ago, Charlie.'

'Since I came back here, I've been visiting her grave several times a week. Did you know that ... that she was buried here, over in the graveyard?'

'Yes.'

Charles almost laughs.

'Of course you knew that.'

It took him a while to find it on his first visit to the graveyard, but there it was, tucked away and uncared for in a lush corner of the surprisingly large area. EVA LEVIN, the headstone read, and he opened his mouth to say something but nothing came out.

'When I heard that you'd met Elsa,' Paul says, 'I can't remember who told me, but it made me happy. That you at least got a few good years with her, after Eva.'

Charles didn't answer. He had never loved Elsa, at least not like he'd loved Eva. But Elsa loved me, he thought. She loved me and I ... I needed her. *Needed*, that's the word. No one deserves to grow old lonely. Then cancer took her, and Charles was alone, again. And that's how it stayed.

'Can I at least see them?' Paul asks.

'See what?'

'The documents. So that I know what's coming.'

'I'd rather not.' Charles drinks some more coffee. It's been a long day, and the tiredness radiates out from his temples, in behind his eyes, and down over his shoulders. 'They're by the computer.'

'Show me.'

Charles gets up and walks into the study ahead of him, over to the desk and the scanner. Paul inquisitively edges up to the boxes standing on the floor and peers down into them.

Paul picks up one of the pictures from out of the box, a black-and-white photograph.

Charles remembers taking it, from a distance, standing next

to Paul one warm spring day. It's the twenty-ninth of May 1985. A white Renault TS is being recovered from Hammarbykanalen, the channel that separates Södermalm from the city's southern reaches. If you squint, you can just make out the silhouettes of two women inside.

'I remember that day,' Paul says, thumbing the picture thoughtfully before he drops it back into the box.

Their deaths were deemed to have been accidental, but strange little details helped give credence to alternative theories: Why was Falck sitting in the driver's seat when it was Gräns' car? Why did they have clean water in their lungs, not the dirty water you'd expect in the channel? What caused the scrapes along one side of the car? And why was Lena Gräns' necklace not around her neck, but found instead on the ground close to the quayside? And so on.

The police investigation that followed was deliberately useless and compromised by hands with dextrous fingers and powerful connections.

Paul picks up another photo: a picture taken in the vicinity of the East German Embassy. It's six months older, taken in November 1984. Johann Kraus' silhouette is easily identifiable, as is Charles. Cats Falck was the photographer.

After putting her and Lena Gräns at the bottom of Hammarbykanalen, they make their way to Falck's apartment, search it for photographs and documents pertaining to the scoop that never was. Paul is shaken, while Charles is numb — his eyes, and his mind, are blank. They burn everything, except a second copy of the photo, which Charles recovers from a shoebox in Falck's wardrobe. He folds it and then puts the photo into his coat pocket while Paul has his back to him.

1984 to 2014. Thirty years in a single breath. It was so long ago, yet somehow it wasn't.

Paul examines Charles' other documents for a while, pulling out papers and reading them, before they both head back to the kitchen.

Charles stares at his friend, and realises that he needs to try to compose himself. He's close to the limits of what he can deal with. The limits are there though, waiting, just under his skin.

He sits down on his chair. He drinks some coffee.

The car outside is still there, empty and in darkness.

'I was looking for you, too,' Charles says, and it sounds like an admission but it isn't. 'In the archive.'

'I know.'

'I didn't find anything.'

'I know.'

It's been gnawing away at Charles for ages, and now, with the end near, it is a question that remains unanswered.

'Back then,' he says, 'you told me that you did what you did because you had once needed help and got it. Gert, I think his name was.'

'Yes?'

'Just like you were helping me. That's what you said.'

Paul doesn't blink.

'And?'

'What did he help you with? I know,' he adds when Paul doesn't respond, 'that you grew up in a foster home near Uppsala, and that's where you met. You must have been very young then.'

'Why are you asking about this now?'

'I need to know. Before ... I just want to know how it all started.'

'This doesn't have to have an unhappy ending, Charles.'

This time, it's Charles who says nothing.

'I was seventeen when we met,' Paul says, eventually. 'At that point, I had been living there, on this big farm, for four years. I had gone into town and came back, armed with a shotgun and a hunting knife to take the lives of my stepfather, his two sons, and the other two foster children. Actually, it was a while before I realised that only two of the children were his, because he treated them all as if they were his own. But with me … I guess it was because I got there so late — I was thirteen when I first arrived. And he never treated me like anything other than a dog.' Paul's lips have thinned to a bitter grey line on his face. 'Gert had spotted me in Uppsala. He was a sergeant at the time, and he'd thought there was something strange about my bag, but also about my general demeanour. So he followed me out to the farm.'

'He stopped you then?'

'That depends what you mean. He stopped me from killing the children, at least. And with hindsight, that might have been for the best. The kids were awful, but they were the way they were because of him.'

'You killed your foster father.'

'I saw it more as a cleansing. In a way, so did Gert. He knew what was going on at the farm, the assaults and the violence, but was never able to do anything about it. There wasn't enough evidence. Anyway, he helped me, made it look like a robbery gone wrong, and I never had to do my time.'

'And then he demanded something in return?'

'Not until much later, when I'd ended up with SEPO. I think that was the first time I was useful to him. He was on the police board at the time, like a wolf in sheep's clothing. A Palme-hating far-right extremist in a Palme-led Sweden.'

'You could have said no.'

He cocks his head to one side.

'Think about what you're saying now. You should know better than anyone that it isn't that simple. But that's not why I, or rather *we* — me and you — did what we did. If you're looking for an absolute starting point, a definitive beginning, then yes, that's how it started. But life can't be reduced to something as banal as one's childhood. I did what I did because … I could. Because I wanted to.

Because it served me well.' He blinks. 'Simple as that.'

'Is Gert still alive?'

'He died of cancer a few years after Palme.'

Charles doesn't know what to say. Then it strikes him:

'Who sent you?'

'I think you know that, if you give it some thought. The personnel have changed, times are different, but the organisation remains the same. You must stop this.'

'I won't be doing that. I should have done this years ago.'

If only he hadn't been such a coward.

Paul bends down and opens the bag, then pulls out a cold, black revolver. He pops the cylinder out to make sure it's loaded, then closes it.

He stands up.

'I'm asking you, Charlie. If not for my sake or yours, then for Marika's. Don't do this.'

'That's funny. I was about to say the same thing to you.'

All of a sudden, Paul looks very tired. He lifts his arm and clenches his jaw.

The deep throat of the revolver's barrel is so black, and only when Charles sees that does it begin to vibrate inside his chest.

We were allies. The great betrayal had all started with a lie between friends.

And he used to think that at some point in his life there'd be a year with such a long summer, and during that summer he would fall desperately in love with someone he could never hurt. By then he would be older, would have learnt from his mistakes, accepted himself for who he was, and he would do whatever he could to spend the rest of his life around people who mattered to him. The years passed, though, and that moment he'd been waiting for never came; instead, his longing had subsided into that murky part of the soul where you keep things that you used to believe in, and it's only now, as he realises that it's too late, that the longing extricates itself and settles close to his heart, like regret. This wasn't the life he had hoped for. This was just what was left behind.

Sweden. He got scared of people and has never trusted anyone.

Voices. Voices in the darkness.

They're talking about me. I slip in and out for a while. The voices blend with the sound of a whip cracking, with a spoon stirring a saucepan. A voice with another accent saying, *If I see you again, I will beat you to death.*

The voices here and now, I hear them saying *collapsed lung*, hear *intubate.* I recognise one of them.

'And now?'

'It's stable now — has been for more than twelve hours. Critical, but stable. He's breathing for himself.'

'Are you sure? He looks so … weak.'

The voice. *Sam.*

It isn't dark. It's me; I've had my eyes closed. The room is strangely pale and the light stings my eyes.

I don't know whether I say her name, but I think so, because my throat feels strange and when I open my eyes I see her face. Locks of her hair fall over me, touching my cheeks, and it's a feeling I have missed and I don't want it to stop, but she pushes the hair behind her ears, seems to be trying hard to smile.

'They had to intubate,' she says. 'Mind your vocal chords.'

Her fingertips touch my lips.

'What day?'

'What day is it? Wednesday. Wednesday the twenty-fifth.'

'Ju …'

'June. They've kept you sedated.'

I realise now how scared she is. I want to say something soothing, but I don't know what.

'Sorry.'

Sam shakes her head.

'Everything's okay. Don't worry. Everything is okay.'

'How's Kit?'

She smiles, a little smile.

'He's very well.'

For some reason, this means an awful lot, and for the first time I see that maybe we're going to get through this after all, and tears start streaming down my cheeks. Sam dries them carefully with her thumb.

'It hurts,' I manage.

Sam puts something in my hand.

'Here. I told them that you'd feel better if you could control your own pain relief. You push here, up or down.'

'Sounds dangerous.'

She lays her hand on my cheek.

'Don't worry.'

'I'm tired.'

'Sleep.' Sam moves her hand, touches my arm. 'I'll be here when you wake up.'

And maybe that is the only thing that really matters.

'Do you know …' I clear my throat, then swallow. 'Goffman …'

'Your colleague arrested him.'

They've given me something that was supposed to be a sandwich. It tastes metallic and makes me feel sick, but I force myself to eat it because Sam seems to think it's important.

My colleague. *Tove*.

'Where is she?'

'Your colleague?'

'Yes.'

'She was discharged yesterday.'

'Did she get injured?'

'Her arm.' Sam purses her lips to a pale line. 'That's about as much as I know.'

I look at my sandwich.

'This tastes …'

'I know. I had one myself.'

'I thought it must've been me.'

She shakes her head with a little laugh. That makes me happy.

My mother and my brother have visited, apparently. There are some flowers on a table in the corner.

'Who are those from?' I ask.

'Which ones?'

'The biggest bunch.'

'From Gabriel.'

'Are they?'

'You haven't spoken to him?' she asks.

'No.'

'He said … him and Grim, something had happened.'

'What?'

'I don't know.'

'Just as well,' I say, still staring at my sandwich. 'I couldn't face hearing about it now anyway.'

'I thought you might say that.'

Time passes. I eat my sandwich. I ask where my phone is, and Sam goes off to get it. I think about Levin.

Sam returns with the phone, and I have a go at trying to use my arms. They're heavier than normal, and the movements are much slower, but at least I can hold it, and dial the right number. Sam's phone rings at the same time.

'It's the gallery,' she says. 'I thought I'd go and try and grab some lunch, too. Will you be okay if I leave you for an hour or so?'

'Don't worry.'

She squeezes my hand before she goes, pushes her lips onto my forehead. Then she smiles. She still hasn't said anything about the state of my face.

I'm left alone with my phone, and I lift it to my ear.

It rings for a long time, and the ringing tones themselves sound slow, drawn out.

When she answers, with her name, it sounds a long way away.

'Hi.' I don't know what to say next. 'Are you in Stockholm?'

'No, I'm at home.'

'Okay. Good. That's good.'

'How are you feeling?'

'Good. I think.'

'I find that a bit unlikely. He tried to kill you.'

'I don't think he ... I don't think he was trying to kill me. He could've shot me in the head in that case.' Silence. 'And you?'

'Me what?'

'How are you feeling?'

'My arm hurts. But it's okay.'

'I ... Thanks. For bringing him in.'

'Strictly speaking, it wasn't me,' she says. 'It was a lorry.'

'Eh?'

'Never mind.'

'A lorry?'

'You'll have to get someone to tell you about that.'

'Will do.' I'm waiting for something, but I don't know what. 'Have you got his ... Levin's documents? The sound file?'

'I've got them. I haven't done anything with them yet, just made sure that no one else has them. Gabriella Halvardsson has been in touch and asked to see them.'

'What do you think?'

'I thought I'd start by asking you what you think.'

I close my eyes. I so wish he was here, that I could talk to him.

'I don't know,' I say. 'I don't know yet.'

'Apparently, they found a sack truck. At Goffman's, in his cellar. They think it was Levin's, that Goffman used it to move the boxes from Levin's house to his car, which was probably parked in a clearing in the woods behind Alvavägen. Söderlund, the technician, photographed some tyre tracks there — did you see them?'

'Yes,' I say, when something in my memory clicks into place: I was standing on the lawn with Tove, there in the gloom behind Levin's house, and looking over at the dark woodland. Something about the woods was unsettling. 'Yes, I think so.'

'The first analysis indicates that at least one set of tracks looks to have come from Goffman's car. So that probably is where he parked the car and the route he took to and from the house. They haven't found any boxes or papers, though. He refuses to say a word in interviews, but they suspect that he has tried to burn them somewhere, perhaps successfully, along with the computer, the phone, and the scanner.'

'Thanks.'

'I thought you'd like to know,' she says. And then, after a short pause: 'There was one more thing, something I was thinking about while I was in hospital.'

'What was that?'

'What Bredström said during the interview, about Eva Levin's car crash, that she almost never drove, and how there wouldn't be any witnesses who had seen her in the car on the night she died. When the investigation into Levin's death got underway, on the Thursday, we pulled up the documents around that incident. I didn't look particularly closely at them then — Davidsson had said that there was nothing strange about it, and I didn't see anything either. But when I was lying there in hospital ...' She hesitates.

'I don't know. It was just something that occurred to me.'

'About what?'

'What is supposed to have happened is that while Charles was down at Brukets Bar having a drink, Eva took their car to go and pick up Marika, who was going to sleep at a friend's but changed her mind. According to Bredström, Eva had a licence but almost never drove anywhere. That's correct — I checked the notes, and it says something along those lines. That statement came from a colleague of hers at the supermarket. That night, she is meant to have got in the car, perhaps because it was easier to pick Marika up that way, I can buy that. That was also mentioned in the investigation — that if she ever did get in the car, it was because she had Marika with her. There's no one in the file though, as far as I can see, who reports having seen Eva in the car, not even the parents at the house that she picked Marika up from, although they were never asked, since the investigators only asked the standard questions, but no one saw the car that night. Weird, eh?'

'Yes. It is. I don't know what to say.'

'It could be nothing,' she continues. 'And even if what actually happened diverges somewhat from what the investigation concluded, it still doesn't necessarily mean that there was any basis to Bredström's accusations.'

'But it is weird. Are you at work?'

'In the graveyard.'

'Oh, okay.'

'I've never been here before.'

Then neither of us say any more, and now I imagine her moving between the headstones, surrounded by the encroaching trees. Maybe she knows which one is his, or maybe she's looking for her brother's name, grave by grave. I try to decide what kind of headstone I think he might have, how big it is. Whether there are flowers on the grave. Maybe Tove's got some with her.

She ends the call. I realise that I don't know what happened to Eva Levin.

I lift up the little remote and turn it right up, so high that before long I'm not thinking anymore.

I'm dreaming. My field of vision is cloudy, and crumbling away at the edges. When the doctor in charge — not the surgeon, another doctor — was here before, she mentioned that they're giving me a cocktail of medication that can interfere with my sleep. Or else it could be the morphine. I might have pumped myself full of a bit more than I should have.

It must be that. I'm having feverish dreams without knowing. I'm anxious and I want to wake up but can't. The door is closed, but beyond it I can hear the gentle movements of someone on the other side.

Then the door handle is carefully pushed down, and eventually the door opens. I realise now that I've been waiting for it, that I'm impatient and very, very happy to be seeing my friend again.

As he enters the room, he allows himself a little smile.

'Leo,' he says, walking over to the chair where Sam was sitting just a few moments before. 'I told you we'd see each other soon.' He sits on the chair. 'Have you been expecting me?'

'Yes.'

'I can't stay long.'

'I understand,' I say. 'A brief appearance in a dream is better than nothing.'

A look of surprise washes over Grim's face, before it's replaced by something that there isn't a word for, just a feeling.

'Yes. Yes, maybe.'

'How did you get out?' I ask.

'Oh, you know.' Grim smiles. 'I had some help.'

'From who?'

'From Gabriel.'

'I don't get it,' I say. 'He shot me. Goffman shot me.'

'I heard.'

'I'm scared. I thought I was going to die. I … Sam … I don't know …' Tears. Tears again, I can't help it. There's something wrong, a dam deep inside me about to burst.

'Kit …'

'It's okay, Leo.'

He leans over, and I can smell my best friend, and for a second it's summer, long ago, and we're lying next to each other on our backs by the water tower in Salem, looking up at the cloudless sky above us. There were rumours of a thick fog due to arrive that evening, but it's still clear and light, and Grim turns to me, squinting because of the sun, says that he'll miss me if we ever have to go our separate ways.

Then I remember.

'Are you going to hurt me?'

'No.'

I daren't trust him; I wish I could. It's going to take more than words this time. He puts his hand on my arm and looks me in the eye, says again:

'It's okay, Leo. Breathe.'

'It hurts. My chest …'

Grim follows the little transparent tube running from the back of my hand and on to something just behind me. He looks around and bends down, and when his hand leaves my arm, my skin is warm and I want him to touch me again. It feels safe, in spite of everything. He comes back up with the little box that controls my pain relief.

'It had fallen onto the floor,' he says, pressing it.

'Again,' I say. 'More.'

When he's finished, he puts it onto the bed next to my hand and glances quickly at the closed door.

'Isn't this …' he says. 'Isn't this a bit too realistic to be a dream?'

He wants me to wake up, I think to myself. I don't want to. I want to stay here. I shake my head.

'Everything's blurred round the edges. Like a sheet of paper that's started burning at the margins.'

'Oh, okay. Yes. Unfortunately, reality doesn't burn up that easily.'

He smiles, makes me want to laugh.

'Exactly.'

'If I disappear again, Leo ...'

'Don't do it.' I search for his hand but don't find it. The effects of the morphine are taking over, making life go quiet and wrapping it all in nice grey wool. 'I don't want you to.'

'I don't want you to go looking for me. I want you to leave me alone. Can you do that?'

'I'm sorry,' I say, 'for what happened.'

'I know that. And I'm going to leave you alone. I'm not going to ...' Grim blinks, doesn't finish the sentence. 'If I don't do anything, I could be in trouble. You've got to believe me. You have to trust me this time, Leo.'

'I don't understand,' I say.

'Say that you trust me.'

'I ...' It's only as I say it that I realise it's true. Only now do I realise how much he means to me. How much I'm going to miss him if he really does go up in smoke again.

'I trust you.'

'Good.' He looks at the door again. 'I think I have to go now.'

'Why did you come, then?'

He smiles, a weak smile.

'To say farewell.'

'No.' I grasp at him, scared. 'No. Why?'

He takes my hand, and for just a second he winds his fingers around mine. I want to hold him there, but I haven't got the strength. The logic of the dream is too strong. It cannot be defied.

I must have nodded off, I think. I'm not sure, but something's happened, anyway, because when I open my eyes the light coming through the window into the room is different. It looks like it's very, very warm out there, and I'm glad I don't have to deal with that.

There's something in my hand: a stiff, folded little note. The way the edges scrape my hand feels nice. I open it.

farewell, leo

at least

until we meet again